BISHOP
AS
PAWN

ALSO BY WILLIAM X. KIENZLE

The Rosary Murders

Death Wears a Red Hat

Mind Over Murder

Assault With Intent

Shadow of Death

Kill and Tell

Sudden Death

Deathbed

Deadline for a Critic

Marked for Murder

Eminence

Masquerade

Chameleon

Body Count

Dead Wrong

WILLIAM X. KIENZLE

BISHOP
AS
PAWN

ANDREWS AND McMEEL
A Universal Press Syndicate Company
Kansas City

ISBN 0-8362-6130-5

CREDITS
Editorial Director: Donna Martin
Senior Editor: Jean Lowe
Production Manager: Lisa Shadid
Copy Editor: Matt Lombardi
Book Design: Barbara J. King
Jacket Design: George Diggs
Editorial Coordinator: Patty Donnelly
Typography: Connell-Zeko Type & Graphics

FOR JAVAN

ACKNOWLEDGMENTS

Gratitude for technical advice to:

Father Harry Cook, pastor, St. Andrew's Episcopal Church, Clawson
Sergeant James Grace, detective, Kalamazoo Police Department
Thomas Hinsberg, ethicist emeritus, St. Joseph's Hospital, Pontiac
Father Anthony Kosnik, S.T.D., J.C.B., professor of ethics, Marygrove
    College
Irma Macy, religious education coordinator, Prince of Peace Parish,
    West Bloomfield
Gwenn Samuel, director of external publications, Detroit College of
    Law
Colleen Flaherty Stuck, director, Ameritech
Rita Sudol, commissioner, Commission on Spanish Speaking Affairs,
    Pontiac
Rabbi Richard Weiss, marriage and family therapist

Archdiocese of Detroit:
Father Robert Duggan, C.S.B., pastor, Ste. Anne, Detroit
Sister Bernadelle Grimm, R.S.M., pastoral care (retired), Mercy Hospital
Father Patrick Halfpenny, pastor, St. Vincent de Paul, Pontiac
Father Donald Hanchon, pastor, St. Gabriel, Detroit
Jo Garcia, Theological Library Service, Sacred Heart Major Seminary
Karen R. Mehaffey, Theological Library Service, Sacred Heart Major
    Seminary
Msgr. Stanley Milewski, chancellor, SS. Cyril & Methodius Seminary,
    Orchard Lake
Ned McGrath, director, Department of Communications
Nancy Ward, Alumni Memorial Library, St. Mary's College

Detroit Police Department:
Inspector Richard Ridling, Vice Section
Inspector Barbara Weide, Criminal Investigation Bureau

ACKNOWLEDGMENTS

Office of Wayne County Prosecuting Attorney:
Timothy Kenny, assistant Wayne County prosecuting attorney
John O'Hair, Wayne County prosecuting attorney
Andrea Solak, chief of special operations

Wayne State University:
Ramon Betanzos, Ph.D., professor of humanities
Anna Ledgerwood, M.D., professor of surgery
Charles Lucas, M.D., professor of surgery
Werner U. Spitz, M.D., professor of forensic pathology

Any technical error is the author's.

In Memory of Father Thomas McAnoy

BISHOP
AS
PAWN

PROLOGUE

Bishop Ramon Diego was dead. And the priests were having a party.

On the surface, this may seem cavalier, even inhuman. But actually, the bishop's battered body had not yet been discovered.

Besides, it was not exactly a party. The occasion was the quarterly meeting of Detroit city priests.

Although the gathering was a regularly scheduled event, not all the priests of the entire archdiocese of Detroit were invited.

Four times each year, the priests assigned to parishes within the actual boundaries of the city of Detroit got together to; pinpoint problem areas in their ministry; share solutions or at least attempted solutions; enjoy each other's company; gripe, and gripe some more.

This also was an excellent opportunity to surreptitiously case any newcomers to the presbyterate of Detroit . . . although almost no priests were any longer volunteering to serve in the inner city.

Some thought a natural differentiation existed between suburban ministries and priestly experience in the dying and dangerous city of Detroit proper. Others felt that priesthood was priesthood, that suburbanites had souls, and that Detroit was neither dying nor dangerous.

Even though this party was of, by, and for inner-city priests, by no means was every one of them in attendance. In all, there are about 150 priests assigned to Detroit city parishes. These dinner meetings were movable feasts. It just so happened that tonight's party was hosted by the Cathedral parish. Tonight only about forty priests had gathered for the light dinner and refreshments at Blessed Sacrament.

Now, as the hour neared 10:00, only ten of the original forty-some priests remained.

Besides these few, there was the service crew—the caterer and two seminarians—who had prepared and served the buffet meal. Now they began removing the leftovers and cleaning up the kitchen.

"This ain't bad," Pete, the caterer, said. "I expected a real crowd."

"'A real crowd'?" Mark, one of the seminarians, echoed.

"Wait a minute . . ." Charlie, the other seminarian, said to Pete. "You don't think the guys who showed up tonight are *all* the priests we've got in Detroit?"

"Well . . . yeah. We got a lot of food left over," Pete replied. "And, what the hell: How could you run a church in a big city like this with . . . what? . . . less than fifty ministers?"

"*Priests,*" Mark, who was ever on the lookout for a possible convert, corrected. "You a Catholic?"

"Naw, Greek Orthodox . . . but I don't work at it."

Perfect, thought Mark. All Pete had to do was make a lateral arabesque to become Greek Catholic, or Uniate, and he would be in union with Rome, so to speak.

"Our priests drink too," Pete said.

"What?"

"Booze. This is just about the way we'd set up for an Orthodox party. Our company's handled a few. Surprised me at first; I guess I just took it for granted that priests didn't drink." Pete smiled. "Course for a while there, I didn't think they went to the bathroom either. But"—he indicated the sideboard well stocked with bottles of liquor and mixes—"your guys drink too."

Mark leaped to the defense. "You didn't see any of 'our' guys get drunk did you?"

"Well . . . the guy who came in late looked like he had a snootful."

"Okay, but he sobered up pretty quick, didn't he? Soon as he got some food in him."

"I guess." Pete dumped the bones of some picked-over chicken in the garbage bucket. "Your guys don't dress up much."

Mark would have preferred a less adversarial conversation. But he was grateful for any opportunity to pursue a religious theme. "You mean they're not all in uniform—clericals. Well, remember, Pete: They're all priests and they all know each other. No need for a uniform." He sidestepped the fact that in any case clericals were no longer worn anywhere near as often as had been the custom some years back.

"Well, then . . ." Pete hesitated. ". . . I guess I can ask . . ."

"Anything, Pete." Things were looking good, Mark thought, for a possible eventual conversion.

"Was the bishop here?"

Charlie guffawed. "One of the reasons these guys get together is to roast the bishops. So the bishops aren't invited. And even if they were, they wouldn't come."

Bishops . . . Pete wondered. "You got more than one?"

Mark leaped at Pete's interest. "There's only one main bishop. He's called the 'ordinary.'"

"The others are 'extraordinary.'" Charlie laughed again.

"Don't pay any attention to him. The others are called 'auxiliary'— 'helping'—bishops. Detroit's a big, important territory; so it's an archdiocese. So the ordinary is an *arch*bishop. Except our archbishop is a *Cardinal*." Mark obviously relished the title. "Cardinals elect the Pope!"

"Would you all mind stacking these boxes?" Pete veered from the topic; the sooner they could pack it in here, the quicker he could get home.

"Then, see . . ." Mark continued while obediently stacking boxes, ". . . the archdiocese is divided into five regions, and an auxiliary bishop is responsible for each region—with maybe an exception for our newest auxiliary, Bishop Diego. He's supposed to look out for the Hispanics."

"I sure thank you fellas." Pete, balancing an improbable pile of boxes and gear, exited without further formality.

Charlie smiled at Mark sympathetically. "I thought for a minute you had him there. Maybe next time."

"If we'd had all the guys here—maybe then Pete would've been impressed. Or, if more of the guys had been wearing their clericals . . . Look: There's about ten guys left and only one of 'em is wearing a 'collar.'"

Charlie snorted. "He probably wears a Roman collar in the shower."

"Huh?"

"Name's Koesler, Father Robert Koesler. He's pastor of Old St. Joe's downtown. I did some work for him last summer. Took census in his parish—almost everybody there lives in a highrise, or an apartment or a condo. A nice guy, but definitely 'old school.'"

"Oh, yeah . . ." Mark brightened. "I remember him. Isn't he the . . . uh . . . ?"

"'Detective priest'?" Charlie grinned. "I guess some people think so. But he doesn't. He told me all he's done is just supply some information to the police from time to time. No big deal, according to him."

"Oh . . ." Mark's attention turned to another related consideration. "Now that I think of it, how come this isn't open to all the priests? When Cardinal Boyle has a general meeting *everybody* shows up."

"I don't know . . ." Charlie grew reflective. "There *is* a difference. Even when there's a general meeting, the suburban guys hang out together and the same for the city guys. Must have something to do with their territory. I guess it's the difference between first, second, and third world countries."

The two young men, now almost done, were packing away the untouched food, which would be distributed to the needy tomorrow. Charlie chuckled. "Reminds me of something my aunt told me a while back." Charlie's aunt was a nun who had a penchant for saying the wrong thing at the wrong time to the wrong people.

"You know how in the old days if the nuns did something wrong, they had to confess it to all the other nuns in their convent? They called it the Chapter of Faults.

"Anyway, a priest used to say Mass at the convent once a week. The nuns took turns making him a pretty damn good breakfast after Mass. Well, one morning when it was my aunt's turn, the priest left some bacon and eggs, which my aunt promptly scarfed down. But then she felt guilty. So at the next Chapter of Faults, she confessed, 'I ate Father's remains.'"

They both laughed.

"By the way," Mark said, "who's the new guy?"

"What new guy?"

"The one who came in with the Ste. Anne's crew?"

"Oh . . . okay . . . I can't think of his name right now, but he's about to become a Detroit priest. Didn't you see the announcement in the *Detroit Catholic*?"

"I must've missed it."

"He's a Maryknoller . . . an older guy."

Actually, the priest in question was a Maryknoll missionary, or, more technically, a member of the Catholic Foreign Mission Society of America.

"I always thought that a missionary vocation would be sort of thrill-

ing," Mark mused. "You know: China, Africa, Japan, South America—
exotic places. Why would he want to work in Detroit?"

"I don't know." Charlie shrugged. "But it's gonna take him a while."

"Why?"

"'Cause the Maryknoll order has to let him go before our archdiocese can 'adopt' him. It's a regular process . . . something about
'incardination' and 'excardination.' I asked Father Kerin, but he said
we'd study it later in Canon Law."

"Yeah, yeah. Just like all the questions about sex and marriage . . ."

"'We'll study it later,'" they said in unison.

CHAPTER
ONE

"I'm being sued," Father Bert Echlin stated.

Father Ernie Bell snorted. "If you lose, you'll have to borrow money to pay off."

"They always think we've got an infinite pile of money back of us," Father Henry Dorr said.

"Well, we have, in a way." Father Frank Dempsey chuckled. "If any one of us gets into enough trouble, they can always sell the Sistine Chapel."

"Who'd want it?" Echlin wondered.

"Why? What are you getting sued for?" Dorr asked.

"My sidewalk."

"You got a sidewalk?" Dempsey joked.

"I got a sidewalk, okay," Echlin said. "It looks like it got bombed. I mean, I'm used to potholes in the streets. But in the sidewalks?"

"So it's an eyesore. What's so different about that?" Dempsey shook his head. "If people in this city sued over eyesores . . ."

"A woman fell on my sidewalk," Echlin said.

"Fell?" Dorr said.

"Fell, or took a dive. Anyway, she's suing. After I got a call from her lawyer, I walked around the parish. I've got the best sidewalk in the neighborhood." Echlin half grimaced. "I think I got spoiled by my previous parish. In Monroe, if you got problems you get a notice from the city: Either you fix it or the city fixes it and sends you the bill."

"Welcome to Detroit," said Dorr.

It was nearing 10:30. The quarterly meeting of the city priests was winding down. The catering crew, having cleared away the food, had departed. The liquor supply and a few priests remained.

Much of the evening's conversation had centered on the city in which these priests lived and ministered. They griped about the mayor, one Maynard Cobb; about the Common Council; about city services, or more realistically the lack thereof; about the provision for snow removal, which was the periodic but fairly dependable forty-plus degrees of temperature; about street lighting, which was spotty at best; about city pockets where police protection was intense in contrast to the larger stretches of the city pretty much left to shift for themselves; about the erratic mass transit boondoggle; about the pervasive presence of drugs with their concomitant violence, which was all too frequently fatal, and at the very least overwhelmingly vitiating.

These were all "safe" topics. Practically every gathering of two or more citizens in metropolitan Detroit, whether in the suburbs or the city, griped about the selfsame things.

Members of the select group of priests who called themselves the "hard core" of the core city were easily as concerned about Big Brother as they were about their wounded and limping city.

Big Brother was embodied by the various layers of Church bureaucracy, which seemed to these priests to be obsessed with how they were functioning liturgically, canonically, and socially.

Some few of their colleagues were aligned quite frankly with Big Brother. Thus, in these meetings, conversation was steered along "safe" paths. That way there would be nothing to report; even bureaucrats complained about the city and its many failings.

However, once those who felt some allegiance to the power structure were not present, the "hard core" group felt more free to talk about what interested them: *their* Church and *their* ministry.

But tonight, their aim was to discover just where this Don Carleson fit into the scheme of things. Their technique, traditionally, was not a frontal assault; rather, they would sound out the newcomer on his opinion of and approach to some of the points of common interest to them all.

Two more priests checked their watches, shrugged, and headed for home. This left the four who had been assessing the sad state of city maintenance, Father Carleson, and Father Koesler.

Ernie Bell had arrived about forty-five minutes late for the meeting.

It was evident that he'd been drinking, and while the meal had sobered him somewhat, he still had not completely recovered.

"So, Don," Dorr began, "you're a Maryknoller. Where were you working before you came here?"

"Oh, just an insignificant diocese in Central America. Nobody's ever heard of it."

"What brings you to Detroit?" Echlin asked.

"I'm tempted to say Northwest Airlines. But I know you're serious. So, I didn't come here blindly. I checked out the major dioceses in the States and this one seemed most promising."

"This one?" Dempsey's tone suggested skepticism. "Pound for pound, we've got more problems than any other metropolitan diocese I can think of."

Carleson shook his head. "You've gone through the Council right from its beginning in the early sixties. Most of the other dioceses ducked Vatican II. They're still fighting their way through it. This thing— adapting to the Council and its spirit—like most other things depended on who the bishop happened to be. Your guy—Boyle—has fought his way through it. Still fighting."

"Yeah, but they put you in Ste. Anne's," Dorr said. "Things are just as poor there as you could have had in the missions."

"No." Carleson smiled. "These people here aren't really poor. Why, most of them have TV sets. In the Third World, there are just two societies: the extremely wealthy and the dirt poor. And when I say dirt poor, I mean it literally."

"So, then," Dorr said, "that's why you came back: The missions were more miserable than you counted on?"

"No, not really. It was the bishops."

"Bishops!" Dorr snorted. "You really lucked into it, didn't you? Getting assigned to Diego!"

Through clenched teeth Carleson replied, "That's only temporary."

"Temporary?" Echlin chuckled mirthlessly. "Not if he thinks he can make your life truly miserable."

Carleson didn't respond.

But Ernie Bell did. He almost exploded. Seemingly, the mention of the bishop's name had roused him. "Diego! That bastard! Diego, that goddam bastard!"

"What's the matter with Diego?" Dempsey wondered.

"You don't know?" Koesler said. "I thought everyone knew."

"Diego discovered that he could make Ernie's life miserable," Echlin said. "And he's been doing pretty well at it ever since."

"How come I didn't know that?" Dempsey asked.

"I don't know." Echlin shrugged. "It's pretty common knowledge, at least among the guys."

"But Ernie, you speak Spanish. You're good at it," Dempsey protested. He looked at the others. "My God, he's at St. Gabriel's . . . right in the heart of the Latino community. Why would Diego give him a hard time?"

"Where've you been, Frank?" Dorr asked. "If you'd get out of the Afro ghetto once in a while—"

"And get into your ghetto?" Dempsey interjected.

"At least get out of your own. What Diego's been doing—and *not* doing—is famous . . . infamous."

"Like?"

"Like he's supposed to be God's gift to the Hispanic community."

"That's what he was in Dallas," Dempsey said.

"That's what he was *supposed* to be in Dallas," Echlin corrected. "Turns out he don't like Latinos very much."

"Doesn't like Latinos!" Dempsey exclaimed. "Why, my God, he's Mexican himself! Why wouldn't he like Latinos? He *is* one."

"I don't know," Dorr said. "Something must have happened to him when they made him a bishop."

"Yeah, it happens. It happens all the time," Echlin said. "Look at Supreme Court justices. Presidents nominate them expecting they'll follow the president's party line. But, often as not, they don't.

"Or look at *our* history. Cardinal Montini was a star-spangled liberal until they put a white suit on him and made him Pope Paul VI and he dug his heels in.

"Or take Danielou. As a theologian he was always in trouble. Then they make him a Cardinal and nobody can find a liberal bone in his body."

"So," Dorr pursued, "why not Diego?"

"The son of a bitch." Bell spoke for the first time since his similar blast earlier in the conversation. "Latinos—Latinos who live in this city—live in barrios. Diego ain't gonna live in a barrio . . . not again."

"He came from one, didn't he?" Dorr said diffidently, trying not to further rile Bell.

"Yeah, he came from one," Bell said. "And he worked in one when he became a priest. But he wanted out. Best ticket out was becoming a bishop. So, he worked his way into getting the red. He'd just about worked his way into the mainstream in Dallas when he got sent here as an auxiliary to Boyle. So he's God's gift to the Latinos here. Back in the barrio. But he's working his way out all over again."

"Are you sure?" Dempsey said. "I mean, that's a hell of an accusation!"

"Yeah, I'm sure. I know how he ticks. I confronted him with the whole scenario. I had chapter and verse. I could tell him the contacts he's made already. I could even tell him the contacts he's planning to make.

"He tried to deny it. But he couldn't: I had him dead to rights."

"So what?" Dorr said. "What could he do to you? I know he's a bishop—but he's only an auxiliary. What can he do to you?"

Echlin shook his head. "Auxiliaries may be daddy's helpers, but they're still bishops. They've got inbuilt clout."

"But, how much clout?" Koesler commented. "Who knows?"

"That's exactly it," Bell said. "Nobody knows. But if he's got as much as he thinks he has . . . I could be in a lot of trouble."

"What? Threats?" Dempsey said.

Bell was silent for a few moments. Finally, "He wanted to close me down."

"Close you down!" Koesler exclaimed. "St. Gabriel's? You've got to be kidding . . . or he is!"

"Bob's right," Echlin agreed. "St. Gabriel's is smokin'. You've got as many programs going—or more even—than any other parish in the city."

Bell shook his head. "We're 'not what we used to be' . . . that's what he said."

"Who among us is?" Koesler said. "The people who built these city churches are either dead or have moved away. I don't think there's a single city parish whose people look like the original congregation—either in color, nationality, or numbers. None of us is what we used to be!"

"There's one big difference," Bell said.

"And that?" Koesler asked.

"And that is that a bishop didn't tell you he was going to do everything he could—*everything*—to close *your* parish."

"I can't believe it. I just can't believe it," Dempsey said. "My God, where would all your people go?"

"There's that giant right down the street," Bell said.

"Holy Redeemer? Oh, it's a monster," Echlin said. "But it's got its own hands full. Put what you've got at Gabriel's in Redeemer and the giant would be choked to death."

Bell shook his head. "Not according to Diego. According to Diego, Redeemer would just be what it used to be. Once more, Redeemer's got enough Redemptorists to take care of the crowd . . . just like in the good old days."

"But . . . closing!" Koesler shook his head. "It doesn't make sense." He shook his head again. "That's just not Cardinal Boyle's style."

Bell winced. "That's where we find out how much clout an auxiliary's got. All by himself, I don't think he could shut me down. And maybe that isn't Boyle's style. But . . ." He looked at the others. ". . . could Diego pressure Boyle into doing it?"

All were silent as they considered Bell's query.

At length, Koesler spoke. "I see what you mean, Ernie. It's the club. It's the bishops' club. Very gentlemanly, very deferential, very you-scratch-my-back-I-scratch-yours. I hadn't considered that. That makes it a very good question. It's not just that the odds are against Cardinal Boyle's doing anything like that. What happens when a fellow bishop, particularly one Boyle has to work with, wants something? Wants it badly . . . ? I don't know . . . it's a new and different ball game, isn't it?"

Silence.

Finally, Carleson spoke. "It's getting kind of late, and I lost my ride. Could I beg a lift?"

"You can go with me," Koesler said promptly. "Ste. Anne's and St. Joseph's are only a few minutes apart."

Neither Carleson nor Koesler proved to be a bellwether. As the two got their coats and hats, none of the remaining four priests made a move to follow suit.

As he left, Koesler noted Ernie Bell returning to the bar. Koesler feared that Bell might drink too much before his drive home. He had come to the meeting late and slightly intoxicated—although he'd recovered well enough as the evening progressed.

Koesler would simply have to trust the others to be responsible.

CHAPTER
TWO

Koesler decided to drive west on Chicago Boulevard to the Lodge Freeway and swing south on the expressway toward downtown Detroit.

He smiled as it occurred to him that the grand inquisition had not fared very well. The "hard core" group of the core-city priests had not learned very much at all about the philosophical and theological convictions of Father Don Carleson.

The well-rehearsed probe had been derailed by Ernie Bell's somewhat apprehensive tirade against Ramon Diego. In that, either Bell had been quickly convinced that Carleson could be trusted, or Bell was taking an impulsive gamble. If what he said got back to Diego, Bell would find himself in deeper trouble yet.

"If you're not too tired," Carleson said, "maybe we could stop at your place for a few minutes."

"Sure, no trouble." Koesler smiled as he kept his eyes on the road and on the overpasses from which heavy objects were, at whim, thrown down at passing vehicles. "In no hurry to get back?"

"No. Besides, I need to unwind a little. I know they didn't grill me as much as they wanted to, but the pressure was there anyway."

Koesler chuckled. "You knew."

"Yeah, I knew."

They drove on in silence. Both priests knew that St. Joe's was not, in anyone's geography, "on the way" to Ste. Anne's. True, they were not terribly far apart, but St. Joe's was east of Woodward—the magic divider—and Ste. Anne's was west. For whatever reason, Carleson definitely was not eager to go home. Additionally, Carleson had pleaded fatigue when he excused himself from the dregs of the Cathedral meeting.

All of this Koesler found interesting. Perhaps the apparent contradiction would be resolved as the evening wore down further.

*   *   *   *

As they were about to enter the completely darkened rectory, Carleson said, "It's like an ancient castle."

Koesler stopped to regard again his benefice. "Yes, it is. I guess it's the rough stone exterior. And it *is* big. And dark. Way too big for one person with just part-time and outside help. I suppose we'll do something about it one day. Sell it, maybe. Though it had better be a pretty big family that buys it," he added.

"You're not worried about its being shut down." The sentence was a question.

"Like Ernie Bell is worried about his place? No. From everything I know about Cardinal Boyle, he's not going to do that sort of thing. He did it just once, years ago—to two parishes: St. John's and Immaculate Conception . . . with disastrous consequences. The city leveled a whole area of what was called Poletown, so a Cadillac factory could be built there. It didn't work to just about anyone's satisfaction. And, as far as Bishop Diego is concerned, wherever he may want to go, I am simply not in his way."

*   *   *   *

"You're not going to deactivate the alarm system?" Carleson asked as he followed Koesler down the hall to St. Joe's rectory kitchen.

"No. Mostly because we don't have any."

"You don't have an alarm system?'

"No. Does Ste. Anne's?"

"You betcha. State of the art."

"I suppose we ought to get one. Just never got around to it."

"Until you do, it might be a smart idea to leave some lights on when you're out . . . to scare off the B-and-E'rs."

"That *is* a good idea." Koesler switched on the kitchen lights. Then, as an afterthought, in keeping with what had just been said, he went to turn on more lights in nearby rooms.

He returned to the kitchen. "How about a cup of coffee?"

"Sure."

Koesler went to the stove and turned the heat on under a pot containing a dark liquid. "I'll just heat this up."

"Okay."

Koesler was mildly surprised. Usually, visitors complained when he served coffee that had been made much earlier.

In quick order, the pot was steaming. Koesler poured two cups and set one before his guest. Carleson blew over the hot brew, tasted it, then smiled. So did Koesler. This was the first time in his memory that anyone had given even the appearance of actually liking his coffee, even when it was made from scratch.

Carleson had hung his hat on a peg near the door. But he hadn't removed his coat.

"May I take your coat?" Koesler asked.

"Thanks, no. I'm comfortable. Actually, it's kind of cold in here."

Koesler immediately felt apologetic. "I turned up the thermostat. It should warm up soon. I usually let it go down to about sixty when I'm out. Otherwise, I keep it at about sixty-eight."

Carleson hunched his shoulders. "It's probably just me. I can't seem to stay warm."

"Actually, this is a fairly mild January. It can get bone-chillingly cold these next couple of months, especially for us. Both my parish and yours are very near the river. That and the windchill can keep one in the cabin."

"It may be mild weather to you and everybody else who's used to it, but it wasn't all that long ago that I was sweating it out in Honduras. I've been back only a couple of months."

"That's right. I read where you were there—what?—about five years."

"Uh-huh." Carleson smiled at the memory. "I was part of an experiment at Maryknoll."

"How's that?"

"Usually a missioner is pretty well grounded in the local language before he's sent anywhere. I was supposed to pick it up on the scene. On the whole, I think it worked out fairly well . . . except for when I arrived in a little village where I had to take a bus to an even smaller village where my parish was.

11

BISHOP AS PAWN

"See, I had everything I was bringing with me in a humongous duffel bag. By the time I got to the bus the luggage compartment was filled. The bus itself was packed with people, right up to the door. And there was I trying to squeeze myself on board with this huge bag.

"Everybody seemed to be yelling at me and pointing to the opposite side of the bus, but I couldn't understand what they were saying. I only had a few Spanish words and phrases.

"Finally, in all this pandemonium, I noticed a man sitting halfway back in the bus. He was motioning to me to pass my bag back to him. Well, he was like a port in a storm. I sent the bag back, and it was enthusiastically passed from hand to hand until it reached him.

"When he got it, he threw it out the window. I thought—my God!—he just threw away everything I own! But what all these people were trying to tell me was that there was another luggage compartment on the other side of the bus."

They laughed.

During the story, Koesler had been studying his guest. Carleson was of average height, perhaps five-feet-eight or -nine. A bit on the heavyset side, which would help keep him warm during the winter once he got used to it. His eyes were attractive and trusting in an open face. His full head of hair was white—perhaps a bit prematurely. Koesler guessed Carleson to be about ten or fifteen years younger than his own sixty-six years. "You liked it there?"

"I loved it."

"Then why . . . ?"

"Why did I leave the missions? Why am I becoming a diocesan priest?"

Koesler opened his hands on the table palms up, inviting a response. "If it's not too personal. Earlier you said something about the bishops . . ."

"The bishops . . ." Carleson's expression hardened. "Yes, the bishops. See, the Church in the Third World is not all that different from the Church anywhere else—here. Bishops, by their very position, tend toward being somewhat aristocratic. The highest rank a bishop can reach, short of the papacy, is the Cardinalate. And Cardinals are referred to commonly as 'Princes of the Church.' The Polish word for priest is *księdz*—which is almost exactly the word for 'prince.' And that's only a priest.

"Bishops—Catholic bishops—are treated pretty much like royalty, if not by everyone at least by Catholics. And that's as true in this country as it is almost everywhere else."

"I can't disagree," Koesler said. "Anytime a bishop presides at the altar, all of the liturgy revolves around him. It's as if he were a king. He even sits on a throne.

"But, as you said, it's a situation common everywhere—in this country as well as Honduras. So, why . . . ? I mean as long as you're functioning as a priest, you're going to have to deal with bishops. And you're still functioning as a priest. . . ."

"It's a good point . . . by the way, could I have a bit more coffee?"

Koesler could have kissed him. Never in his life had anyone come back for seconds of Koesler's brew. Most people never finished the first cup. Gladly did he refill both their cups. And, mercifully, that did it for the leftover coffee.

"Let me try to clarify my point." Carleson blew across the surface of his cup. "Since bishops are treated like royalty, I suppose it's only natural that most of them seem to identify with the movers and shakers of society, with the Establishment, with those in power.

"But, see, in the Third World there are only two classes: those who have everything and those who have nothing. Nothing connects the classes. Nothing exists between them. You must be for one side or the other. No matter with which side the local bishop relates, his priests have to choose. If the bishop joins the aristocracy, the priest does also. Or else the priest finds himself in opposition not only to the rich but also to his bishop."

Carleson smiled grimly. "The priests get together periodically, much like the meeting we attended this evening. And down there we divided ourselves about the way you do.

"This evening, I paid very close attention to what was being said by whom. Everybody kept the conversation confined to noncontroversial subjects like the services the city doesn't provide or the mayor or the council. I watched the departure of the guys who pretty much sided with the Church bureaucracies. I could tell because as they left, the conversation drifted to subjects not so safe.

"And then they wanted to find out which side I was on. But their investigation was short-circuited by—who was it . . . Ernie Bell?—and his problems with Bishop Diego.

"The priests' meetings in Honduras—and the other countries where I've served—are about the same. Except that the stakes are higher. Probably because there are no neutral areas. It's either poor or rich . . . the haves or the have-nots.

"Do you get the picture, Bob? Who the bishop happens to be and what his social ethic is are of tremendous importance. And, in the final analysis, the diocesan priests down there have a bit more mobility than the priests who come in as missionaries. They can move to a different jurisdiction, especially before they're ordained. And while that's not an awful lot of consolation, it's better than the missionary who's sent to a particular locale by his superior. There isn't much of anything he can do about it."

Koesler had been concentrating so much on what was being explained that his coffee had gotten cold. He pushed the cup aside. "You make it sound so . . . so dismal. As if the bishops in mission territories have abandoned the poor to mingle with the rich. It can't be that bleak."

"It isn't. But it comes close. Sure, you've got your Helder Camara in Brazil or Romero in El Salvador. But you've also had the all-but-complete opposition to Aristide by the bishops of Haiti.

"If I'm painting with too broad a brush, I'm sorry. There's no doubt it's tough to be a bishop in the Third World and champion the poor. That choice would put you in opposition to not only the wealthy but the rulers as well as the military. Is it any wonder that a significant percentage of those bishops have sided with the wealthy class?"

"I guess it makes sense," Koesler said after some hesitation. "But if that's the case with the bishops, what about the priests? I mean the ones like yourself who choose to work with the poor? See, here in Detroit once you get an assignment to the inner city, bureaucracy pretty much forgets about you. Now that means different things to different people. But the interpretation of Church law for the inner-city priests is, to put it mildly, neither rigid nor strict. Didn't you find it like that in the barrios? I don't think the Vatican's Church would make much sense in the barrio."

Carleson laughed. "Hardly. We undoubtedly went a lot further than you do up here. If a couple showed up and wanted to be married in the Church, I was so surprised and happy I never thought of asking questions like had either of them been married before. It was no place for the nonactivist. The ethical judgments we had to make were not found in any approved theology textbook."

Koesler appeared skeptical. "I don't know that we play it *that* loose up here."

"I'm counting on it," Carleson said firmly.

Koesler paused thoughtfully, then looked up brightly. "Would you like more coffee? I could make some fresh in a minute."

"Thanks, no. But it was very good."

Koesler could make coffee for this gentleman forever.

Carleson glanced at his watch. "Hey, I'd better get going. It's almost midnight."

"I'll drive you home. But . . . one more thing: If you made your choice and decided to work among the poor and you could feel free to provide them with what they needed—freer, I assure you, than you will be here—why leave?"

Carleson shook his head. "I didn't leave of my own accord."

"You didn't—"

"In effect, the bishop threw me out. More politely, he requested my superiors to change my assignment and get me the hell out of Honduras."

"But why?"

"Because I committed the unforgiveable sin. I began talking about how unfair it was. Jesus did not keep still when he encountered a priestly caste that imposed gratuitous burdens on people. I thought He would not be silent when a few kept everything to themselves while leaving the majority with nothing."

Koesler nodded. "Liberation theology?"

"If you will. It seemed the essence of the Christian message. It seemed inescapable if you read the Gospels. I didn't even say it loudly. I just said it. And some of the bishop's men heard about it. They told him. And he told me. It wasn't a long interview. He asked me if I had 'got the people all disturbed.' A few words later I was packing my duffel bag.

"That's when I decided to start choosing my bishops. Mark Boyle and Detroit seemed about the best choice in the States. I knew he must be surrounded by a self-fulfilling bureaucracy. It seemed inevitable. But one could be relatively free here."

"And if Cardinal Boyle were to pass on?"

"I would take a careful look at his successor. I might apply for another excardination. I might get a somewhat unsteady reputation. On the other hand, the bishop I'd select to work for might feel that I'd given him an unsolicited testimonial."

"And Bishop Ramon Diego?"

Carleson froze.

Koesler was startled. But he had encountered similar reactions. People under great emotional stress—illness, family tragedy, or the like—enjoy some time of relief, a happy distraction. Sometimes they forget their troubles. They lose themselves in the joy of the moment. Then, inevitably, they are forced to return to reality. The change in their emotions, in their very appearance, can be profound.

So it was with Don Carleson. It had been a pleasant evening, with an entertaining chat between two like-minded priests. But now it was time to return to the real world. From his expression, it was clear that Carleson dreaded what must be. It was inescapable.

"It's after midnight," Carleson said softly. "I guess we'd better go."

During the brief drive to Ste. Anne's, nothing more was said. Koesler let Carleson out at the front door to the rectory. Koesler glanced at the showy string of lights that garlanded the Ambassador Bridge. Then he started his return drive.

Cinderella did not want to go home from the dance. Carleson didn't want to go home from his evening out. And he didn't have a fairy godmother.

CHAPTER THREE

Father Koesler shuffled into the kitchen of St. Joseph's rectory. He wore his pajamas, a robe, slippers, his glasses, and his ever-present watch.

He was grateful St. Joe's scheduled no early-morning Mass. Much of his priesthood had been marked by parish Masses programmed for 5:30 or 6:00 in the morning. A 7:00 or 8:00 A.M. Mass was an invitation to sleep in.

Now, with the daily Mass offered at noon he had the leisure to wake up gradually and prepare a more thoughtful homily. Habit, however, kept him waking and rising at 7:00.

Neither the housekeeper nor the secretary, Mrs. Mary O'Connor, would be in for another couple of hours, thus the informal attire.

With yawns and stretches punctuating his movements, he added a banana and skim milk to cold cereal, and turned on the small radio. Station WJR was halfway through its news broadcast. "And now with the weather, here's John McMurray."

Koesler lifted the coffeepot from its stand. Empty. Then he remembered having drained the pot last night with Don Carleson. Koesler decided he could wait until after breakfast.

"There is a mass of cold, arctic air invading the area from northern Canada," John McMurray announced. "It will be accompanied by a strong high-pressure system which will usher in clear skies and plenty of sunshine. However"—McMurray pronounced it "howevah"; a native New Yorker, Koesler assumed—"the windchill factor will make our high temperature today of twenty-eight feel like it's only five above zero. And I'll be back in twenty minutes with WJR's exclusive three-day forecast."

Koesler regarded the banana. The last of its bunch, it had seen the better part of its life. He hoped it would not be too ripe. He preferred bananas to be bright yellow—even greenish—and firm. He'd have to remember to get more today.

"Recapping our lead story," the newscaster said, "a Detroit bishop was found murdered in the rectory of Ste. Anne's church just west of downtown Detroit. Police are on the scene and their investigation has just begun into the death of auxiliary bishop Ramon Diego. We'll be bringing you more details as we get them."

The radio continued to play, but Koesler no longer heard it. His mind was whirling. He went to the front porch and retrieved the *Free Press*. He paged through it, but found no mention of the death. Of course not; the story must have broken long after the *Freep*'s final edition had gone to press.

What had the announcer said? Diego's body was discovered. . . .

The bishop couldn't have been found before Koesler delivered Carleson to the rectory. Otherwise the neighborhood would have been teeming with police cars. He remembered how dark and apparently peaceful Ste. Anne's had been last night.

Then who . . . ? Could it have been Don Carleson who found the body? It almost had to be. Obviously everyone else had gone to bed. The four Basilians who staffed the parish had left last night's meeting relatively early. That was why Carleson had no ride home. That was why Koesler had volunteered a ride.

Evidently, the four had not found the body . . . or the murder had not taken place before their return.

It must have been Carleson who discovered the body . . . probably only moments after Koesler had driven off.

Why hadn't Carleson called him?

On second thought, why would he? There was nothing Koesler could have done. He must have called the police.

Of course, that must have been it.

He wondered what was going on now, at this very moment. None of the priests at Ste. Anne's could have gotten any sleep last night. Poor Don Carleson to have found the body.

For the first time, Koesler wondered how the bishop had been killed. Had it been messy with blood and gore? Or, perhaps, just the innocent little hole a bullet might make?

On second thought, would it have made any difference? In all the time Carleson had spent in Third World countries, he must have witnessed death in all its stark varieties.

Instinctively, Koesler dialed Ste. Anne's. *Busy.* He pictured the turmoil that must be engulfing that scene. This was not an opportune moment for him to barge in.

He would wait to see when—or if—he was needed. No point in intruding where one was not wanted.

Still, he could not help wondering what was going on.

*　*　*　*

"I don't care. I don't like it, Zoo," Sergeant Phil Mangiapane said.

"Sometimes it works," Lieutenant Alonzo Tully replied.

"Maybe. But not when you got Quirt," Mangiapane insisted.

Tully shrugged. "Look at it this way, Manj: Lieutenant George Quirt didn't ask to head this task force—"

"As far as you know!"

"As far as I know. Okay. Just make sure your head's on straight. We gotta close this one, and fast."

"But what I can't figure, Zoo, is why Koznicki put us on the same case with Quirt. And then, on top of that, to put him in charge of the case! He's gotta know that we—especially you—and him don't get along."

"Walt Koznicki didn't fill in the cast of characters, Manj."

"No?"

Tully lifted his eyes heavenward. It was the only show of emotion he would allow himself. "Far as I know, this came down right from Cobb himself. And it was Cobb who insisted on Quirt leading this thing."

"Just what we need: the Mayor messing in the squads!"

"Pull it together, Manj. And get those interviews in. We're gonna debrief pretty soon."

It had been Father Carleson who had called 911. The uniformed officers who responded quickly determined that this was no run-of-the-mill homicide. When they called it in, they made sure it was clear that the deceased was a bishop.

That led to calling in a number of homicide detectives who had expected a complete night's sleep. It also occasioned the waking of Maynard Cobb, mayor of Detroit.

The mayor sounded out his chief of police. They quickly were of one mind that this was one the national media would feast on. Bishops died from time to time, but they weren't murdered.

Cobb could envision the leads in newspapers, on radio and TV. "Only in Detroit . . ." The stories would enumerate the actual totals along with the per capita numbers of murders. Then the Cobb administration would try to find at least a bronze lining. Washington, D.C.'s murder rate was higher per capita. Or Los Angeles or New York had a higher total. Or Detroit's record was not as high as last year's. And that—the search for light at the end of this long, dark tunnel—made up the administration's major effort to control this gun-crazy city.

While Cobb and his police chief did confer on the necessity for and composition of this task force, still they were not in complete agreement.

The chief was uneasy about putting Tully and Quirt on the same squad. It wasn't that Tully was black and Quirt white: That was not a racial problem as far as those two were concerned. It was the disparity in their methods and personalities that occasioned the chief's hesitation. Each was a lieutenant leading a homicide squad. Equal in rank, the two were, under the circumstances, likely to be on a collision course.

As far as the mayor was concerned, he simply figured that Tully and Quirt were the two most effective detectives in Homicide. They'd make an airtight arrest in the briefest possible time.

That Quirt was to be in charge merely indicated that the mayor wanted a speedy close to the case. Tully was more likely to be deliberative but accurate. Quirt tended to be swift and expeditious but slipshod. Cobb thought them a good mix. Quick but sure, with the emphasis on getting a body into jail in the least amount of time and the media off the mayor's aging back.

Not surprisingly, the mayor's view won out.

*　　*　　*　　*

"Hey, Zoo, whaddya think?"

Thinking was exactly what Tully had been doing before Quirt's sudden approach.

The two men were about the same height. Tully's hair was close-cropped. He was lean, fit, and dressed conservatively. Quirt, almost completely bald, was noticeably overweight. He wore mostly bright colors and suspenders.

"I dunno, Quirt. A little early."

"Good lookin' guy."

"Who?"

"The dead guy." Quirt's impatience was obvious. "The bishop."

"He didn't look that good to me. Just dead."

"Yeah, kind of messy. But look here . . ." Quirt motioned Tully into the bishop's office. "Look at all these pictures on the walls. Good lookin' guy?"

Tully had noted the pictures earlier. He had put them on the back burner for later study. Now that his attention had been drawn, he considered them more carefully.

"Looks like a movin'-pitcher star," Quirt suggested. "Looks like . . . who's that guy . . . you know, the spic in those commercials for the car . . . the . . . oh, hell . . . the Cordoba?"

"Montalban. Ricardo Montalban."

"Yeah. Don'tcha think?"

The late bishop was, or rather had been, indeed a handsome man. But that was not what interested Tully. Each photo showed Diego with one or more people. Without exception, the others in these candid shots were among the wealthiest and most prominent men and women in the metropolitan area. Tully recognized almost everyone. Not one was or appeared to be Hispanic.

"He was Latino?" Tully asked.

"Yeah, sure. Whaddya think he was doin' in this part of town? There ain't many people left around here. But what's here are spics."

Tully stepped back into the hallway. Quirt followed.

By far the most conspicuous fixture in the long, narrow, ancient corridor was a larger-than-life bust, done in some sort of black material. The officers approached it with some curiosity.

Quirt bent to read the identifying plaque. "'Father Gabriel . . .'" He paused. "'Richard.'" He pronounced the surname as the English given name.

"'Richard,'" said a voice behind them, giving it the French inflection. Quirt and Tully turned. "It's 'Richard,' said the tall man in clerical collar and black cassock buttoned from neck to ankles. The material was stretched to the breaking point at his ample midsection. "Richard," the tall man repeated, "like the former Montreal hockey player, Maurice 'the Rocket' Richard."

"Yeah, Richard." Tully pronounced the name correctly: *Reesharrd*. "There's a statue or a park somewhere . . . near Belle Isle?"

The priest nodded. "And here in Ste. Anne's parish where Father served as a pastor almost two hundred years ago. In fact," he continued, "Father Richard is buried right here in this church."

Quirt whipped out his pen and notepad. "And you are . . . ?"

"McCauley. Father David McCauley. I'm one of the priests assigned to this parish. I'm also"—a tone of modest pride crept into his voice— "a bit of a local historian.

"Maybe, since the bishop died here, and I suppose much of your investigation will be conducted here, maybe you'd like to hear a little bit about Ste. Anne's?"

"Okay," Tully said, on the off chance that this history lesson might lead to a better understanding of the murder.

"It all began," said Father McCauley, "on July 24, 1701. Twenty-five canoes docked at what would become the city of Detroit. At that time it was just a wilderness," he explained. "In the original landing party were Antoine de la Mothe Cadillac, fifty artisans, fifty soldiers, and two priests. These few men began immediately to build Fort Detroit.

"One of the first log structures was a chapel dedicated to their patroness in the wilderness, Ste. Anne, mother of Mary the Mother of Jesus." He smiled. "It is the second oldest parish in the United States, after St. Augustine, in Florida.

"Eventually, the church of Ste. Anne became Detroit's first cathedral, anchoring the newly created Diocese of Michigan and the Northwest, which included Ohio, Indiana, and Illinois, along with part of Wisconsin."

Father McCauley was warming to his subject. Quirt looked fidgety. Tully looked patient.

"By far the most important pastor in the history of Ste. Anne was Father Gabriel Richard. He belonged to the Society of St. Sulpice, which was dedicated to the education of seminarians—future priests," he explained. His listeners nodded. "In Fort Pontchartrain du Detroit there were no seminarians to teach, but Father Richard made up for that by bringing the first printing press to the area. He published the area's first newspaper and printed books. He opened schools and helped create what is now the University of Michigan. He was the first priest elected to the United States Congress. He formed a nursing corps to care for the sick during the Asiatic cholera epidemic in 1832." Father McCauley smiled again, this time sadly. "He became the disease's final victim.

"The present church," he continued after a moment, "is the eighth dedicated to Ste. Anne. In each of its seven reincarnations, it has never moved far from the spot it originally occupied just inside the fort."

Quirt was definitely fidgeting. Tully continued to be attentive.

"In the beginning, Ste. Anne's served a basically French congregation. Over the years, it has seen many ethnic groups come and go. Today it serves a multi-ethnic, bilingual neighborhood. It is part shrine, part historical treasure, and part geographical parish. Inside the chapel, which is"— McCauley gestured in the direction of the church building— "inside the church, there's an impressive sarcophagus containing the remains of Gabriel Richard in his original coffin. And the altar in the chapel is the same one used by Father Richard.

"Since 1886, the parish has been administered by the Basilians, an order of priests dedicated to teaching. Today the parish is statted by a number of our order. All of us speak Spanish as well as English," he said.

"And all of us," he added after a moment, "are dedicated to the Latino community—which in turn relies on this beautiful old Gothic structure for all manner of help and centering.

"Now, as you may know"—he looked at both of his listeners in turn—"large archdioceses can comprise substantial ethnic or racial groups, such as Polish, Italian, Irish, Latino, Chaldean, and African-American." Quirt nodded impatiently. Tully just nodded. "Detroit surely runs true to this form. And among these groupings, the African-Americans and the Latinos have each been most vocal about wanting 'their' bishop now.

"Bishop Diego, up from Texas, was the archdiocese's fairly recent gift to Detroit Latinos." Quirt stopped fidgeting. Tully's alertness was obvious. "When Bishop Diego came to Detroit, he reached an agreement with Cardinal Boyle that he would be at Ste. Anne's church in residence only . . . with no specific parochial duties.

"This was not a unique arrangement for auxiliary bishops," Father McCauley explained. "You see, the thought was that the bishop would become a leader of, and an advocate for, Latinos—"

"Never hurts to bone up." Quirt, who had already learned more than he ever wanted to know about all this, smiled crookedly. "Well . . ." His voice rose. ". . . look who's here."

Tully scarcely needed to look. From the tenor of Quirt's greeting, but mostly from the nature of this case, it had to be Brad Kleimer.

Tully turned to see Kleimer advancing toward them, hand extended. Kleimer, an assistant prosecuting attorney for Wayne County, was of small stature, perhaps five-feet-six, but there appeared to be three-inch lifts on his shoes. His physique evidenced fidelity to pumping iron. As usual, he wore a natty, three-piece suit. The gray at his temples highlighted his dark, blown-dry hair.

Tully well knew that Kleimer and Quirt had a lot in common: Both men actively sought out the high-profile cases. They coveted the publicity attached to such cases. Each fully intended to measurably improve his status in life. And each was effective at what he did. Quirt made arrests. Kleimer got convictions.

There was no doubt in Tully's mind that Quirt had called and invited Kleimer to this made-for-prime-time circus case. If this scenario was accurate, Kleimer would owe Quirt one. And the debt would be repaid.

It was grotesquely out of the ordinary for anyone on the prosecutor's staff to get involved in a case before the police completed their initial investigation. At that time, attorneys appropriate to the various levels of indictment would be assigned to the case.

Tully—and practically everyone else in the system—knew that Kleimer operated well outside the prescribed process. Somehow, more often than not, he managed to get the word when a headliner case occurred. And somehow, more often than not, he contrived to get the assignment.

Tully was not privy to Kleimer's machinations within the prosecutor's office, but it was obvious how he had cultivated the police connection. There were certain cops who did business with him on an indebtedness basis.

It was quid pro quo. Certain officers would cue him in when they chanced upon a case that merited a great deal of media coverage. In return, he would do his best to get them whatever they wanted— within reason. These favors ranged from rather modest gifts to preferential consideration for promotions. It depended, largely, on the case's potential to attract publicity.

Of all Kleimer's departmental connections, none was situated better or more willing to cooperate than George Quirt.

As far as Tully could judge, there was nothing specifically illegal in this maneuver. Ethically . . . ?

"You're just in time, Brad." Quirt shook Kleimer's hand in greeting. "We're just gonna get it together. You remember Zoo Tully . . ."

"Of course." Kleimer turned to Tully, who nodded perfunctorily.

"Come on in here, Brad. We sorta took over the dining room . . ."

Father McCauley, finding himself totally and completely ignored, hesitated, then walked away. He had work to do.

It was just 8:30. The task force members were filing into the large rectangular room. Dark mahogany constituted the decor. The large table, the chairs, and the cabinets were either ancient or appeared to be. The table was filling with notes, diagrams, and bits of what might become evidence.

The first group of officers into the room seated themselves at the table, with here and there a few chivalrous gestures.

"Okay." Quirt took command, much to the resentment of Tully's people. "What've we got? Mangiapane?"

Mangiapane, jaws tight, looked to Tully, who merely nodded.

"Okay," Mangiapane began, "the time of death looks to be between 4:00 and 6:00 last night." He looked up. "That's subject to the M.E.'s report. The autopsy's not completed yet. But, so far, it looks like a good guess.

"This place is wired for sound," Mangiapane continued. "They got wires in every door and window. The alarm company's central office reports the system was operating last night, but there was no single intrusion registered."

"Which means the perp either was in here before the system was activated or he was admitted," Quirt said needlessly. "Was there anybody else besides the deceased in here last night that we know about?"

Mangiapane shrugged. He didn't have that information. Quirt looked around the room.

Sergeant Angie Moore, of Tully's squad, raised her hand.

Quirt recognized her. He was not disturbed that, so far, none of his own squad had spoken. But, particularly since Brad Kleimer—an outsider—was present, Quirt was conscious that Tully's people had taken the lead.

"There are four—no, five—other priests who live here," Moore said. "Four of them have been working at this parish for from three to ten years. They belong to a religious organization called Basilians. There's another priest who's been here only about three months. He has some sort of special assignment to the victim. I wasn't able to get that too clearly. He's not here now—"

"Who?" Quirt was peremptory. "The guy with the special assignment?"

"Yeah."

"What's his name?"

"Uh . . . Carleson. Father Donald Carleson."

"Where is he?"

"He said he had to go to the hospital. Some patients were expecting him this morning."

"While an investigation was going on?" Quirt was growing truculent. "Which hospital?"

"Receiving." Moore, in spite of herself, felt intimidated.

"Get him back here."

"He answered all our—"

"I wanna know about this 'special' assignment with the bishop. Get him back here! For Chrissakes, this is a homicide investigation!"

Moore fumbled her papers together and left the room.

Tully would have intervened except that, fundamentally, Quirt was not only in charge, but correct: The priest shouldn't have been allowed to leave while the investigation was going on. But after this briefing, Tully would have some strong words with Quirt. He had no business treating Moore like a rookie and publicly embarrassing her. She was a Catholic, and that, added to the normal respect most officers have for the clergy, had led her to make a mistake . . . a minor, nonirreparable one.

"Anybody got anything else on the priests here?" Quirt asked.

Williams, one of Quirt's people, raised a hand. Quirt eagerly recognized him.

From Quirt's change of expression, Tully saw where this was going—and he didn't like it. Quirt was setting up a contest—his gang against Tully's. If this task force was going to do its job, it would have to blend into a single investigative unit. Silently, he damned Cobb for meddling where he had no expertise whatever.

Williams consulted his notes. "I was working with Angie and we questioned all the priests."

Williams's mention of a name from the rival team did not endear him to Quirt.

"All five of them left to go to a meeting of a bunch of other priests at the Cathedral at 9844 Woodward."

"They went together?" Tully asked.

"Yeah, one car."

"What time?"

"They left about 5:30. The meeting was at 6:00 and they figured it wouldn't take more than a half hour to get there, what with Sunday traffic and all."

"What about the bishop?" Tully continued.

"He told them earlier in the day that he wasn't going." Williams lowered his notes momentarily. "For one thing, bishops aren't exactly welcome at these meetings. The priests said most of the meetings they have eventually get down to griping sessions. And some if not most of the griping is about the bishops."

The group laughed, recognizing that the priests were no different from a bunch of cops getting together for a similar session.

"What time'd the meeting end?" Quirt was not laughing.

Williams scratched his head. "No set time. There's usually some sort of light dinner, then the gabfest. People leave whenever they want. They just drift out as the evening goes on."

"When'd our five leave?"

"Four," Williams corrected.

"Four?"

"Carleson wanted to stay. So the others left together sometime a little after 9:00. They came right back here."

"But they didn't find the body." Tully's statement implied the question.

"No." Williams sensed he needed to amplify. "They came in by a side entrance. The alarm system they got here is top of the line. If you know the codes, you can program the thing to cover whatever areas you want. So when they deactivated the alarm for that area, they didn't know the system that controlled the front door had already been deactivated. After they entered the house here, they reactivated the alarm for the rear area. They just assumed the front alarm system was on. There weren't any lights on and everything seemed okay."

"They didn't check on the bishop?"

"Like I said, there weren't any lights on. The door to his room was shut. He's got—he had—a suite on the second floor—a bedroom and den. There's three floors in this building, all occupied.

"Anyway, they didn't see any light coming from under the door to his room. So they just figured that he'd gone to bed early."

"So, when did Carleson get in?" Quirt asked.

"Uh . . ." Williams hesitated. "Angie's got those details in her notes."

Quirt was about to say something when Sergeant Moore appeared at the door of the dining room with a priest in tow.

"Father Carleson?" Tully asked.

"Yes," the priest replied. "Sorry about this. I thought I was finished here, so I started making my rounds at the hospital. When Sergeant Moore told me you wanted me, I came right back."

Quirt gestured toward one of the detectives who was seated at the table. "Sit down, Father."

The designated officer scrambled to vacate his chair in favor of the priest.

Acutely aware that he had become the center of attention, Carleson was uneasy.

"The other priests here say you did not return with them last night," Tully said.

"That's right," Carleson agreed. "Last night was my first chance to meet the other city priests. I wanted to get to know them and let them get to know me. The meeting was old hat to my colleagues here. It was a first for me. So I turned down their invitation to leave early."

"So what time did you leave?" Quirt asked.

"I guess it would have been about 10:00 or 10:30."

"But," Quirt pressed, "you didn't notify the police until after midnight. It take you that long to get from Woodward and Boston Boulevard to here?"

"I got a ride from another priest. We stopped at his rectory and talked for a while."

"This other priest," Quirt said, "he got a name?"

Carleson bristled. He felt the insult in Quirt's tone and choice of words. He also felt he was in no position to state anything but simple facts. "Koesler," he said. "Father Robert Koesler. He's the pastor of St. Joseph's—near downtown. He's the one who drove me home."

Koesler! The name struck several chords with Tully. He had worked several cases using this priest as an expert resource. The guy was no detective, but he knew his way around the Catholic Church—as did, undoubtedly, most of the other priests. But there was something about this guy. Maybe it was his willingness to help. Maybe it was his attention to detail. Till now in this case, Tully had felt himself in a morass of religious minutiae, what with religious orders, teachers in parish work, some historical priest Tully had been aware of only vaguely, a bishop in residence. It was a happy accident that Koesler was already involved in this case. Much more of this religious stuff and Tully himself might have called on the priest.

"So," Quirt continued, "this Father Koesler dropped you off here shortly after midnight?"

"That's right. Then he left immediately."

"What did you do then? Give us every detail you can remember."

"Okay." Carleson paused, attempting to recall the events accurately and completely.

"I opened the front door with my key. The only possible complication there would have been if someone had turned the dead bolt. I still could have opened the door, it just would've taken longer. And once you fiddle with the door, you've got only thirty seconds to deactivate the alarm."

"And did you get to the alarm in time?"

"That's what started me wondering really. I got to the alarm in plenty of time, but the code showed that the system for that part of the house wasn't on. I couldn't understand that. We're very careful about the security system. I was sure the other priests had come home earlier. They would have to have deactivated the system when they came in and then activated it again after they closed the outside door. I figured they must not have noticed that one area of the house wasn't covered.

"But I wondered more why the front door wasn't protected. The bishop's office is right next to the door. I thought maybe he had shut it down because someone had come to the door. He'd have to have deactivated it before opening the door. Then, maybe after the caller left, he'd forgotten to reactivate it. Still, that didn't sound like something he would forget. That's when I decided to look around a little. I went into the bishop's office and turned on the light. And . . ."

"And you found him?"

Carleson nodded. "I found him. And I called 911 right away. Then I woke the other priests and we waited for the police. We were careful not to touch anything. I guess that came from watching movies about murders—"

"We've got just a few more questions," Quirt said.

CHAPTER FOUR

After summoning Father David McCauley, the Basilian priest whom Quirt and Tully had already met, Quirt sent the detectives back to work.

Quirt, Tully, Kleimer, and Fathers McCauley and Carleson then moved to a less spacious room nearby. With the considerable group of detectives no longer hanging onto his every word and gesture, Carleson felt less nervous.

Tully could not gauge how deeply Carleson was affected by all this. He seemed to be holding up rather well. But Father McCauley was definitely nervous.

Quirt began by telling the priests that while it was not a crime to lie to the police, it could be a really disastrous mistake. If they were to lie or not tell everything they knew, it would all come home to roost eventually.

McCauley was deeply impressed. Carleson had been bullied by more threatening characters.

It was obvious that Quirt intended to get down to the nitty-gritty immediately. Tully would have preferred to explore some background first. But, what the hell, the ball was in Quirt's court.

"What we got here," Quirt proceeded, "is we got a dead man. So he happens to be a bishop. Still, he's dead. So we go through this thing by the book." He paused and glanced at Tully. "Near as I can see." Tully remained impassive.

"First thing," Quirt continued, "who would want him dead?"

No response.

"Did he have any enemies?"

Carleson and McCauley looked at each other. Each seemed to expect the other to speak.

Their reaction did not escape Quirt. "Father McCauley?"

McCauley cleared his throat. "This is hard to say . . . but to be as truthful as I can: With some exceptions, the only people who liked him were the ones who didn't know him very well."

Quirt was surprised. "What . . . what do you mean, 'didn't know him'?"

"Well, like when he would visit a parish for confirmation . . ."

"Wait a minute," Quirt protested. "What is this 'visit for confirmation'?"

More than ever, Tully wanted Koesler around. That, he promised himself, would come later.

"Bishops," McCauley said, "especially auxiliary bishops, travel around to parishes in this archdiocese—there are more than three hundred of them—and give the sacrament of confirmation to the children and adults who have been prepared for this sacrament.

"The bishop—in this case Bishop Diego—comes in just for that occasion. Maybe he has dinner with the priests of the parish and probably some priest-guests. Then there's the ceremony over which he presides. Then he leaves.

"Those are the people who like him—the ones he meets very briefly in church. Bishop Diego could be charming. But not over the long haul. But . . . well, if anybody could speak to that it would be Don here . . ." He indicated Carleson.

At mention of his name, Carleson froze. McCauley immediately regretted having putting Carleson on the spot, so to speak.

"Oh, yeah," Quirt said, "I was gonna get to that. Something about a 'special assignment'? What's that all about?"

Carleson took a deep breath, then exhaled as if he were about to embark on a dreaded journey.

"To put it as simply as I can, I've been a priest for some thirty years. Nearly all that time I've been a missionary priest in different countries. Now—well, as of the past several months—I've been in the process of joining the archdiocese of Detroit.

"I've got considerable background working among Latinos. So it was only natural that I serve in this community here in Detroit. But . . . I haven't had much experience ministering in a large, urban, American setting. So . . . so it was determined that the 'perfect' assignment"—the sarcasm was unmistakable—"would be for me to work with Bishop Diego. The bishop is . . . uh, was . . . Hispanic. He'd been in a Latino community in Texas."

"And just what did this assignment involve?" Quirt sensed a possible suspect. It was his favorite scent.

Carleson bit his lip. "To be pretty much at his beck and call."

"Well, let's see if I got this straight . . ." Quirt was warming to the possibilities. "According to Father McCauley here, to know Bishop Diego was not necessarily to love him. In fact, the less you had to do with the guy, the more likely you were to get along okay. Whereas the better acquainted you got, the more you disliked him.

"Seems to me, you gotta be pretty high on the list of people who might even like to see him dead."

"Wait a minute. You can't be—"

"Father . . ." Quirt was unctuous. ". . . all I'm doing is putting together what was just said by Father McCauley and *yourself*. Nothing more than that. Now, let's just see where everybody was last night. Father McCauley, where were you between the hours of 4:00 and 6:00 P.M. yesterday?"

"Really!" As intimidated as McCauley was, he certainly had not expected to be treated as a murder suspect.

Quirt let his very authentic nasty side show through. "This is a homicide investigation. I don't give a damn whether this Bishop Diego was a living saint or a son of a bitch. He's dead. And I'm gonna find out who did it. With a guy who made as many enemies as this guy seems to have made, the line of possible suspects can get kinda long. But no possible suspect is excused just because he happens to be clergy.

"Now, Father McCauley, Father Carleson, you can answer our questions here and now, or . . . we can go down to the station. It's just a short drive. But it ain't as pleasant there as here.

"What'll it be?"

McCauley lowered his head and nodded.

"Okay." Quirt resumed. "Between 4:00 and 6:00, Father McCauley?"

"I was tired. We always are after the weekend schedule of Masses. And I was looking forward to the evening meeting of the priests. But I wasn't looking forward to it very eagerly. And since we were committed to going, I decided to rest up and maybe take a nap—"

"Wait a minute," Quirt interrupted. "How come you were 'committed'? I thought it was voluntary. How come you had to go?"

McCauley hesitated. "Well, we had promised Don. He had never been to one of these meetings—uh, they're actually parties. So we agreed to go for his sake."

Quirt looked at Carleson. "Funny how you keep popping up at the center of things, isn't it, Father?" He turned back to McCauley. "So you took a nap? Conveniently from 4:00 to 6:00."

"No. I went up to my room about 3:00 in the afternoon. I read for a while. Watched a little basketball on the TV. And then napped a bit. Until about 5:00, I guess. Then I got ready to go. We left about 5:30. The dinner was at 6:00."

"Anyone who can corroborate your whereabouts during this time?"

McCauley smiled lopsidedly. "No. We each have our own separate rooms. As far as I know, the others did just about what I did."

"But you can't know for sure. Maybe we should get the other three priests in here. One of you could have been with the bishop, couldn't that be true? Maybe, since no one can testify that you spent all that time in your room, maybe you spent some time with the bishop. Eh?"

"Not hardly," McCauley said.

"No? Not hardly? Why's that?"

McCauley looked almost helplessly at Carleson.

"He couldn't have spent time with the bishop," Carleson said.

"Why not?" Quirt's question was expectant.

"Because," Carleson explained, "because the bishop was with me."

"Between 4:00 and 6:00?"

"There wasn't anything odd or out of the ordinary about it." Carleson chose to ignore the implication in Quirt's question. "Given my druthers I'm sure I'd have spent the afternoon the way Dave did. It's sort of natural, especially for guys our age. That weekend liturgy can sap you. So, I was going to relax a while before leaving for the Cathedral. But the bishop wanted to go out."

"Out?"

"An afternoon cocktail party in Grosse Pointe."

"The bishop doesn't own a car?"

"The bishop doesn't . . . didn't . . . even own a driver's license."

"You were his chauffeur?" Quirt sounded incredulous.

Carleson simply nodded.

"Did the bishop go out much? Travel?"

"A bit."

"And with Detroit's mass transit being what it is, and, I suppose, the bishop being a bishop, he wouldn't want to depend on that. All in all, I guess you had to haul him around quite a bit."

Again Carleson nodded.

"So, yesterday," Quirt said, "just what did you and the bishop do and when did you do it?"

Carleson sighed. "He waited until about 1:00 in the afternoon to tell me. To be honest, I tried to beg off. But he insisted that it was important—'essential' was the word he used—for him to be at this gathering. He said there would be important people there—people who could do lots for the Latino community—"

"From your tone of voice," Quirt interrupted, "I gather you didn't believe him."

"That depends. That there were many wealthy people there was probably true. That any of them would lift a finger for the community was . . . well, doubtful.

"Anyway, I don't think the bishop would ask anybody to show some genuine commitment."

"You didn't want to do it," Quirt said. "You didn't think there was any point to it. But you did it anyway? Sounds kinda heroic!" The tone was laced with sarcasm.

"Look, Lieutenant, I'm no hero, or martyr, or saint. The way this arrangement began, it was supposed to be a short introduction to this urban ministry, sort of a brief probationary period."

"What happened? You keep signing up?"

Carleson snorted. "The deck was stacked. Diego loved the arrangement. Out of nowhere he got a slave. Each time I was due for an independent assignment, Diego would pull rank with the head of the Curia—the one who proposed assignments."

"Couldn't you go over this . . . this guy's head?"

"I'm not a crybaby . . . at least I try not to be."

"Back to yesterday," Quirt ordered.

"Yes, well, there was no getting out of it. So we left here about 2:00. The party started at 1:00, but Diego always likes to make an 'entrance.'

The party was at Harry Carson's home. He's an executive with Co-merica Bank. There must have been about fifty people there . . . at least while we were there."

"You attended the party?"

Carleson smiled briefly. "I *am* a priest. I would never have been left alone to wait in the car. Actually, I would have preferred that; I just hang around on the fringes on these occasions. Anyhow, Diego had promised me we would leave by 5:00 so I could join the others here and go with them to the Cathedral.

"But as the afternoon wore on, he showed no inclination to leave. That is, until this guy showed up at the party. It was about four o'clock, maybe a little later. He acted surprised to see Diego there. But the minute he spotted him, he headed for him like a guided missile. They had a few hot words before Carson steered them into another room.

"After a while, Diego came out looking somewhat the worse for wear. He was obviously embarrassed. He came right over to me and said we were leaving right then and there. He didn't even say good-bye to anybody. That was about 4:30. We got back here about 5:00. I went upstairs immediately to freshen up for the party. I don't know where Diego went . . . I suppose to his office."

Tully was alert for almost the first time during this interrogation. "Who was the guy who created the scene with Diego?"

"I don't know. I never saw him before. But that doesn't mean much: Lots of people at these affairs Diego dragged me to I would meet for the first, and often the last, time."

"Then," Quirt said, "you were the last one to see Bishop Diego alive."

"Not quite, Lieutenant. I was at least second last. Whoever killed him would have been last."

"Now, see here, Lieutenant, this is becoming patently unfair!" Mc-Cauley said forcefully.

Quirt was about to reply in kind, when experience and instinct told him to swallow it and see what happened next. So, rather than trump McCauley's ace, Quirt put on an attentive and agreeable face, encouraging McCauley to complete his thought.

"You seem determined to twist everything we tell you into some sort of statement of guilt. I'm speaking mostly on behalf of Father

Carleson here. Aren't you supposed to read us our rights or something?"

"I'm not arresting anyone. Or even charging anyone with anything." Quirt was downright benevolent.

"We've tried to tell you," McCauley forged on, "in the most tactful manner at our command that the late Bishop Diego was . . . a difficult man. And I say this cognizant of the maxim *nil nisi bonum.*" He slipped into the Latin aphorism.

"What?" Quirt meant to halt any incursion of a foreign tongue, and especially Spanish.

"*Nil nisi bonum,*" McCauley repeated, and then clarified, "*Nil nisi bonum de mortuis* . . . nothing but good of the dead. Say nothing about the dead except good things."

The explanation seemed to satisfy Quirt, so McCauley continued. "In spite of the *nil nisi bonum* disclaimer, we have been very open about the actual, and largely abrasive personality of, uh, our fallen comrade. All right, he *was* difficult to get along with—a challenge, to say the least.

"Speaking for my fellow Basilians, after we learned what to expect from him, we were not enchanted with the prospect of his being here with us. But that was the arrangement the diocese made, and we were ready to live with it. That did not imply that any or all of us wished him harm, or, *per impossibile,* that any of us would kill the man.

"And, all right, Father Carleson was much more involved with the man than the rest of us were. But that was the decision of the diocese and Don was willing to live with it. It had to end sometime!

"Bishop Diego was a most difficult man. He made life pretty miserable for any number of people—mostly priests. And Bob Carleson was not alone in being a special target of the bishop."

Quirt thanked his instinct and experience for letting McCauley ramble on. This was exactly what he was hoping for—another lead, maybe someone as good a suspect as Carleson. "And who would that be? Someone who was a 'special target' for the bishop?"

McCauley blanched. Too late he realized he had fallen into Quirt's trap. Now he had no recourse but to implicate another priest as a possible murder suspect. In the brief interlude that Quirt gave him to consider what he'd say next, McCauley tried to rationalize his blunder.

Eventually, Ernie Bell would have become entangled in this investigation. Among priests particularly, Bell's combat with Diego was common knowledge. If he, McCauley, had not revealed this fact, someone else surely would have.

McCauley's attempt at self-exculpation wasn't entirely effective. But it was the best he could muster at the moment. "Well," he said at length, "Father Ernest Bell has had some problems with the bishop."

"No, no, Father," Quirt said unctuously, "you and your friends here have had 'problems' with the bishop. Father Carleson has had his life made miserable by the bishop. Father Bell have much the same experience?"

Reluctantly, with much hesitation, McCauley told of the enmity that had grown steadily from almost the first meeting of Bell and Diego. Bad chemistry, McCauley declared. In any case, the conflict had escalated to the point where it was now larger than just the two men. Bell's very parish was under attack by the bishop. Everyone involved in the Latino community was in agreement that St. Gabriel's parish was vibrant and growing, doing great work, really. But would the power structure downtown realize that? Or would they be influenced by a bishop who had been brought into the diocese for the very purpose of providing leadership to the Latinos? Bell, understandably, was beside himself with concern for his parish and his people.

Quirt did not grasp the essence of the dispute between the clergymen. But he very clearly recognized a suspect when he saw one. And this Father Ernest Bell surely qualified. "So," Quirt said, "if I got this right, you, you're saying that this Father Bell felt threatened by Bishop Diego."

"Yes, I guess that's a fair statement."

"The power structure of the local Church could close down a parish if it wants to?"

"Well, I don't want to give the impression that they'd do such a thing capriciously. But, with the clergy crisis and all, sometimes a closing does solve a bunch of problems. Especially if a nearby parish can take over the displaced parishioners."

"But now"—Quirt's tone was eager—"now Bishop Diego is dead. And Father Bell's problems seem to be solved . . . don't they?"

"Well . . . yes," McCauley admitted. "But that doesn't mean—"

"Lieutenant," Carleson broke in, "are we quite done here, at least for the moment? I'm way behind, and getting more so, on my hospital rounds. Do you mind if I leave now?"

Quirt, pleased with his progress and eager to begin checking out his theories, did not bother to answer Carleson, but merely waved him away.

Carleson left immediately.

McCauley was about to follow suit, when Sergeant Mangiapane stuck his head in the door. "Zoo," Mangiapane said almost breathlessly, "the autopsy's over—"

Tully shook his head and inclined it toward Quirt, who was obviously not pleased with what he took as a slight.

Mangiapane shrugged and turned to address Quirt. "This'll make more sense, I think, if we go to the bishop's office."

"Let's go." Quirt led the way.

Return to the scene of the crime, thought McCauley. *All those crime movies weren't a complete waste of time after all.* . . . Although he assumed that he had been dismissed, he decided to tag along.

The rectory's entrance, appropriately enough, fronted on Ste. Anne Street. A sidewalk led to a rise of wooden steps. The heavy door opened to a small foyer that in turn led to a long hallway. Bishop Diego's office was the first door to the right after entering the corridor.

The office itself was moderately large. Had there been much furniture or bric-a-brac, it would have looked crowded. However, it was sparsely outfitted. The eye-catching feature was the previously mentioned collection of photos adorning the walls. They came close to constituting a Who's Who of Detroit, with the bishop's image the only constant in each of them.

Now assembled in the office were Mangiapane, Tully, Quirt, Kleimer, and Father McCauley.

"Doc Moellmann," Mangiapane began, referring to Wayne County's medical examiner, "says that the bishop was hit once—a powerful blow to the back of the head between the crown and the neck. The weapon was a blunt instrument—a pipe, or a heavy bottle, or a baseball bat. We haven't turned up anything yet.

"We found the bishop sitting in this chair and slumped over the desk. This figures out pretty good. The fatal blow was at a slightly downward angle. The bishop was kinda tall, almost six feet. If he'd been standing, to get that kinda angle, the perp'd have to be a giant.

"But if the bishop was sitting, then the perp'd be in the neighborhood of five feet six or seven—someplace between five-five and five-eight.

"Also, the time of death that we were estimating at between four and six o'clock yesterday evening is on the nose.

"As far as prints go, they're all over the place. Everybody and his mother's been in here touching things—and they don't spend a lot of time dusting. One of the guys said they probably got Gabriel Richard's fingerprints in here." Mangiapane was alone in thinking this quite humorous.

"We been through this office and the bishop's room upstairs," he continued, "but we didn't find anything out of the ordinary."

"Nothing unusual!" Father McCauley exclaimed. "You don't think all that money is unusual?"

"All what money?" Quirt was feisty.

"The bishop always kept some money—he called it petty cash—in the office here. We advised against it, of course. We told him it could be an irresistible temptation. We told him he'd be lucky if the worst that happened would be that somebody would steal it."

"You mean Diego kept money here in the office?" Quirt pursued.

"That's right."

"And it was commonly known that he did?"

"Well . . ." McCauley hedged, "I wouldn't say that it was common knowledge. Not everybody on the street would know about it. Sometimes the 'deserving poor,' as the bishop referred to them, or a family in desperate need of food or clothing—things like that. Well, the bishop liked to help such people. . . ." McCauley looked at the policemen. "He wasn't a complete villain, you know. And"—he gestured to include the pictures on the walls—"he had friends in high places. He could—and did—tap some pretty wealthy people. With them he called it his 'discretionary fund.' They usually contributed generously.

"Anyway, I thought you would find that unusual or out of the ordinary," he concluded.

Mangiapane was furious. "We didn't know about it! We didn't know anything about it. Where does he keep it?"

McCauley, rocked by the vehemence of Mangiapáne's reaction, spoke almost apologetically. "Why, right here in the cabinet."

It was an ordinary metal cabinet, about five feet high and two feet wide. Its double doors swung open to reveal four shelves. McCauley reached toward a container about the size of a cigar box.

"Don't touch it!" Quirt shouted.

McCauley nearly leaped back from the box. His nervous system could not stand shocks like these.

After a moment, as everyone stood transfixed by the nondescript box, Mangiapane picked up a small stack of file folders from the desk, slid the stack under the box, and lifted it to the desk. Then, taking a letter opener, he flipped the catch lock and, with the opener, raised the lid.

The box was empty.

"How much did he keep in there?" Quirt asked, after a moment of silence.

"Oh, $4,000, maybe $5,000," McCauley said.

"Could he—would he—have given it all away?" Tully asked.

McCauley shook his head slowly. "I don't think so. I've never known him to let the supply dwindle down to nothing."

"Mangiapane," Quirt said, "get the techs back here. I want the box dusted."

Mangiapane was dialing before Quirt finished the order.

Tully's mouth curled in a slight smile. "Well, well, possibly a robbery/murder."

"Or," Kleimer said, "somebody wants it to look like a robbery/murder."

Tully looked quizzical. Quirt seemed puzzled, but recovered quickly. "What do you want to take, Zoo?"

"I'll take the quarrel at the party yesterday, and hit the streets."

"Check," Quirt said.

Tully and Mangiapane left without further comment.

Kleimer's eyes went from McCauley to Quirt, who got the hint. "You can leave now, Father."

That was all the word McCauley needed. He was gone.

Quirt turned to Kleimer. "What'd you mean about somebody *wanting* this to look like a robbery/murder?"

"Sit down for a minute," Kleimer invited.

The two sat facing each other, knees almost touching.

"Picture this as a news story, George." Kleimer's gestures conjured up headlines. "'Bishop Killed by Crackhead,' or, 'Bishop Killed by Wealthy Socialite'—or 'Bishop Killed by Priest.'" He looked at Quirt fixedly. "You get it?"

Quirt thought a minute. "That pretty well covers the possibles we got now."

"Yes, but more . . ." Kleimer edged his chair closer. "'Bishop Killed by Crackhead': How does the public react to that?" He didn't wait for a reply. "It's old hat. The big, important thing is the word 'Bishop.' But that he was offed by some nobody, some street kid with a head screwed up with crack or whatever—that's run of the mill. Killings like that are in the news all the time. Everybody knows these punks will do anything for a fix. So he kills a bishop . . . too bad. But that's life in the big city.

"Now"—Kleimer's tone grew emphatic—"take, 'Bishop Killed by Wealthy Socialite.' Better. Why would one of the movers want to take out a bishop? Would he do it himself? Or would he hire somebody? People would want to know. There's a juicy story for you."

Quirt's face was expressionless, but he was listening intently.

"But . . ." A gleam appeared in Kleimer's eyes. ". . . 'Bishop Killed by Priest.' Now we really got something! This is right out of the Middle Ages, Thomas à Becket and all that."

"Who?"

"Never mind. Just remember this: 'Bishop Killed by Priest' is going to be written up forever. And that's just how long our names are going to be in the public eye. It'll be the biggest bust you ever had or ever could have. And," he added with some satisfaction, "the biggest conviction I ever had."

Before the lieutenant could respond, Kleimer swept on. "Now, get this: I'm not suggesting that you rig this investigation. But let's say if one of our priest suspects does prove to be the killer, he didn't do it for the money. Now don't get me wrong . . ." He waved his hand. "I'm not saying a priest couldn't steal money. But . . . Carleson and Bell both hated this guy's guts.

"So now what does it look like? Like somebody got in here for the purpose of robbing the bishop and, for some reason—or for no reason—killed him.

"But I ask you, George: If I'm a priest, and I got to get rid of this guy, how do I throw the cops off the trail?"

Quirt's visage slackened in the light of recognition. "You take the money. You don't spend it right away. Maybe never. And we go out on the street where Zoo is, and we start looking for some loser out there who has suddenly started buying acid like he never has before."

Kleimer said nothing. He extended his hands, palms up. A grin lit his face. Then he grew grim again.

"And let's think of this: No matter who you arrest, and no matter who I convict, that's no sign that the poor schmuck is guilty. Let's face it, if that were the case, there'd be no innocent people in prison. And you and I know that not everybody who's in jail is necessarily guilty.

"The upshot of all this, George, is that if you arrest some punk and I get a conviction, we might very well be sending a loser—an innocent guy, but a loser—to prison. And neither one of us is going to profit from it. The story'll be dead just like the publicity we won't get.

"On the other hand, if we arrest and convict a priest, he may or may not actually be guilty. But we're going to get ourselves some media exposure we couldn't buy. . . . Have I made myself clear?" Kleimer's extended trip through a tortuous path of rationalization was concluded.

"Perfectly."

"I'm grateful to you, George. And just to prove it . . . I hear that Koznicki will be looking for a new number-two man to back him up in Homicide. You know Hunter's taking an early leave. I'll just see what I can do to get the right man in that job."

Quirt was grinning from ear to ear.

Kleimer gave him a friendly pat on the shoulder and left.

Quirt knew what he had to do. But for a few moments he would savor his prospects.

Quirt understood Kleimer's motives and aspirations as well as his own. The two were cut from the same cloth.

For months—no, more like years now—Quirt had been observing Kleimer's unswerving, persistent ascent in the prosecutor's office. With some 170 lawyers and legal interns on the staff, a person could get lost in a hurry.

Kleimer reminded Quirt of Silky Sullivan, that marvelous racehorse of yore. He had a habit of getting out of the gate slowly, and in no time he was lost in the pack near the rear. But, if you knew what to look for, and kept your eye on him, he would just gradually—almost leisurely—move along, overtaking one horse at a time until, approaching the finish line, he would be in the lead and pulling away confidently.

So it had been with Kleimer. He had moved up through the ranks steadily. At one point, he was one rung removed from chief prosecuting attorney. That, under a previous administration, was the highest-profile position in the office. Of course it was not *the* prosecutor, but, arguably, as far as media attention, and as a recognition factor, the C.P.A. got more ink, more coverage and exposure than even the boss. Kleimer was on the edge of genuine fame.

However, under the present prosecutor's administration, the attorneys were required to specialize in various categories of crime. So that they would become expert in specialized fields. For all practical purposes, that nipped Kleimer's career just as it was about to come to full bloom.

But just as that door was closed on Kleimer, he surreptitiously opened a window.

Most of the court cases in any large metropolitan venue are handled backstage. Out-of-court settlements and plea bargains clear a good percentage of the docket. Lots of other cases come to trial, but by general consensus, the media pass on them.

Then there are the crimes particularly heinous, bizarre, or abhorrent, as well as those involving the rich, famous, or celebrities that show up on the screen, the front page, and the top of the newscast. By no means always, but increasingly, the attorney of record and the talking head on television was Brad Kleimer.

Most readers, listeners, viewers, simply took it for granted that if a crime was notorious enough, Kleimer would be trying it.

Quirt was watching and learning.

As often as feasible, Kleimer tried to insinuate his presence early on in these cases. He became the presence whom police technicians had to walk around.

When it came time to assign the case to a prosecutor, Kleimer frequently could claim truthfully that he had been in on that case from the beginning and was far more familiar with it than anyone else on the staff.

There were times when this argument was dismissed. For one thing, nearly everyone on the staff was on to him. He was neither Mr. Popularity nor Mr. Congeniality.

But—and this was a large condition—he did get his share and more of convictions. Kleimer had a talent not only for coming up with favorable rationalizations but also for getting judge and jury to go along with his predisposed logic.

Thus, even though the method of his success was no secret to others on the staff, he still got much more than his share of plum cases.

While Quirt watched this recurrent yet successful technique with fascination, he could only guess at Kleimer's goal. Though the possibilities were obvious.

One day Kleimer would cash in on all this valuable publicity. He certainly wasn't building this reputation just to remain anywhere near his present position. He would assuredly move on—very likely into elective office. Perhaps prosecutor. More probably, governor, Congress, a presidential administrator. Who knew; maybe even president of the United States.

Nothing mattered to Kleimer but his advancement. He would sacrifice anything to be Somebody. This ruling passion had already cost him his marriage and the custody of his children. That hurt. But it was a price to pay for his advancement, and by damn, he would pay it.

Once Quirt had learned what was going on, he'd decided to attach himself as securely as possible to Kleimer's coattails.

For Quirt too had aspirations. He did not want to spend his time until retirement in the police horse stables or watching over parking meters. His first desire was Homicide. That was where the preponderance of action was. That was a unit so elite that, in the early years, one needed a sponsor even to be considered for admission.

Quirt sowed his seeds of cooperation with Kleimer very carefully. Of course, there were severe limitations to what Quirt could do for Kleimer. But, as one of the patrolmen frequently first on the scene of a crime, he could at least try to guess where these cases might go. Each time he found one that was promising, he would call Kleimer.

Kleimer could recognize a promising source when he found one. It was clear that the higher this patrolman advanced, the more fruitful a source he would be.

Kleimer found a sponsor for Quirt and he was admitted to Homicide.

Quirt, in turn, was not without talent. His investigations of homicides, while tending to be shallow, were bolstered by some pretty good instincts, as well as considerable luck. Quirt was a true believer in the tenet, I'd rather be lucky than good.

In due time, Kleimer needed only minimal influence to see his protégé move up to the rank of lieutenant—and become head of one of Homicide's seven squads.

This, for Quirt, was almost enough. He would have been happy to remain right there until retirement beckoned.

However, a satisfied Quirt was not desirable as far as Kleimer was concerned. A satisfied Quirt would be complacent and not at all motivated to cue Kleimer into promising cases.

So it was simply a matter of advanced planning for Kleimer to suggest that the number two spot in Homicide might be in Quirt's future. Quirt's ambition was renewed.

The important thing, as Kleimer saw it, was to keep the carrot just beyond Quirt's grasp. A hungry Quirt resulted in prime tips for Kleimer.

If everything worked as planned, there would come a time when Kleimer would need no help from any police officer. He would be far above that. Once he had advanced beyond the prosecutor's office, he would drop Quirt like a child's outgrown toy. Nor would Kleimer care that he was responsible for having someone promoted way above that individual's competence.

Neither Kleimer nor Quirt cared for anything or anyone but themselves.

CHAPTER

FIVE

Father Don Carleson briefly considered visiting Father Koesler. Further thought convinced him that would not help.

Carleson was deeply disturbed, nervous, anxious, and felt great stress. Any conversation with Koesler would necessarily concern Diego's death. Definitely counterproductive.

No, he would do what he'd told the police he was going to do: visit the sick at Receiving Hospital.

He parked in the underground garage and took the elevator to ground level but headed for Emergency rather than the general reception area.

Receiving's Emergency Department was an exemplar of such facilities. In addition to the usual everyday outpatients, there were the medically uninsured who wandered in instead of consulting a private physician they couldn't afford. Ambulances disgorged the injured of the inner city. The ER staff never knew from one day to the next what fate was about to hurl at them.

In short, the perfect place to distract one from personal preoccupations.

As Carleson entered the waiting and intake area, he heard a fast-approaching commotion behind him. He hugged the wall as three occupied gurneys raced past, propelled by EMS personnel. From their faces, Carleson knew this was no ordinary emergency.

The EMS teams peeled off into various trauma rooms. Organized turmoil became routine in each compartment.

Carleson, careful to stay out of the way, listened just outside the doorway of the first room. With the arrival of the gurneys, an overpowering stench had pervaded the entire area. Carleson could not identify the odor. But if the entry doors had not been left open, everyone in the area could well have passed out.

Work in this first unit was cursory. It was obvious this victim was dead on arrival. The staff knew they were just going through the motions. But they went through the motions anyway.

One of the EMS drivers was standing next to Carleson. "Ain't this somethin', Father?"

Carleson's nose wrinkled. "What on earth is that?"

"Oh . . ." Seemingly for the first time, the driver realized his clothing was tainted. "This stuff? It's sewer slime." He grimaced. "I'm gonna take a shower." He shook his head. "I don't know how in hell—oh, 'scuse me, Father—I don't know how we're gonna get it out of our trucks."

"Those people were in a sewer?"

He nodded. "They were supposed to clean it. The first guy barely got down the ladder before the fumes got to him and he keeled over. That sh—uh, stuff was about a foot-and-a-half thick. The second guy went down to rescue him. He keeled over. That's the guy in here"—he gestured—"who was DOA. Then the third guy went down. Gutsy. He was just barely able to get the first guy up and out before he da— darn near passed out."

He moved on to the next trauma unit. Carleson followed.

Things seemed less chaotic here. "This—if I remember right—this is the third guy," the driver said. "The only one who got out safely." He addressed one of the nurses. "How's he doing?"

"Pretty good. He'll make it. He'll probably be ready to be released after they oxygenate him."

Carleson could see her relief. "He's the father of the kid"—she indicated the third trauma room—"in there."

Carleson and the driver moved on to the last sphere of this three-ring circus. An ant colony was filled with white- and green-clad people squeezing by each other and calling out to one another as they maneuvered.

One of the nurses who had been with the dead man was now taking in the activity. She turned to the two men standing beside her. "It'll be a miracle if this guy makes it." She smiled at Carleson. "That would be right up your alley, wouldn't it, Father?"

The priest smiled and shook his head. Miracles had never been his strong suit, and never less so than lately.

As Carleson proceeded through Emergency, he marveled at how easy it was. Receiving Hospital prided itself on its security. They functioned on the theory that they expected trouble—which expectation was regularly fulfilled.

All well and good when it came to extroverted troublemakers who were loud and/or violent. At the first sign of that sort of trouble, the hospital security force as well as Detroit police assigned to the facility would smother the fracas like foam on a fire.

But what of the casual intruder?

A hospital this size had a staff so large it was virtually impossible to keep track of everyone. Anybody could stuff a stethoscope in a pocket or drape it around his or her neck, and most people—visitors and staff alike—would simply assume he or she was merely a doctor visiting patients.

Or, of more immediate moment, what of himself? What gave him license to walk wherever he wished? Only the sliver of white at the collar of his black suit.

In an institution that boasted of its tight security, anyone in clerical garb could nevertheless travel unchallenged through the general areas of the hospital, such as patients' rooms.

Of course Carleson had the advantage of being known by many in the hospital, particularly the Emergency staff. As part of his missionary training, he had become a paramedic. This had prepared him to administer, in effect, first aid.

However, it did not suit his personality to observe restrictions when the needs of people cried out for assistance. More often than not in areas he had served, there was no doctor for uncounted miles. So Carleson elected to do whatever he could to respond to the sick.

Even when procedures clearly exceeded his training—surgery and the like—he would pray and then act. In every such instance, if he had not acted, the individual would have died anyway. The worst that could happen, then, would be death on a makeshift operating table instead of death in a hut or in a jungle. More often than not, the patient survived. That Carleson freely attributed more to prayer than to his meager skill.

He never spoke of his medical operations in the bush. It was among those thorny topics better left unmentioned.

Yet, in some extrasensory perceptional way, the medical staff of the average hospital somehow sensed the link that joined Father Carleson to them.

So it was with Receiving Hospital in Detroit. Other religious personnel might be able to enter restricted areas, but they very definitely would be limited in where they could go and what they could do. Nothing of an offensive nature. Just a firm easing of the person out of sensitive areas.

But based on that implicit camaraderie, Carleson virtually had the run of the place.

Today the hospital was doing for Carleson what he had hoped—distracting him from his personal concerns and letting him lose himself in the lives and pains of others.

All Emergency personnel who were not otherwise engaged were either inside or at the door of Trauma Room Three, where a senior resident, numerous interns, nurses, and technicians were doing everything possible to save a young man who had been overcome by toxic fumes.

Carleson continued on his unplanned tour through Emergency toward the hospital proper. He smiled as he passed a gurney on which sat a rather good-looking man engaged in a seemingly reasonable discussion concerning treatment for pain. The doctor was insisting on a prescription for Motrin. The patient was arguing, with decreasing composure, in favor of codeine.

Carleson well knew the powerful difference between the two analgesics. He also knew the young man was going to need a fix of something soon or he would slip into withdrawal symptoms.

At this point there was still an element of humor in the exchange. Before long, the black comedy would disintegrate in the face of the patient's desperate craving for drug release.

There was nothing Carleson could do about it. No prayer or blessing, no offer of understanding and friendship could supersede the patient's yearning for oblivion.

The young doctor was being quite resolute . . . although in actuality, there was little else he could do. Inevitably, what was now a fairly amicable difference of opinion would segue into a demeaning—even violent—pleading, demanding in the face of intractable refusal.

Carleson moved on.

An elderly man whose face testified to his having weathered many an intemperate northern season sat gingerly on a gurney. Loudly he gave witness that these doctors and nurses were badly underpaid. For this unsolicited testimonial he received affectionate support from the staff. At Carleson's approach, the man generously included the priest among those insufficiently compensated. Carleson thought the man didn't know whereof he spoke. Nonetheless, the priest gave him a bright smile and a thumbs-up.

The attendant, about to wheel the man to surgery, informed Carleson that the patient had tucked a pint of liquor in his back pocket, then absentmindedly plumped himself down on a cement curb, thus emptying the precious liquid directly into the sewer to the delight of thirsty rats. And, of course, lacerating his rump.

He certainly didn't seem to feel any pain. Undoubtedly he had consumed some of the contents before the container smashed.

Last in the parade of trauma scenes was a gurney holding a naked man covered only with a hospital-issue sheet. Standing at the patient's head, an intern attempted to determine what was wrong. Had he been drinking?

"A beer . . . maybe two."

"C'mon . . . two?"

"Two! Maybe three. No more'n three."

The intern began inserting a nasal-gastric tube through the patient's nostril. The patient began to gag.

"Swallow, man, swallow," the intern urged.

Suddenly, the patient began throwing up. Quickly, the intern turned the patient's head to one side so he wouldn't drown in his own vomit.

To Carleson, it was a repulsive sound and a nauseating odor. A nurse standing nearby obviously was similarly affected. "I've seen it a million times," she said, "but it still makes me gag."

Carleson was grateful.

A heavy, pungent odor permeated the room. "Three beers, eh? Smells more like whiskey to me," the intern said.

At the foot of the gurney, a nurse shook her head with certainty. "Jamaica rum!"

Before leaving Emergency, Carleson glanced back. Trauma Room Three remained the center of activity. The beehive continued to swirl and an attentive audience was absorbed in the goings-on.

That's what it was all about. The life of one person. The most sophisticated and expensive machinery available—and the most knowledgeable and dedicated personnel—bent to the purpose of saving a life.

Carleson thought again of his work in regions that were considered advanced if there was clean water available. If there was electricity, one felt that one had entered the twentieth century.

The TV series "M*A*S*H" referred to near-frontline doctors' work as "meatball surgery." Compared with what went on here in Receiving, the Korean front was rudimentary. But measured against Carleson's capabilities in the jungle, "M*A*S*H" was the Mayo Clinic of the Far East.

Whatever, his journey through Emergency accomplished the hoped-for. His own concerns and problems were forgotten for the moment.

He left ER and proceeded to the pastoral care department to check on the patients he hoped to visit.

There weren't many. Most on his list were people who, after previous casual visitation, had asked him to return. Actually, only one elderly man was a bona fide parishioner of Ste. Anne's.

Checking further, he found that quite a few on his list had been released. One had died. That left only five, including the parishioner, to call on.

As luck would have it—as his luck frequently had it—four were not in their rooms. CAT scan, X rays; two in physiotherapy.

But good old dependable Herbert Demers was in.

Herbert seldom went anywhere. Doctors periodically tried to have him transferred out, claiming that the treatment he was getting in the hospital could just as well be administered in a nursing home. And—this was an extended busy period—they needed his bed.

But, inevitably, just as arrangements were complete, Herbert would lapse again into a critical condition, requiring extensive, sometimes intensive, care.

Herbert's condition was further complicated by an order to resuscitate.

That had come about shortly after he was admitted. Herbert's family consisted of a grandson and the grandson's wife. A doctor didn't want to take the time and trouble to explain to them the various options available. So he used the catchall, "Do you want us to do everything we can for your grandfather?"

The couple would have been perfectly disposed to waive extraordinary measures and let Grandpa expire in peace. If Grandfather had been able to express himself, he very definitely would have been of the same mind.

But Herbert couldn't express himself. And the family could not bring themselves to come right out and say, "No, we don't want you to do everything you can for him."

The doctor won that one. He was spared having to take the time to explain that, under certain circumstances, he could direct that if Herbert were actually dying, the staff could be ordered not to attempt resuscitation. Herbert could mercifully be allowed to do what his body demanded—die.

So Herbert lingered on. The vital signs were there, just barely. He did not need oxygen tubes; intravenous tubes connected his frail body to medication and nourishment.

No one knew what, if anything, was on his mind.

To Carleson, Herbert was the ultimate source of motivation. No matter what problems or troubles one experienced, there was always Herbert Demers. Nothing haunted Carleson as much as the thought of having his soul imprisoned in his body rather than animating it.

Herbert occupied a semiprivate room. The bed next to the window was empty. Carleson hesitated at the door. "What happened to Mr. Girondello?" he asked a passing nurse.

"Oh . . ." She stopped to recollect. ". . . he expired during the night." She continued on her course.

Carleson mulled that over as he stood in the doorway.

Did Herbert know his roommate was gone? Did he understand? *Could* he understand? Had he heard Mr. Girondello breathe his last? Had Herbert wished it had been himself?

Who knew?

"So then, Herbert, how goes it today?" Carleson expected no reply. His goal today, as always, was to try to provide a little distraction for his

parishioner. Without knowing whether the man could even understand what was said, the priest did know that Herbert could hear and
see. Those were simple functions to test.

Carleson laid his overcoat and hat on the chair near the window
and drew one of the more comfortable chairs close to Herbert's bed. "I
bring you greetings from the Ambassador Bridge," Carleson said. "You
remember the Bridge . . . from a little distance, especially at night
when it's all lit up, it looks like a rainbow. And if it were a rainbow, I
guess your house would be the pot of gold . . . 'cause that's where it is:
right at the foot of the bridge.

"Your house looks fine, Herbert. Just the way you left it."

Herbert's home indeed was in good repair for a structure that went
back nearly a century. He had taken exquisite care of it for as long as he
could—which was up to only a few years ago. And though no one had
taken over Herbert's careful maintenance, his work endured even now.
The priests of Ste. Anne's were hopeful some young couple would buy
the roomy home and raise their family there. Hope for a renewed
neighborhood was part and parcel of the Ste. Anne's community whose
pastor fervently declared that he did not come to Ste. Anne's to be
curator of a museum but pastor of a parish.

"There've been some people—some young people—looking at your
house, Herbert. Be nice if they moved in, wouldn't it? Your father raised
his family there and so did you. Now, please God, it should be somebody else's turn."

Carleson considered it futile to pretend with Herbert that he would
ever return to his old home. If the old man was aware of anything, it
was that he was going nowhere except heaven.

"Herb, did you hear the one about the priest who visited a parishioner in a hospital just about like this? The patient had oxygen
tubes in his nostrils and seemed to be asleep. The priest leaned over the
bed to get a better look at the man.

"All of a sudden, the guy's eyes popped open. He gasped a few
times. And the priest thought, 'Oh, my God, the poor guy is breathing
his last.' The patient made a motion as if he wanted writing materials.
A last message to his loved ones, thought the priest, as he slipped a pad
and pen into the poor soul's hands.

"And while the guy scribbled on the pad and wheezed and gasped, the priest anointed him. Just as he finished absolving him, the guy gave one last gasp and died.

"'What a blessing and grace it was—really providential—that I could be with the poor man just as he breathed his last,' the priest thought. 'I'll just have to get this final message to his family.'

"So the priest slips the pad out of the guy's hand and looks at what's written there. It reads, 'You're standing on my air hose!'"

Carleson looked at Herbert. Nothing. That was what the priest had expected. But, against all expectations, he had hoped for some sign. A twitching at the mouth. Something in the eyes. An alertness.

Nothing.

Was he talking to a vegetable? Was there any use to this? He might as well be talking to himself.

He'd felt this way on previous visits.

"You know that bishop I've told you about, Herbert. You remember him, don't you?"

Nothing.

"Ramon Diego's the name. He certainly wasn't what I bargained for when I signed up for Detroit. I know I've told you all about this before, Herbert, but something big has happened, and you're about the only person I can confide in.

"At first, Herbert, I figured it wouldn't be too bad. Somehow, as it came out of the mouth of Cardinal Boyle, it sounded as if the diocese was giving me a break." He smiled. "It must be that soft, Irish brogue he can't quite get out of his speech.

"Anyway, I should have known better, but as Boyle explained it, it made some kind of crazy sense. I had all the experience I'd ever need for working with a Hispanic group. But I was kind of light on ministry in a big American urban setting.

"That's where Ramon Diego was supposed to come in. His Texan background was supposed to fill in the gaps for me.

"And I bought it! Can you imagine!" He shook his head. "I thought, well, maybe I've spent just about all my time in the sticks, but it can't be that hard to get used to a big city and racial instead of just economic prejudice and bigotry.

"Maybe it was because Boyle mentioned this experience-gathering would be only for a limited period of time." He shook his head again.

"When he didn't put a cap on it—a few weeks, a month or so—
I should have tumbled . . . and renegotiated.

"But . . . I didn't.

"I certainly should have realized that life is going to get very complicated if I let a bishop look over my shoulder all the time. But . . .
I didn't.

"I should have checked with some of the priests working in the
Latino community and found out just what kind of guy this Diego was.
But . . . I didn't." He looked directly at the motionless figure in the bed.
"And there you have it, Herbert: I set myself up. But in my wildest
dreams I couldn't have guessed how bad it was going to get.

"Oh, it's not just that he's not a good bishop . . . he isn't even much
of a Christian."

He stopped and sat in thought and then, as if shaking himself,
continued. "But then, I'm not getting down to what I have to tell you,
Herbert. Especially not when I talk about Diego in the present tense.
It's not that Diego *isn't* much of a Christian; he *wasn't* much of a
Christian.

"And this is what I want to tell you, Herbert: Bishop Diego is dead.
Murdered. What do you think of that, Herbert?" He sat back in his
chair. "Now I'm going to tell you what happened to him."

Carleson had been talking to Demers but for the most part not
quite focusing on him. Now that he was reaching the essence of his
story, the priest shifted in his chair and pulled it closer to the patient.
And, with this newly paid attention, he noticed something for the first
time.

Demers was moving his fingers. Almost imperceptibly, but there
was some sort of movement. "You're moving your hands, Herbert. Are
you trying to tell me something?" Carleson was suddenly excited.

Demers seemed to catch Carleson's intensity and feed upon it.
Now, unmistakably, Demers was making a motion with his right hand
that clearly simulated writing.

"I'll be damned! You were listening to me after all! You want to
write me something? A message?"

But Demers appeared to be able to do no more than give the
slightest indication that he wanted to write. Quickly, Carleson grabbed
a white, disposable bag. It would have to serve as a pad. There was

nothing else immediately available, and he didn't want to waste a precious second. Propping the bag atop a small tissue box, he fitted the makeshift writing pad into Demers's left hand. From his jacket pocket, Carleson took a ballpoint pen and inserted it between the thumb and forefinger of Demers's right hand.

The priest watched spellbound as Demers tried feebly to put pen to paper. There were a few wavering passes, but no contact. Finally, defeated, he let the pen fall to the sheet.

This was not going to work.

"Can you tell me, Herbert? Try! Try to tell me!"

Demers let his head fall to the right so he was directly facing Carleson. His lips twitched faintly. Carleson placed his ear as close as he could without blocking Demers's lips.

Nothing.

Carleson turned his gaze toward Demers. "Try to move your lips! I'll try to read your lips!"

He watched intently. There was a slight movement. "'Heh . . . heh . . .'" Carleson spoke trying to articulate the expression forming on Demers's lips.

"'Heh . . . hel . . . help . . .' 'Help'? 'Help' . . . is that it?"

"'Help m . . . help me . . .' 'Help me'? 'Help me'? Is that it, Herbert? Help you what? What do you want me to help you with? Another word, Herbert! Give me another word!"

"'D . . . da . . . die.' 'Die'? 'Help me die'? You want to die?"

Of course he does, stupid, Carleson told himself. *Wouldn't you in his condition?*

Demers, having delivered his message, relaxed. He seemed to sink back into the pillow as if he were part of the headrest.

"I'll tell the doctor what I just saw you do, Herbert. Maybe the doctor can help you die now that we know what you want. Hang in there. I'll do everything I can." Carleson took the man's right hand and held the bony appendage firmly.

He had serious doubts that anything would come of this. The doctor would have no proof of Herbert's desire other than the word of one priest. Carleson was certain Demers could not repeat his performance. Carleson was certain the status would remain quo.

This poor man wanted only one thing: release. Eventually, of course,

God would take him. Meanwhile, he would be imprisoned in his shell of a body.

But, wait. Demers had asked *him*. The old gentleman had said it with all the strength he could summon. *"Help me die."* That's what he'd said. *"Help me die."*

It was a desperate plea that would continue to haunt and torment the priest.

Could he? Would he?

Carleson had no immediate answer.

CHAPTER
SIX

"This old Springwells area isn't what it used to be." Sergeant Neal Williams was driving.

"What *is*?" From the passenger seat, Lieutenant George Quirt scanned the storefronts, small business establishments pressed so close to one another it seemed impossible to insert a dime between them.

The two officers had spent several hours interviewing several priests who had attended last night's gathering. The groundwork had been done by other officers on the task force.

These preliminary investigations had disclosed that four of the priests—Fathers Echlin, Dorr, Dempsey, and Bell—had been at the party until the very end. Two others—Fathers Carleson and Koesler—had left only a short time before the party broke up.

The importance of these six lay in the fact that one or another or more had been present through the entire evening. So, together, their recollections of the event would cover everything that had happened or been said.

Of course, the police had already interrogated Carleson. And, since it had been determined from their questioning that Koesler had said little at the gathering, he had not been questioned.

"I remember this neighborhood," Quirt said. "European. Irish, Polish, Slavs, Germans, French. Now look at it. Spics took over." He slowly shook his head. "Might just as well be Mexico City."

"Maybe," Williams said. "But they're keeping it up pretty well. Not a lot of boarded-up storefronts. And look at the housing down the side streets. Pretty good shape."

Quirt grunted. Williams was too young to know what always happened in areas like this. You get your blacks and they're shiftless and lazy. And they look different, for Chrissakes. They're used to living in the dirt down south, in houses that are falling apart. Let 'em get in a decent neighborhood up here and—instant slum.

"Now, your spics can fool you. Most of 'em look like whites. But give 'em a little northern winter and watch 'em hibernate. Too many of 'em can't even speak the language. They expect us to speak spic." Quirt smiled at the phrase he was sure he had just created. *Speak spic.* He'd have to use it on the guys soon.

Quirt was by no means Williams's favorite human being. But he was on the lieutenant's squad so there wasn't much he could do about that. Williams wasn't alone in his feelings toward Quirt. Most of the rest of the squad was only too well aware that as a detective, Quirt was no better than average. His arrest record was a combination of diligent—even superior—police work by the squad topped off by Quirt's eagerness to close each file expeditiously even if somewhat prematurely.

The squad's record of arrests leading to convictions was good. But that, in turn, could be attributed to luck and the fact that Brad Kleimer prosecuted most of their high-profile cases. And Kleimer was good—quite good.

Right now, Quirt, with his totally gratuitous ethnic slurs, was driving Williams up the wall. But early on he had decided to wait the lieutenant out. With any luck, Quirt'd be off the squad before too long. With Quirt's luck, Williams thought wryly, the so-and-so'd be promoted.

"Hey, Williams, you're a Catholic, aren'tcha?"

Williams smiled. "My wife would give you an argument on that."

"Like that, eh? Well, you're still closer to that scene than I am. When we get there, feel free to lead off."

"Whatever you say." Williams didn't see where his nominal Catholicism gave him any edge in this investigation, but he was just as glad to take the lead. Quirt stood a good chance of messing it up. "Well, no sooner said than done. Here we are."

St. Gabriel's plant covered one small block of West Vernor Highway between Inglis and Norman. The rectory was tucked between the church on the corner of Inglis and what appeared to be a school on the corner of Norman. A driveway separated the school building from the rectory. Williams pulled into the driveway and parked next to the rectory in what seemed to be an asphalted school playground.

When they stepped out of the car, the officers could plainly hear children's voices through the closed windows and doors of the building. "Now," Williams said, "that surprises me."

"What's that?"

"That they've got a school. I didn't think that was possible."

"Why not?"

"At best this is a lower-middle-class neighborhood. I assume most of the Latinos are Catholic. But I wouldn't have thought they'd have enough money to support a school."

"This . . ." Quirt's gesture encompassed everything they could see. ". . . this is middle class?"

Williams shrugged. "There's an Arbor Drugs right across the street, and I noticed a Farmer Jack market on one of the cross streets. I don't think you'd find them—or any other quality stores—in a rock-poor neighborhood."

Quirt let it stand. But Williams's observation about the school was well taken and informed. No matter what Williams's wife thought of his religious observance, Quirt was glad he'd brought him along.

The two officers reached the rectory's front door to find a man in a black suit and a clerical collar awaiting them in the open doorway.

"You Father Ernest Bell?" Quirt asked.

The priest nodded.

Quirt showed his badge and identification. "I'm Lieutenant Quirt and this is Sergeant Williams. We're from the Homicide Division."

Again the priest nodded. "Someone—I guess it was your secretary—called and said you were coming over. I've been expecting you."

As they entered the rectory, the detectives caught the vague odor of Scotch. They sensed the priest's nervousness and concluded this was a scared man who had tried to bolster his confidence with a belt of liquor. Interesting.

Father Bell led them through the main floor to a furnished, winterized porch at the rear of the house. Each of the officers selected a chair on either side of the couch. They repositioned the chairs to face the couch, leaving that as the logical place for the priest to sit. He would, in a sense, be surrounded. The maneuver was not lost on Bell.

"Would anyone like something?" the priest asked. "I've got booze or beer. Or I could get you some coffee."

"No, nothing for us." Quirt seated himself. "As you probably know, we're investigating the death of Bishop Ramon Diego."

"Yes, yes, I know that." Bell clearly was edgy. "What can I do . . . ? I mean, I don't know what I could . . ."

Quirt, without looking at Williams, nodded. The ball had transferred courts.

"What we have, Father," Williams said, "are questions—lots of questions. You can help us with some answers." His tone was calming, reasonable, reassuring. Yet it appeared to have little effect on Bell's tenseness.

"First off," Williams began, "do you know anyone who might have a reason to kill the bishop?"

Bell did not reply immediately. "No," he said finally. "He may have had some enemies," he added, "but then, who doesn't?"

"Let's talk about these enemies." Williams flipped open a notepad and looked expectantly at Bell.

"Well, I don't know, really." Bell was defensive. "He didn't travel in our company very much. He preferred the jet set, as it were."

"We're looking into that. But how about your 'company'? For instance, just to drop a name, Father Carleson. He had some problems with the bishop . . . at least that's what we've been told." Williams looked at Bell expectantly.

The priest was torn. It would be unrealistic for him to deny the feud; the conflict between Diego and Carleson was common knowledge. If he claimed to know nothing, the detectives would be suspicious. On the other hand, an admission that he knew how Diego had treated Carleson might very well lead to the subject of the bishop's meddling in St. Gabriel's affairs.

He would go with the latter. "Yes, Father Carleson had problems with the bishop. Or so I've heard. But the whole situation was awkward. In effect, Don became the bishop's secretary. None of us thought that was how their relationship was supposed to have developed."

Williams wrote a few lines. Then he spoke. "Yes. At his age, and with his experience, he would expect to get a parish—be a pastor . . . wouldn't he?"

Bell, convinced and regretting that he'd been correct about the direction this conversation now was taking, nodded.

Quirt smiled inwardly. Smart move bringing Williams and letting him play the lead. He had to admit that he himself would never have thought to steer the questioning in this direction.

"If Father Carleson becomes a pastor," Williams continued, "you'd know how he'd feel, wouldn't you . . . you being a pastor, and all?"

"I suppose."

"How is that? I've always wondered."

"I . . . don't know. I don't know what you mean."

"Well, there are lots of parishes around. And, if I read the papers right, there's a shortage of priests. So . . ." Williams spread his hands, palms upward. ". . . is one as good as another?"

"What do you mean? Is one *what* . . . ?" Bell was by no means inebriated, but he was trying to clear his head of the shot he'd taken before the police arrived. This was no time to be fuzzy.

"I mean: If someone told you you couldn't be pastor of St. Gabriel anymore, you'd just move on to some other parish, wouldn't you? There'd be no great problem, would there be? Or am I wrong?"

By concentrated effort, Bell tried to figure out the next chess move. These cops gave every indication they had done their homework. Probably they'd talked to one or more of the guys—Dempsey or Dorr or Echlin. They weren't just blindly groping for answers. It would be futile—maybe even fatal—to take the bait and agree that it would be no great shakes to leave St. Gabriel's. To stand by as they put his beloved parish in mothballs. For one, it would be the wrong move for the diocese to make. For another, it would be like watching a loved one die.

And he knew this whole mess was the work of Diego. The question was: Did they know?

"No," Bell answered at length. "It's not like that. When you're in a parish for any length of time, you get to know the people—some better than others. They—many of them—make you part of their family. You don't just pull up stakes and move on without caring—very much."

Williams turned a page. A change of subject was signified. "This parish, St. Gabriel, tell us something about it. Let's start with the school."

Bell looked at Williams questioningly. "What could that possibly have to do with Bishop Diego?"

Williams smiled disarmingly. "Like I said, we've got questions. Humor us, if you will, Father."

Bell looked out the window at the school building. "We don't have a school."

The two detectives looked surprised. "We just walked past it," Williams said. "We could hear the kids."

Bell smiled. "Those are the Head Start kids. That's a federally run program. They use our school—what used to be our school."

"You *had* a school."

"Yes."

"I remember the basketball team. Pretty darn good. Used to win league championships, didn't it?"

Bell nodded. "Yeah, that's right. But we—I wasn't here then—we had to cut back. The cost of running a high school got to be prohibitive. We started running out of nuns. Had to hire lay teachers at lots more than we paid the sisters. The high school was closed in '71."

"And the elementary school?"

"Same thing. We tried to keep it going. But the expenses kept skyrocketing—salaries, mostly. Even though our teachers made great sacrifices—we couldn't pay them anything close to what their counterparts in the public schools got. So the tuition had to be raised almost every year. At the same time, the makeup of our parishioners was changing. The Latino community was growing. They weren't rich by any means. The handwriting was on the wall. We finally shut down the whole school about . . . oh . . . six years ago."

"Then the Head Start program came in."

"Uh-huh." Bell was almost offhand.

"But the Head Start program could be carried on anywhere there was an empty building. You just happened to have one," Williams said matter-of-factly.

"What are you getting at?" Bell leaned forward. His manner was combative.

"There was talk of closing down St. Gabriel's."

Bell said nothing. He had to be most cautious here. How much had these officers been told about his situation in this parish?

"Earlier, Father," Williams said, "you mentioned what it was like to be pastor of a parish. You said"—here he consulted his notes—"that the pastor can become part of his parishioners' families. That if you were assigned some other parish, you couldn't just pull up stakes and move on without caring very much."

Bell gazed at Williams intently. This was clearly The Enemy.

"Well, I was wondering, Father," Williams continued, "if it is so difficult to move along to another assignment after being so wrapped up in your former parish, how much more difficult it would be if the parish you loved but had to leave just . . . ceased to exist."

Bell cocked an eye. "Why are you so interested in St. Gabriel's? We're not going out of business. The buildings are in full use and they're in pretty good repair. We've got a zillion programs going on. Lots of the good people here depend on this parish for help in everything from food and jobs to counseling to immigration. And we respond! We make a realistic contribution to the CSA. In a word, we're healthy! So why are you harping on this parish closing down?"

"The word we got was that Bishop Diego was considering closing it."

"He couldn't do it!" The tone was aggressive.

"A bishop couldn't do it?"

"Are you a Catholic?"

"Yes." Williams did not qualify his answer as he had with Quirt. If he were to admit he was no longer a practicing Catholic, Bell would dismiss out of hand his competence in the matter. Besides, Williams had gone to school in his earlier questioning of the other three priests.

Bell had not expected so absolute a response. Taken aback somewhat, he said, "Bishop Diego was an auxiliary bishop. He was here to help Cardinal Boyle. The Cardinal is the archbishop. *He* runs this diocese, not an auxiliary bishop."

"Still . . . a bishop . . ."

"Why are you leaning on this? Are you trying to come up with some reason why I would hate or resent Bishop Diego? God Almighty, are you trying to accuse me of . . . of killing the bishop?!"

"We're not accusing you of anything, Father." Williams tried to sound reassuring. "Like I said, we've got a lot of questions. We're looking for answers. As much as anything else, we're trying to figure out what kind of man this Bishop Diego was."

"Then you'd better ask the high-priced lawyers, the judges, the top brass at G.M., Ford, Chrysler. Those were his buddies."

"We're asking them. What we want to know now is, what was he to you?"

They knew. Or, they thought they knew. Well, better they hear it from his own lips. "He was a pain in the ass to me."

The detectives were relieved at the self-revelation. But they showed no emotion. "He wanted to close St. Gabriel's," Williams pursued. "If it's as active and relevant as you say, why would he want to do that?"

Bell hesitated. Reluctant to give any further explanations, he would hesitate now before each reply. He would try to do no more than confirm some of the more innocuous information they'd already gathered.

"What you've got to understand," Bell explained, "is what Bishop Diego meant to the Hispanics of this archdiocese. All the people knew of him was that he was one of them. He grew up in a barrio in Texas. To the people, he was almost another Messiah."

"And that made you jealous?"

"Jealous? Hell, no! Sight unseen, I hoped for the same thing. If we in the southwest corner of Detroit need anything, it's a friend in high places." He shook his head. "No, we welcomed Diego with open arms.

"Then some of us came to know what *he* had in mind. Becoming a bishop—even an auxiliary—was nothing more than a launching pad as far as he was concerned. He was going to be every rich white Catholic's token Hispanic. He couldn't have cared less for our people. Only . . . only they didn't know. When he came for a visitation or a confirmation or anything like that, he was the hail bishop well met. He had 'loose change'—rumor has it quite a bundle—to pass out like an out-of-season Santa Claus.

"Well, I was the one who was willing to blow the whistle on him."

Williams and Quirt recalled the pictures on the walls of the late bishop's office. Diego and Bob Mylod; Diego and Maynard Cobb; Diego and Tom Litka; Diego and J. P. McCarthy; Diego and lots more . . . but only the rich, famous or well positioned. Neither officer doubted Bell's theory on Diego's master plan for himself. But . . .

"But . . ." Williams said, "he was a bishop. And you're a priest. *You* were going to blow the whistle on *him*?"

Bell nodded. "I think so. Whatever else happens, my people trust me. I've been with them in the trenches for . . . for a long while. It would be a close call, I guess. But I think—I'm sure—they would believe me over him. And that's beside one major factor . . ." A pause. "I've got the truth on my side."

"So," Williams said, "that's the way it was up till yesterday. You with your threat to expose him. And he with his threat to close you down."

Bell half smiled. "It's almost a pun, but we had each other in a Mexican standoff."

"And that," Quirt broke his long silence, "as Sergeant Williams just said, was the way it was till yesterday. But today's another day. And the Mexican standoff is over. I take it nobody else is trying or threatening to close your church."

"I . . . I haven't thought of it in exactly those terms," Bell said. "I was sorry that a man was murdered. Especially one I know pretty well. And I was shocked that it was a bishop. But . . . I suppose you're right. That threat is just about over."

"Convenient." It was almost sotto voce. Then in a normal tone, Quirt said: "Tell us about your yesterday. What did you do?"

"What did I do?" Apprehensive, defensive. "What I ordinarily do on Sundays: said Mass."

"That was the morning. And then?"

"I had several meetings yesterday afternoon. Briefly with some of the parish council members. A longer meeting with the worship commission. They're pushing for more Masses in Spanish. It's a ticklish situation. We've got—"

"About when did you get done with those meetings?" Quirt asked.

"I don't know . . . about 4:00 in the afternoon, I guess."

"And then?"

"I was tired. But I wanted to go to that meeting at the Cathedral. So I had a drink or two, just to unwind."

"And when did you leave to go to the meeting?"

"I don't know. The meeting—well, the dinner began at 6:00. So I must've left at about 5:30." It was not particularly warm on the porch, yet Bell was beginning to perspire.

"Not necessarily," Quirt said.

"Not . . . ?"

"You were late. Late for the dinner."

Bell seemed to be searching his memory. "Are you sure I was late? I don't remember being late. How can you be sure?"

"That's what all the other priests we talked to say. They say you arrived twenty minutes to half an hour late. You were the last one to arrive."

Bell's brow furrowed. He appeared to be trying to connect two remembered incidents separated by a vacant space. There were the meetings yesterday afternoon. He remembered them in some detail. Then there was that supertired feeling that had been recurring more frequently of late. He could remember pouring himself a drink—a martini. Was there another one? Three? That component had gone hazy.

Then there was the dinner with all the priests gathered. The food gradually sopping up the alcohol. Things got clearer then. Toward the end of the evening everything was crystal clear. Except . . . he had talked too much. Expressed his contempt for, fear of, and anger with Diego far more openly than he ought.

But the middle part. It was gone. And that was scary. Especially now with two detectives who demanded chapter and verse for everything he had done yesterday.

And slowly emerging from this daze was the importance of remembering what seemed utterly lost to memory.

He was in trouble. That he knew.

"So, Father Bell," Quirt said, "there's some time missing from what you told us you did yesterday. How about it?"

"I . . . I can't recall right now. But . . . I . . . I think I should call a lawyer."

"You can if you want, Father," Quirt said, "but, by the time he gets here, we will be long gone."

"Wait: There's one thing I want to get straight: Are you accusing me of murder? Are you accusing me, a priest, of actually killing a bishop?"

Quirt and Williams stood and slipped into their coats. "No, we're not doing that," Quirt said. "We're just gathering information. But it is interesting, isn't it? Bishop Diego allegedly is upset—maybe threatened—by your intention to, as you say, blow the whistle on him. In retaliation, he threatens not only to have you moved from your parish, but to close the whole place down.

"Then, the bishop is murdered sometime between 4:00 and 6:00 yesterday afternoon . . . a time when you are unable—you say—to remember where you were or what you did.

"However, the upshot of all this is that your problem is solved: The bishop can't do anything to you now."

The two detectives, fully garbed now for the outdoors, made no move to leave.

"If I was you, Father Bell," Quirt said, "I'd try real, real hard to remember what went on during that time of your mental lapse. And I would hope—maybe pray—that somebody was with you and can testify that you didn't even see Bishop Diego yesterday. Yes, sir, I certainly would do that."

A serious Williams and a smiling Quirt departed.

Once in the car and headed back to Beaubien, Quirt rubbed his hands together in near glee. "It's moving along like clockwork. We should have this on a platter by tonight . . . tomorrow at the outside." He turned toward Williams. "Just one thing: The part I don't see as real. That plant, St. What's-its-name . . ."

"St. Gabriel."

"Yeah, St. Gabriel. It seems to be going full speed. I mean, that school building isn't going to seed like so many institutions in this city. And, say that Bell has all these programs going . . . seems to me that the threat to close it down was pretty thin. How would Diego have handled all those kids, all those programs?"

Williams, driving east on Vernor, had just come to the complex that was Holy Redeemer. "This is how." As they cruised slowly, Williams pointed out first the gymnasium, then the auditorium, followed by the elongated rectory embracing the corner of Vernor and Junction.

He turned south where, after the rectory, the huge church stood. Then an extended parking area where the teaching brothers' home once stood. Then the school, which continued around the corner of Junction and Eldred. More school. A huge and largely unused convent. Then through an alleyway to more school and north on Calvary back to Vernor. "That's how," Williams repeated.

Quirt's mouth hung open. "For Chrissake! I had no idea . . ."

"Just a mile down the road. He could have shipped the kids, the programs, the church services to Redeemer. *But*," Williams emphasized, "a move like that would have disrupted the whole shebang. And for no good reason I can see except to neutralize Bell's threat."

"Okay, then, that wraps it up. And we got not one but two first-class suspects: Carleson and Bell. Both of 'em have a credible reason to want the bishop out of the way. Carleson is forced to become an indentured slave—"

"A bit strong?"

"Sure. Okay. Carleson comes to Detroit expecting to have his own parish to run. Instead, he's talked into apprenticing under the guidance of Bishop Diego—for what is promised to be a short time. But Diego keeps pulling strings to keep Carleson around to run errands, be a chauffeur and the like. And besides keeping Carleson on a tight leash, Diego is no sweetheart.

"Carleson was with Diego all the early hours of yesterday afternoon. He could have rattled the bishop's brains before he joined the other priests on their way to the meeting. Before they leave, Carleson shuts down the alarm system for the front door. He takes the money Diego keeps in the office to make it look like robbery/murder.

"Then he comes back about midnight, fortuitously 'finds' the body, and calls us.

"Not a bad plan . . .

"Or . . . Bell is really as worried as he seems to be that Diego will close down his parish to keep Bell from broadcasting that Diego doesn't give a crap for the spics.

"So how's this for a scenario: Bell's got a drinking problem. He even had a shot just to face us. He's got this nagging grudge against Diego. There's a priests' meeting that'll include just about all the priests in this neck of the woods. *But not the bishop.* Bishops aren't welcome at what turns out to be these bull sessions.

"So he does just what he told us he did. He has some meetings. We can check that out. But I'm pretty sure we'll find it's so. No reason to lie about that.

"Then, he does what he says: He makes himself a drink—or two or three or more . . . whatever amount it takes to put him in a black-out. He said it himself: He doesn't know what he did from the time he had his drinks until well after he finally got to the dinner, where he sobered up.

"We know he didn't drink himself into complete unconsciousness and flop on a bed until the stuff wore off. He was still blacked out until after he got to the dinner. He musta actually driven there without consciously knowing that he did it.

"So, supposing that instead of driving directly to the meeting, Bell drives to Ste. Anne's. If he rang the doorbell, Diego would certainly let him in. To do that, Diego would have to kill the alarm for the front door. Bell comes in. They go to Diego's office. Bell is quite obviously drunk—and abusive. They argue. Bell clobbers Diego, leaves and goes to the meeting, where he sobers up. But before he leaves the rectory, he takes the considerable stash of petty cash.

"He knew it was there, okay. Did you hear him just now: He said that Diego kept a considerable amount around to quiet the natives—"

"Isn't that an awful lot for a guy who's dead drunk to do?"

"I'll bet you I can find a hundred shrinks who can testify that it's not only possible but not all that uncommon.

"Yessirree, this case is ready to bust wide open. We just need one more break. And I got a hunch we're gonna get it. It's right around the corner."

"You forgetting about Zoo?"

"What about him?"

"He's got some of the guys following other leads."

"Tough luck. We got the goods."

"But . . ."

"It'll work out. Man, this is terrific! A bishop murdered and two priests the prime suspects."

"What's so good about that? I think it's kinda sad."

"You won't feel so bad when you read about it in the papers. On the front page, yet!"

So that's it, Williams thought. *We're going for the publicity.*

On that level, he was forced to agree with Quirt: It was a story right out of the Middle Ages. As far as Williams was concerned, and prescinding from the publicity this virtually insured, the case against either priest was better than average. Both Carleson and Bell had motive and opportunity. Which was not even enough to arrest either one, let alone get an indictment or a conviction. Quirt might be celebrating a mite early.

They *were* terrific leads, though. And Zoo would have to agree.

Thinking of Tully, Williams wondered how he was doing. When last seen, Zoo was headed out to track down the guy who had angry words with Diego at the cocktail party yesterday afternoon. He was also going to sound out the street, on the chance that it was what it looked like—robbery/murder.

Williams shuddered to think how complicated life would get if this thing ended up on the street. The possibilities would spread to include everyone from acidheads to the desperate poor.

Meanwhile, Quirt was thinking about how happy Kleimer was going to be when he found they had not one but two priest suspects . . . and both of them real, genuine prospects.

Quirt hadn't even thought about Tully since they parted earlier this morning. But there was nothing to worry about on that score. Carleson and Bell were bona fide suspects. Tully might even be a help in nailing one of them. Quirt began to chuckle.

Williams wondered, but didn't ask.

Quirt was thinking that, left to his own m.o., Tully would probably spend weeks on a case like this.

That was an exaggeration. But Tully was known to be painstaking and methodical. Too much so for Quirt.

Yessir, it was a stroke of good fortune for everyone that he, Quirt, had been picked to lead this task force.

Good ol' Mayor Cobb.

CHAPTER SEVEN

Sergeant Phil Mangiapane chattered as he drove. Lieutenant Alonzo Tully listened only sporadically.

The lieutenant was lost in labyrinthine theories. He had been convinced that it was very possible—easy even—to dislike this Bishop Diego. The questions were: How many ways were there to do this, and how many people were involved in this dislike?

Father Carleson was one candidate. The interrogation at Ste. Anne's rectory indicated that. Another possible candidate was this Father Bell. Quirt was following that.

Up to his metaphorical ears in bishops and priests and auxiliaries and pastors and threats to close parishes, Tully had given serious thought to seeking guidance through this ecclesiastical maze from good old Father Koesler. This priest had been of use in some previous investigations when things Catholic threatened to obscure clues.

Little did Tully know that Father Koesler had been virtually waiting by the phone for just such a call. As the day wore on, the priest was taking care of parochial duties, but in a semidistracted way. In the past, he had been reluctant to take time from his parish to become a resource for the police. But now in this matter, he was almost eager to participate.

He had come very close to being part of this case from its inception. It was he, for instance, who had accompanied Father Carleson to the door of Ste. Anne's. If Carleson had invited him in, Koesler would have been there when Carleson discovered the body. And so, Koesler made it a point to tune in to the hourly newscasts. But each was the same as the previous: There was no progress to report. Nonetheless, Koesler stood ready.

Only, no one was calling.

In Tully's mind there was no point in seeking Koesler's assistance . . . not just yet, anyway. Quirt and his team were covering the "Catholic angle." Meantime, Tully's crew was mostly on the street, tracing leads and seeking informants.

Tully, along with Mangiapane, was checking into the incident at yesterday's cocktail party where someone had ripped into Diego. The ruckus had been quieted quickly. But, occurring as it did only hours before Diego's murder, it certainly was worth checking.

The peculiar expertise possessed by Koesler was needed neither on the street nor in Tully's exploration.

Mangiapane and Tully had just left the downtown headquarters of Comerica Bank, where they had spoken with Harry Carson about the fracas at his residence.

Carson had been cooperative to a point. He readily revealed the identity of the man who had accosted Bishop Diego. Michael Shell, a lawyer, had lost no time in challenging the bishop. An attendant had taken Shell's coat, and no sooner had his arms left the sleeves than he had charged Diego.

Carson had stepped between them before anything physical could happen. He insisted they repair to the den and straighten things out. Things did not level off in the den. Shell was on the muscle, and Carson, to protect the bishop, stepped between them again. It was then the bishop declared he was leaving. After the bishop had departed, Carson had had strong words with Shell; the altercation had come close to ruining the party. Shell, in a huff, then left Carson's home. The party wound down and died.

What was the fuss about? Carson would rather not say. It was a personal matter that the police might better discuss with Mr. Shell.

Tully saw no point in pressing Carson further. If they had need of him, Carson would be there. Meanwhile, no better next stop than Shell's Southfield office.

As Mangiapane took the Nine Mile exit from the Lodge, Tully became aware that the sergeant was talking about Angie Moore, a member of their squad.

". . . so, since Angie was off duty and on her way home, she didn't pay much attention at first. Then, after a while, she thought there was someone following her. So she made a bunch of quick turns and, sure enough, the guy stayed right on her tail.

"Well, she was real close to home. So she just drove into the driveway and turned off the engine. Then she took her gun out of her handbag and waited.

"The guy pulled in behind her, got out of his car, came up and opened her door. 'Whattya say, Babe, wanna get it on?'

"And the next thing he knows, he's looking down the barrel of her service resolver. 'No, and I don't think you do either.'

"So the guy starts mutterin' and sputterin' as he backs—he *backs*—down the drive to his car. And he takes off without even turnin' his lights on." Mangiapane paused for the expected laugh.

"She should've headed for the nearest precinct station," Tully said soberly.

"Yeah, Zoo. She said that too. Only she just didn't think of it."

Drawn as he was to the image of the creep finding his prospective victim with a gun in her hand, Tully began to chuckle. Mangiapane joined in. "It *is* funny," Tully admitted.

With that, they pulled into the small parking lot adjacent to the law offices of Shell, Shell and Brown. As they parked, Tully spotted a man entering a car. The man, carrying a briefcase, was obviously in a hurry. Tully thought he recognized the man from newspapers and TV.

As the man turned on the ignition he looked up to see two men standing directly in front of his Lincoln. The black man was holding up a police badge. The man hit the car's window button.

"Michael Shell?"

"Yes."

"I'm Lieutenant Tully, Detroit Homicide. This is Sergeant Mangiapane."

"It's about yesterday, isn't it?"

"Uh-huh."

"Well, look, I'm late getting downtown for a deposition—" Tully's expression arrested Shell. "I know, I know: We can talk about it at headquarters or here. Okay."

Shell's office was of average size and, by anyone's standards, grossly cluttered. In addition to a modest bookcase crammed with what appeared to be legal manuals, the room was filled with bric-a-brac, appar-

ently souvenirs of past victories. It seemed unlikely Shell commemo-
rated defeats.

After motioning them to a couple of upholstered chairs that were
too large for what was left of this space, Shell picked up the phone.
"Henry, will you cover my deps today? . . . well, as a matter of fact,
right now. Yeah, I know it's short notice, but something came up. No
. . . no, Henry, that's impossible. This is something I've got to—*I've got
to*—take care of now . . . right now. And my client needs one of us for
the deps. Okay, okay, Henry. Thanks; I owe you one."

Shell took a deep breath and exhaled slowly, then hung up. Tully
took stock. Shell stood perhaps five-feet-six or -seven. Both his hair and
his mustache were thick and dark. His glasses were near-Coke bottle
bottoms. Overweight—lots of baby fat—about 210 to 220. Fast food on
the run—but that was all the running he did. His own firm at a relatively early age. He lived for his work.

If Tully's hypotheses proved true, he could extrapolate much of
what went on in Shell's life—at work and at home.

The scenario according to Tully: Shell was on his third marriage.
Present wife blonde, a knockout, some thirty years younger. She has no
children. He has two kids from his first wife, one from the second.
Present wife knows where her ultimate well-being lies; she does not
wander off on separate vacations. She supplies plenty of steamy, if
brief, progeny-free sex. She tans at a studio. He is bright, totally aggressive, and has the utmost confidence in himself, especially if he can get
past the judge and play to the jury. He works thirty-eight hours a day,
spends most of his time seated, and eats whatever, whenever. If she plays
her cards just exactly right, she'll spend her golden years aboard an end-
less series of cruise ships while Mike tries to pass that Great Bar in the Sky.

Shell sat in his contour-fitted chair. From a desk drawer he took
three candy bars. He offered two to his guests. They declined. Shell
unwrapped one and bit into it.

So far, thought Tully, right on, dietetically.

"Coffee?" Shell's guests declined. Shell poured himself a mug from
a pot on a hot plate on a remote corner of his king-size desk. Eyebrows
raised, he looked at the detectives. He knew, of course, why they were
here. He also knew not to volunteer information. The conversational
ball was, for the moment, in their court.

"You know that Bishop Ramon Diego is dead . . . that he was murdered."

Shell nodded slowly. No "Shocking," "Sorry," "That's too bad," "That's good," or "I did it."

"Yesterday afternoon," Tully proceeded, "at a gathering at Mr. Harry Carson's home, you had words—angry words—with the bishop."

"That's right." Useless to deny it; there were a couple dozen witnesses.

"What was that all about? We know Mr. Carson was with you during the entire exchange," Tully added, "but we want to get it from you."

Shell took another bite of the candy bar. "It was about my wife."

"Your wife?"

"My wife and the bishop."

"Your wife and . . ." This did not fit into Tully's scenario.

"It's complicated," Shell admitted.

"Let's try to simplify it," Tully said. "Your wife. She's your first wife?"

"Second."

Fewer than expected.

"Here's her picture . . ." Shell took a framed portrait from his desk and passed it to Mangiapane, who glanced at it and passed it to Tully.

Well, I never claimed to be infallible, thought Tully. She was a good-looking woman. But a beautiful dark-haired matron rather than the vapid blonde toy he had envisioned. "A recent photo?"

"Couple of years."

"So, what about the bishop and your wife?"

"It started just after he got here from Texas. When was that . . . maybe a year ago. See, her maiden name is Ortiz . . . Maria Ortiz. She's fluent in both English and Spanish. She's quite active in Hispanic affairs—fund-raisers and like that. So, she was excited when he got here and became bishop . . . you know, God's gift to the Latinos." He grimaced. "Some gift!"

"What's that mean?"

"She—Maria—introduced him to her friends—society, club women mostly. And that's where he began to spend most of his time: bashes, soirees, tennis, golf. Oh, not always with the women; he'd pal up with the men too. But the men spent most of their days at work. So the bishop would be the fourth for tennis or cards. Offer the invocation at parties, then stick around for a few hours."

A cynical grin appeared briefly. "Times when he would spend most of the day in high society must have been a relief for that poor schmuck priest . . . Carleson. At least the poor bastard didn't have to play chauffeur those days." It was a parenthetical remark.

"We were on thin ice then, Maria and me . . . have been for the last few years."

"What's the trouble?"

Shell hesitated. "You'd find out soon enough, I guess. It's common knowledge in our group . . . and with the gossip columnists. She claims I spend too much time at work . . . neglect her for the business."

For the first time, Tully could empathize. He himself had lost a wife, kids, and later a significant other for just that reason.

"We went to a counselor—Maria's idea—but what could he do? Damned-if-I-do and damned-if-I-don't. She wants the good life, I gotta earn it. I cut back at work, she loses the life-style.

"Well, anyway, the whole thing settled into a routine. We'd go out occasionally on Saturday nights, once in a while Fridays. And every now and then we'd go to one of those fund-raisers. I mean, our social life was not a complete bust. But to do all this and live the kind of life we've got means I put in twelve- to fifteen-hour days.

"Not that I mind. I like it. In fact, I love my life just the way it is. But . . . she can't see it that way." He thought for a moment. "And I'm sorry about that. I'd like her to be happier with our life the way it is. Because—bottom line—this is the way it has to be.

"But, like I said, she doesn't see it that way. And I know most of the time, she's just been going through the motions." He leaned forward and in a man-to-man tone, said, "That's the way our sex is. It's like making love to a board. And, believe me, that's not the way it was in the beginning: She was one hot-blooded Latina lover."

The last thing Tully wanted was to go through the grunts and groans of Shell's sex life. "You mentioned earlier . . . the bishop . . . Bishop Diego and your wife . . . ?"

"Yeah. Well, you needed some background. Like I said, we were already on thin ice when Diego came on the scene." Shell paused.

"Are you saying that Diego and your wife were having an affair?"

"Well, yes and no."

"'Yes and no'? Were they or weren't they?"

"You got to understand this Diego character."

"Do you?"

"I think so. He's upwardly mobile. That I know. What I don't know is where he wants to go. Pope?"

"Go on."

"He uses . . . he used people. And if they became his friends, he recycled them. But he would never—*never*—do anything to compromise his ambition. It was easy for him to charm the women. He was a handsome son of a bitch."

Tully nodded. He was growing weary of hearing about Diego's movie-star looks. "What's understanding Diego got to do with whether or not he was having an affair with your wife?"

"Like I said, it's complicated and it's not easy trying to make it simple.

"Let's do it this way: Suppose I answer your question: No, they didn't have an affair." His jaw tightened. "Jeez, I even had them followed. They met, okay. For one thing, she was always in the group that attached themselves to him. On top of that, they met, just the two of them, from time to time. But they never did anything They never went to a motel. They never went to our house together. They'd maybe go on a picnic or something like that.

"And it wasn't that they didn't care for each other. My P.I. reported that he never saw a couple so infatuated with each other. *But they didn't do anything.*

"At this point, you'd guess that not getting physical was my wife's idea. It's always the little women, eh? But it wasn't. He's the one who kept it innocent. And why? *Because he's upwardly mobile.* He's going places. And he's not going to get to be Cardinal or Pope by having a physical affair with some good-looking Spanish broad."

"You know this for sure?" Tully asked. "That staying out of the sack was his idea?"

Shell extended his arms, palms up, as if to say, what other explanation makes sense. "Fits his profile."

"So," Tully concluded, "the simple answer to my question is no."

"Not exactly."

"What?"

"It wasn't a physical affair. I'm convinced they never had intercourse . . . not even close. But they had—a what?—a spiritual affair."

"Huh?"

Shell unwrapped a second candy bar and bit into it. "I can't explain it. I've never seen anything like it. The guy could have had her, easy. She was bananas for him. He could have, but he didn't.

"The way I see it, he just wouldn't compromise his future. Must have taken a lot not to accept what he was freely offered. I'll give the bastard that. But then, see, she changed. It was something like that character in *Man of La Mancha*—you know, Dulcinea. She's a scullery maid and a whore. But the crazy Don Quixote keeps calling her 'My Lady' until she changes completely and starts acting like a highborn lady.

"Not that Maria was a whore, you know. But what I mean, she changed. Oh, she was willing to throw herself at him. But he's Don Quixote. He's going to teach her how to love 'pure and chaste from afar.' Okay, so she becomes Dulcinea . . . and I lost my Maria."

"You mean—"

"I told you our relationship was on thin ice. Sex for me was like making love to a board. Well, Maria took the board away and left me nothing. Nothing."

No one spoke.

"As far as I know," Shell said finally, "I'm the only guy in history to have been cuckolded by a couple of practicing virgins."

Mangiapane barely suppressed a burst of laughter. Tully, with some effort, kept a straight face.

Shell, who was quite serious, continued. "Now, what the hell could I do about it? How could I say Diego was guilty of alienation of affection? He didn't do anything except mesmerize her. She didn't do anything but fall under his spell. The upshot of the whole thing was I lost my wife. I lost her to a goddam bishop. And there wasn't a goddam thing I could do about it.

"It was awful. We'd be together, say at dinner, and she wouldn't say anything—nothin'—just answer questions. With one word—the fewest possible syllables. She began sleeping in the guest room.

"I was going nuts.

"What happened next reminds me of a story. . . ." Shell smiled briefly. "Seems this doctor—a surgeon—was on trial for using abusive and obscene language. Trying to explain his side of it, he says to the judge, 'You see, Your Honor, on the day in question, I woke up about eight o'clock. The alarm didn't go off. I was scheduled for extremely delicate surgery at 9:00. So I tried to hurry. Naturally, I cut myself shaving. I started breakfast before I took my shower. There wasn't any hot water. After the cold shower, I found I'd set the microwave for too long and burned everything. In my haste to get dressed, I ripped the trousers of my suit. The car wouldn't start. I lost two taxi rides when people pushed me aside so they could take the cabs. I was nearly an hour late by the time I got to the hospital. The elevator that took me to the OR stopped just a few inches short of the floor. I tripped on my way out. I fell flat on my face and broke the glasses I needed to perform the operation.

"'At that point, a nurse came up to me and said, "Doctor, we just received a shipment of a thousand rectal thermometers. What do you want me to do with them?"'"

The two detectives couldn't help but laugh.

"Funny," Tully said after a minute, "but what's that got to do with you?"

"Just remember," Shell said, "how completely frustrated I was. For all practical purposes, I had lost my wife. It was like being with the living dead. And there wasn't a thing I could do about it. And I owed it all to this son-of-a-bitch bishop.

"That's exactly the state of mind I was in when I walked into Carson's house and saw the bastard standing there in the middle of a bunch of fawning sycophants. There he stood like Cock Robin in his black and red robes. I never even met him before. Just saw his picture in the papers, caught him a few times on TV. This was the first goddam time I was ever in the same room with the bastard.

"So it was like when the nurse asked what to do with all those damn thermometers. I blew it. I blew my stack."

"Were you going to hit him?"

"I don't know. Maybe." He shrugged. "Carson stepped in before anything could happen."

"Then Carson got you and the bishop to go to another room together. So then what?"

"I kept at it. I called him everything I could think of. I told him to stay the hell away from my wife—even though I knew it was too late to do any good. Then I made some idle threats—like anybody in my position would've done."

"How did the bishop react?"

"Completely on the defensive. He didn't say a word. First his complexion matched his red robes. Then he got real pale. That was when I knew I'd reached him. About that time he muttered a few excuses and beat it."

"And then . . . ?"

"I was too worked up to remember what Carson said to me. Something about telling me to leave in no uncertain terms . . . that I had wrecked his party."

"And then . . . ?"

"I left."

"And then . . . ?"

"And then I didn't kill him."

After a short silence, Tully spoke again. "So what did you do then? Where did you go?"

"The boy got my car." Shell snorted. "Hell, the motor hadn't had time to cool. I must've set some kind of world's record for the briefest time spent at a party. Oh, I didn't mind being asked to leave." He grinned lopsidedly. "I've been thrown out of better places than that.

"But I was still steaming. So I forced myself to park for a while to cool off. I didn't want to add an auto accident to all the rest of my misery.

"When I felt a little less like tearing Diego limb from limb, I started out Jefferson. I wasn't heading anywhere in particular. I ended up in a bar in St. Clair Shores . . . what the hell is the name of the place . . . uh . . . I've never been there before. It's around Nine Mile and Mack . . . uh . . . The Lazy Dolphin. Yeah, that was it."

"What time would that have been?"

"Geez, I don't know. That's where I went from Carson's house, driving slow . . . I guess maybe 3:00, 3:30."

"How long were you there?"

"A couple of hours . . . about 5:30 maybe."

"Would anybody remember your being there between those hours?"

"Uh . . . I don't know. . . . I don't think so."

"You were there two hours and no one can attest to that?"

"The bar was crowded. I don't know . . . maybe the bartender."

"We'll check that out."

"Am I still a suspect?"

"Who said you were a suspect?"

Shell smiled. "I've been in court a few times. I'd say someone who gets into a violent argument with somebody and that somebody gets killed later on the same day, I'd say the police might get a little suspicious. Might even come over to the guy's law office asking questions."

"Just checking things out, Mr. Shell.

"Thanks for your time."

*   *   *   *

Mangiapane, who had been taking notes throughout the session, slid into the driver's seat. Tully spent a few moments taking in the atmosphere before entering the passenger seat.

Mangiapane started the engine. "Off to see Dulcinea?"

Tully smiled. "Yeah, Dulcinea. Know where they live?"

"In Troy. I looked it up before we got started."

"Good man."

Mangiapane would take Telegraph Road north, then cut east on Square Lake. "He seemed kind of open, didn't you think, Zoo?"

"That the impression you got? Yeah, I guess he did volunteer a lot of information for somebody who's under suspicion. But when you think about it, it's all stuff we're probably gonna get from the other people we talk to."

"Maybe the stuff that went on in Carson's house. But how about what was going on with his wife and the bishop?"

"Yeah, how about that? Going over what he said, there's the fracas at Carson's. All the guests heard what he said to Diego. Even when they went in the other room, Carson was there. And I'd be surprised if at least some of the guests didn't hear him through the closed door. He was pissed and he was likely yelling.

"Then there's that bit about him and his wife and his wife and Diego. Remember he said that a number of people, even some gossip columnists, were in on that. It figures: The Shells are society. They're in the spotlight. If their marriage is on the rocks, people know. And people talk. And the bishop was popular with those society women. Mrs. Shell was a member of that group. Whadya wanna bet that some of those dames knew what was goin' on. Hell, they probably wanted to trade places with her. So we're gonna get some info about Shell and his wife, and the wife and the bishop, from a lot of people.

"And, we're on our way to interview the wife. Shell knew we would. He knows what she's gonna tell us.

"What this comes down to is that Shell wanted to tell us first what we were gonna learn anyway. That way he appears open and aboveboard. A nice, frank guy who certainly wouldn't kill anybody.

"ManJ, right after we get done with Mrs. Shell, I want you to start checking this guy out. Use as many of the team as you need. By this time, the guys must know whether they're gonna get anything from the streets.

"If I were Mr. Shell, I'd start hoping that barkeep's got a real good memory."

CHAPTER
EIGHT

It was not a pretentious house. But considering the neighborhood, the address, and the 48098 zip code, it probably went for about $500,000. Frankly, Tully had expected more from the Shells' conspicuous consumerism. Perhaps more was coming.

The snow, somewhat deeper here this far north of Detroit, lay in neat rectangles, squares and other geometric shapes demarcated by crisply clean driveways, walkways, and streets.

Mangiapane pulled into the Shells' driveway. One of the fringe benefits of riding with Manj, mused Tully, was that he knew his way around the city and its environs as well as or better than any cab driver. You not only never got lost riding with the sergeant, you got to your destination as quickly as possible.

They were met at the door by a maid in black dress and white apron. Tully displayed his badge and identified himself and his companion. The maid, displaying neither surprise nor awe, led them to a drawing room, where she announced them to a woman seated in a white deeply upholstered chair near the window. A white robe covered her from shoulder to ankle. Her complexion was a dusky tan. Though her eyes were obscured by shaded glasses, it was obvious she was the woman in the photograph on Mike Shell's desk.

Tully introduced himself and Mangiapane. She acknowledged that she was Maria Shell, wife of Michael.

They declined her offer of coffee or tea. The maid was dismissed.

Mangiapane flipped open his notepad and prepared once again to record the session.

"You are aware of Bishop Diego's death?" Tully asked.

Maria Shell nodded slowly. Despite the dark glasses, Tully could tell there was puffiness about her eyes. She seemed composed, but barely. He guessed she'd been crying.

"Why are you here?" She spoke softly and deliberately with no trace of accent.

"We just visited your husband."

Tully expected a reaction, but Maria Shell appeared to be waiting for more explanation for their presence in her home.

"The bishop was murdered sometime between the hours of 4:00 and 6:00 yesterday afternoon. Your husband had angry words with him shortly before that time."

"You think my husband killed Ramon?"

Tully, startled that she had used the bishop's given name, quickly recovered. "We're just conducting an investigation now. We haven't accused anyone. Did you know about the altercation between your husband and the bishop?"

She nodded. "A friend told me."

"You didn't accompany your husband to the party."

"I seldom do."

"I would have thought that since the bishop was going . . ."

"He must have made up his mind at the last moment," she interrupted. "I didn't know he would be at the Carsons'. In any case, I wouldn't have gone with my husband. We seldom go anywhere together." She paused. "What did you say those times were?"

"The bishop's murder? Between 4:00 and 6:00."

"My husband's outburst?"

"Sometime between 2:30 and 3:00."

"Michael was not home at all yesterday afternoon or evening. He didn't come home until approximately 10:00 last night."

Interesting. *The wife goes out of her way to destroy her husband's alibi sight unseen.* "He didn't claim to be home, Mrs. Shell."

One corner of her mouth turned up. She shrugged. "Did he . . . suffer . . . much?"

The question derailed Tully. It seemed related to nothing. "Your husband?"

"No!" Her tone indicated she couldn't have cared less if her husband had been hanged, drawn, and quartered. "Ramon."

"Oh. 'Suffered'?" Tully had not given the matter any thought. But the answer was not difficult, nor did he have to bend the truth. "No, I don't think so. I think death came instantly. If death wasn't instantaneous, he was at least unconscious and died in that condition."

A tear trickled down her cheek. She made no move to brush it away. It was a poignant moment, and Tully paused, almost in memoriam to the bishop and the evident affection Mrs. Shell had for him.

"Your husband stated that your marriage for quite some time has been . . . I think his words were, 'on thin ice.'"

Her generous lips pulled tight. "How would he know?"

"Beg pardon?"

"He was seldom here. Business *interfered*"—she spoke the word bitterly—"with his home life. I was his . . . seminal wastebasket."

Now, there's a descriptive phrase, Tully thought. "Whatever. Your husband stated that your already shaky relationship went downhill after Bishop Diego came on the scene."

She made a disparaging sound. "If it hadn't been for Bishop Diego, my marriage to Michael would have ended."

Apparently, thought Tully, Maria had some mechanism, perhaps subconscious, that dictated whether she used the bishop's given name or his title. It might be important to understand this choice. "Your marriage 'would have ended'?"

"I'll be frank with you, Lieutenant: If Ramon had shown the slightest interest, I would have left Michael in a minute to be with him!"

Tully was willing to reconsider Diego's power to mesmerize. Quite a statement! And to the police . . . "One of the things we're trying to find out"—Tully shifted the conversation slightly—"is just what sort of man Bishop Diego was. It might help us determine who might want him out of the way. Of all the people in this area, you probably would be best able to help. Would you?"

As she leaned back in the chair, her robe opened to the knee. Both detectives noted a very shapely leg.

"What can I say? Ramon was a kind, generous, dedicated priest." She turned her head from side to side as if looking for something to say that would be more relevant.

"It has been mentioned"—Tully did not state how often and how forcefully it had been mentioned—"that the bishop was ambitious."

"'Ambitious'?" It was as if she'd never heard the word before.

"Quite a few of the people we've interviewed seem to think that Bishop Diego was using Detroit as a jumping-off platform to bigger things." Tully left Diego's ultimate goal vague because Tully had no idea where one went from bishop. Pressed, he probably would have guessed Pope.

A joyless smile spread on Maria's face. But it quickly disappeared. "I know what you're talking about, Lieutenant. But it simply isn't true. To the best of my knowledge, Detroit has never had a Hispanic bishop before. And there is a large and growing Latino community here. So, I suppose, when Ramon was called from Texas and made a bishop here, many people just put two and two together and got five.

"He became the Great Spanish Hope. Just because he happened to be Hispanic and was assigned to the archdiocese. It happens. A black bishop comes to a diocese and the black community assumes he's there for them alone. But that just isn't the way it works."

Tully smiled engagingly. "You'll have to explain that a little more for my benefit, Mrs. Shell. That's the way it works for me."

"You're not a Catholic."

Tully shook his head but did not bother clarifying how far from being Catholic he was.

"I think," Maria began, "St. Paul said something about that for the Christian—they did not use the term Catholic in those days, but it was the same thing—"

It was? Tully wondered.

". . . there was no such thing as Jew or Gentile, male or female, bondsman or free man. We are all one in Christ."

"Excuse me, Mrs. Shell, but it doesn't seem to work out that way in practice. Does it?"

"My very point, Lieutenant. I am speaking of the ideal. That's what we all strive for. At least that is what we ought to be striving for. But, in practice, we regularly fail in this objective. So African-American Catholics feel separated from other Catholics. And if a black bishop is sent to their diocese, they feel he is God's gift to them. Or, in this case, a Latino bishop is sent to Detroit and the Latino community believes he has been sent to them."

"But he hasn't."

"But he hasn't," she confirmed. "He is sent to the archdiocese of Detroit and to all the Catholics of this archdiocese. Do you see?"

"Yes." Tully nodded. "I think I see. But do you see how the Latinos could hope that he came for them?"

"Yes, of course I understand. But they are wrong."

"Let's just go a little further with this, if you don't mind, Mrs. Shell."

She nodded. But she was beginning to fidget. He was going to have to wrap this up. "Earlier today, I was in the late bishop's office. Have you ever been there?"

"Yes."

"It's a simple, modest office. I would have expected that a bishop would have had something much more elegant."

She smiled more unreservedly, with a sense of pride, Tully thought.

"But," he continued, "I was struck by the photos on the walls of the office. You know the ones I mean?"

She made no response whatsoever. It was as if he had not posed the question.

"I think," Tully said, "that the bishop is in every picture. Which is not surprising in itself. But just about everybody else in these pictures—at least all I managed to see—they were all prominent people, well known in this area." He paused.

"So?"

"So, I was wondering just who the bishop had come to Detroit to save or serve—whichever way you want to say it."

She said nothing.

"There weren't any 'ordinary' people in any of those photos. Just the rich and famous."

"Do not the rich and famous have souls?"

"I'm not in position to be an expert on souls and salvation. I'm just a cop with a problem. The problem is that a prominent citizen of the city of Detroit was murdered yesterday and it's my job to find out who did it. Bishop Diego seems to have been a focal point for two local groups. One is the Latino community who expected him to spend pretty much his every effort on their behalf. The other group was the Catholic movers and shakers who had his interest just about all the time.

"Now, it's pretty likely that somebody in one of these groups, for whatever reason, wanted him dead. One group, his own people, if you will, feel betrayed and accuse him of being ambitious. The other group has his complete attention. But maybe one or more of this group doesn't appreciate his involvement with them . . . your husband, for instance."

"You are intimating that my husband could have killed Ramon?"

"Could he?"

She reflected on this for a few moments. "He could not believe in his wildest imagination the type of relationship that Ramon and I had. Michael sees only one use for women. Most of his closest friends are similarly limited. If anyone were to tell them that Ramon and I communicated on a purely spiritual level, they would laugh themselves sick. But that's what really happened. It was on the specific urging of Ramon that I stayed with Michael."

"Your husband claims that your relation with Bishop Diego caused you to stop speaking to him . . . caused you even to sleep in a separate room."

Maria snorted delicately. "What came first, the chicken or the egg?"

"But, would you agree with your husband that your relationship was on shaky ground—or thin ice—at about the time that Bishop Diego got here, and that it subsequently deteriorated?"

She thought for a moment. "I'd have to admit that, wouldn't I? I've already let pass that we are no longer talking, and that we're sleeping in separate beds."

"Your husband hasn't asked for a divorce?"

"I think he thinks he can win me back."

"Can he?"

"No."

"But he won't take no for an answer?"

"Apparently not."

"Going back to my original question: Could your husband have killed Bishop Diego?"

She turned her head to the window. With her eyes shaded by the glasses, it was impossible to tell what possible message might be communicated through her gaze. "If he were . . ." She hesitated. "If he were . . . I think something would have had to have happened. Something like drink. Michael would have had to be drunk—not comatose drunk, but very high. Or using drugs. And I don't think he's ever been on drugs. Not more than a marijuana cigarette on occasion." She turned back to Tully. "So, yes, under certain circumstances, I guess he could have."

"Do you think he did?"

"I don't know. I sincerely hope he did not."

"You care about your husband, then?"

"It would ruin his life. And it would not do wonderful things for my life either."

CHAPTER
NINE

"What do you think, Manj?"

Without taking his eyes from the road, Mangiapane shook his head. "I dunno, Zoo. I'd hate to live with that broad and have to keep my hands off her."

"There's that."

"Drive a guy nuts."

"Nuts enough to commit murder?" Tully was asking himself as well as Mangiapane.

"I think so."

"Notice she said she thought he'd have to get loaded to off somebody."

"Yeah." Mangiapane started to smile. "And he said he went from Carson's house to a bar."

"Wasn't that helpful of him to tell us that? Now, if anybody in that bar can remember Shell in there that night, the next important thing to check out is how long he stayed there."

"Makes a pretty good case, Zoo. Shell bumps into Diego unexpectedly. He's surprised the bishop is at this party. He doesn't have a chance to get himself in control. So he blows his ever-lovin' stack. Then he storms out. He drives around until he happens into this bar. He goes in, gets a few snootfuls. Not dead drunk, just high. Like the lady said, he needs to get some liquid courage. He's sober enough to drive, and plastered enough to scramble the bishop's brains."

"Or," Tully suggested, "she's underestimating her husband. Maybe he doesn't need to get juiced. Maybe his stop at the bar is in his head. Maybe he did happen on this bar, took a look, and saw there were so many people there no one would be able to testify whether there was a stranger there or not. So, he can tell us he was there, sure that nobody can say for certain whether he was or wasn't there. Whatever. No matter what, we're going to have to ask somĕ questions there."

They drove on for several minutes before Tully broke the silence.

"Manj, you're a Catholic. How well do you have to know a bishop before you call him by his first name?"

"Yeah, I caught that too. And I dunno, Zoo. I never knew one well enough to call him Fred or Charlie. They got a title, and I don't even remember that. It's Your Grace, or Your Excellency or Your Eminence, or something. Now that I think of it, I don't even know anybody who calls any bishop by his first name."

"What the hell kind of Catholic are you, anyway, Manj?" Tully was chuckling softly. "Not only don't you know, you don't even know anybody who knows."

"There you got it." Mangiapane was also chuckling. "I just sit in the pew and wait for the priest to tell me what to do."

"No, actually"—Tully grew more serious—"you told me something by not knowing. I'm going to guess that it's very uncommon. And I'm going to guess that Mrs. Shell knew the bishop very, very well. And, you know what else I'm going to do? I'm going to quit guessing."

"Huh?"

"Manj, drop me off at . . . oh, what the hell is it . . . the parish where Koesler is pastor."

"Old St. Joe's?"

"Yeah, that's it."

Mangiapane was grinning. "Finally going to call on Uncle, huh?"

"This stuff is getting too deep for me. I got a hunch Quirt is gonna come in with a lot of heavy stuff on those two priests. I also got a hunch he's not gonna know what he's talking about. I'm gonna go to school before this case gets much older.

"After you drop me off, get somebody—Angie, if you can—to take over that bar investigation. I want you to talk to everybody who's been on the street. See if anybody's come up with anything."

"Sure thing, Zoo. . . . Uh, don't you think you ought to call and make sure Father Koesler's available?"

*   *   *   *

Available? It was as if the second shoe had been dropped.

He'd been distracted most of this Monday waiting for a phone call about the murder of Bishop Diego. After all, it wasn't that he was a stranger to police investigations when they had to do with things Catholic. And what could be a more Catholic homicide than the murder of a bishop?

His surprise, if it could be termed that, was that the call came from Lieutenant Tully rather than Inspector Koznicki. Of course, Koesler knew the lieutenant. But Koznicki had become a dear and close friend.

In any case, he was about to get in the swim.

With some hesitation he asked Mary O'Connor to clear his calendar for the rest of the day. His reservations concerned two appointments he had scheduled—one late this afternoon, the other early this evening. Neither person was likely to take the postponement graciously. Neither could lay claim to either tact or diplomacy. Mary would have to suffer their predictable reactions. Koesler tended to believe Mary when she assured him that the job would be easier for her. The recalcitrant parishioners would be disappointed when she gave them the message—but they would save their venom for their pastor.

So he wouldn't miss the dreaded appointments by putting them on the back burner.

Awaiting Tully's arrival, Koesler thought about the two troublesome parishioners.

Mrs. McReedy belonged to the Church of Vatican Council I. In a sense, that was a comfortable Church. There were so many rules and regulations. Practically no one challenged their existence or relevance. The very keeping of them led to feelings of peace and comfort. The rules offered salvation. And salvation was comfortable. And, should one by and large keep the rules—such as fasting and abstaining and attending Mass on the appropriate days—one would go to heaven.

Mrs. McReedy would be objecting to the absence of many of these rules and regulations from Father Koesler's homilies, ministries, and total life philosophy.

She would have been at the rectory at 3:30 sharp had not Lieutenant Tully rescued him.

Also headed off by Tully's visit was Frank Parker, who thus would not be here at 7:00 this evening.

Frank belonged to a Church that might arise from some future Vatican Council. To call Frank an activist was like saying that John F. Kennedy liked women.

And Frank wanted his parish—Old St. Joe's—to dive in no matter where the waters might lead. Some of his projected programs: March and parade through Lafayette Park to support AIDS research. A regular monthly Mass for and by Catholic gays enlisting a homosexual priest to celebrate the Mass. A regular evening weekly Mass for and by women—with a designated woman as celebrant each week. Remove all the remaining religious artifacts from the church's interior. Have concelebrated liturgies regularly with Protestant and Jewish clergy.

Koesler believed Frank Parker's heart was in the right place, but that his mind and his viscera had bonded.

Looking at this day that wasn't going to happen, Koesler was again reminded that it didn't matter whether you were killed by conservatives or liberals—you were just as dead either way.

He could remember the mid-fifties when he had been ordained a priest. How sure and certain things were then.

It had become a joke, but in those days—and for long years before—the Church structure resembled a triangle with the Pope at the summit. It was *his* vision and commands that trickled down to the bishops, from them to the priests and finally to the strong but subservient base of the laity.

The joke was that the hierarchy, for the most part, continue to think that nothing has changed. The hierarchy should consult with its priests, who are being squeezed from all angles.

Today's canceled appointments surely were a case in point.

There was Mrs. McReedy, who, with the Lone Ranger, wanted to return to the days of yesteryear, and expected Koesler to lead the way. Then there was Frank Parker, who wanted to go, with the Trekkies, where no man has gone before. He expected Koesler to ignite the avant garde blast-off.

Yet were today's priest to toy with one of the Parker programs, organizations such as Catholics United for the Faith, in close step with the bishop, would stamp on his obtrusive toes.

On the other hand, implementing Mrs. McReedy's most fervent

prayers would alienate many Catholics whose faith and interest had been awakened by Vatican Council II.

One of the many blessings of an inner-city ministry was that the more "inner" one got, the less anyone outside cared what was going on. Unhappily, Old St. Joe's was on the outer fringe of "inner." Thus the McReedys and Parkers could still stir things up.

The doorbell. Probably Lieutenant Tully. Fortunately, it would be neither Loretta nor Frank.

Footsteps resounded on the hardwood floor. The clicking heels of Mary O'Connor ushered in a male of light but firm foot. Mary brought Tully to the dining room door. Ordinarily, Koesler received callers in his office. But Tully was special and did not come close to being a parishioner.

Declining Koesler's offer to take his coat, Tully draped the garment over a chair and seated himself on another, more comfortable one.

"Could I get you a cup of coffee?"

Tully appeared eager to accept, then hesitated. "Is it already made?"

"No, but I can whip up some instant—"

"No! No! That's all right. I've had too much today."

It made no difference to Koesler whether the lieutenant wanted coffee, but the vehemence with which his offer was declined startled the priest. And yet so many reacted in that fashion. It was almost as if he were incapable of making a simple cup of coffee that was potable. But that couldn't be true; just last night Father Carleson had enjoyed his coffee.

Was that just last night? It now seemed days ago.

"Who calls bishops by their first name?" Tully always got right to the heart of things.

"Who calls bishops by their first name?" Koesler was utterly perplexed by the question. "Well . . . I suppose . . . their parents, for two."

Tully did not seem satisfied. "I guess I could take that for granted. Who else?"

Koesler pondered. He always took people seriously no matter how bizarre the question. "Don't take it for granted. I can remember parents who stopped calling their little boys 'Johnnie' and started calling them 'Excellency' or 'Bishop.'"

"No shi— Sorry." Usually, Tully monitored his language better.

This revelation was a genuine surprise. And he was not often taken by surprise.

"As a matter of fact," Koesler said, trying to put the officer at ease, "I remember a rather close friend who became a bishop. The first time I met him after that happy day, I was pleased to address him by his new title. And he said, 'Don't give me that bishop shit. I'm still just plain Joe.'

"So, there's more to it than that.

"Now that I think about it," he mused, "it all seems to depend on the bishop, the person who's addressing him, and the circumstances."

Koesler stopped in midthought. He had expected—hoped—he could be a consultant regarding the murder of Bishop Diego. And here he was fooling with bishops' given names and who would dare, or be permitted, or invited to use them. "Is this of any importance?"

"It could be. It's something I don't completely understand. And I think I should."

Koesler tilted his head and smiled. "Okay. Bishops in most instances, at least from the earliest days of the Christian Church, were usually selected from the ranks of the priests.

"In modern times, priests were given the title of 'Father.' It was only a few years ago that the title became virtually expendable. Some contemporary priests discard the title and encourage everyone to use their given name. Others insist on the title's use. Others will excuse close friends from using it.

"That's pretty much the case with bishops. Except that far more bishops than priests will want the title—along with the reverence.

"An example: Probably no one is a more complete churchman than the Cardinal Archbishop of Detroit. Whenever he comes to mind—no matter how casually—I automatically think of him in terms of His Eminence Mark Cardinal Boyle.

"Even his priest secretary who lives in the same home, travels with him frequently, and shares his meals, regularly refers to him as Eminence. About as casual as this gets is when the secretary, when speaking to another priest, refers to the Cardinal as 'the boss.'

"And yet, I've heard Joan Blackford Hayes call him Mark."

"Who's Joan Blackford Hayes?"

"You don't . . . Well, I suppose you might not know her if you're not Catholic. She's the founder and head of the Institute for Continuing Education. In effect, she's part of the local Church administration. It's as if she's a member of Cardinal Boyle's cabinet. Still, I'd never have guessed she was on a first-name basis with the Cardinal if I hadn't heard her call him Mark."

"How about Maria Shell?"

"Who's Maria Shell?" Koesler assumed Maria Shell was someone he was expected to know. And he didn't. It happened with discouraging regularity. Here he was a native Detroiter for all of his sixty-five years and there were so many well-known Detroiters he'd never met, did not know, or recognized only from reading about them.

"That's just the point," Tully said. "Who *is* Maria Shell? You tell me about a woman who's been selected by the bishop to be a member of his team. And still you were surprised to hear her call her boss by his first name.   •

"See, yesterday afternoon, Father Carleson drove Bishop Diego to a cocktail party thrown by a prominent guy named Carson. . . ."

It happened again. Koesler did not know the prominent Carson.

"Turns out a guy named Michael Shell showed up at the party and had it out—strong words, not blows—with Diego. Then, a couple to a few hours later, the bishop is murdered."

"And this Michael Shell is a suspect?"

"Of course we're interested in anyone who exhibits violent anger at someone who later is murdered. It gets complicated. But Shell is positive that Diego was a good part of the cause Mrs. Shell is estranged from Mr. Shell. He doesn't allege that the two had illicit relations . . . but he does accuse the bishop of alienating his wife's affections.

"The point is, I just interviewed Mrs. Shell. Half the time she talked about 'Bishop Diego.' The rest of the time, he was 'Ramon.' Granted, I don't know much about institutional religion, but that's the first time I've heard an ordinary person—*a woman*—call a bishop by his first name. And you say he might have invited her to do that?"

"Yes, especially in this case."

"Why especially here?"

"I didn't get to know the bishop personally. But we priests do talk. So from pretty reliable hearsay, I think I have a fair idea of what made Bishop Diego tick.

"I hate to say this, because it's practically the opposite of what a bishop should be, but Bishop Diego used people. Bishops—priests for that matter—ought to be serving people in any kind of ideal way. But a sort of consensus would tell you that Bishop Diego manipulated people.

"Although I don't know them, from the way you referred to them, I take it that Mr. and Mrs. Shell and this Mr. Carson who gave the cocktail party yesterday are pretty important people. Rich and, I suppose, Catholic."

Tully nodded.

"Then," Koesler continued, "they're the type of people that the bishop wanted—needed.

"See, shortly after he got here from Texas, our priests, who sort of have a sixth sense for this sort of thing, agreed that Diego was just passing through Detroit on the way to his own diocese. And, if he had any way of influencing it, the diocese he would be given would be big and important."

"Getting his own diocese, that would be a promotion?"

"Very, very much so. And, as you can easily see, getting a place like New York or Chicago or Boston is a great deal different than, say, Saginaw. So, everything he did here had a lot to do with where he would be going. That's why it was so necessary for him to get to be part of the socially and financially important circle of the archdiocese."

"Have you seen the late bishop's office at Ste. Anne's?" Tully asked.

"No."

"Never mind. It just sort of illustrates what you've been saying. His formula for success seemed to be working quite well. But it doesn't explain Michael Shell or Maria Shell."

"I don't know Mr. Shell. And I'd never heard of Maria and her relationship with the bishop. But I think I could guess what was going on."

"By all means," Tully invited.

"Let me call it the 'forbidden fruit.' You're familiar with the forbidden fruit in the Garden of Eden?"

"Adam and Eve?" Tully smiled. "Yeah, even I know about them."

"Well, this law we have of celibacy sort of makes priests and, I suppose even more, bishops a kind of forbidden fruit. I don't want to seem to be bragging about this. We priests certainly are no better catches than the average man. But the fact that we are—how shall I say it?—out of bounds sometimes seems to add a certain attraction.

"It's something like the company that gets a new computer system. And the president announces to the employees that this new system is foolproof: No one can break into it and solve its secrets—"

"Don't tell me," Tully interrupted. "It's a challenge. Somebody's going to take on the challenge and try to beat the system."

"Exactly. The owner is, in effect, hurling down a gauntlet. He's implying that none of his employees is smart enough—talented enough—to break into the computer system. In the face of that, someone is almost certain to try—maybe even succeed.

"The author of Genesis used this sort of example to begin the explanation of how evil came into the world. Adam and Eve could use this garden of paradise in any way they wished. There was only a single command. Inevitably the fruit of the one forbidden tree became the most desirable of all.

"Now, nothing in this story that suggests that the tree of the knowledge of good and evil was any better or more nourishing or tastier than that of any other tree. Only that it was forbidden.

"Well, that's what I'm suggesting here. Priests aren't guaranteed in any qualitative way to be more attractive than any other man. But the requirement of celibacy makes them a forbidden fruit. Some women can be attracted for that reason alone. But it can work the other way too. The forbidden fruit and the tempter can become one and the same agent.

"Take Bishop Diego, for instance. If we grant that he was an almost shamefully ambitious person, his game was working quite perfectly. In a situation like that, he could become quite bored."

Koesler was becoming animated as the flow of his argument carried him along. "There's a scene in *My Fair Lady* where Henry Higgins takes his new creation, an elegant Eliza Doolittle, to a fancy ball. Everyone in on the experiment is very tense until Eliza seems to be carrying off her innocent deception perfectly. Higgins is bored to tears . . . so much so that he welcomes the acid test provided by another speech teacher and grammarian—Zoltan Kaparthy.

"This, I think, is what may have happened with Bishop Diego. His plan was working so well that he was willing to introduce another element—just to liven up the game. And so he could welcome his own Eliza Doolittle. He wouldn't become so carried away that he would compromise the limitations his celibacy called for. But he would dally— just to add a little spice to his now humdrum program. What's her name . . . Maria Shell? He would lead her on to a sort of chaste love affair.

"Now maybe he made a mistake there. Maybe he didn't count on treading on the already fragile relationship between Maria and Michael Shell."

"And maybe," Tully continued the speculation, "that was a serious— maybe even a fatal mistake."

Koesler leaned back in his chair. "Maybe."

The hint of a smile played around Tully's lips. "Now, about that Adam and Eve story: Does it say what Eve thought of the snake?"

"I'm sorry?"

"The snake caused all the trouble, I mean by tempting Eve. Did she get sore about that?"

"Hmmm. That's not part of the story. Life just goes steadily down-hill for Adam and Eve after their disobedience."

"But she should get angry, shouldn't she?"

Koesler pondered a moment. "I suppose so. Of course the original disobedience was her responsibility. She could have rejected the offer. She should have. But, on the other hand, she probably would have stayed on the straight and narrow if she hadn't been tempted. So, yes, I suppose that would be one conclusion you could draw from the story. But . . . wait a minute . . . you're saying . . ."

"I'm saying, What if Maria Shell wised up to Diego? What if she realized that no matter how bad her marriage was, it got a whole lot worse after Diego came on the scene? What if she thought or assumed that her relationship with Diego was going to get serious, get physical?

"At one point when I was talking to her today she as much as said that if he had called, she would have answered. She was ready to pack up and leave with him. Suppose she tumbled to what you just said: that Diego was using her, just the way he was using everybody else. After all, why should he change his m.o. for her alone? She's a smart lady, she could have come to that conclusion eventually. Why not now?

"Then we've got two people instead of one, whose lives would be significantly brightened with Diego out of the picture." Tully looked thoughtful. "That could be interesting.

"Okay," he said after a moment, "that clears up my perspective on the Shells. Now, one more thing: What about those two priests—Carleson and Bell—and the bishop?"

"Don Carleson and Ernie Bell? *They're* not suspects!?"

"It's part of the investigation. We've been tracing movements of just about everybody who crossed Diego's path yesterday, and as far back before then and as completely as we can. Mostly from that meeting last night, Carleson and Bell surfaced. You were at that meeting. I'm surprised they didn't question you."

"'They'? Aren't *you* conducting this investigation?"

Tully explained the makeup of the temporary task force and the fact that Lieutenant Quirt was heading it. "You know both these priests, don't you?"

"Yes. I know them . . . Ernie Bell far better than Don Carleson. Ernie's entire career as a priest has been in this archdiocese. We were together in the seminary. Father Carleson is in the process of joining us from the foreign missions. But he and I had a long talk just last night. So I have some little knowledge of him. What would be helpful for you to know?"

"Let's start with Bell. The problem between him and Diego seems to be about some threat to close his parish."

"Yes, that's my understanding."

"Tell me a little about that from your experience. I mean, it's not like the guy is going to lose his job, is it? He'd just go to another parish, wouldn't he?"

Koesler smiled. "Sure you wouldn't like some coffee? It'd just take me—"

"No! No, that's all right. I'll be just a few minutes more."

"Hmmm. Well, you're right, of course, Ernie surely wouldn't lose his job if St. Gabriel's were closed. There are lots of parishes that need someone, particularly someone like him.

"But that's not the complete picture. It may very well be that Ernie is so close to what he's doing there that he doesn't realize how that parish has become an extension of himself."

"An extension . . . ?"

"Yes. So many parishes like St. Gabriel in the inner city of Detroit have changed drastically, radically. Mine, for example, used to serve a German community. You'd never guess that from the fairly cosmopolitan congregation we've got now.

"St. Gabriel's was a working-class parish. Blue collar. Now it's predominantly Latino. Ernie Bell has helped—no, he made that parish over to provide essential services to the Latino community. He is so involved in all that goes on in that parish, that the parish has become, in a very real way, that extension of himself."

"So, if they closed it . . . ?"

"They would, in effect, be taking a part of him away."

"And what would happen to the people he took care of?"

Koesler shrugged. "In all likelihood, they'd be encouraged to attend and get their help from Holy Redeemer parish. It's about a mile east of Gabriel's and it's mammoth."

"So, why should Bell be so torn up? It's not like his folks wouldn't be helped."

Koesler smiled sadly. "That's the way the Chancery would look at it. The people in charge downtown would claim that nobody was being abandoned. That the priest shortage is forcing a consolidation. But past practice says that it wouldn't be that neat.

"Lots of Gabriel's parishioners are elderly, and many of them speak only Spanish. Many of them would be lost. They wouldn't understand. They would feel themselves truly abandoned. They couldn't grasp that they were expected to affiliate with a different parish—even if some transportation were provided. They would almost barricade themselves in their homes. Many would go hungry, get sick. It's not unlikely some would die.

"And the ones who made a successful transfer to Redeemer? Well, there's no doubt that Redeemer is a monster parish. But it's up to its ears taking care of its own. I doubt even Redeemer could take the influx without cutting back its service to its own, let alone everyone who came from Gabriel's.

"That, you see, is how Ernie Bell looks at it. He's seen it happen to others and he knows what to expect."

Tully toyed with an ashtray that was going unused. "And you: Do you agree with Bell's evaluation?"

"Yes," Koesler said without hesitation.

"This threat to close the parish came from the late bishop," Tully said. "The way I got it, the bishop was responding to a threat from Bell to show him up for what he was—a greedy, ambitious manipulator. To me, it sounds like an idle threat. What could Bell do to Diego?"

Koesler leaned back, seeming to envision what Father Bell might cause to happen. "Innuendo comes to mind. Innuendo and the news media. Find some enterprising journalist—maybe the *National Catholic Reporter* or the *News* or the *Free Press*, and intimate what, on the one hand, is expected of Bishop Diego and, on the other, what he was doing, who his constant companions were. How much his people needed him and how little he gave.

"It wouldn't be that difficult to drop names of some of the wealthiest Catholics around and how tight they were with the bishop. Offer interpretation of what was happening and what the bishop's goals were. That should get the ball nicely rolling."

"And what would that accomplish?" Tully asked. "What trouble could that cause?"

"It could—and it very likely would—cement Bishop Diego right here as an auxiliary bishop for the rest of his life. And that could be like purgatory—if you understood purgatory as just like hell only limited to a certain period of time."

"Why? Why would that force him to stay here?"

"Rome makes the final judgment when it comes to bishops—who becomes a bishop and where they all go. And one of the last things Rome wants is a bishop tainted by controversy.

"It's sort of like the first two nominations President Clinton made for attorney general. The first had broken a law in hiring illegal aliens. The second had done the same thing before the practice had been a law.

"The idea was, there should be not even a hint of a scandal or any impropriety. Which would have been the case with Bishop Diego if it had become common knowledge that he sought power by any means necessary—making friends of powerful and wealthy people while neglecting the ones who were obviously in desperate need of him.

"Most Catholics in other dioceses would not want such a bishop. And, with this in mind, Rome would not want to send him. He'd be mired here in Detroit with few responsibilities and practically no power.

"So you see, both threats could have been very real."

Tully nodded his understanding. "Okay. Then what about Carleson? Seems no secret that he didn't like Diego. And Carleson was closer to Diego than maybe anyone else. Something about being a chauffeur—a servant?"

"That situation would come as no surprise to most of the priests here." Koesler took a deep breath, held it for a few moments, then exhaled. How much should he tell Tully?

"Lieutenant," he said at length, "when I say that something is common knowledge among priests, I don't mean everybody knows about it. But we do get together almost as often as we can—and we talk. I don't suppose it's much different than with the police: You talk about your work and you talk about each other and you talk about your superiors.

"So, many, if not most of us, were aware, at least in a general way, of what was going on.

"The sort of treatment Bishop Diego dealt out to Father Carleson was not all that rare years ago. There were certain pastors—and, for the most part, we knew who they were—who treated priests assigned to them shamefully. And they got away with it. For one thing, it was a seller's market and there was little recourse.

"Now the demeaning treatment of priests has all but completely disappeared. There aren't that many priests around and it's a buyer's market. There are so few priests left that they become pastors far, far sooner than in the past. As a result, there just aren't that many priests who are assistants. If a priest is a pastor and he's lucky enough to have help in the person of an assistant priest, that assistant is likely to be treated very, very well. If not, the assistant may request a transfer. And he'll probably get it—and the pastor will be all alone. As his reputation spreads, no one will go to work with him.

"So the relationship that grew up between Father Carleson and Bishop Diego was, I think, so rare as to be unique.

"From my conversation with Father Carleson last night, I would guess that he's been sticking it out partly out of respect for Cardinal Boyle, who was the main reason Don chose Detroit for his diocese. And also partly because he was convinced it couldn't go on much longer."

"I gather you like your Cardinal," Tully said.

"I do."

"Then how come he didn't do something about this problem? I presume he has the power to do it."

Koesler shook his head. "Not everybody is a saint. Now, Cardinal Boyle doesn't have many flaws that I know of. But one flaw might be his appreciation of his fellow bishops. It's a large, select, exclusive, and inbred club. Cardinal Boyle is a member in very good standing. It would be most unusual for him to intervene in another bishop's affairs. Most unusual . . . but not impossible.

"That's why I think the Cardinal doesn't realize how impossible the situation had become. He would be reluctant to step in, but if he knew . . .

"That's the only sense I can make of it: He didn't know.

"What made it worse for Don Carleson was that he's no fledgling priest. He's a mature man and he's been very much in charge of everything wherever he has served. From what he told me, he is not the type to debate a course of action endlessly. Someplace in the Gospels, Jesus says, 'Be ye not hearers of the word only, but doers.' That's Don Carleson: a doer."

Tully nodded. "And now that the bishop is no longer humiliating him and cramping him, he's his own man once again. Interesting. With the death of Diego, a man gets rid of the guy who he thinks is seducing his wife. A woman gets revenge for having been manipulated. A priest doesn't have to worry about losing his parish. And another priest can go around singing, 'Free at last! Free at last! Thank God Almighty, I'm free at last!' And we haven't even heard what our detectives have picked up on the street." He shook his head. "It's rare that one death clears the decks for so many people."

The phone rang in the front offices, as it had several times during Tully's visit. Either Mary O'Connor was handling the calls herself or she was taking messages for Koesler.

The click of Mary's approaching footsteps said that this call was different. Either it had to be for Tully or it was an emergency for Koesler.

It was for Tully, and he could take it in the kitchen.

"Zoo"—unmistakably it was Mangiapane—"this is Manj."

"Yeah, what is it?"

"You better get down here."

"What happened?"

"They found something in Father Carleson's car. They think it's dried blood. They took it down to the lab. Quirt is all over it, he's so sure it's Diego's blood. Anyway, you better get down here."

"Manj, just where the hell is 'here'?"

"Oh, sorry, Zoo. We're at headquarters and just about everybody's here, including Carleson and that prosecutor, Kleimer. This comes about as close to a lynching as I've seen. If that sample they took doesn't turn out to be Diego's, I think Quirt will have a heart attack."

We should be so lucky. "I'll be right down, Manj. Hold the fort and check to make sure we're legal on all the procedures."

He hung up and returned to the dining room. Father Koesler was not going to be happy with this news.

CHAPTER
TEN

As often as Koesler had visited the Homicide Division of the Detroit Police Department—which was not all that frequently—his overwhelming impression was that it was a busy place. Very, very busy. The
present activity did nothing to mitigate that impression.

People shuffling papers, walking purposefully from room to room
carrying files, talking to others as paths crossed; people intently talking
on the phone, or just as intently listening.

Quirt's task force had occupied Squad One's large but now crowded
rectangular room. Mangiapane, evidently on the lookout for Tully,
stood in the hallway just outside the door. When the sergeant spotted
Tully approaching with Father Koesler, his face lit up. "We're still waiting for the lab results, Zoo."

"They lifted the substance from Carleson's car? Where?"

"The dashboard, passenger side."

"Warrant or consent?"

"Consent."

"Did he sign?"

"Yeah, Zoo."

Tully partially turned to Koesler to explain. "From the top, it
doesn't help Carleson that the substance was on the passenger side. We
know that Carleson drove Diego. So, whatever it is, presumably it came
from Diego.

"Ordinarily, we'd have to get a warrant to search a car. That is,
unless the owner gives us permission, which Father Carleson did. But
in Detroit we devised this document that, in effect, attests to the
granted permission. That way, if we get into court and the defendant
denies giving permission, we've got the document that he signed giv-

ing permission. They sent the sample to the Police Crime Laboratory."
He turned back to Mangiapane. "When'd they do that, Manj?"

"Couple hours or so."

Tully turned back to Koesler. "It shouldn't be long now. With a
priority like this, they usually come up with an answer in two or three
hours. They probably want to be extra precise on this one, so it may be
more like three.

"You probably remember some of these people. . . ." Tully's gesture indicated those in the squad room.

Koesler, a bit taller than Tully, had no trouble seeing everyone in
the room.

"The guy sitting on the desk just in front of us, chewing on the unlit
cigar, is Lieutenant Quirt. Like I told you, he's heading this task force."

Noted, thought Koesler. He studied Quirt for a few moments, then
looked around at some of the others. As Tully had said, there were a few
familiar faces. One of the unknowns, a heavyset man, stood out in that
he was carefully, expensively groomed; his three-piece suit was definitely not off the rack. "Who is that gentleman?"

"Which one?" Tully followed the line of Koesler's gaze, at first
unsuccessfully.

"The three-piece suit."

Tully spotted him "That is Bradley Jefferson Kleimer, an assistant
prosecuting attorney for Wayne County. And he shouldn't be here."

"Shouldn't be here?"

"You ever see that TV series, 'Law and Order'?"

Koesler nodded. "I've always thought it was well done. Though I
must admit, I don't know how it stacks up against real life."

"Pretty good. The prosecuting attorneys for a big city usually number lots more than two. And there are some other mistakes they make.
But one thing they do well is to separate police and legal work. Cops
carry through the initial investigation and maybe make the arrest—on
that program, they always make an arrest. They turn over all they've
found to the prosecuting attorney, who takes over. Somebody in his
office will determine what the charge will be—or if there will even be a
charge. That office decides it all: whether there'll be plea bargaining,
how much bail to request, and the rest."

"What you're saying"—Koesler was paying close attention—"is

that police work is still going on. No arrest has been made. So—what did you say his name is?—Kleimer is here a bit prematurely." He looked puzzled. "So, I give up. Why *is* he here now?"

"He wants this case. He wants to prosecute it. It's a celebrity trial. A bishop is murdered. That's gonna get lots of ink locally—nationally— hell, probably internationally. This isn't the first time he's pulled this stunt."

Koesler thought for a moment. "Yeah, I remember that name. I've read about cases he's handled. I've seen him on TV and heard him interviewed on the radio. He always came on like the celebrity prosecutor. But, now that you mention it, it's the defendant who's usually the celebrity. . . ." Koesler hesitated. "But he does, doesn't he . . . usually get convictions, I mean?"

Tully, his expression unfathomable, nodded. "That's the only reason the police cooperate with him at all. Most of us don't like him personally. He's a headline-grabbing son— He's a grandstander. But cops like to see bad guys put away. So, more often than not, they cooperate with Kleimer. Some cops go a bit further." He paused. "Let's say it's no accident that he's on this scene, laying claim to it, and that Quirt is leading the investigative task force."

Koesler was appreciative of Tully's ability to enlighten effectively as well as succinctly. Tully was grateful that Koesler was such an apt pupil.

Tully, with the easy familiarity of one in his own work space, continued to survey the room. "Back there in the corner"—Tully indicated the far reaches of the squad room—"there's your man, looking like he hasn't got a friend in the world—which may be damn near true right now." Tully inclined his head in Carleson's direction. "You might want to talk to him."

Koesler brightened. "I would indeed. May I?"

"Sure, go ahead. Nothing significant's gonna happen until we get the lab report."

Koesler made his way through the swarm, conscious of the quizzical stares following him. Outside of Father Carleson, he was the only one in clerical garb.

He was halted halfway toward Carleson by a man who stepped directly in his path. "Excuse me," the man said in a friendly manner, "I'm Brad Kleimer from the prosecutor's office. And you are . . . ?"

"Koesler, Father Koesler."

"Is that K-e-s-s-l-e-r?"

"No, the German way: K-o-e-s-l-e-r."

"May I ask what you're doing here?"

Koesler was tempted to ask Kleimer the same question, and, utilizing what he'd gleaned from Lieutenant Tully, add that whatever Kleimer was doing here, he shouldn't be here in the first place.

But, true to his innate courtesy, Koesler replied only, "I'm here with Lieutenant Tully." That seemed inadequate, so he added, "A few times in the past I've supplied information to the police when questions regarding Catholicism or the Catholic Church were part of their investigation. I'm also a bit of a friend of Father Carleson. I was just on my way to visit with him, if you don't mind."

Kleimer made no move to get out of Koesler's path. Rather, the attorney studied the priest for a few moments with an expression of dawning recognition. "Yeah," he said finally, "I remember. I've read about you in the papers. But you haven't been on TV, have you? I don't remember seeing you."

"No, I haven't. You didn't miss me. I'm surprised you remember me at all." Koesler had the impression that according to Kleimer no one's fifteen minutes of fame began until the TV cameras were there to film it.

"What was it you said you helped with?"

"When the police need some insights into things Catholic. There are times when, without an insider's direction, the Catholic Church—its rules and regulations—can seem a bit of a maze."

"I see," Kleimer said. "As when a bishop is murdered?"

"Well, not on the surface, I suppose. But there can be complications like—oh—the role of an auxiliary bishop or the possible values of priests." Koesler found this conversation increasingly awkward.

"Interesting."

"Now, if you don't mind . . ."

"Oh, you wanted to see Father Carleson, didn't you? Sure. Go ahead." He stepped aside.

Tully, meanwhile, was trying to find out what news there was from the street.

Odd; there wasn't much. That was ominous.

"Ordinarily the Latinos are tight," Sergeant Moore explained, "but this is different. No leads or breaks at all. Vice cooperated with us. We called in our markers, talked to our snitches—all we could find quickly. But . . . nothing."

"What's the water temperature?"

"Warm," Mangiapane said. "Maybe under the surface it's boiling. Something's going on out there, Zoo. Like, overnight there was new bread on the street. But we can't find anybody who'll say how much or who's dealing."

Tully ran his tongue between his lips and teeth almost as if trying to taste the object of all this secrecy and silence. "The guys turned all the screws?"

"Tight as a drum," Mangiapane replied.

"Nothing?"

"That's it. Nada. Zilch."

"Now," Tully said, "we ask ourselves what does all this mean?"

"All that new money on the street," Moore speculated, "and close to five grand may have been taken from Bishop Diego just last night. A connection?"

"Could be," Tully acknowledged. "But then, why this solid brick wall? Given all the pressure we put on, how come we've got no names? If some punk hit the bishop for as much as five grand, and if this punk starts stockpiling dope, you'd think there'd be a leak someplace down the line."

"Maybe it's not a punk," Mangiapane said. "Maybe it's a big hitter."

"Maybe," Moore offered, "it's a punk—but maybe a real dangerous punk. Maybe it's fear that's keeping everybody quiet."

"Two very good maybes," Tully said. "If either of them eventually points to the killer, we'll have to program our investigation to find a really big hitter or a very dangerous punk. We gotta get back on the street and start looking for somebody who fits one or the other of those profiles."

"But Zoo," Mangiapane said, "what about Father Carleson?"

"The fat lady hasn't sung yet."

Father Koesler had finally made his way across the crowded room. As he neared Father Carleson, the priest's face lit in recognition. "Boy,"

WILLIAM X. KIENZLE

Carleson exclaimed, "are you a sight for sore eyes! Welcome . . ." He hesitated. ". . . friend?"

Koesler smiled warmly. "Of course, 'friend'; what did you think?"

"Right now, I can't be too sure. But if anybody ever needed one, I sure do."

"I think you'll find you have lots of them. Maybe not in this room, but certainly among the priests and people who know you."

Carleson smiled wryly. "What? They think I killed Public Enemy Number One?"

Koesler was instantly quite serious. "Of course not. Because they know you didn't do it."

"That 'they' definitely excludes most of the people in this room."

Koesler looked about. His gaze met the deadly serious expressions of the detectives around them—some covertly glancing at the two priests who seemed to have sealed themselves off from the larger group. Reluctantly, he had to agree with Carleson's dark observation.

"What are you doing here, anyway?" Koesler asked. "You haven't been arrested."

"You know that?"

"I've been with Lieutenant Tully for the past few hours. So I pretty well know what's going on."

"Tully. The nice-looking black guy? He sure didn't have much to say when I was being questioned at Ste. Anne's."

"This is a task force. I gather it's kind of rare for them to put together one of these things. But Lieutenant Tully isn't in charge . . . which is, I think, a mistake. Lieutenant Quirt's the one in charge."

"That's not good news to me."

"But you haven't answered. What are you doing here?"

"I kept saying yes. Yes to looking through my car. Yes to coming down to headquarters while they were processing what they found in my car."

Noting Koesler's expression, Carleson concluded the question was not yet satisfactorily answered. "It just seemed to be delaying the inevitable," he said. "They assured me they could get a warrant to search my car. They didn't look like they were kidding. So I agreed to let them look. Even signed a paper giving permission. Don't know why I had to do that: I'd already agreed.

"Anyway, they scraped something off the dashboard. That's what they're examining at, I think, the crime lab.

"As to why I'm here: They asked if I would accompany them and wait for the results of the test. Well, they took my car down here. So it seemed sensible to go along. I wasn't going to go far without a car, and I didn't want to impose on anybody by borrowing a car.

"So, here I am."

From an offhand manner, Carleson grew quite somber. "Bob, I've got a hunch I'm not going to leave here anytime soon."

Koesler was shocked. "Why? Why do you say that? Hey, we'll probably leave here together. Let's go to Carl's Chop House. On me."

Carleson shook his head. "I'm pretty sure what they're going to find."

"You . . . you are?" Koesler was almost afraid to ask.

"I'm pretty sure it's blood. I wouldn't be that sure except they seem to be that sure. They haven't said it in so many words, but that's what they believe. I know that."

"Blood!" Tully had said "substance," and Koesler hadn't given it any further thought. "But how . . . ? Whose . . . ?"

"It didn't make any impression on me at all at the time. It happened a couple, three days ago. I was shipping the bishop somewhere—I forget where. It doesn't make a great deal of difference. But he sneezed. Diego sneezed. And the sneeze was the beginning of a nosebleed. I didn't pay much attention. I was driving and looking out for traffic. I didn't know he had a problem until he complained. Then I glanced over at him. He was holding a handkerchief to his nose, and the handkerchief was bloody.

"I told him to lean his head back, put some pressure on the bridge of his nose, and breathe out through his mouth and in through his nose. Pretty soon the bleeding stopped.

"That was about the extent of it.

"But when he sneezed, some of the blood must've hit the dashboard. I didn't pay any attention, and I didn't notice anything. That's got to be what they found."

The explanation sounded unconvincing. But Koesler had believed Carleson to this point. He would stay the course even if he had to suspend disbelief to a degree. "If you're so sure, did you give your explanation to the police?"

"Yeah, but they weren't buying any of it." He shook his head. "For the most part, they weren't even listening."

Koesler surmised that the officers preferred not to arrest Carleson before they had identified the substance and, at the same time they didn't want to cloud the Miranda warning. "Are you sure . . . I mean are you certain that what they got from your dashboard was Bishop Diego's blood?"

Carleson nodded, then hesitated. "No. I can't be absolutely sure. What do I know? Like I said, I wasn't paying attention. I didn't even know there was anything on the dashboard except dust." He shrugged. "But what else could it be?"

His brow knitted. "Maybe I'm just preparing myself for the worst. I don't know. All I know is I'm pretty darn miserable. I wish I'd never heard of Detroit. I wish Ramon Diego had stayed in Texas until he rotted."

Carleson did look drained. Koesler could think of nothing else to say. He put one hand on Carleson's shoulder. The gesture was intended to be supportive.

At that moment there was a commotion near the door. Without knowing for certain, Koesler felt that the first "verdict" in this case was in. His grip on Carleson's shoulder tightened.

The detectives, like the parting of the waters, peeled back to let Lieutenant Quirt through.

The lieutenant seemed barely able to control his pleasure. He squared off dramatically in front of Father Carleson. "Father Donald Carleson, I'm arresting you for the murder of Bishop Ramon Diego." Without turning, he said, "Charlie, read him his rights, and book him."

For Carleson as well as for Koesler time seemed to stand still. It was as if everything were happening in slow motion. Neither priest was able to focus on the words of the Miranda warning. Each of them had heard at least the beginning of the cautionary statement on TV and in the movies.

"You have the right to . . ." There was something about a lawyer and something about what you said could be held against you.

But none of this was truly sinking in.

Next, Charlie Whoever-he-was was taking Carleson away. And Koesler stood numb, unable to make sense of what had happened.

There was a sense of elation in the room. An arrest had been made in a complex murder case. By anyone's standard, this was high profile. The media had concentrated its considerable attention on this case. And now it looked to have been solved in record time. Almost twenty-four hours to the minute.

Of course, not everyone was an instant convert to the validity of this arrest. But when they heard Detective Williams read aloud the finding of the crime lab—that the substance found in Carleson's automobile was not only blood, but the same rare type as Bishop Diego's—almost everyone was swept away with the sense of accomplishment.

Father Koesler, overwhelmed and confused, sought out Lieutenant Tully. In the emptying room, it wasn't difficult to locate him. He was near the door, talking with several people. Koesler recognized Sergeants Mangiapane and Moore. The others he assumed were members of Tully's squad.

As Koesler approached the group, he could hear Tully's quietly earnest tones. While Koesler couldn't make out every word, he gathered that Tully was ordering some of his people to thoroughly check out both Mr. and Mrs. Shell. Talk to friends and business associates and see what they had to say about the Shells' relationship with each other and especially with the late bishop. Others were to return to the streets and see if they could break through the silence that had met their earlier attempts.

Koesler stopped short of the group and waited until Tully's squad members had left. He was buoyed by the impression that Tully's group, at least, was continuing the investigation. Tully's expression invited Koesler forward.

"I couldn't help overhear," Koesler said. "I'm really pleased you haven't given up the investigation."

"This?" Tully motioned toward the departing detectives. "A precaution. From what I've heard, we've got a pretty good case against Carleson. But, you never know. There were other leads, some of them pretty good. If, by any chance, the case against Carleson doesn't go down, that's a bad time to have to go back to square one."

In the moment it took for Tully to explain his continuing with the case, Koesler's budding hopefulness deflated like a leaking tire. "Just finding that blood?" Koesler protested. "Father Carleson has an explanation of how it got on his dashboard."

"So does Quirt," Tully replied. "According to his scenario, this thing started sometime yesterday between when Carleson and Diego left the Carson residence and when they got back to Ste. Anne's. Probably when they arrived at Ste. Anne's. That part is incidental. Anyway, Carleson's animosity toward Diego has already been established. Yesterday it exploded. Carleson struck Diego either with his fist or some hard object. Diego was hit flush on the nose, causing the blood flow, some of which got on the dashboard.

"Diego was unconscious. Probably Carleson then checked inside the rectory and discovered, as he'd anticipated, that the other priests were all in their rooms. He dragged the unconscious bishop into his office and propped him up in his chair. Then he got whatever weapon he used—a bat, a piece of pipe, a thick bottle—and struck the lethal blow. One very powerful blow and it was all over. We know that Diego sustained a nose injury and that there was blood. In the beginning, we thought the blow from behind had knocked Diego forward so he had hit his face against the desk top. But knocking him out in the car makes just as much, if not better, sense.

"Then Carleson took the money that he knew Diego kept in his office. He could have done anything with the dough. It didn't matter—stash it, throw it away. The money wasn't important. Killing Diego was. But taking the money could make it look like robbery/murder.

"Carleson, of course, knew the combination to the alarm system. So he was able to shut it down for the front of the rectory to make it look as if Diego had admitted his assailant.

"And there"—Tully spread his hands wide—"you have it. Our crime lab established that the sample taken from Carleson's car was the same blood type as Diego's. In a few days they'll be able to complete the DNA to determine that the two samples not only match—they're identical. We're pretty confident that'll be the outcome."

Koesler was glum. "There's no chance that Father Carleson's explanation is what really happened?"

Tully shrugged. "That possibility, along with the possibility that something may fall apart during the trial, is why I'm going ahead with the investigation. But—" He squeezed his eyes shut and shook his head. "—I wouldn't count on any miracles at the trial. Kleimer doesn't fumble very often."

"Kleimer'll prosecute?"

"I would guess he's on his way to the chief of operations right now. I'd say Brad Kleimer is a happy man. This case just could be his ticket to making his name a household word. I wouldn't bet against it."

There was a pause. Tully had things to do. But Koesler had been so co-operative, Tully was determined to leave the priest a satisfied customer.

"What's going to happen now?" Koesler asked.

"You mean with Carleson?"

"Yes. All I know is right about now, Joe Friday says something like, 'Book him on a 420 and turn him over to the psychiatrist.'"

Tully smiled briefly. "You mean, What do we really do now?"

Koesler nodded.

"Right now," Tully said, "he's going through the PCR—the preliminary complaint report. Charlie, the detective who took Carleson into custody, is probably typing the report. It just includes technical information: the date, time, location, and why he was arrested—for murder, in this case. They'll write up an arrest ticket.

"Then they'll make fingerprint cards—four of them. One for the feds, one for the state, and two for the city. Then he'll have to wait for the fingerprint search, to find out if he's wanted anywhere. And that, by the way, will tell him how he's gonna be treated."

"How he's going to be treated?"

"The fingerprint search will take between two and three hours. The question is where's he gonna wait and what's he gonna do.

"A decision'll be made whether to let him relax someplace like the Complaint Room, where he can watch TV if he wants to. Or whether he'll be taken to a holding cell.

"If he doesn't spend those two or three hours in a cell, eventually he'll be released to appear—sorry, that's sort of police shorthand. Whatever else happens, he'll be going to court tomorrow. If we feel confident he'll show up for court on his own, he'll probably be watching TV during the fingerprint search. And he'll probably be released to go home and return for his court appearance. If we decide that's a bad risk, we'll keep him in a holding cell on the ninth floor until court time."

"Who makes this decision?"

"In a case like this, lots of people are in on the decision. This is going to be a media-crazy case. So everybody up the line is being informed, from Inspector Koznicki to Mayor Cobb."

"What happens in court tomorrow?"

"Well, the prosecutor either will or will not recommend the issuance of a warrant. And a judge either will or won't sign it. Put your bottom dollar on the warrant and the signing. Then, if everything goes according to Hoyle, we'll arrest him again. He'll be arraigned and the judge'll set bail. Then, within twelve days—counting Saturday and Sunday—there'll be a preliminary exam . . . sort of a mini-trial. A few people will testify, the object being to establish that there is reasonable cause to believe that a crime—murder—was committed—that it wasn't an accident. The bail probably will be continued and, eventually, there'll be a trial."

"So," Koesler said, "if I've got this right, what happens to Father Carleson now—whether he's kept in a cell or not—is pretty important."

"To him, definitely. Overall, yeah, it has its importance. That'll probably be decided by Quirt and Koznicki."

A detective approached. "Pardon me, Zoo, but the boss wants to see you. Now."

Tully fixed Koesler with a look. "By Quirt and Koznicki and me."

"Would you let me know how this goes?" Koesler asked. "I'll wait here if I may."

Tully nodded as he left.

It was a brief distance from the Homicide squad rooms to Inspector Koznicki's small office. Tully was surprised to find Kleimer seated just outside the door. "Well," Tully said, "I thought you'd be over at the chief's office."

"All in good time. All in good time," Kleimer said affably. "May I accompany you?"

Tully smiled wordlessly, knocked perfunctorily on the Inspector's door and entered, leaving Kleimer to tag along in his wake.

Koznicki and Quirt were seated. Tully slipped into the only other chair.

At the sight of Kleimer, Koznicki tensed and leaned forward in his chair, giving the impression that he was about to vault over the desk and assault the lawyer. Neither Kleimer nor Tully wanted that to happen. Kleimer didn't want to die. Tully didn't want to witness his death.

"You are not involved in this case at this point." Koznicki spoke through clenched teeth.

Perspiration appeared at Kleimer's hairline. "I'm just following through, Inspector. It just so happened that I chanced on this case shortly after the investigation began."

Koznicki glanced at Quirt. The inspector very well knew how Kleimer had "chanced" upon his case. "It just so happens," Koznicki borrowed Kleimer's phrase, "that you are not supposed to be here now."

"But . . ." Kleimer began to protest.

Pushing with large powerful hands, Koznicki half rose.

Kleimer turned so abruptly that he tripped over his own feet. He would have fallen had he not grasped the doorknob.

It was not the most graceful of exits. As Kleimer hurried down the hallway, he vowed that one day he would make Koznicki pay dearly for this.

Tully, hiding his smile in his heart, closed the door and resumed his chair.

"Lieutenant Quirt has reported our progress in this investigation," Koznicki said. "We seem to have built a rather strong case on circumstantial evidence. What is your opinion, Alonzo?"

Having Tully brought into the decision-making process did not please Quirt. On the one hand, he had to admit that both he and Tully were of equal rank and that each commanded his own squad. But, on the other hand, he, Quirt, had been hand-picked to head this task force. In fact, he was honored that the hand that picked him belonged to the mayor of Detroit.

Soon, Quirt was certain, he would be the inspector in charge of Homicide. Kleimer would come through for him. Both he and Kleimer now had scores to settle with Koznicki—and a few others who had treated them badly. Given a little more time, they would straighten things out.

Tully shook his head. "This is Quirt's collar. It looks pretty good.

Carleson had motive and opportunity. The blood in his car is hard to explain away."

Koznicki nodded slowly. "I think with what we can bring the prosecutor's office, they will issue a warrant." He seemed saddened.

The sadness was not shared by a supremely self-satisfied Quirt. "And I broke the case in one day. Twenty-four hours. That's gonna make a lot of people happy, up to and including the boss—Mayor Cobb."

Koznicki turned to Tully. "You uncovered no suspects?"

"Suspects? Sure. There's the guy who had it out with Diego yesterday afternoon. A Michael Shell who claims his already shaky marriage was further damaged by Diego. There's his wife, Maria Shell, who could've reacted to Diego's manipulating her. And we've got a feeling that something's going down on the streets."

"What!" Quirt was incredulous. "Listen, we've got the guy: It's Carleson. It'd be silly to wait another ten to twenty years while we interview every punk on the street. Come on!"

"Anyway," Tully said evenly, "we're gonna check out these leads and see where they go."

"You can't!" Quirt was angry. "We're goin' to court tomorrow morning. What'll it look like if we bring in a suspect for arraignment and you're still working the case?"

Tully regarded Quirt. "What'll it look like if Carleson is acquitted and we've got no other leads? Look at it this way, Quirt: At worst we're covering your ass. You ought to be grateful."

Quirt's sputtering response was unintelligible.

Koznicki gave every evidence that he was pleased at Tully's decision to continue his investigation. "One final decision before we go home, gentlemen: Where is Father Carleson now, and what do we do with him overnight?"

"He's in a holding cell." There was belligerence in Quirt's tone. "And that's where he should stay."

"You put a priest in a holding cell!" Koznicki was not happy.

"He's a murder suspect," Quirt said defensively. Much would now depend on whether Tully would support his decision.

"Your opinion, Alonzo?" Koznicki asked.

"I'd have to agree with Quirt. I know how you feel about priests,

Walt. But we've got to consider that not only do we not know much about him, nobody around here—not even the other priests—knows much about him. Like Quirt said, he's the prime suspect. And you know what would happen if we released him from custody and, say, he killed somebody else tonight. . . ."

Koznicki bowed his head in agreement. "I believe you are correct, Alonzo. Should that happen, I would be looking for another job tomorrow."

With that prospect, Quirt felt a passing urge to recommend the release-to-appear of Carleson, just on the off chance the priest would kill again and Koznicki would be somewhat prematurely out of the way. Quirt kept this urge to himself.

"Very well," Koznicki said. "Father Carleson stays in holding."

The meeting was over. Now Tully would have to inform the waiting Father Koesler that his buddy would be kept at least overnight. One of those messages that was never easy to deliver.

CHAPTER ELEVEN

It had been long and tiring—but at last this demanding day was at an end. That was the good news. The bad news was that tomorrow would be just as taxing.

Ned Ferris, chief of operations for the Wayne County Prosecuting Attorney's office, leaned back in his chair as far as he could and stretched tired muscles.

Wayne County comprised many Michigan cities, chief among them, by anyone's measure, Detroit. Detroit with its long, interesting history. Detroit, the onetime "Arsenal of Democracy." Where they built—or used to build—cars. Detroit with its pockets of wealth and its acres of poverty. With that glorious river linking the Great Lakes. With consistently looming violence and murder, this prosecuting attorney's office was among the busiest in the country. With the responsibility for, among other things, determining what charges to bring against suspects, and selecting attorneys to try cases, the position of chief of operations would not soon be out of business.

One element of current crime that most troubled Ned Ferris was child murder—children being murdered, children being murderers. This very day was a case in point.

A fifth-grader walking to school was gunned down when a drive-by shooter missed a house in which his enemy lived. Talk about not being able to hit the broad side of a barn!

That was this morning. This afternoon, an eighth-grader had demanded an expensive jacket from a classmate. The jacketed youngster ran and was shot four times, twice to the head, twice to the back. The boy was dead before he hit the ground. The shooter explained that it was his classmate's fault: He ran away after being ordered to give up his jacket.

None of these kids was doing especially well in math or English. Their primary school was the street. And the primary lesson of the street was how to get a gun and how to use it.

The drive-by shooter had yet to be picked up.

But the eighth-grader was in custody. How should he be tried? Was he what he looked like: a little boy just starting his teen years? As such he would go through the juvenile justice system and, if convicted of an extremely serious crime such as murder, he would be incarcerated with other juvenile offenders until he was twenty-one. Would he learn anything helpful in those years? Or would he emerge older but just as lethal?

If he were fifteen or older, he could be tried as an adult and, if convicted, spend the rest of his long life in prison without the possibility of parole.

Ferris shrank from the prospect of such a young life, promising everything and anything, being buried forever—first in prison, then in the ground.

But, unless he missed his guess, that was the drift of the public's reaction to kid crime. Such children, the consensus seemed to run, were beyond redemption as well as rehabilitation.

These cases were among the most difficult he had to juggle. But juggle and evaluate them he would. That's what he was paid for.

He was about to turn out the light and call it a day—though not a good one—when his intercom sounded. He considered ignoring it. But he knew his secretary wouldn't bother him at this closing hour unless something special had come up.

Brad Kleimer wanted a few moments of his time.

Through this day, Ned Ferris—just as every other power-wielding person in the city government—had been kept informed on the developments in the Diego murder. Had he not been so absorbed in the jacket shooting, Ferris surely would have been more actively involved in the Diego case. But the alleged perpetrator of the grade-school shooting was in custody and being processed—a procedure in which Ferris was actively involved.

And of course, with the priest charged in the bishop's murder, that case too was in Ferris's lap. And now the other shoe had dropped.

"Priest Kills Bishop," and similar headlines, would be flashed on TV newscasts, on front pages and feature articles probably around the world. Undoubtedly, a scrum of prosecuting attorneys would be vying for this case. For just as surely as the case would engender headlines, so would the name of whoever prosecuted this case become famous.

Now why, Ned Ferris wondered whimsically, would he associate the arrival of Brad Kleimer with the Diego case? When considering a trial that could catapult the prosecuting as well as defense attorneys into national prominence, why on earth would Kleimer's name come to mind?

Ned Ferris was bone weary and desperately wanted to go home. But he could always find time for a charade of musical hot seats: Which assistant prosecuting attorney would get the final chair?

Ferris loosened his tie and unbuttoned the top button of his shirt. He bade the secretary let loose Kleimer.

Kleimer entered with studied nonchalance and took the chair that Ferris indicated. He took out a handkerchief and dabbed at his forehead. Some of his perspiration stemmed from the bum's rush at the hands of Koznicki just a few moments ago. Part was due to his headlong dash to the chief's office. It was not the cool entry he would have chosen, but he wanted to reach the chief before the other staff attorneys did. He fervently hoped he had.

Kleimer consciously willed his heart to slow. "I suppose you've been following the Diego developments."

Ferris nodded benignly.

"Then you must know," Kleimer continued, "that a Father Carleson has been arrested and charged with the murder?"

Ferris nodded again. "The news beat you here by only a few minutes."

For a moment Kleimer pondered the speed of sound. He could scarcely compete with that. Nonetheless, since the chief had just gotten the word, there couldn't have been any applicants ahead of him.

"Just as a matter of curiosity," Ferris said, "how did you happen to know about this? I mean, I only just now got the word."

"One of the Homicide guys needed some direction on procedure."

"Oh? Who?"

Kleimer needed no time at all to come up with a name. "Lieutenant Quirt," he lied. Quirt would know enough to back him.

"Quirt. Hmmm." Ferris was noncommittal. He rearranged several objects on his desk without any apparent purpose. "Looks heavily circumstantial."

"True. We've had lots stronger cases. We'll have to use every advantage we can." Actually, Kleimer considered the case to have many strengths.

"I wonder . . ." Ferris looked at the ceiling. "It'll be tough finding the right person to try this case." He looked at his desk. "But I'd better come up with someone soon . . . very soon." Ferris was having difficulty keeping a straight face.

"Well . . ." Kleimer stood and began to pace. ". . . I was thinking: I've already been helping them on the case. I'm most familiar with it." He looked at Ferris. "I'd like to try it."

There it was, out on the table.

"You!?" Ferris treated Kleimer's offer with the astonishment it should not have merited.

"Yes, me." Kleimer was nettled by the chief's reaction. "As you've said, this is going to be a tough one. Well, right off the bat, I've got an arm and leg up on any of the special-assignment prosecutors. I've been in on this almost from the very beginning."

Ferris's eyes widened. "Just how much procedural direction did the Homicide guys need!"

"Well, you know how it is. One thing leads to another. Anyway, I was present while suspects were interrogated. And I'm well aware of who the various suspects are. And I can tell you straight out that this Carleson is a good arrest. Just let me get to that jury and that priest will be spending the rest of his life behind bars. No parole!"

"Murder One! Think we should go for the first degree, eh?"

"Absolutely." Kleimer returned to his seat. "Murder One. And I'll nail him." He leaned forward. "I don't need to remind you my record is pretty impressive. . . ."

Ferris studied Kleimer. "I do believe you're right, Brad," he said at length. "Barring any complication—and I don't foresee any—you're the logical choice to handle this trial. So, let's go with this. And Brad"—his gaze pinned Kleimer—"keep me informed: about everything—*everything* . . . understand?"

Kleimer was on his feet. "Yes, sir. I'll get on this right away. Nothing to worry about." Kleimer's expression was one of simultaneous reassurance and gratitude. "And Chief: Thanks for the vote of confidence."

The two men shook hands. Kleimer departed.

Ferris gathered the documents he would take home for study. His mind wandered over this meeting with Kleimer. He was reminded of something conductor Zubin Mehta once said about Richard Wagner, the ethnically prejudiced German composer: that he was a fourth-class human being but a first-class musician.

Something on that order could be said of Brad Kleimer.

As far as Ferris could tell, Kleimer had only one moral code—if one could speak of it in terms of morality—and that was self-advancement.

Ferris did not relish dealing with Kleimer. But one thing Kleimer had proven repeatedly was his skill in the courtroom. He could charm and sway a jury, sometimes even a judge. As long as the judge and jury did not have to live with the man, Kleimer would be effective. But so far, no one had had the stomach to stay with him for the long run. It was no surprise to anyone when his marriage had collapsed. If anything, Kleimer's colleagues were astounded that it had dragged on as long as it did.

So the bottom line was that Kleimer was the logical choice for this trial. And he would've gotten it without groveling.

The position of chief trial attorney had been created under a previous prosecutor's administration. It had been his responsibility—the position had never been filled by a woman—to handle high-visibility cases. Kleimer lusted after that position. The present prosecutor had strong convictions that there should be, if the case warranted, a top female assistant prosecutor, a top black assistant prosecutor, a top white assistant prosecutor, and so on.

This case involved a white and a Hispanic. So it could have fallen under either heading. But since the alleged perpetrator was white, in all probability it would be given to a top white assistant prosecutor.

Under that category, Kleimer was qualified.

And if Kleimer had not fit the appropriate niche, Ferris had been prepared to refuse him steadfastly.

Lately there had been a considerable intrusion by Kleimer into, for him, marginal categories. In his own obtrusive way, he had begun to insinuate himself into cases more suitable for others. In effect, Kleimer was trying to refashion the function of the office of chief trial attorney and fill it himself. Along the way, he was alienating a lot of fellow attorneys and making not a few enemies.

Whatever, the Carleson-Diego case was now his.

Ferris was torn. On the one hand, he wished Kleimer good fortune. After all, the business of this office was to get convictions. On the other hand, Ferris quietly hoped that this case would prove to be Kleimer's launching pad to fame and would get him the hell out of the prosecuting attorney's office.

Ferris was about to extinguish his office lights and finally head for home when one final question came to mind.

He dialed Homicide and got his answer: The priest would spend at least this night in a holding cell. Ferris was surprised. Locking up a priest before arraignment! Was nothing sacred any longer?

TWELVE

Don Carleson sat on the edge of his cot. He was the sole occupant of the cell. Probably, he thought, a special favor arranged by the officer in charge. He must be a Catholic; he had "Fathered" Carleson to pieces.

Favor or not, he was grateful. He'd had some little experience in like surroundings. This was not Father Carleson's first time being locked up.

But it had been so long ago.

Noisy. His small space was invaded by the sounds of men in other cells. Some were angry, some crying, some hallucinating. Some were trying to climb the walls in search of some substance that would open for them a door to blessed oblivion.

It hadn't been like this the other time, the first time.

Carleson lay down on the cot and freed his mind to return to that other time.

*   *   *   *

It had been warm. Hot. Not cold and damp, as it was now.

Many years ago. In Nicaragua. In a tiny village called Sandego near the banks of the Rio Coco on the border of Honduras.

The village was so insignificant and remote that he had actually felt insulted when he first laid eyes on it. What must his superiors in Maryknoll think of him to send him to such a godforsaken spot?

Then he began to learn that his little town actually was the antithesis of a place abandoned by God.

The inhabitants were Catholic . . . Catholics with simple, childlike faith. They had been promised that a priest was being sent to them. So they had pooled their meager resources and put together a makeshift but practical chapel.

On his arrival, the entire village turned out to greet him. All were wearing their very best rags. In all his time with them, he never discovered how they knew when he would arrive. It was their happy secret.

Happy was the appropriate word for these people. In the face of their constant lighthearted effervescence, he began to believe he'd been given the best assignment Maryknoll had. He found himself pitying priests missioned in major cities like Managua or, save the mark, Chicago or New York. Such priests were reduced to inventing games to attract people to the Church. Helpful too was the threat of hellfire for absence from Church services.

Here in Sandego, he just rang a bell when it was time for services and everybody came with incandescent smiles.

In a word, the spirit was contagious. In no time, Father Carleson was one with his villagers, his congregation, his people.

He had brought with him not only Mass vestments, missal, and an initial supply of bread and wine, he also carried basic medications that would make life at least less painful for the people.

Of all his earliest accomplishments, Carleson was perhaps most proud of the well. Each evening, he would read from the do-it-yourself manual for finding a water supply and digging a well.

The villagers pitched in enthusiastically if blindly. They had no real concept of what he was attempting. They just sensed that the poor man wanted to dig a hole and he needed help. So they pitched in, smiling and throwing dirt. The hole became so deep that they had to pass the dirt up in baskets. And they were forced to help each other up and down the sides of the hole.

And then, a miracle.

Water. Cool, refreshing, and pure. And available.

It didn't take long for them to realize that they no longer had to carry water from the river. Or fear the diseases river water often brought.

Now the water was right in their midst. They had access to it anytime. There didn't even have to be a special need or necessity. It was theirs and it was pure.

It was a miracle. And Padre Don was the miracle worker.

In time, Carleson almost forgot there was a world beyond Sandego. He forgot he was living in greater poverty than he had ever experienced or imagined. Sandego and the lovely people he served completely fulfilled him.

There was a cloud on the distant horizon. It lay just beneath the consciousness of the inhabitants of Sandego.

It was a band, a group, an army called the Contras. The Contras were at war with the revolutionary Sandinista government of Nicaragua. Later, it would sicken Carleson to learn that the U.S. government had overtly and covertly subsidized the Contras.

It had been more than a year since the Contras' previous visit to Sandego. But that visit had been so savage that the inhabitants had not been able to forget it.

Carleson of course knew of the Contras, but gave them no more than passing thought. He was certain they would never inflict themselves on the sleepy hamlet of Sandego. It would be like bombing a small town in the Louisiana bayous. Why?

They arrived one night as the stars were fading. As soundlessly as a stalking jungle cat. With the dawn, men armed to the teeth roughly awakened the villagers—including their priest.

The villagers—even the children—were ordered, pushed, clubbed into a single line and forced to remain motionless and silent while the officers toured the village. After their investigation, they reviewed the assembly. They noted with special interest the Yankee priest.

As far as Carleson could tell, everyone—captives and captors—was Catholic. All spoke Spanish. And that meant nothing.

He was only slightly fearful—not at all for himself. He viewed the invaders as a form of purgatory. No matter how nasty things got, it would be over and done with eventually. The Contras would have to move on sometime.

A man with the insignia of a colonel appeared to be the ranking officer. He addressed the assembled villagers. It was mostly badly memorized propaganda. After the canned lecture, he got down to reality. They would not stay long. They needed supplies. They would take whatever fitted their needs. During their stay, the villagers would be required to work for the Contras and not themselves. Their degree of cooperation would dictate the longevity of this occupation.

With that, the soldiers took over. The villagers were forced to begin gathering up everything this little town had.

The colonel, along with another officer with the insignia of major, took Carleson to the well. They showed much interest in it. They had been here before. They knew that the well raised the value of this land. They asked question after question. Carleson answered them all. It didn't matter to him whether they dug their own well. Probably back at base camp there were women and children that could use the convenience of their own water supply. At one point, he simply gave them the book he'd used to bring water to Sandego. The colonel cursorily paged through the book and handed it to the major, who looked at it, shrugged, and tossed it aside. They were illiterate.

From time to time, Carleson would note the gratuitous cruelty of the soldiers. Twice he moved toward intervening. Each time, the colonel's aides jabbed rifles into his ribs.

Finally, the day was done. The villagers were forced to prepare food and serve it to the invaders. The residents were allowed nothing. If any Sandegan dared smuggle a morsel for self, one of the old people or a child was beaten.

Carleson was excused from serving the dinner. He was even invited to eat. He refused. It made absolutely no difference to the Contras. He could starve for all they cared.

After the meal, the soldiers gave the scraps to the stock animals that they would take with them when they left. They had shot all the village dogs.

A young soldier walked across the firelit circle, knelt next to the major, and whispered something. The major whispered to the colonel. Both laughed heartily. The colonel waved his hand signifying permission.

The soldier, with four comrades, walked slowly around the circle of attending villagers. They stopped before a strikingly beautiful girl barely out of childhood.

Two grabbed her and dragged her screaming to the center of the circle near the fire. Her parents shrieked their pleas for her. They were clubbed back, as were the others who objected.

Slowing, savoringly, they stripped her. While four pinned her to the ground, the young soldier lowered his trousers and gleefully raped her, thrusting more brutally with each of her screams, which seemingly added to his enjoyment.

Villagers tried to look away, but the soldiers forced them to watch.

Carleson, seated near the two commanding officers, was not observed so carefully. He shut his eyes so tightly that tears rolled down his cheeks. He pressed his hands against his ears, but could still hear the girl's horrible screams.

For the first time in his life, Carleson knew rage. He felt hatred. There was not an ounce of forgiveness or understanding remaining in him.

He opened his eyes to see the other four soldiers raping their helpless victim in turn.

There was no clear thought in his mind. There was an explosion.

While all around him were absorbed in the entertainment, he noticed a guard, who, in his glee, had loosened his grip on a machete.

In one fluid movement, Carleson rose, grabbed the machete, and with a sweeping arc severed the colonel's head.

It was as a freeze-frame. Even in peripheral vision, everyone had seen the sweep of the blade. Everyone saw the colonel's head fall to the ground, followed by his spurting blood.

No one moved. The raping soldier halted in midthrust.

Seconds later, when Carleson made no further threat to anyone, a soldier raised his gun to the priest's temple, finger on the trigger. Before Carleson could even think his last thoughts or pray his last prayers, a shouted command from the major halted the soldier's straining trigger finger.

It was at once evident to the major that he was now in charge. But, what to do?

To buy time, he ordered Carleson placed in captivity. The villagers were commanded to construct a bamboo cage. When it was finished, the soldiers shoved Carleson into the cage and lowered it into the well. There they left him while what passed for a judicial board was created.

Some on the board plumped for Carleson's immediate execution. Others preferred torture and death. A few pointed out that this Contra unit itself was in considerable trouble.

After all, they had not been in combat with the Sandinista army. They had been sent to terrorize a helpless village. How to explain a security so vacuous that the ranking officer is killed by a Yankee priest?

And that reminded them that the assassin was, indeed, Yankee. Without knowing exactly how such things worked, they knew the priest belonged to some organization—a diocese, a religious order?—in North America.

If they killed the priest, it would cause an uproar in the United States. Their financing could be interrupted—even crippled.

Of course, they could kill the priest and all the villagers—and no one would be left to tell the tale. Such wholesale slaughter was not beyond their experience. But if there were no villagers, there would be no village—and no stock or crops to sustain them in future raids. Amazing how these villagers managed to grub up food out of nothing.

The major had never perspired so freely.

In the end, he decided to leave the priest caged for the few days required to round up all possible supplies. Then, after a brutal beating of the priest, which all the villagers were forced to watch, and graphic threats of what would happen should anything concerning this episode ever be made public, they would return to their base camp. They would report that their colonel had been infected by some lethal bug and had been buried on the trail.

Carleson had no idea what his fate might be. He assumed he would be executed. He hoped his death would not include torture.

He had ample time and seclusion to reflect on what he had done. The thought of killing anyone had never ever occurred to him. Now he'd done it, and it had proved not all that difficult or strange . . . oddly, almost natural. If he had it to do over—God forgive me, he prayed—he would do what he had done.

Three days passed. Carleson was terribly weak, having had nothing to eat or drink. He was beaten within an inch of his life.

The Contras packed all they had commandeered and left. The villagers nursed Carleson back to relative health. They began the arduous and dogged effort to return to their former condition.

When his superiors at Maryknoll learned what had happened, they quickly arranged his return to the New York headquarters. There he was professionally cared for, physically and emotionally.

What had happened to the Contra colonel was never mentioned. It was part of no readily accessible report.

When he recovered, he was returned to another Central American mission. And then another and another. But he no longer had patience with red tape and institutional protectionism.

He realized he would have to take more command over his own life. He no longer could trust the bishops with whom he had to deal. Thus his request to be incardinated into Cardinal Boyle's Detroit.

*   *   *   *

The cell block in Detroit Police Headquarters was quieting down. Still, Carleson couldn't sleep.

Compared with those three days in his cage in Sandego, this could realistically be described as comfortable.

Still he lay awake. What would happen to him? Was he a disgrace to the priests of Detroit?

And the most disturbing question of all: Would anyone reveal or discover what had happened when the Contras had invaded his precious little village?

Prayer did not come easily. But it was his only consolation. He prayed.

CHAPTER
THIRTEEN

It had snowed overnight, an inch or so. Just enough to put a quiet white cover over the outside.

Father Koesler had retrieved the morning *Free Press* almost as it hit the porch. He'd pulled off the plastic cover and unfolded the paper on the dining room table.

Three separate stories relating to Diego's murder and Carleson's arrest on page 1A. Two of them jumped to an inside page where there were more sidebars and photos. Those seeking saturation information would not be disappointed.

He'd already heard the radio news, where the essence of the story kept being repeated. Radio did not have as much time as the newspapers had space. Television, with film of Ste. Anne's and its neighborhood, as well as a series of talking heads— mostly priests—had somewhat more personalized coverage than radio.

And the story had gone national. The networks were picking it up from their Detroit affiliates.

Seldom had Koesler been this interested in a breaking story. Normally he was content to let each new drama play itself out. In his sixty-five years, there were few varieties of story that he had not experienced before.

This one was different. He could not recall in his lifetime a priest being charged with killing a bishop. Of course, that was the fascination everyone else was experiencing. People couldn't get enough of this developing story with its bizarre if sketchy details.

And of course the media were in a feeding frenzy. No matter how they tried, they couldn't keep up. Too much was happening behind the scenes where the media were not allowed.

No one could possibly be tracking the story with as much absorption as Koesler. He had noted the frequent appearance on radio and TV of attorney Kleimer and Lieutenant Quirt. Koesler wondered what impression he might have had of them had he not met them both yesterday. As it was, having been briefed at least partially by Lieutenant Tully, Koesler had some notion not only of the roles they were playing, but also what the stakes were.

From redundant interviews with both of them, it was crystal clear (a) that Lieutenant Quirt had broken this case and made the arrest and (b) that Brad Kleimer was going to prosecute this case.

Kleimer brought to mind Alexander Haig immediately after Ronald Reagan was shot. Haig had been near manic in insisting that all was well because he was now in charge of the country.

It was difficult for Koesler to settle into his usual routine. He had appointments to keep and things to do. But, in a desire that was, for him, almost unprecedented, he wanted to get involved in this case. The problem was that, after his briefing of Lieutenant Tully yesterday, no one seemed to want him anymore.

*   *   *   *

Brad Kleimer was running on adrenaline.

He had slept only a few hours, fitfully at that. He'd had no breakfast, just coffee, black and lots of it. To say that everything he did now was important was to beat the life out of the obvious.

The arraignment that would take place in just a couple of hours was, he felt, pro forma. He had no doubt that Carleson would be bound over for trial. But there must be no slipups. Kleimer was painfully aware of the pitfall of overconfidence. He was making sure that everything was being done by the book.

In a sense, the media interviews had been a distraction. In another way, they were part and parcel of the grand plan. Detroiters were no strangers to Kleimer's voice and image. But this trial was going to make the impression he created indelible. Of much greater importance, in this case he was playing to the country. To the world!

Everything seemed in place. But time was running short.

What made it particularly frustrating for Kleimer was that he was not actually involved in these early steps. The public generally is un-aware of the layers of specialists in the prosecutor's office. Today's show would be handled by the Warrants Section. This was the intake department of the office. They decided whether or not there would be a charge. They were the experts at getting a warrant signed by a judge for a specific charge which they would determine.

The next process that would occur no more than twelve days later was handled by the Preliminary Examination Unit. They took charge of the preliminary hearing. This was a formal hearing before a judge to deter-mine whether there was sufficient evidence to hold the defendant for trial.

Only after these procedures could Brad Kleimer take center stage and take responsibility for the trial he'd been promised.

So this was a nerve-wracking time for him. All the attorneys who handled the early prosecution maneuvers were veterans of the system. Especially given the importance of this case, only the most experienced prosecutors would move things forward. Nevertheless, Kleimer wor-ried. He needed this trial. It could well be his ticket to the big time. Meanwhile, he was getting the word out that when everything was on the line, he would carry the ball.

He stopped pacing, thought a moment, then picked up the phone and dialed.

It was answered on the second ring. "Yeah."

"Quirt, this is Kleimer."

A guttural laugh. "You're all over the place, ain'tcha? We can't turn on the radio or TV without finding you."

"Forget that. What's going on at headquarters?"

"With the Diego case? I talked to Koznicki first thing . . . got him to dissolve the task force."

"Good! Very good. No problems?"

"I don't think Tully's very happy about it. But I headed this investi-gation and I said it was over. That's by the book . . . and Koznicki goes by the book."

"Okay. Now, we don't know what bail will be. And we don't know whether Carleson can make it. But we've gotta be ready. If he stays locked up, that's one thing. But if he makes bail, I want somebody from your squad to hang loose on him. Not a tail, not surveillance—just check on him from time to time.

"But whether he's locked up or cut loose, I wanna know more about him. Who he's close to, who he hangs with, what he does with his free time, stuff like that."

Kleimer was, once more, out of line. He had no authority to commandeer any Homicide officer's authority. But he was secure in the presumption that Quirt would prove cooperative. One hand washing the other once again.

"Okay, okay." Quirt was stung by Kleimer's brashness. "Only, don't forget: You owe me for this one. You owe me big."

"You got it." Kleimer hung up without further nicety.

No sooner was the receiver down than the phone rang.

Kleimer was sick to death of the phone. But you couldn't tell: Maybe the networks had sent their teams in by now. To this point, the national media were tapped in to their local affiliates. Pretty soon the big boys would be here. It was inevitable. Maybe now. "Yes?" he answered brightly.

It was his secretary. "There are a couple of gentlemen out here to see you."

"Who, Marge?"

"A Mr. Walberg and a Mr. Turner. From Los Angeles."

Kleimer's eyebrows arched. He had expected the biggies to come from New York. "Send them in."

Walberg and Turner were tanned to the degree of leather. Neither was dressed for northern winter. But both were outfitted stylishly. Tall and slender, they moved in a studied graceful manner that brought to mind synchronized Olympic swimmers. As he shook hands with each of them, Kleimer noted both had very soft hands.

"So, gentlemen"—Kleimer indicated chairs, which they took—"I'm a little pressed this morning. What can I do for you?" No cameras, from the wrong coast . . . could these guys be something other than representatives of the media?

"We'll be brief," Walberg said. "We represent Gold Coast Enterprises—an independent film studio . . . perhaps you've heard of us?"

Kleimer shook his head. *The movies?*

"It doesn't matter," Walberg dismissed that. "To be frank, this is some story you've got going here. Have any other studios contacted you?"

Again Kleimer shook his head.

"Super! Our project is in the form of a made-for-TV movie. The religious angle is irresistible. 'Priest kills bishop.' Out of the Middle Ages. Tell me, is there sex?"

"Sex?"

"You know—a woman. Someone they fought over. A broad plays one against the other. Or maybe there isn't a woman. Maybe they're gay lovers—the bishop and the priest. Maybe the bishop is unfaithful and his significant other offs him. . . . Any of that? It'd be perfect."

Kleimer counted the change. He'd have to play his hand most carefully. This—a movie—had no place in his plans. Although, confronted with the reality, he should've figured on this. But . . . a *movie*. Did he want to get involved in this?

"Would you like some coffee?" His visitors accepted. He could have had his secretary bring it, but he went for it himself. He needed time to consider their overture.

A movie! It *was* attractive. That was indisputable. It might be fun. And everyone knew Hollywood is where the bucks are.

Of course money was a consideration, but in his priority system not the primary one. If money were high on his list, he'd be in private practice.

No; he had established his agenda and it was working very well. He had made a name and reputation for himself far faster and far more dependably than he might have as a moderately big fish in a gigantic pond.

Then too, movies were chancy. No matter what kind of offer these two slimeballs would make, once they got going, he would have little input, and no control whatever of the finished product. Their stupidity easily could rub off on him.

No; all things considered, getting in on their deal made no sense for him.

But he'd have to let them down easy. If they got their cockamamy idea off the ground, and if he left them with a bad taste, they could easily screw up his character in the movie.

So, how to let them down gently?

Quirt. Of course! Quirt would be thrilled to be part of moviemaking. To top that, he owed Quirt some sort of immediate favor. This was tailor-made.

Quirt would assume that Kleimer, having been offered this opportunity, desperately wanted it—who wouldn't?—but had given up his opportunity for Quirt's sake. That would have to be the way this scenario worked out.

Whether he took it on or not, Quirt would have to believe that Kleimer had sacrificed his own chances to pass on this golden opportunity.

The welcome reality would be that it cost Kleimer nothing. He was dumping what to him was garbage. And Quirt would see it as a gourmet offering.

Kleimer returned to his office with the coffee for his guests. He leaned back and sat on the edge of his desk. As he looked down at them, he smiled. "Gentlemen, I don't think I can help you. I'd like to, but I don't think I can."

Walberg and Turner exchanged a smug smile.

"Don't be so modest, Mr. Kleimer," Walberg said. "You have an inside track on a terrific story. We want to tell this story through the eyes of the one who sees that justice is done."

"You're right on the money. But it's not my eyes you want to look through."

Walberg smiled. "Think Perry Mason."

"Mason's a defense attorney," Turner interjected.

"It doesn't matter." Walberg had lost some of his ebullience. "There's that series . . . 'Law and Order.' Yeah, that's the one—the one where the prosecuting attorney wins."

"He doesn't always win," Turner reminded.

"It doesn't matter," Walberg snapped. "That was just an illustration. Moviegoers are in the mood to see that justice is done. And, Mr. Kleimer, your job is to see that justice is done."

"Let me return for just a moment to that program you were just talking about," Kleimer said. "The one called 'Law and Order.' The first part of that show is how the police prepare the case for trial. Then the prosecutors take over."

"Yes, but . . ."

"Hear me out, please. All I'm suggesting is that you consider filming your movie through the eyes of the police rather than the prosecutor."

"But . . ."

"I can tell from the kinds of questions you were asking a few minutes ago that you want to talk to the police. This business about sex, for instance. From the police investigation of this case, I think you're on the right track. But I'm not at all sure it'll come up during the trial."

Turner exuded triumph. "See? I told you, Teddy: It's a *police* story. If I said it once, I said it a million times: It's a police story."

Good, Kleimer thought. One of the idiots is happy. Now to make sure the other one doesn't go away angry. "Actually, this approach may make your job easier. I suppose one of your problems is that the real-life story isn't over yet."

Kleimer had not recovered from his initial amazement that they would attempt to portray an event whose conclusion was still unknown. He suspended disbelief for the moment. "You know your business far better than I, but it seems to me you'd be doing yourselves a favor by starting your film with the police work on this case. Then time would be on your side. You could work right into the trial. Like I said, you know your business better than I, but this procedure does seem logical."

"You're absolutely right." Turner was enthusiastic. "It's a police story."

Kleimer was drawing the obvious conclusion that Walberg was a court nut while Turner loved police work.

"Well . . ." Walberg had lost an edge on his self-assurance. ". . . you *are* going to convict, aren't you . . . the priest, I mean?"

"Put your bottom dollar on it." Kleimer smirked.

Good-byes were said with promises to get back together as this venture proceeded. The odd couple left.

No sooner were they gone than Kleimer was on the phone.

"I know this isn't the kind of return favor we talked about, Quirt, and we're still in the ballpark of working on a promotion for you. But I've got something that will tide you over for a little. Are you alone?

"Well, then, find a place where you can be alone. You're about to get some visitors who just might change your life. I'll tell you all about it. . . ."

*　*　*　*

With Kleimer's forewarning, Quirt was preparing himself.

First he secured an interrogation room, guaranteeing privacy for himself and his prospective visitors.

Then he used his electric razor, patted down his thinning hair, and tightened his belt several notches until he had a real problem breathing comfortably. Finally, he made sure someone would greet the visitors and have them cool their heels for a while. He didn't want to seem too eager.

All was ready. Quirt was prepared. At the last moment, he decided to let them wait just a little longer.

*   *   *   *

Armand Turner looked about with ill-concealed disgust. "This reminds me of the sign you've got on your desk."

"Which—oh, you mean 'This Mess Is a Place.'"

"Exactly."

"You're right, of course. But isn't it perfect?"

"It doesn't look like any police headquarters ever seen on TV. Most of them look as if someone has at least mopped within the previous five years."

"Forget TV for a moment, Mondo. This quite obviously is reality."

"Screw reality! Audiences will never accept such a tawdry scene. Our headquarters will have to measure up to what the audience expects."

"Tsk, tsk, tsk. Remember our budget. What if we can get them to let us film here? We've got to keep thinking economy. Already I'm thinking about that church . . . what was it?"

"Ste. Anne's."

"Ste. Anne's, right. I'm sure they'll let us use the interiors. Save us a wad not having to build those sets. Add a measure of reality, too. We can use this kind of stuff in the teasers: 'The actual room where the bishop was clubbed to death,' 'Where he prayed before being martyred' . . . that sort of stuff."

"You've got a point, Teddy. I must admit I wouldn't be unhappy losing these vomit-green walls." His face brightened. "But hey, now that we're talking budget, just what do we have? I mean, just to recapitulate. The event?"

"The cold-blooded murder of a Roman Catholic bishop by a Roman Catholic priest."

"That does have a ring to it. The TV players?"

"Gold Coast Enterprises and a cable network."

"Right. The reaction time?"

"A month or less. There's a very definite limit to audience attention span when it comes to murder in Detroit. Even when both the victim and murderer are Catholic clergymen."

"Right. The payoff?"

"We can look for a ceiling of about two seventy-five. So far we haven't had to pay off anyone. But that'll begin soon enough."

"The problem is, everybody thinks TV pays like the big screen where six figures are what's served for breakfast."

"Let's just hope our detective—what's his name? . . . Quirt . . . doesn't think he's worth auctioning Disney Studios for."

"Moving right along: the story spin?"

"How 'bout, 'Changing Church explodes as priest kills bishop.'"

"Mmm . . . a little weak . . . but okay for beginners," he concluded. "And, lastly, the problem?"

"No ending."

"The price you have to pay for being first on the scene."

"Wait a minute! Wait a minute! Mondo, I just remembered something. It just dawned on me why I thought this place was so perfect. *Beverly Hills Cop*! Remember?"

"How could anyone forget *Beverly*—oh, I see: The opening was filmed in Detroit. Right here in these rooms, wasn't it? Okay, so I guess if the movie had the 'typical Detroit headquarters,' viewers would wonder why Detroit had cleaned up its act. We almost have to use these interiors, for the simple reason that Eddie Murphy did."

"And"—Walberg rubbed his hands together—"think of the savings!"

Quirt entered the hallway. Self-introductions were made. The lieutenant ushered the moviemakers into the small room ordinarily used for interrogations.

"We were admiring your decor. . . ." Walberg waved his arm in an encompassing way.

"Our *what*?"

"The colors, the furnishings." More gestures.

Quirt's eyes popped. He leaned forward. "This shit?"

"We were thinking of it more in terms of vomit," Turner said.

"Yeah," Quirt agreed, "puke is more like it."

"You must've been here when they filmed *Beverly Hills Cop,* weren't you?" Walberg asked.

Quirt nodded.

"Did you have to vacate the premises while they filmed?"

"What?" Quirt looked mock-astonished. "They didn't shoot here. They couldn't. This is a pretty busy place. They had to build their own sets." He nodded. "But they did manage to capture the pukey atmosphere all right."

"Well, Teddy . . ." Turner turned to his partner in slime. "At least it won't be very expensive to recreate this place. And it'll be an appropriate setting for the language."

"The language?" Quirt's brows knotted questioningly. "You gonna have cops wandering around using the F word the way they did in *Beverly Hills Cop*? I gotta tell you guys, that ain't real. I mean, our guys are not unfamiliar with the word. They just don't talk like that . . . especially on the job."

Turner sighed deeply. "We're not in the business of teaching viewers about reality. We give them what they're familiar with."

"But"—Walberg changed the subject—"speaking of business, I guess Mr. Kleimer called and told you what we wanna do."

Quirt nodded enthusiastically.

"We want," Walberg continued, "to tell the tragic story of Bishop Diego's murder, and help people understand why it happened."

"Why it happened?" Quirt repeated. "Even we don't know that for sure. We think Diego pushed the priest—Carleson—too hard."

"Don't worry," Walberg said. "We'll find more than one reason."

"Was there any sex?" Turner asked.

"Sex?"

"Were either of them—or both—gay?"

"Gay! No, nothing like that."

"A woman?" Turner persisted.

"A woman . . . ?" That was one of the leads Tully had uncovered. Quirt couldn't recall her name . . . but there was something about some broad who might have had it in for Diego.

Tully would know all the details, of course. But one of the last things Quirt wanted was for anyone else—especially not Tully—to get in on this. "A woman . . . yeah, there was something about a broad who might've been a suspect before we nailed Carleson."

"A suspect? No. No," Turner said. "We don't want to confuse the issue. We'll have the woman as a love interest. We can get explicit there. The bishop in mufti, sneaking up to her apartment. Climbing into bed among the shadows."

Quirt's mouth was open. "You guys don't get real worked up about reality, do you?"

Walberg disregarded this. "I think we can get this show on the road. Do you have an agent, Lieutenant?"

"Me? An agent? You kidding?"

"Then we'll have our lawyer get in touch. About compensation. We'll be telling this story through the eyes of the detective . . . through *your* eyes."

"No shit! Who you gonna have . . . who you gonna get to play me?"

"We've been negotiating with a bit player you wouldn't recognize. But now that Mr. Kleimer has changed our direction, we're thinking of Chris Noth . . . you know, one of the detectives on 'Law and Order.'"

"No kidding!" Quirt was delighted. "Hey, he's a good-lookin' guy!" He paused. "Chris Noth as me! Oh, yeah; I forgot about you guys and reality."

Quirt was being paged. He left the room to take a phone call.

"Just wanted to check: How're things going?" Brad Kleimer asked.

"Great, just great. This could be a lot of fun," Quirt said.

"Fun?"

"Guess who they got playing me in this movie? Forget it, you'd never guess. Chris Noth!"

"Chris Who?"

"The guy who plays one of the detectives on 'Law and Order.' And guess what else? I'm gonna get paid! This is movie money. Big bucks! They wanna tell this story through my eyes. I'll probably have my name up there in the whatchamacallits—the credits. This is a *gas*. I gotta thank you, Brad. Wait'll I tell the wife."

"Slow down, George—"

"Say, Brad, do you remember anything about that dame Tully came up with? The one who might've had a motive for offing Diego?"

"No. Forget her, George. What about all that follow-up on Carleson I asked for? You haven't forgotten that, have you?"

"Don't worry, Brad; I'll get someone on it."

"Dammit, I don't want 'someone'; I want the best you've got!"

"Don't worry. I'll get you somebody good. Listen, Brad, I gotta get back to the movie guys. I'll talk to you later."

Slowly, thoughtfully, Kleimer lowered the receiver until it rested on the base.

Christ! He hoped he hadn't outsmarted himself.

CHAPTER

FOURTEEN

It was disastrous. The only excuse Brad Kleimer could dredge up for his blunder in introducing George Quirt to the movie people was that he'd been caught off guard. Chalk it up to shortsightedness.

Kleimer had not foreseen in any way the advent of Hollywood. Once he had determined that his involvement in a movie would be counterproductive, he should simply have washed his hands of the matter and left Walberg and Turner to their own devices. Instead, he had to be too clever by half and bring Quirt into it.

He shouldn't have done that. He now realized that if an airtight case was to be built against Carleson, he himself would have to personally take care of the nitty-gritty.

Kleimer was miserable.

News from the Thirty-sixth District Court, where Carleson had been arraigned a short time ago, didn't help. Oh, the priest had been indicted on a charge of first-degree murder all right. But the judge had set bail at only $25,000. It could have been—should have been—much higher.

The special problem was that the archdiocese of Detroit had gotten into the act.

They—Cardinal Boyle actually—had put up $2,500, the 10 percent bond needed for Carleson to be freed on bail. On top of that, Boyle had retained Avery Cone, one of the area's top trial attorneys, to defend Carleson.

Thus, with Carleson free to come and go, Kleimer was deprived of the luxury of checking into the priest's past while he was confined. Now Kleimer would have to get more deeply involved and take care of the pavement work that he'd expected to delegate to Quirt.

In addition, no matter how capable Kleimer was, Cone was a most worthy opponent. This was no walk in the park to begin with. It was becoming more of a challenge by the minute.

Kleimer was about to consider his next move when the phone rang. This might still be the long-awaited national news media. Masking his beleaguered mood, he greeted the caller in as upbeat a manner as he could muster. "Brad Kleimer. How can I help you?"

There was a silence, as if the caller had gotten the wrong number. Then a decidedly female voice said, "My, aren't we being sweet today. I didn't expect that."

"What? Who is this?"

"How soon they forget."

It was Kleimer's turn to pause. "*Audrey?* Is that you?"

"The ex-Mrs. Kleimer herself."

It had been almost a year since he'd heard from her. Now it all came tumbling back. He was not handling surprises well this morning.

When Audrey remarried about a year ago, he had been released from the obligation of alimony. This as the result of a clever little clause he had worked into their divorce papers. When he stopped paying for her, he also stopped thinking of her. Which is why he hadn't immediately identified her voice. "Well, Audrey, what brings the pleasure of this call?"

"What makes you think it's going to be a pleasure?"

"Because I'm no longer paying for you. You know: Alimony payments can break my bones, but names will never hurt me. So what gives?"

"I've been inundated with you this morning. The newspaper, the radio and TV, the phone interview with J. P. McCarthy! Everywhere I turn, there you are with the upcoming trial of the murdered bishop. Up to your old tricks, honey? Digging into a celebrity case while the homicide dicks are still investigating it?"

"Don't bad-mouth it, kid. Those old tricks are what paid for your clothes and jewels—not to mention those unlamented alimony payments.

"But, all that aside, this isn't the first time since we said good-bye that I've been in the news. What brings you out of the mothballs now?"

"Just a coincidence, that's all. Just a coincidence."

"Audrey, this is fun, and I'd like to play twenty questions with you some more. But, as you can probably guess, I'm up to my earlobes. Is there a point to all this?"

"Uh-huh. The coincidence is that you are going to prosecute the priest who married me."

That stopped him cold. As he tried to absorb this unexpected statement, he didn't stop to envision the delighted smile on his former wife's face.

"Cat got your tongue?"

"Audrey, what in hell are you talking about? You married a priest?"

"No." She chuckled. "No, he witnessed my marriage. Father Carleson witnessed my marriage. He married Lou and me."

"Have you been drinking? You and Lou got married a year ago. What did you do, wander around South America until you ran into this priest?"

"It's kind of complicated. Lunch?"

Kleimer checked his watch and shook his head. "I shouldn't, but . . . okay, I've got to. It'll have to be a quickie."

"You were always so good at those."

He ignored it. "Where?"

"Certainly not downtown Detroit."

"Kingsley Inn?"

"Fine."

"Let's beat the crowd. Eleven-thirty?"

"See you."

*   *   *   *

Brad Kleimer arrived at the Kingsley first. He was seated, and ordered a Bloody Mary.

He looked around the room. It was early, so there were only a few scattered diners. The crowd was yet to come.

Kleimer had formed a habit of looking for recognition. After all, he had been in the news often enough to expect people to draw the connection between all those photos of him and the real live celebrity. Every time he caught someone's eye, he assumed the identification had been made.

He had just placed the napkin on his lap when Audrey arrived—Audrey Schuyler since her second marriage.

Either she had checked her coat, or she'd left it in her car and used the valet parking. In any case, he was happy she wasn't wearing any sort of wrap. She had such a trim, attractive figure, it was a pleasure to watch her walk into a room like this. Both men and women regularly did a double take when they saw her. In addition to being beautiful, she exuded confidence and charm.

She came straight to his table. He neither stood nor attempted to; she expected no chivalrous gesture on his part. She merely slid into the chair opposite him.

"Well, Audrey, still looking smashing. How nice that Lou can keep you in the style to which I accustomed you."

She ordered Perrier with a lemon twist. As she removed her black kid gloves, she said, "And you're looking prosperous, especially for a humble prosecuting attorney."

"There are some perks, speaking fees, things like that. And, of course, I'm not paying for you anymore." He leaned toward her and spoke in a confidential tone. "Seriously, I didn't look forward to seeing you again. But now that you're here, it brings back a lot of pretty good memories."

"Thanks, I wish I could say the same."

"Hey, lunch was your idea, remember?"

"So it was. Sorry."

Leaning still closer, he said, "I really haven't got time this afternoon, but, by God, I'd be willing to make some. You know, this *is* an inn. We could get a room. . . ."

"The suggestion was for *lunch*."

He shook his head sadly. "Too bad. You always were a terrific piece of ass."

"Oh, Brad, you have such a way with words."

The waitress brought their drinks. In keeping with Kleimer's pressing schedule, they each ordered a small salad.

This modest order was not great news for their waitress. Her only hope was a tip out of all proportion.

Kleimer unnecessarily smoothed the tablecloth with the palms of both hands. "Well, let's come to the point of all this. Four years ago, you and I were married. We were married in a Catholic ceremony at, as I recall, St. Owen's in Bloomfield. Not far from where we are now. You were Catholic. I was Protestant. The Catholic Church has problems with that sort of situation. We needed a dispensation. We got it.

"You may remember I went a bit further than that. Partly because I'm fascinated by all law—civil or canonical—and partly because I didn't want to leave you any loopholes, I looked up all the laws of your Church governing marriage. I made damn sure that when we 'exchanged consent'—much more canonically correct than 'speaking our vows'—you were locked into this until death do us part.

"You wouldn't agree to a prenuptial agreement. So my only consolation was that you'd never be able to remarry in your Church as long as I was alive.

"I never had the opportunity of telling you before now, but that's why I was doubly delighted when you married Lou Schuyler. Not only was my financial responsibility for you ended, but you had to be married by a judge."

They fell silent as the waitress brought their salads.

"You really are something else, Brad." For the first time there was anger in her tone. "If you went hunting, you wouldn't just shoot the deer, you'd torture it to death. But . . ." She softened. ". . . all's well that ends well."

"Yes," Kleimer said, "that does bring us to what you mentioned earlier. You claim you were married by this priest—Carleson. I find that incredible. I would stake my considerable reputation in the law that you had no escape whatsoever from our marriage—as far as Church law is concerned. We could have gotten ten divorces in civil law and it wouldn't have cut any ice with the Church.

"If there'd been any way out in canon law, you never would've had to be married by that judge. I'm sure you can see why I consider your statement incredible."

She stabbed a portion of lettuce and inattentively dabbed it in the dressing. "I didn't pay that much attention when we got married. I knew you seemed terribly interested in the impediments to a Catholic marriage and to the dispensation I needed to marry a non-Catholic. It was silly, but I thought you might actually be interested in the Catholic Church and that one day you might convert."

He almost choked as he started to laugh and then abruptly stopped in favor of breathing.

"I know. I know. I said it was silly. But it wasn't until Lou and I wanted to get married that I finally tumbled to what you'd been up to. We visited quite a few priests to see what we could do about our marriage—yours and mine, I mean. Some of those priests were pretty knowledgeable—we even saw a reasonably kindly priest in the Tribunal. But they all said pretty much the same thing: I didn't stand a chance in hell of getting an annulment. The only possibility I had was if you were to cooperate unconditionally. Even then the Tribunal priest judged our chances as somewhere between slim and zero.

"That was when I swallowed a whole lot of pride and called you. Remember?"

"Absolutely!"

"Remember how you responded?"

He nodded vigorously. "It gave me the laugh of a lifetime."

"That's when it came through crystal clear. You'd contrived the whole thing at the time of our marriage. Your laugh slammed the door on any hope I might have had."

Kleimer pushed aside his all-but-empty salad plate. "Which brings us, at last, to the bottom line. Mind explaining what you said earlier about Carleson?"

"Of course." The waitress removed their dishes and took their order for two coffees.

"Lou and I continued going to Mass, but we never joined a parish because we couldn't receive Communion. That was carefully explained to us before we got married out of the Church. We were 'living in sin.'" She looked at him intently. "It just occurred to me: It didn't bother you in any way, shape, or form that Lou and I had to live a sort of tortured life. Oh, we were very happy together. But it takes some of the enjoyment out of life when you can't forget that you're going to hell. Far from that disturbing you, you enjoyed our dilemma."

He merely smiled.

"Well, anyway, one day a friend told me about this priest who, very quietly, handles cases like mine. Lou and I talked it over—we didn't want to go through any more disappointing, doomed procedures. Finally, though, we agreed to give it a try.

"Enter Father Carleson and dear old Ste. Anne's. We explained everything to him. We didn't leave out any detail. And he took us through the whole process step by step.

"The basic condition was our consciences, he said. Lou hadn't ever been married. So that wasn't the problem. It was my marriage to you, as you well know.

"So, Father told us it was our decision—not his, not the Church's. Did I—did we—consider my marriage to you a genuine, loving relationship in which we both grew and developed? Or did we honestly consider it a nice try but, unfortunately, a failure?

"He insisted that we be brutally honest with ourselves. We could fool him with no great trouble. But we certainly could not fool God or ourselves.

"If, finally, we were satisfied and at peace in our consciences about our marriage—Lou and me—he would witness our marriage. He said at best it would be a convalidation.

"So"—she smiled broadly—"a couple of months ago, we did it. And since then we've been ecstatically happy. And I'm sure"—her tone dripped sarcasm—"you're happy for us."

Kleimer sat agape. Only slowly did he close his mouth. "He can't do that!"

"He did it. *We* did it."

"It's a direct violation of Church law."

"We went over that. He showed us how little Church law had to do with the law of Christ. Canon law was by no means infallible. It's constantly changing."

Kleimer thought about what he might be able to do. "He violated his own Church's law. I could report him."

"We kept everything very quiet. There wasn't any scandal because there wasn't anyone around to be scandalized. Father said if anyone brought it up it would be of no importance to the media, particularly since the divorce happened so long ago. And, anyway, he said he was willing to take his chances with Cardinal Boyle. This was one of the reasons he had chosen to work in the archdiocese of Detroit."

"I'll—!" But he could think of no other threats.

"There's something else, Brad, that hasn't occurred to you. But it would after you gave this whole thing more thought."

"Oh?"

"Actually, Lou thought of it—credit where credit is due. You won't be able to try him."

"What?! You're crazy!"

"No. You see, Lou takes much more interest in law than I do. Picture it, Brad: You're in the middle of the trial when the judge finds out that the defendant blessed the remarriage of your ex-wife. Supposing the defense attorney questions the defendant, and the jury discovers what I've just told you. You no longer are the disinterested seeker of justice: You've got a very serious personal stake in this. Your prosecution could be perceived as a vendetta—revenge. Wouldn't that sort of cloud the jury's judgment? Wouldn't the judge have to ask you to remove yourself from the case?"

If it were possible for a brain to fry and the smoke to escape from one's nostrils and ears, Brad Kleimer would be vaporizing. He'd had his dream case in hand. And now, like a bird set free, it was gone.

There sat Audrey, not gloating, not smirking. Passive and tranquil. Metaphorically, she had dislodged the weight of the world from her shoulders and dumped it on him. She had anticipated this moment as one of victory and triumph. She just was not cut from Kleimer's cloth.

Kleimer threw his napkin on the table, and jumped to his feet. "We'll see about this!"

It was a flaccid response, and he knew it. Under the circumstances, it was the best he could do. He stormed out, leaving Audrey to pay the bill. That too was neither classy nor effective. This was not Brad Kleimer's finest moment, and he knew it.

Audrey glanced at the check, covered it with her American Express card, and waited for the waitress. Audrey would leave a generous tip. It was the least she could do.

FIFTEEN

If Brad Kleimer were keeping score—and in a vague sort of way he was—this day was beating him badly.

The priest—Father Carleson—had been indicted for murder in the first degree. To date, that was Kleimer's sole bright spot. The bail had been set too low and, with the totally unforeseen interference of the archdiocese of Detroit, the priest had been able to meet it. Acting again in a most unpredictable way, the archdiocese had engaged Avery Cone to defend Carleson. Cone was good, one of the best.

Next, there were those insane people from Hollywood who'd almost inveigled Kleimer into wasting his time helping them. In what he had believed to be a coup, he had steered the madmen to George Quirt, thus ridding himself of them and, at the same time, further ingratiating himself with Quirt.

Then that had backfired when Quirt became infatuated with moviemaking to the degree that Kleimer would not be able to depend on him to press the investigation into Carleson's past.

The cherry on the top of this unpalatable sundae was his former wife's revelation that Carleson had somehow convalidated her marriage to Lou Schuyler. Not only did that negate Kleimer's painstakingly planned revenge, it also tainted his prosecution of Father Carleson.

The score, as Kleimer tallied it, was about six to two in favor of the opposition.

After serious and solitary consideration of the latest development, Kleimer decided to broach the matter of Carleson's involvement in Audrey's marriage with the chief of operations. Better this way than to launch into the trial all the while looking over his shoulder for the subject to surface, leading to a possible mistrial. After all, Kleimer had intended on using this trial as a springboard to fame, not as a catapult to infamy. Being a laughingstock was *not* in his plans.

And so, as if to treat the whole thing as if it were a ludicrous possibility, Kleimer told the chief, in a most sketchy way, of the cloud that cast a "slight" shadow over the coming trial of Father Carleson.

Unfortunately, the chief wasn't buying the "slight" possibility that this coincidence could haunt Kleimer in his effort to convict. Kleimer argued the point until it became clear that the chief wasn't going to budge on the one hand, and that he was about to lose his temper on the other.

Make that seven big ones to two.

And then, the tide turned.

"Don't get me wrong, Brad." It was the frustrated voice of Lieutenant Quirt on the phone. "I know you were only trying to do me a good turn, but those Hollywood guys are nuts!"

"What's the matter?" A glimmer of hope in what had seemed an ocean of depression.

"These guys think the real world is named after Disney!"

Coming from Quirt, an imaginative metaphor.

"They don't give a damn for any of the facts of this case," Quirt fumed. "As of now, the Hollywood version of the story is that either Diego or Carleson was a fruit. Or maybe both of them were gay. Or maybe they weren't gay; maybe they were both in love with the same broad. Take your pick. Any one of those or some combination of them will be *their* motive for the murder.

"I tried to convince those flakes that something really happened here—that there was a perfectly good murder that wasn't committed for any of those reasons. But, you know, it's like I wasn't there.

"On top of that, they wanted me to arrange for the mayor to give them the key to the city, and to make sure the news media was there to cover the ceremony.

"And that's not all! They wanted me to be with 'em like twenty-four hours a day!"

"So?"

"So, I told them to go to hell."

Kleimer was smiling. But he managed to sound seriously concerned. "How about the money? Wasn't the money good?"

"Hell, I couldn't even pin 'em down to anywhere near a firm figure. They kept trying to tell me that stuff made for TV wasn't in the
same league as the big screen. After a while, I kept trying to tell them,
Okay, I believe you. But they were still vague. They were 'on a tight
budget. . . .'" Quirt went into an exaggerated imitation of Walberg and
Turner. "'We don't know how much we're gonna have to pay the stars
. . . or rental costs' . . . or"—Quirt returned to his natural voice—"any
of the rest of that shit! They like to sweat bricks when they found out
they were gonna need a contingent of our guys to be with them every
minute they were working. *And* that they were gonna have to pay the
cops' full salary, including overtime!"

"So you're outta there completely?"

"Brad, I'm all yours. That is, when I'm not working on the constant
supply of murders this city keeps coughing up."

"George, I really appreciate that. It just comes a little late."

"What? Whaddya mean 'late'?"

Kleimer briefly explained the circumstances that had forced him
out of the trial. "So that's it, George," he concluded. "I don't mind
telling you I'm feeling pretty damned embarrassed about the whole
thing. I had some great—really great—publicity going there. Everybody expects me to be the prosecutor. I haven't even figured out a PR
way to soften the fact that I'll be on the sidelines."

"Geez, Brad, that's rough. After all you already put into it. Sorry. I
wish there was something I could do. But . . ."

"Wait a minute." Kleimer searched for an elusive thought. "Now
that you're not tied up with the movie guys anymore, maybe there is
something we can do . . . if you're willing."

"Sure, Brad, anything—within reason, that is."

"This is well within reason, George. You're still tight with the
mayor's press secretary, aren't you?"

"Yeah . . ." Quirt slowly acknowledged.

"Suppose you were to go see him—I think this'll work best face to
face—suppose you go see him and tell him how I've been kicked off
the case. You can even tell him why—only soft-pedal it . . . like the
remarriage thing is no great shakes. Put in the fact that the accused has
Cone for an attorney. Push the fact that I'm better prepared than any of
the other guys. Pull out my track record and all. See if he won't go to

the mayor. Maybe a word from Cobb will do it. . . ." He tried to make his voice impelling. "How 'bout it, George?"

"I don't know. . . ." Quirt hesitated. "Wouldn't it work just as well if you did it?"

"No. It would sound too self-serving. Believe me, George, it'll work better if it comes from you. We've been on cases lots of times before. We've worked good together. You make the arrests and I slap them behind bars. Cobb, above everybody, wants this mess cleaned up fast. I'm the one can do it." Again the compelling tone. "How about it, George?"

"What the hell. Sure, Brad. I'll do my best."

"Right now! There's not a moment to lose."

"You got it!"

There was hope. Just a glimmer. But there was hope.

He was in a sort of limbo. There were other cases he could work on. But he had planned to focus on and devote most of his efforts to the Diego murder. Now, he didn't know whether it was his or not.

A few moments ago he was down and out. He would have, once he worked through the distraction of self-pity, devoted full attention to other, nagging matters. But that was before he'd had that brainstorm of having Quirt intercede for him.

He wanted to stay busy; he just couldn't decide what to do.

His thoughts returned to the abbreviated luncheon with Audrey. That had initiated this latest flurry of activity. Now that he had a leisure moment to consider what she had told him, he wondered again how Carleson had pulled off that validation. *Damn!* Kleimer had been so sure he had covered every possible exit from the Church wedding he and Audrey had gone through.

But how to handle this development? Surely somewhere he could find a commentary on the new code of canon law.

But that was the long way. No, his best bet for the brief time before Quirt would report on his success or failure was to ask someone who would be qualified and willing to walk him through it.

Who? He didn't know any Catholic priests; at least none came to— Wait a minute: What about the guy he met yesterday at headquarters . . . that priest who had helped in previous investigations?

Kleimer had no idea how that priest had been drawn into police work. But the guy had to have a better-than-average knowledge of things Catholic—even for a priest. Plus he probably was of a cooperative nature. Just the two traits Kleimer was looking for.

The name, the parish, escaped Kleimer. A call to his secretary, several calls by her and he had it: Father Robert Koesler, St. Joseph's parish: 393–8212. So close by Kleimer didn't even need the 313 area code.

His first impulse was to engage in a phone conversation with Koesler. However, that would leave both open to interruptions. No, better still, getting out of the office while Quirt was trying to work something out with the mayor might prove a diversion and ease Kleimer's nervousness.

A quick call revealed first, that Koesler was at his rectory and, second, that he would be able to see Kleimer in the few minutes it would take to get there. Kleimer was happily aware that his luck was beginning to turn.

As he drove the few short blocks between the Frank Murphy Hall of Justice and St. Joseph's, Kleimer debated with himself as to just how he would present his question. As a purely speculative problem? Hardly. He had to assume that Koesler was of above average intelligence; he would see through that device easily. The problem of some unspecified third person? Perhaps. But there was the same possible pitfall; undoubtedly Koesler would tumble to his deception.

No, Kleimer settled on the truth—but as little of the truth as he could get by with.

Koesler, as he awaited Kleimer's arrival, began to rue his earlier eagerness to be involved in this case. It was one thing to try to assist a fellow priest in a troubled time; it was another to help the police charge that same priest with murder.

Of course, his aid had not actually contributed to Father Carleson's arrest. That was the work of Lieutenant Quirt. To this point, at least Koesler's involvement had not consumed too much of his time. But the prosecutor's call might very well change that. Kleimer would explain nothing on the phone; rather, he had been politely insistent that they meet.

Fortunately, Koesler did have a break in his schedule now, so he was able to receive Kleimer. But this could get hairy if it escalated too much.

Koesler saw Kleimer in the rectory office. Not having much time, Kleimer immediately launched into the history of his marriage. He emphasized the marriage itself. At the time of their wedding, both parties were of age and neither had been previously married. They filled out and signed the necessary forms. He agreed to everything required of him. He promised he would not interfere in any way with Audrey's practice of her Catholic faith. He declared himself open to the possibility of having children. He promised that if children came, he would cooperate at least passively in their being raised Catholic. There was only one obstacle to their marriage: He was not a Catholic. He had been baptized as a child in the Episcopal Church.

None of this surprised Koesler. He had led uncounted couples through that procedure.

What did startle him was Kleimer's account of how he'd made sure that Audrey both understood and agreed to her part of the bargain. As part of the Catholic ritual, she also had some promises to make. Namely, that she would be open to having children, that she would raise them as Catholics, and that she would live her faith in a way that might lead her husband to convert.

In no other instance that Koesler could recall—in his own experience or that of any other priest he knew—had the non-Catholic partner in a mixed religious marriage gone to such trouble and detail to make certain sure that the validity of the marriage could never be challenged.

Kleimer concluded his narration. "As far as I was able to guarantee, the only sticking point was that impediment of my not being Catholic. But the priest requested a dispensation. And it was granted. I know; I studied the dispensation when it arrived from the chancery. . . ."

Koesler had to wonder why Kleimer had been so meticulous about his marriage's validity. It was, he thought again, in his experience, unique.

". . . I mean," Kleimer said, "isn't that something like Henry VIII?"

"Beg pardon?"

"Henry VIII, king of England."

"Was someone executed, and I haven't heard about it?"

Kleimer thought for a moment. "Come to think of it, she was one of four of Henry's wives who wasn't executed."

"Where are we going with this?"

"Oh. The point is that Henry's first wife, Catherine of Aragon, had been married to Henry's brother, Arthur. Arthur died a year after the wedding. Then she married Henry. But before they could be married, they had to get a dispensation because she was too closely related to Henry by affinity—the marriage to his brother.

"The Pope dispensed them. Then, when Henry wanted to divorce Catherine and marry Anne Boleyn, he claimed that his marriage to Catherine was invalid because she had been his brother's wife. In effect, he wanted the same Pope who had dispensed them from the impediment to invalidate their marriage because of the impediment he dispensed them from."

"I'm familiar with that story. But what's it got to do with you?"

"Just this: When Audrey told me that her marriage to Schuyler had been validated, I blew my cork. But later, when I got to thinking about it, I figured she must be confused. A priest couldn't do that . . . he couldn't just run roughshod over all those laws. I mean, they're *your* laws—laws of the Catholic Church. He's not some kid priest; he's been around.

"When she married Schuyler, they couldn't get around her previous marriage to me. I made sure all the *i*'s were dotted and all the *t*'s crossed. I guess they thought they had some small chance if I were to cooperate. Of course, I refused any cooperation." He laughed sharply. "Why in hell would I be cooperative when I went through all that trouble to make certain there were no loopholes?"

"Why, indeed?"

Koesler noted repeatedly during this narration how inordinately pleased Kleimer was that he had been able to foil his former wife's every attempt at happiness. And how disgruntled, how angry he was, that somehow, despite his best efforts, she had somehow achieved that happiness.

Kleimer by no means was the only person Koesler had ever known who was so filled with hatred. Oddly, this sort of venom was frequently found between people who had once been the best of friends or even lovers.

When a marriage went sour, it was most rare that the process of dismantling the relationship was accomplished amicably. From time to time, Koesler would reflect on a couple who at one time had sat in his office planning their wedding. They could not be more in love. They looked at each other with adoration and hunger.

Then, sometimes, years later, the same couple would be back for marriage counseling. Now, they refused to look at one another. The animosity was palpable.

What had happened? The chemistry was so precarious.

While, in Koesler's experience, there were many contenders for the title of "meanest former spouse," at this point Kleimer was the leading candidate.

One of Koesler's weaknesses—at least he considered the trait less than Christ-like—was his dislike for persons such as this. No, he did not much care for Bradley Kleimer. But the priest tried not to betray his feelings. There was always the possibility, no matter how slight, that such a person might turn about and learn to forget rather than harbor vindictiveness. To love rather than to hate. To rejoice in the good fortune of a former friend or spouse rather than seeking vengeance.

But, to be perfectly honest, he did not hold out much hope for Kleimer.

"Anyway," Kleimer was saying, "after I had a chance to reflect on what Audrey told me, I had to think there was something else going on. But what? Then I thought maybe Carleson was able to find something wrong with that dispensation we got from the impediment of mixed religion. But what in hell could've gone wrong?

"That's when I thought of Henry VIII, who got a dispensation and then challenged the validity of his marriage because of the dispensation—just as if it had never been given. Could that have happened to me? Could they have found some flaw in the dispensation we got?

"Well, you're the expert when it comes to Church law. What do you think?"

Koesler did not appreciate the corner Kleimer had forced him into.

To begin, Koesler had no way of knowing what had happened between the Schuylers and Father Carleson. Perhaps Carleson *had* discovered a loophole. Unlikely . . . but possible. Or he might have worked out an arrangement whereby they agreed to live together as brother and sister rather than as husband and wife.

At very best, such an unrealistic relationship was awkward. At best it would be strained; at worst, intolerable.

There were several other possible arrangements that might have been found and agreed upon. But, in short, Koesler did not know exactly what had happened. However, after his conversation with Carleson Sunday night, Koesler knew full well that the priest was fully capable of doing just what Audrey Schuyler had implied. He knew that in Detroit some priests retained the approach that requires anyone with a previous marriage to acquire not only a civil divorce but an annulment—a ruling by the Tribunal or Church marriage court that the previous marriage was null, that it never existed. Indeed, such is the letter of the law.

Other priests might counsel such a couple to get married in any manner recognized by the state and just continue receiving the sacraments. This is sometimes referred to as "the pastoral solution."

Still others, mainly in low profile, perhaps in the core city, will witness the remarriage—in direct contravention of Church law.

Father Carleson, however, never even asked couples who came to him whether there was a previous marriage to be dealt with. Koesler had concluded that Carleson was a *do*er, not merely an observer. He might well have waved aside all restrictions plus lots of laws, and simply witnessed the couple's marital promises.

"Well—?" said an impatient Kleimer.

"Well, I don't know what happened. It's like when a surgeon performs an operation. Then someone like yourself goes to a second doctor to ask what the first doctor did. Doctor number two would have to be at a loss as to what happened. He'd have to have been there, seen the X rays, shared in the examination, witnessed the operation." Koesler hoped Kleimer was understanding all this. "I have no clue as to what Father Carleson found or did."

Kleimer checked his watch. He should get back to find out what Quirt had or hadn't accomplished. But he wanted some answers from Koesler more satisfying than a plea of ignorance. "Okay. Lemme ask a couple of procedural questions. If Carleson somehow was able to validate that marriage, shouldn't there be a record of it somewhere?"

"Yes," Koesler answered truthfully, if with some reluctance. "There might be a notation in the marriage register at Ste. Anne's. There also ought to be a notation in the baptismal records of both parties."

"So . . ." Kleimer felt he was finally getting someplace. ". . . if there's nothing in the records, they're still locked out of the Church as much as they were when they married in the civil ceremony."

164

WILLIAM X. KIENZLE

"Not necessarily. They might have agreed to a brother and sister living arrangement."

"Oh, yeah; I read about that when I married Audrey."

Once again, Koesler was impressed by the extent of Kleimer's preparation for his eventual vindictiveness.

"But," Kleimer continued, "if they agreed to that, they couldn't have intercourse. It'd be a sin for them to do anything sexual more than a brother and sister might do . . . right?"

Koesler, with an increasing sense of distaste, nodded wordlessly.

Kleimer seemed quite satisfied that the Schuylers, even though squared away with their God, would still be miserable. Then furrows formed in his forehead. "Hey, wait a minute! I'm thinking of what kind of guy this Carleson is. Diego seems to have made a lot of trouble for a lot of people. But nobody does anything about it but Carleson. He's an action guy. He doesn't wait around for things to happen; he makes them happen. He killed a bishop. It'd take a lot less to say the hell with some Church marriage laws and just witness the marriage of a couple of people who canonically couldn't get married . . . no?"

"You're jumping the gun badly. Father Carleson has been accused of murder. That doesn't mean he's guilty. Your premise is unfounded." But Koesler feared that the astute attorney had detected his unspoken fleeting agreement with that premise.

"Son of a bitch . . ." Kleimer was no longer addressing Koesler, or anyone else for that matter. He was talking to himself. "This thing works both ways. If he can overlook every law of the Church and act out his contempt for those laws, why couldn't he do the same with another law against murder, and just do what he feels is necessary?" He had him! "Sure! I'm gonna hang that bastard!"

Kleimer rose and slipped into his overcoat as Koesler said, in an alarmed tone, "Wait a minute, Mr. Kleimer. You're dealing with two different kinds of law here. God's law is not always the same as Church law."

As he continued to try to reason with Kleimer, Koesler became somewhat incoherent.

Kleimer, wrapped up in his own elation, walked out the front door. As he went down the steps, he waved offhandedly. "Good-bye, Father Koesler. And thanks."

The priest could only stand and watch as Kleimer got in his car and drove off.

Slowly, Koesler became aware that Mary O'Connor was staring at him, shocked. She had never seen him so flustered. "Are you all right, Father?"

Koesler did not respond immediately. He shut the door slowly, thoughtfully. "Yeah. Yeah, I'm all right, Mary. But I'm afraid a friend is in an awful lot of trouble."

CHAPTER
SIXTEEN

After Kleimer left the rectory, Father Koesler stood silent and still, watching the prosecutor bound down the steps and into his car parked at the curb. The priest felt as if he had betrayed a friend merely by truthfully answering questions. He knew he could not have done otherwise. But he felt bad regardless.

Mary O'Connor was surprised when Koesler asked her to hold all his calls. He scarcely ever did that.

Koesler went upstairs to his study. The room's one small window admitted little light to brighten this gray day. He chose to sit in the gloom and think.

This matter of marriage, divorce, and remarriage was handled differently in various faiths. For one whose marriage had disintegrated, this could easily be life's lowest point. And divorce, depending on whether and how it was contested, could be brutal.

To Koesler, this was the moment when an understanding, solicitous, forgiving, and welcoming Church was most needed. He was embarrassed to admit that his Church, the Catholic Church, was perhaps the least helpful of any major faith in this respect.

Koesler had friends who were priests, ministers, rabbis, so he knew something of their procedures.

Among Orthodox Jews, the bill of legal divorcement is enacted by a husband giving a "get" to his wife. There is no trial, or precise laws that must be observed. A rabbinical court finalizes the "get" by making cuts in the paper bearing the decision. This "cut" is a statement that the case may not be reinstated. It is final.

According to Jewish law, a husband may divorce his wife at will, with some restrictions. That the husband must approach the rabbi precludes such whimsy as dismissing the wife over, say, breakfast. However, the wife needs the permission of her husband to seek a divorce. Which may be another definition of "fat chance."

One further indication of the wife's standing is that a wedding cannot be witnessed on the Sabbath. One cannot conduct business on the Sabbath. The connection being the perception of a wife as comparable to chattel—property.

Reform Jews, with whom there is a current tendency toward more traditional practices, are, by and large, not in the divorce business. Things are pretty much up to the individual rabbi. In this, there can be a good bit of shopping for the right rabbi, since it is perfectly possible for the one rabbi, for reasons of his own, to refuse to witness a specific marriage.

The Conservative wing of Judaism is somewhere between the Orthodox and the Reform.

So, unless one is the unhappy wife of an Orthodox Jew, it seems not all that difficult to be remarried in the Jewish faith.

The Episcopalian Church in the United States of America is far more structured than Judaism.

Until the mid-seventies, in this branch of Christianity, it was not canonically possible for a divorced person to be remarried. Then, in the convention or synod of that time, the U.S. Episcopal Church altered its stand to permit remarriage in the Church.

The responsibility for the care of these cases falls to the parish priest. In fact, the total response for all Episcopal marriages is in the lap of the parish priest.

The process begins with a parish member in good standing. He or she is a communicant of a given parish. The communicant approaches the parish priest and the process begins.

There is a minimum of sixty days or a maximum of six months notice given. During this time there is a studied preparation. This requirement is meant to remind all those involved that this will be a union as set forth in the Book of Common Prayer. If one—or both for that matter—is a divorcé or divorcée, the priest may ask that person to express what happened in the previous marriage, why it happened, and what was learned.

Whether or not the marriage includes a divorced person, there are informational forms to be filled out. If there has been a divorce, the form will inquire into the care of the children, if any, of the prior marriage.

Finally, if a divorced person is involved, a letter must be sent by the priest to the bishop, asking canonical permission to witness the vows.

Rarely would that permission be denied. For one, almost all the time the bishop has no way of knowing the people involved. He relies on the priest's judgment. The bishop's attention might be piqued if one of the parties were a celebrity or, perhaps, notorious.

If a priest were to exercise atrocious judgment, the bishop might well level a punishment—in effect, denying the priest permission to function as a priest for a given time.

In the Episcopalian Church in the United States of America, attention certainly is given to the existence of a prior marriage. Steps are taken to learn from the past, and an attempt is made that a sad history will not be repeated.

"Shopping" for a sympathetic priest seems fruitless, at least in the directives of Episcopal Church law, since the communicant is directed to consult his or her parish priest.

But such restrictions, rubrics, processes, and laws fade into a mild attentiveness when compared with Roman Catholic law regarding marriage, nullities, dissolutions, sanations, privileges of the faith and remarriage.

Give the Catholic Church this: It has been around a long time to build up these laws, or canons. And the Church has used this time assiduously.

Koesler pulled a huge volume from his bookcase. *The Code of Canon Law—a Text and Commentary.* These 1,752 canons, published in 1983, comprised Catholic Church law.

He switched on the overhead light and returned to his seat with the book. He pulled a pen and a pad from his desk.

He'd never thought of it before, but now he decided to tabulate how many of these 1,752 laws applied to marriage and remarriage. After a few minutes of counting, he came up with 146 laws.

Perhaps the pivotal law is Canon 1060, which states: *Marriage enjoys the favor of the law; consequently, when a doubt exists, the validity of the marriage is to be upheld until the contrary is proven.*

This is at the hub of remarriage after a civil divorce. Remarriage, by definition, indicates there is a prior marriage. There is no doubt about the validity of the first marriage until and unless one or both parties want to marry someone else. At that point, if the second marriage is to be in a Catholic ceremony, the party or parties must prove, not that the previous marriage was a failure, a bad but sincere effort, a mistake, etc; but that the previous marriage was *null from its inception*. It must be proven that only some ceremony took place, but that nothing happened.

Koesler considered the most simple example: Church law requires that for a valid marriage, among other things, the Catholic wedding must be witnessed by a priest and two other witnesses. What happens if the Catholic is married, say, by a judge? Obviously, the marriage is invalid, since it was not witnessed by a priest. Thus, the Catholic is free to marry; since no valid marriage existed, there is no valid marriage to block another marriage.

However, that first marriage, according to Canon 1060, *"enjoys the favor of the law."* In order to remarry, the Catholic must challenge the validity of the first marriage. That is what created the "doubt." Now the Catholic must "prove" the first marriage was nothing from its inception.

This, while it can be a serious problem depending on circumstances, is still one of the easiest cases to process. Koesler had handled several over the years. One first secures a recent copy of the Catholic's baptismal record. Recent, because when a Catholic marries, the fact is noted in the baptismal record. Now, the fact that the record is issued without notification of marriage indicates that the Catholic has never contracted a Catholic—i.e., valid—marriage.

Next, one secures a copy of the marriage certificate signed by the officiating party not a priest. Finally, both parties of the first marriage are questioned, and both testify that they were married in civil law and that the marriage was never convalidated. Additionally, there may be a demand that witnesses be called to testify to the truthfulness of the parties.

But . . . there it is. The simplest of all Catholic marriage cases. After that, it goes steadily uphill.

Many, perhaps most people, assume that Catholic laws on marriage and remarriage affect only Catholics. Not so. Good old Canon 1060's *"Marriage enjoys the favor of the law . . ."* applies, in the eyes of the Church, to everyone. So, for instance, two Protestants marry and divorce. Later, one of them wants to marry a Catholic and, since the previous marriage involved no Catholics, assumes there will be no problem. Then, the surprise: Church law assumes that Protestant, Jewish, Islamic, whatever, marriages are valid. The non-Catholic will bear the burden of proving to the Church's satisfaction that the previous marriage was invalid—null—from its very inception.

There are countless variations of these processes. But the point is: It's not simple.

Of the matrimonial court procedures of the Roman Catholic Church, there are those who say it is a "healing" process that helps people learn what went wrong and how they might improve.

Others claim it is the "shark in the pool syndrome." As in: A motel resident goes to the pool and finds a shark in it. He complains to the manager, who explains that the shark is quite benevolent. The resident insists it has nothing to do with benevolence; *there should not be a shark in the pool.*

Father Koesler felt that the Church should not necessarily be in the business of granting or withholding annulments. After the misery of a divorce, the Church should be in a welcoming, not a judgmental mode.

He flipped pages until he came to Canon 1141: *A ratified and consummated marriage cannot be dissolved by any human power or for any reason other than death.*

At last, something that endures until death do we part.

By "ratified" is meant mutual consent, freely given between baptized persons and with no impediment blocking validity, to be followed by sexual intercourse.

The Catholic Church considers all marriages indissoluble to a certain degree. Only the ratified, consummated marriage is absolutely indissoluble.

It seemed this was the sort of marriage had by Brad and Audrey Kleimer. It was this sort of marriage that Father Carleson seemed to have dismissed in witnessing the subsequent marriage of Lou and Audrey Schuyler.

To witness the Schuylers' marriage, Father Carleson would have to be, in effect, ready to flush 146 laws down the drain.

Father Koesler was left disheartened. Could Brad Kleimer be right? Was Father Carleson willing to brush aside any law he judged inapplicable? Even the law against murder?

CHAPTER
SEVENTEEN

Brad Kleimer's desk looked as if a flamingo had been shot while flying over it. Pink slips were scattered about profusely. Undoubtedly the result of his having received lots of calls while he was out, plus his secretary's abandoning any effort to keep them in a neat pile.

It didn't matter. This put him pretty much in the driver's seat. He would be busy on the phone, but he would be able to discard the inconsequential calls while taking the others in the order of his choice.

He fingered through the messages, casually dropping many in the wastebasket. He was disappointed that there was no call from any of the national media or networks.

That would come. All he had to do was get reinstated as the designated trial attorney. And the slip he was now fondling just might open that door. That call was from Ned Ferris.

It had to be a green light. The chief had no reason to call him now unless it would be about the Carleson case. If Quirt had failed, the call would've been from him.

With some satisfaction, Kleimer dialed the number. "Chief?"

"Brad. Listen, there's been a reevaluation on the Carleson trial."

"Oh?" Kleimer tried to mask his smug triumph. He wanted to give the impression of surprise followed by gratitude.

"Yes. The boss wants you to try the case."

"That's great news, Ned. I had pretty well figured I was out of it. I'm really grateful. The boss does know about that marriage business, doesn't he?" *Of course he does,* thought Kleimer.

"He's aware, yes. And he wants you to get it out of the way as quickly as you can. It's manageable, isn't it?"

"Absolutely, Chief. Right off the bat, I can tackle the issue. After all, it makes no difference to me what my ex-wife does. My responsibility ended when she remarried a year ago. The final bond was dissolved then. When she married her present husband, the alimony—which was all that was left of our marriage—ceased. After that, she could've had her marriage blessed by a rabbi or a priest, or an ayatollah for that matter. Obviously, it made no difference to me. It's no more than a coincidence that the priest who killed his bishop also blessed her marriage. If anything, that's *her* problem."

There was an extended pause before Ferris said, "Sounds good. Just get it out of the way early on."

"Absolutely. The only thing is that I wish I could get into it. Witnessing her marriage, it turns out, was a damn good example of how impulsive and spontaneous the priest is."

"Oh? How's that?"

"Just that the guy apparently didn't touch all the bases in his Church law. It seems he just up and did it. It'd be a good example of how the guy functions. If he feels something needs doing, he does it. If a bishop needs to be disposed of, he eliminates him."

"Hmm . . . not bad . . ." Pause. "But don't touch it! The boss was very clear he wanted this marriage of your former wife taken out of the picture early, once and for all. He doesn't want a single juror to think you've got any kind of vendetta going. No confusion. Not a doubt. I can't emphasize that too strongly."

"I read you loud and clear, Ned. I've got some people looking into Carleson's past. I'm sure we'll find all we need and more to show what kind of guy we're dealing with."

"Stay in touch."

"Will do."

As he replaced the receiver, Kleimer felt good—very, very good.

Leafing through the remaining pink slips, he found none that needed urgent attention. Still, he ought to get through them as quickly as possible and clear the decks for a really intensive investigation into Carleson's past—and present.

The phone rang. You never knew; it might be a network.

It was George Quirt.

Kleimer felt magnanimous. Quirt it was, after all, who'd done the leg work to get Kleimer back on the case. "I owe you, George."

"Yeah you do. But I gotta tell you, it was downhill all the way. I didn't even have to go through all our reasons. I was about to tell him how you've been on this case from day one. Remind him of your track record, about the fact they've got Cone on their team.

"But I didn't have a chance to get them on the table. The mayor's man like to hit the ceiling as soon as I told him the chief took you outta the trial. That's it! That's all I had to say. He went right off to see the mayor. And, I found out from some other guys that the mayor is having one of those days. He ain't seeing anybody. But to brass tacks: Did you get the call? Was it from Ferris?"

"Yup. Obviously, the mayor had an offer my boss could not refuse. Pretty tricky with the mayor in city government and us in the county. Anyway, however he worked it, it happened in a hurry.

"But listen, George, you can free yourself up now, can't you? I mean, you haven't been shanghaied by that movie bunch, have you?"

"I'm keeping my distance. It's getting so I can smell them."

"And you can clear some of your people to sniff around Carleson's doings?"

"We're kinda loaded as usual. But I think I can cut a couple of the guys loose for it."

"Can you spare Williams and his partner?"

"I guess . . . that what you want?"

"For now, yeah."

"You got it."

"Stay in touch."

"You bet. How else am I gonna be close enough to you to collect on all these IOUs you been handing me?"

"That's the boy, George."

They laughed and hung up.

Kleimer was only too aware of Quirt's extensive limitations. He knew that Quirt had risen to his present position through a combination of luck, elbow grease, and, mostly, having excellent personnel on his squad.

It was not all that difficult to wring deals from Quirt by dangling rewards; his cravings were near insatiable. After that, it was important to ease George out of the nitty-gritty and get him to sic one or more of his excellent staff onto the investigation. This is what Kleimer had just accomplished. He was content.

The phone rang. One of these calls simply had to be a network.

Not this time. "This is Father Koesler. We met just a little while ago. . . ."

"Yeah, right. What's on your mind, Father?"

"I haven't been able to think of anything but your visit since you left."

"Yeah, you were a lot of help. I owe you."

"You don't owe me anything, Mr. Kleimer. I'm afraid that you have a wrong opinion of Father Carleson. He really is a very fine priest. From what he's told me of his work in the missions, he's a dedicated Christian. That he might take a human life is . . . well, it's just beyond imagination."

Kleimer was chuckling to himself. "Don't worry, Father. That'll be the argument of the defense attorney. The thing is, I'm not going to be a part of the defense. I'll be prosecuting."

"I understand that. But you seem to have the notion that Father Carleson is the type who would justify the means by the end. And I want to assure you that even if he might handle a marriage problem with more charity than a strict interpretation of law, that has nothing to do with his deep and abiding respect for life."

Koesler could almost hear Kleimer's head shake.

"Father," Kleimer said, "you didn't do anything. So stop feeling guilty. I got this idea all by myself just in talking to you about Carleson and my former wife. But you should remember that you are not going to convert me into a Carleson believer. Even if I wanted to—and I don't—my job is to prosecute him. So, first chance I get, I'm gonna check out the books at Ste. Anne's and the parish where Audrey was baptized. I don't expect I'll find any notation that would indicate that this wedding is recognized by the Church.

"But that's okay, Father. If this works out the way I think it will, this'll be one more indication that I've got the right guy. I'll be prosecuting the right man."

Kleimer could almost hear Koesler's shrug. "There's nothing I can say that will influence you or change your mind, is there?"

"No. Not really. But I insist I owe you one. How about coming up to my place some evening? You like classical music? I've got some recordings. You like any kind of music, I've got it. We could toss down a few . . . get to know one another better."

The offer was not one of unalloyed generosity. Koesler had proven himself a useful resource person. He very well might serve as such again. Kleimer would like to have this priest in reserve for future use.

Koesler, for his part, would respond only to an offer he could not resist. Which, in Kleimer's case, would be a summons to confer sacraments *in extremis*. And, since Kleimer was not Catholic, Koesler was not likely to take Kleimer up on his invitation.

But the priest did not wish to needlessly offend the attorney. "Thank you very much for your invitation. I've kind of fallen behind in my parish duties the last day or so." That much was true. "How about I take a rain check?"

"You got it, Father. Any time."

This day was beginning to redeem itself. Kleimer was retrieving his self-satisfaction with interest.

And there was still the national media to come.

CHAPTER EIGHTEEN

Free at last.

Thanks to the good offices of Father Dave McCauley of Ste. Anne's parish, Father Don Carleson had escaped the mob of newspeople who had pinned him down after his release on bail.

They had their job to do. Carleson was able to admit that. He understood it. But he didn't have to like it.

It was nightmarish. First, there was the swarm of reporters who pressed in around him, firing questions; the print people scribbling notes that later they would organize into a story with, they hoped, a snappy lead; the radio news hounds thrusting microphones like voodoo rattles at his jaw.

The ones he minded most were the photographers and camera people. He found it most difficult to give any thought at all to what he was saying, as he tried to answer the questions shot at him from every side, while cameras clicked relentlessly in his face and the shoulder-balanced TV equipment loomed like hungry vultures, zoom lenses lunging in at him.

Fortunately, after some fifteen minutes of that steady, persistent interrogation, Carleson noticed McCauley in his car with the passenger door ajar. He calculated his angle of escape and bolted, pursued by the cameras and the yawp of shouted questions.

Fortunately, too, McCauley placed himself at Carleson's disposal. Nothing was prescribed. Whatever Carleson wanted to do was fine with McCauley.

After a moment's thought, Carleson opted for the freedom of movement his own car would afford. He had no clear idea of what he would do now. But his own car, with no passenger, would provide unencumbered mobility and opportunity for thought.

They drove to Ste. Anne's, where Carleson showered and changed last night's slept-in clothes. Then, before the media could catch up— for they, too, had decided to try Ste. Anne's—he drove off. Aimlessly at first, he kept the car in motion, trying to decide what he might do to forget himself and his troubles.

He recalled a saying of his mother's. She was fond of reminding him of the man who considered himself destitute because he had no shoes until he saw a man with no feet. Or, as his father expressed the same idea, if someone hits you on your toe with a hammer, you'll forget every other misery you've got.

With a slight smile, he headed for what had become a home away from home—Receiving Hospital.

As usual, he left his car in the parking garage and went through the Emergency entrance.

Immediately, he sensed a difference. It was as if the familiar staff were shrinking from him—or was it merely his imagination at work? Certainly he was conscious that being charged with murder simply had to change the way people related to him.

Suddenly, from among those who seemed to be standing back, a man stepped forward briskly. It was Dr. Schmidt, a most capable young intern. "Yo, Father Carleson, read any good murder mysteries lately?"

It broke the ice. All the others, none of whom seriously thought this popular priest could have murdered anyone, gathered around Carleson, offering support.

Smiling and shaking hands, Carleson said, "I know this is a cliché, but you've really made my day."

Camaraderie was so thick and spontaneous that it seemed as if it were a birthday celebration.

In the next few seconds, everything returned to normal. Business was slow at this moment; no one had been rushed in for some time. A few patients were reclining or sitting on gurneys with Emergency personnel asking questions or administering medication.

As Carleson made his way to the door leading to the hospital proper, he was flagged by a nurse who had been talking to one of the resident surgeons. Carleson, with an expectant look, crossed to them.

"I was just telling Pete here about something funny that happened yesterday, Father," the nurse said. "I thought you'd get a kick out of it."

Carleson tightened the small circle with his presence. There was no doubt in his mind, he could use some diversion.

"This happened to my pal, Annie, who works in oncology," the nurse said. "She had a patient who'd been hanging in there by a thread for several weeks. He's got a wife and two kids, both girls, teenagers.

"About a week ago, we got the wife's permission to take the guy—Clarence—off life support. They expected him to check out rather promptly after that. But he didn't. He's been in a coma pretty much since then. The doctor's been wanting to get Clarence out of here—home or a nursing home—but everybody's afraid to move him. He could check out easily while he's getting transferred. In general, nobody quite knew what to do, how to handle it.

"Then yesterday, Annie took the wife aside and explained about giving him permission to leave."

The resident nodded knowingly; Carleson looked puzzled.

"See, Father," the nurse amplified, "sometimes a moribund patient will hang on to life because he thinks there are things unresolved that he has to take care of. He thinks he's needed, and somehow that gives him enough will power to fight off death.

"So, anyway, Annie tells the wife she ought to make it clear to Clarence that he can let go.

"Later, Annie is walking down the corridor and she can hear Clarence's wife yelling. She's yelling, obviously 'cause Clarence is in this coma. And she yells, 'Clarence, I forgive you every mean, rotten, nasty, vicious thing you've ever done to me! Girls, kiss your father good-bye! Clarence, die already!'

"And he did. Right then."

Both the resident and Carleson laughed.

Carleson, upon reflection, was aware of the phenomenon of clearing the way for imminent death. But he had never heard a more illustrative, yet humorous, anecdote demonstrating the theory.

Still chuckling, Carleson made his way into the hospital.

It didn't take long to wipe the smile from his face. The intake department overflowed with patients and their relatives and friends. Most of them were so used to being put on hold that they fully expected to sit in these chairs watching mindless television forever. Forever was the time it took to process the sufferer into a room, a cubicle, or an Ace bandage and out.

No one seemed to identify him as that clergyman they'd seen on TV news or on the front page. He was grateful.

As he made his way down the corridors, he took care to share a confident smile with the worried visitors searching for the room that held their loved one.

Some of the visitors and a few of the patients pushing IV stands paused to talk to him. Somehow they sensed that this was a priest who really understood what it meant to be alone, to be abandoned, to face overwhelming odds. Some asked for a prayer. Others bowed their heads for a blessing.

In some strange way, these interventions, far from sapping his energy, gave him strength. Busy hospitals such as Detroit's Receiving communicated to him the sense that this was where he was supposed to be. These people—so frightened, so alone—were, in a special way, *his* people.

Now he found himself on the floor where Ste. Anne's one and only hospitalized parishioner should be. Carleson made his way toward the nurses' station, hoping that Herbert Demers was no longer here. No longer, indeed, in this life.

Ann Bradley, R.N., looked up from the screen where she'd been searching for records. "Oh, hi, Father. Come to see Mr. Demers?"

It was no surprise that she recognized the priest. By this time, almost all the hospital employees knew him. He'd been there for, in the course of time, all shifts.

"He's still here?"

Bradley nodded grimly. "That's about the way we feel, father. Every time any of us comes on duty, there are a certain few patients we expect to find gone. Mr. Demers certainly is among that group. He doesn't really cause us any trouble. But there's so little we can do for him. Make sure the IV tubes are working. Turn him. Talk to him. Funny thing," she said, thoughtfully, "every once in a while I get the feeling he's trying to tell me something." She shrugged. "Of course he isn't. It's something like a baby: We get the impression we're communicating but, outside of maybe he feels our touch, nothing."

"What if . . ." Carleson hesitated. "What if he did? What if he did communicate with you?"

"What do you mean?"

"The last time I visited him—I know this isn't going to make much sense—but I'd swear he formed words with his lips."

"Really!" Bradley lost all interest in the computer screen. "What did he . . . uh, 'say'?"

"He said . . . he said, 'Help me die.'"

"He said that? Are you sure?"

"Yeah. I really am positive. I'd just told him a story—a joke, actually—about a patient in one of those old-fashioned oxygen tents. Somebody was accidentally standing on the oxygen hose killing the patient." He stopped, then shook his head. "I can't tell you why in the world I was telling somebody as sick as Herbert Demers such a black joke. I guess I just felt I should say something. And I didn't think Herbert would know what I was talking about anyway.

"But, after this joke about a visitor killing the patient, Herbert very slowly and very deliberately mouthed those words: 'Help me die.'"

"Weird!"

"My thought exactly. But what would you do if you had that experience? What if Mr. Demers asked you to help him die? What would you do?"

"Well, I'd note it in the log, make sure the doctor knew about it."

"That's it?"

"It? Oh, you mean would I act on it? Well, no. Of course not. You must know, Father, there are lots of patients—terminals, people with a lot of pain—who want to die. But that's completely out of bounds." There was surprise, mingled with a touch of shock in her manner. As if the last thing she ever expected from a priest was the hint of approval for euthanasia.

"Yeah, sure, of course," Carleson said. "Just wondered. I think I'll go see Herbert now. See if he wants to mouth any more messages."

Carleson's offhand demeanor convinced Bradley that he hadn't been seriously suggesting euthanasia. Just considering all possibilities.

Carleson entered the room. The second bed was vacant and tightly made up, awaiting the next patient.

Herbert Demers lay motionless in his bed, his skin almost as white as the sheet. The rise and fall of his chest was almost imperceptible. Carleson took the elderly man's hand. He felt a pulse—barely.

After a lengthy period of sitting and stroking Demers's hand, Carleson recalled the story he'd just heard in the Emergency Room. What the hell, he thought, it might just work. It certainly was worth a try.

Carleson slid his chair as close as possible to the bed. He squeezed Demers's hand tightly. There was no answering pressure.

"Mr. Demers . . ." Carleson spoke loudly. Then, considering the old man was in a coma, the priest decided to throw caution to the winds and shout. "Mr. Demers . . . Herbert . . ." Carleson shouted, "it's all over. Your family is all grown up. They love you, but they don't need you anymore. You've had a good, long life. It's over now. You can go to God. He's waiting for you. All you have to do is let go. Let go, like you were going to sleep. Let go and go to God, Mr. Demers. Let go and go to God, Herbert."

Carleson repeated the exhortation twice more, in more or less the same words. At the end, he was actually perspiring. He had poured so much of himself into willing Demers into eternity that he was nearly exhausted.

After he had been silent for several minutes, Ann Bradley entered the room. Evidently, she had been waiting in the corridor for Carleson to finish.

She stood next to the bed across from Carleson. She grasped Demers's wrist and held it several seconds. She placed his arm gently on the bed. She placed her fingers on the patient's neck, feeling for the carotid artery. She looked at Carleson and shook her head.

"He's gone?" Carleson was willing at this point to believe in magic.

"No," Bradley said. "Sorry. He's still very much with us. But"—she smiled—"nice try." She left the room.

Carleson remained seated, close to Demers. This doesn't make much sense, he thought. There should be some provision for cases like this. Demers had concluded his life long ago. There was no doubt whatsoever in Carleson's mind that Demers had communicated. He had pleaded for help in dying. So, this was no vegetable lying on this bed. There was a soul in prison, longing to be free.

With nothing much better coming to mind, Carleson decided to recite the rosary aloud. Maybe that familiar prayer would strike a chord in the old man's memory.

Carleson took his beads, signed himself with the cross, and, fingering the crucifix, prayed aloud the Apostles' Creed.

All the while, he thought of Demers's request for help to die. It would be so easy. So easy.

NINETEEN

The networks and national news media giveth. And the networks and national media taketh away. Bradley Kleimer was not—definitely not—disposed to bless either party. *And that,* he thought, *goes double for the local gang.*

In interviews with reporters from the *News* and *Free Press* and all four local TV newscast stations, followed closely by sessions with stringers from national and international news services, Kleimer could see the writing on the wall.

As was their practice, today's media had already tried the case. Unlike most of their previous excursions into the predicted verdict, this time they had acquitted the accused.

Kleimer soon got the impression he would be persecuting—not to be confused with prosecuting—an amalgam of Mother Teresa, Jimmy Carter, and Jeanne d'Arc.

And the deeper the media dug, the worse it got.

In their probe of Carleson's background they were not turning up the mud Kleimer was hoping Quirt was finding; instead, what was emerging was the portrait of a selfless, sacrificing, dedicated missionary, who served the poorest of the poor with quiet, unassuming distinction. Also emerging ever more markedly was the strong image of a bishop who was the antithesis of the talented missionary whom he had forced into a sort of involuntary servitude.

This, for Kleimer, was not a happy turn of events. He remained unshaken in his belief that Carleson had murdered Diego. But something had to happen. Something had to turn this media-triggered momentum around.

The phone rang. Kleimer had long since lost his eagerness

to answer it. But it could scarcely get much worse. And one never knew. . . .

It was Quirt. This could go either way.

"Geez, Brad," Quirt said with emphasis, "have you been listening to the radio or catching the TV news?"

"Most of it," Kleimer said glumly.

"Makes you wonder, don't it?"

"What? You too? Don't tell me *you're* second-guessing us!"

"Oh, no. No, we got the right guy. But I think the media want us to give Carleson a medal instead of life in Jacktown."

"Yeah, well, fortunately the media aren't going to be in the jury box."

"That's true. But it makes you think, don't it? Hey, Brad, is it possible for the prosecution to ask for a change of venue?"

"No—that's just for the defense. Besides, where would we go? This is getting national—hell, international!—coverage." With little hope, Kleimer asked, "Any of your guys come up with anything?"

"Nothin' you could bottle. Williams thinks he's on to something, but it's pretty vague. Nothin' to get your hopes up for."

"Is he there with you?"

"Yeah."

"Put him on."

"It's not much more than a hunch."

"Put him on!"

"Okay, okay. Just a second."

No one had to caution Kleimer to rein in a rampant exuberance. His single comfort, and it wasn't much, was that things couldn't get much worse.

There was a click on the line. "Williams?"

"Yeah. Listen, this is just a feeling—"

"Yeah, yeah," Kleimer interrupted. "Quirt's already given me the disclaimer. Whatcha got?"

"Well, I was checking Carleson's past assignments with Maryknoll headquarters in New York. Most of what I got was the same stuff they've got on radio and TV. It'll be in the papers in more detail later today and tomorrow. But there's one thing I'm pretty sure they haven't got."

"What's that?" Kleimer tensed and leaned over his desk. The pen he'd been toying with he now poised over a legal pad.

"It was a routine question," Williams said. "This priest . . ." Kleimer assumed Williams was checking his notes. "This priest—a Father Weber—was giving me a list of Father Carleson's assignments—missions, I think they call them. Like I said, it was routine. He was giving me names of places—mostly Central and South America—and dates, and if anything outstanding happened because Father Carleson was there . . . you know, like chapels or housing units built, or wells being dug—stuff like that—"

"Yeah, yeah. So?"

"Well, he got to one place—Father Weber, I mean—it's called . . . uh, Sandego. It's in Nicaragua—close to Honduras—and, well, anyway, when he came to that point, this Father Weber hesitated. It wasn't a long pause. But I got the impression that he was surprised by something to do with that assignment. I think he came across something, and he was trying to decide whether to tell me. And then he decided not to."

That was it. Williams apparently was finished. "That's it?"

"I said it wasn't much."

"What did you make of it?"

"It could've been anything. A word that was smudged and Weber was trying to make it out. Maybe his glasses got dirty. Maybe he got tired of reading through all these dates and places."

"Did you press him on it?"

"Yeah. I did. I thought he spent too much time brushing it off as 'nothing.'"

"Your gut feeling?"

"Without any real good reason, I got the idea that Father Weber was covering, uh, I don't know what. Something that, for whatever reason, Maryknoll wants kept quiet. Father Weber—and I'm just guessing—well, I think he knew what was in the record. But then when he was reading me all the assignment stuff, he almost went too far. He stopped himself at the last minute.

"But I gotta tell you: All this is just one king-size guess . . . nothing more."

Kleimer was no longer taking notes. He was tapping his pen on the desk pad. After a minute, he spoke. "Go there!"

"You want me to go to Ossining?"

"That's it. I want you to read that record for yourself. Who knows; it could be the break we need. But we'll never know with you here and that record in New York. See if you can tap a contingency fund. If not, I'll see if I can free up some travel expenses here. Hell, if worse comes to worse, *I'll* pay for it! Just go!"

Kleimer broke the connection and sat lost in thought.

What could it be? Something Maryknoll is trying to hide? Something Carleson did that nobody's proud of? Molesting children? That sort of thing had become more common recently, it seemed. Maybe knocked up a local virgin?

Get serious, Kleimer admonished himself. Carleson may have reached the end of his rope and offed a bishop. *But, be real: He's not the venal type.*

Nicaragua. What comes to mind? The Contras. Civil war. Thugs in uniform. Villages destroyed. What would a guy who didn't give much of a damn for rules and regulations do in a situation like that? Certainly not sit on his hands. He'd do . . . *something*. Maybe something violent. Something that would lead a jury to believe he was no stranger to violence?

Kleimer turned off his daydream machine. Such speculation could inject a little hope into a largely hopeless situation. But, face it: The odds were heavy that Williams would find nothing more than that the Maryknoll priest has emphysema and that when he read as far as Sandego, he just needed to take a breath real bad.

Kleimer wasn't sorry he was sending Williams on this fishing expedition. But he knew there was no way he could count on miracles.

No, he was going to have to work like hell, starting right now. He decided to check the fax machine and see what Quirt's people had turned up on Carleson. Kleimer needed to get inside that guy's skin and find out what made him tick.

*   *   *   *

"Have you seen this afternoon's *Detroit News*?" Phil Mangiapane asked.

"Yeah, I did," Angie Moore replied.

Zoo Tully, focusing on reports, paid only peripheral attention to their conversation.

"I didn't get past the front page," Mangiapane said, "but—wow!—I think they're gonna canonize Father Carleson."

"You should see the rest of their coverage. They've got stuff on a whole bunch of cases that depend on circumstantial evidence, interviews with lawyers, and reactions from just about all the Hispanic spokespeople. I can't remember when I've read about a less likely killer."

"Things don't look good for our side."

"Scratch 'our side,' and make it, 'Things don't look good for Quirt and Kleimer.'"

Tully put down the reports and gave full attention to his sergeants. His squad, like the other six, could boast of outstandingly competent officers. Experience had taught Tully that Moore and Mangiapane were his most dependable. And with this investigation going in many directions, dependable officers were a prime necessity. This was especially true since the case of Bishop Diego's murder had been closed. A suspect had been arrested, arraigned, and was now free on bail. Thus, this ongoing inquiry had to be handled with extreme delicacy.

The squad was expected to move on to the next in the never-ending caseload of homicides. So most of their investigation into the Diego case now would have to be carried out on their own time.

This was no problem for Tully personally. Normally he would be hard-pressed to distinguish between his time and company time. It was a measure of the respect in which he was held by his squad members that they would follow his lead in this sort of situation.

"Let's see what we've got," Tully said. The three were alone in the squadroom. "There's Michael Shell. One of the oldest motives around: alienation of his wife's affections. Opportunity?"

Moore shook her head. "Donnelly checked out that bar he said he was in Sunday afternoon . . . the Lazy Dolphin. The bartender remembers Shell. Donnelly showed the guy several head shots. He picked Shell out of the pack right away."

"What made him so sure?"

"The length of time Shell spent at the bar. The barkeep remembered that Shell got there early to midafternoon and stayed until early evening. He remembers because Shell had been drinking pretty heavily, and he considered cutting him off. But then he talked to Shell and Shell voluntarily switched to a couple of soft drinks. Then he left. But by the time he left, it was a couple of hours at least after the time of Diego's murder."

"Okay," Tully said, "that's a dead end. How about his wife . . . Maria?"

"That's still a live one," Mangiapane said. "Patterson's been following that up. The opportunity was there: She hasn't got anybody who can account for her time that afternoon, or that evening. The motive wasn't all that strong, but it's getting healthier. Patterson's been talking mostly with friends of Mrs. Shell—including some that aren't all that friendly."

"Oh?"

"I got a hunch Moore's gonna kill me for this . . ." Mangiapane smiled. ". . . but Patterson spent some time in the beauty shop where Mrs. Shell goes—like regularly. And while Patterson sat there, the girls talked. Their candid opinion seems to be that there was one hell of a lot more going on between Maria and the bishop than what the lady told us. *They*—her 'friends'—seem to think it's not all that impossible she coulda done it."

"Girl talk?" Moore was sarcastic. "How would she know Diego was at Ste. Anne's rectory that Sunday afternoon?"

"One of her friends was at that Grosse Pointe party," Mangiapane replied. "Patterson heard the lady say she called Maria and told her about the fracas with hubby. She could've guessed easy enough that Diego didn't have another party up his sleeve. Plus he'd probably be too shook up to do anything more than hole up after he almost got beat up. She had nothing to lose going there. When she got there, she found him in the office alone. One word led to another and—bingo!—she creamed him."

"Interesting," Tully commented. "See if Patterson can find if any of those talkative ladies maybe actually heard Mrs. Shell express some threat. It would help.

"What about that priest . . . the one Quirt and Williams interrogated?"

"Father Bell?" Moore said. "Same as he was when Quirt abandoned that theory and latched on to Carleson. Plenty of motive and plenty of opportunity."

Tully sighed. He hated to ask any more of his squad than they already had volunteered. But this was a bona fide lead.

Moore seemed to read Tully's mind. "I'll take Father Bell," she said. "I've already got a list of his closest friends—clergy and parishioners. Let's see if they've got anything interesting—or implicating—to say."

Appreciation was evident in Tully's manner. "Thanks, Angie. Now— and I think this is the last thing—what do we hear from the street?"

Neither Moore nor Mangiapane spoke for several seconds.

"We were just talking about that before you came in, Zoo," Moore said slowly.

"Yeah," Mangiapane agreed. "It's spooky. We've tapped just about every source we've got and . . . nobody'll open up. I talked to a few people who clammed whenever it looked like we were getting close to anything."

"Same with me, Zoo, and with just about all our guys. Which leads to several theories . . . none of 'em with much water. Maybe nobody actually knows. Maybe some vagrant wandered in, saw the cash supply, and decided to help himself. Maybe the guy who did it has so much clout nobody'll rat on him. And maybe . . . maybe it just doesn't involve anybody from the street. Maybe Carleson or Bell or Maria Shell did it.

"Whatever. The bottom line is we've got nothing from the street."

Tully thought for a moment, then, with deliberation, said, "I've got one large marker out. Maybe this is the time to call it in." He glanced briefly at his two sergeants. "You guys follow these leads we talked about. If there's anything on the street, I think I'll know before today's over."

With that, Tully bundled up against a very cold January and hit the bricks.

CHAPTER
TWENTY

Tully would walk the short blocks from Police Headquarters to the Millender Center, on Jefferson across from the Renaissance Center. The Millender was a combination business and residence structure—and posh. RenCen partially blocked what otherwise would have been an impressive view of the river.

As he leaned into the strong wind coming off the water, Tully pondered what he was about to do.

It had been a great many years since he had talked at any length with Tony Wayne. Not since the death of Tony's only son some . . . could it be that long? . . . twenty-five years ago.

Tully, then on the force only a couple of years, had been one of a battery of uniformed officers responding to a shooting. It was not Tully's first exposure to a murder scene. But it was his first experience with a massacre.

He would never forget it.

It happened at the close of the sixties, a time of great unrest in Detroit and in the nation. A white mayor was trying to maintain a tight cork on a surge of civil unrest. The city was trying to recover from one of its most destructive riots. Forces contended for control of organized and random crime. And it probably didn't help that the first waves of the Second Vatican Council were beginning to engulf the world's Catholics.

In Detroit, two powerful men contended for the title of Number One Crime Boss. And should Mafia domination falter—as indeed it eventually did—one of these local crime organizations would reign supreme.

In one corner was Malcolm Ali, a.k.a. the Kingfish. Black, in his early thirties, the Kingfish and his gang held a tight rein on crime within the boundaries of the then confined black ghetto. By no means content with, in effect, overseeing a reservation, the Kingfish's appetite drove him toward dominance of the city—with the suburbs in the offing.

Blocking him, and ever jealous of his territory, was Anthony Wayne. Only a close few were allowed to use his nickname: Mad Anthony. The original General Anthony Wayne had a colorful career as an officer in the Continental Army fighting first the British, then the Native Americans. Detroit still holds a fort named for him. And, of course, Detroit is part of Wayne County.

Tony Wayne was by no means as impetuous and hotheaded as his namesake. But it was only natural that one so ambitious and, at least by his lights, so successful, who lived in this region and whose name was Anthony Wayne, would take on the famous general's nickname. And, as has been observed, only a precious few could use the name with impunity.

It was a matter of territory.

It was anyone's guess whose terrain was more lucrative. It was evident whose was larger. Mad Anthony controlled much of the organizational crime in close to half of Detroit proper as well as in a good part of the suburbs. The Kingfish made do with what was left. Given the nature of these beasts, it was inevitable that they would find themselves on a collision course.

From time to time the "soldiers" of these crime families clashed, always bloodily. Of the two, Tony Wayne was more receptive to peaceful overtures.

And so it was, on a pleasant day in May of 1969, that a tentative probe for peace was scheduled in an unpretentious Coney Island eatery near the Farmers Market on the eastern outskirts of downtown Detroit. The parley was to consist of ten of the top soldiers, five from each family. Among the representatives of Tony Wayne was his only son, Freddy. Elaborate precautions were taken to ensure that none of the participants was armed. Neither food nor drink was served. The restaurant announced it would be closed that night. Participants sat on opposite sides of a long buffet, composed of several small tables pushed together.

Tony Wayne's group took the floor for the first presentation. Freddy opened with the preamble to their initial offer.

Imperceptibly, the Kingfish group began to slide their chairs back from the table. Since it was his territory, the Kingfish knew of something Wayne's group had not discovered in their search of the premises—a concealed trapdoor dating back to prohibition days. It had remained unused since that time. Now the sound of scraping chairs masked its use.

As young Freddy Wayne read the documents he assumed would be the basis for their discussion, beneath the table a portion of what seemed to be a solid wooden floor was moving.

The next few seconds had been carefully and repeatedly rehearsed.

The trapdoor flew open. The buffet tables were upended as three men carrying automatic weapons erupted from the basement.

Chairs were overturned as the Wayne group sprang to its feet and stampeded toward the back wall. Several instinctively reached for the weapons that had been taken from them.

The shooting seemed as if it would go on forever.

The bodies of the victims jerked in a macabre dance of death. Some extended their arms and hands as if these ineffective extremities could ward off the bullets that tore through flesh and bone.

In seconds the slaughter was over.

Kingfish's men advanced cautiously. Each of the victims was checked to make certain none lived. All were beyond death. The victors stayed only long enough to congratulate each other.

Proprietors of neighboring businesses, after waiting to make sure the shooting was over, called the police.

Among those first at the scene was Patrolman Alonzo Tully. He alone was able to identify those of the victims who still had a face left. And he could guess the identity of the others. Even in those early days, Zoo Tully lived for his work: He had memorized the names and faces of the mug shots of both the Kingfish's and Mad Anthony's gangs.

Tully had never before seen such carnage. However, it was the attitude of several of his fellow officers that surprised him. Once the identities of the corpses had been tentatively established, several of the officers treated the event as if it were a cause for celebration.

Five hoods wasted. Five men the cops would no longer be bothered with. Five reasons to make merry. Tully noted a sergeant using his nightstick to stir the brains of one victim. There seemed little if any respect being paid to this crime scene—or to the victims of this crime. And Tully well knew the prime importance of preserving intact the scene of the crime as the one and only inerrant clue.

The uniformed detachment was closely followed by several homicide detectives. Outstanding among them was the stereotypical larger-than-life Sergeant Walt Koznicki. His fame in the department had little to do with size or strength. More impressive was his meteoric advancement. He had been scarcely out of his rookie phase when he was tapped for the prestigious Homicide Division. After nine years, his record for solving cases was storied.

It took Koznicki only a few minutes to assess this situation.

It was a gangland slaying of a rival gang. And the crime scene was being trivialized by some cops who were celebrating the destruction of enemy forces. Forgotten was the responsibility for solving a crime. This was not a legal execution; it was mass murder. The police officer's duty was to determine who had done it, find proof, and make the arrest.

Instead, these officers had by and large contaminated the crime scene.

This execution was a professional job that had been done by the numbers. There would be precious few clues left behind, and most of them, Koznicki expected, had been obliterated or tainted by the careless and sloppy approach now evident.

Koznicki, somewhat out of character, blistered the police who had responded to this call. A thoroughly embarrassed silence supplanted the former festive scene.

It was then that Koznicki discovered Alonzo Tully.

It was not Tully's place to reprimand superior officers for their unprofessional conduct. But, quietly, he had been surveying this for what it was, the scene of a crime.

Carefully steering clear of the blood and gore, he had uncovered something. He called Sergeant Koznicki over and showed what he'd found.

Freddy Wayne had sustained multiple gunshot wounds to the head. He was undoubtedly dead before he hit the floor. His body was in a curious position, arms and hands flexed as if holding something. But only a scrap of paper remained clutched between thumb and forefinger of his right hand. Scattered about were several sheets of paper, the top sheet missing its lower corner. Tully explained his theory: These must have been what Wayne had been holding when he was shot.

Evidently one of the killers had ripped the papers out of Wayne's hand and then discarded them. If Tully had not recovered them, they would have been saturated by the conglomerate blood that spread across the floor.

With great care, so as not to destroy any latent prints, Tully and Koznicki studied the sheets of paper. Clearly, the whole constituted a position statement, an overture toward peace on the part of the Tony Wayne faction.

Whoever had ripped the papers from Freddy's hands must have glanced through them and, finding nothing of consequence, discarded them. That was a mistake. And if the killer's prints could be found, it would be a mistake compounded.

Koznicki gingerly handed the papers to one of the police technicians who had just arrived. To aid the techs in a projected search for identities, Tully enumerated at least fifteen of the Kingfish's top hoods. Both Tully and Koznicki simply assumed that these killers belonged to the Kingfish gang.

For Koznicki and Tully, it was respect at first sight.

Tully wanted to follow this investigation through, and he was invited in by Koznicki.

It proved to be one of those cases when everything worked in favor of the good guys. On the sheets of paper that had been cast aside, three sets of prints were found: those of Fred Wayne, his secretary, and Juahn Carter, the Kingfish's right-hand man.

Carter was easily located and picked up. No credible way could he explain away those prints.

Sergeant Koznicki, with Alonzo Tully sitting in, explained with seeming concern Carter's options. He could remain silent and take the fall. In which case he would most certainly be convicted and sentenced to life in prison with no possibility of parole. In which case, additionally, Mad Anthony most assuredly would put out a contract for his son's killer. The life sentence would thus be considerably abbreviated— by execution.

Or he could cooperate with the police and implicate everyone who had participated in this massacre, including the one who masterminded it—the Kingfish. No deal without the Kingfish.

At that point, Koznicki left the room so that Tully, with the same degree of consideration that Koznicki had shown, could explain, in as many ways as possible, these options, over and over again.

It required many and assorted explanations to get through to Carter the value of fingering the Kingfish. Carter was only too aware of the Kingfish's talent for torture before execution. In comparison, prison seemed a downright pleasant choice. Tully reminded Carter that Mad Anthony's men would be waiting in Jackson—and there was little the authorities could do about that.

On the other hand, for his cooperation with the police and the prosecuting attorney's office, a deal might be worked out whereby Carter could vanish from the scene and surface elsewhere to live to a ripe old age in peace and freedom.

Understandably, Carter's confidence in the law's ability to protect him needed much reinforcement. The very name of the Kingfish was enough to send shudders up and down Carter's spine.

Finally, with the encouragement of a near-exhausted Patrolman Tully, Carter saw the wisdom of the police offer. Carter sang beautifully, giving the prosecutor's office seven convictions of first degree murder. The Kingfish himself was the eighth.

The conclusion to this affair:

Malcolm Ali, a.k.a. the Kingfish, was sentenced to life without parole. He lived in relative peace in Jackson Prison for almost a year. That lull led the authorities to believe that the Kingfish might live many more years in captivity. As a result, they relaxed their guard . . . and the Kingfish was found eviscerated with a homemade knife.

In much the same way, nine years prior, that Walt Koznicki had been inducted into the elite Homicide Division, Koznicki now became rabbi for Alonzo Tully, who promptly became "Zoo" to his fellow detectives.

Tony Wayne exacted revenge for his son's murder. And, gathering power steadily, Mad Anthony waited for what he foresaw as the Taming of the Mafia. Eventually he became Numero Uno of metropolitan Detroit's crime arena.

Finally, although Tony Wayne well knew who had murdered his son, he was appreciative to the young officer who had pursued the investigation so professionally instead of writing it off, thankful that the gangs were wiping each other out.

In effect, Tully had inadvertently set up the Kingfish by getting him convicted. In any event, Wayne would have gotten the Kingfish; it was just made easier when the law put him in a cage. Two reasons for feeling obligated to Alonzo Tully.

So, after Kingfish's trial and conviction but well before his execution, Mad Anthony arranged a clandestine meeting with Tully. In an emotionless tone, Wayne thanked Tully. Wayne laconically declared himself in debt to Tully. Mad Anthony owed Zoo Tully one—one very big favor.

Wisely, Tully had not cashed in his premium, then or thereafter.

But now Tully was walking the streets of Detroit, intent on finding out if the debt was still on the counter and collectible.

TWENTY-ONE

The office-and-business directory listed Metro Development on the second floor.

The title did nothing to explain what sort of business Metro Development was. It wasn't supposed to; Metro Development did whatever Mad Anthony Wayne wanted it to do. And the business it did changed, sometimes by the hour.

The attractive receptionist smiled when Lieutenant Tully asked to see Mr. Wayne. The smile said, Thank you for dropping by but you've got a snowball's chance in hell of seeing Tony Wayne.

Tully returned the smile and showed the receptionist his badge. That helped. Tully gave his name, rank, and position in the Homicide Division. That helped more. Still, no entree, merely a phone check with someone with more clout. Tully was invited, sweetly, to take a seat and someone would be here shortly.

Ten minutes later, a man who did not fit the adverb "shortly" appeared. He was one of the largest men Tully had ever seen.

"Come this way, please."

It can speak—and politely—Tully noted.

Even though he was quite good at this sort of thing, Tully would have had trouble retracing their route. As near as he could make out, the journey through the Millender Center, from office to residential suite, was a series of going down to go up and vice versa.

Finally, they were in the luxury suite of Tony Wayne. Due mostly to the back-lighting from the windows, Tully did not immediately recognize the figure behind the king-size desk—until the figure stood and stepped forward.

In the past twenty-five years, Tully had seen Wayne's photo likeness in newspapers, magazines, and on television with irregular frequency. He had seen the mobster fleetingly in person a few times. But this was the first time in all these years that Tully had the opportunity to study the man.

Mad Anthony seemed shorter than Tully had remembered him. Wayne stood about five-feet-seven or -eight. His salt-and-pepper hair was wavy and tight to his scalp. He was trim and moved smoothly. His complexion, just as Tully remembered it, was swarthy. Whether that was its natural shade or the result of overexposure to the sun, Tully could not say.

Most interesting was Wayne's expression. It was totally ambiguous. Was Wayne happy to receive his visitor, or was he about to explode with mad fury?

The gigantic guard stood just inside the door, almost leaning against it in an at-ease stance.

Wayne stopped several feet short of Tully. "It's *Lieutenant* Tully now, isn't it?"

"The department would be embarrassed if I was still a patrolman."

There was that enigmatic look again. Did Wayne see the humor in Tully's statement?

"Come, sit down." Wayne gestured toward a padded straight-back chair in front of the desk. Tully seated himself, and Wayne returned to his high-back chair. "It's been a long while. . . ." Wayne paused. "Twenty-five years."

Tully nodded. "Twenty-five years. You remember?"

"Like it was yesterday. Even now there's an emptiness in my heart. Freddie was a good boy." Wayne pinched the bridge of his nose. To forestall a tear?

Yes, a good boy, thought Tully. If his son had lived, Mad Anthony probably would be considering retirement so that Freddie could take over "the business."

"I remember too," Wayne said, "you performed a service for me then."

"It wasn't that much," Tully stated in all honesty. "I did my job."

"True. But we didn't expect it. Hell, we thought the cops'd be glad to get rid of us." Was there a hint of emotion on his face? "You almost make a guy respect the law." He gazed at Tully thoughtfully. "Anyway, you treated Freddie with dignity . . . like a person who'd been wronged. I don't forget that."

"That's why I've come."

"I thought as much."

Tully shifted in his chair and inched forward. "Twenty-five years ago you offered me a favor."

Wayne waved his hand. "It's been an uncashed check all these years. Is this the time?"

"You know of the murder of the Mexican bishop?"

"He was a fool."

"A fool?"

"All that money . . . there for the taking."

"You knew?"

"Hell, everyone knew. It was just a matter of time."

"The street's hard to read. Something seems to be going on, but we can't break the silence."

Was that amusement ever so briefly on Wayne's face? "What do you think?"

"My best guess would be . . . it's not a heavyweight. That wasn't enough bread for anybody to risk his reputation and a lucky collar. It just wasn't enough.

"On the other hand, it wasn't a drifter or a street punk. A guy like that would get coughed up. We've got some pretty reliable snitches, but they're not talking. They'd give the guy to us if he meant nothing to anybody."

"So . . ."

"So I figure somebody important is protecting the guy."

Wayne leaned forward. "You have an excellent suspect under arrest."

"The priest? Maybe. But I've got a feeling."

"And you want the guy from the street."

Tully nodded.

"This will clear the table for us."

Again Tully nodded.

"You're sure you want to spend your marker on this?" It was obvious he thought that Tully was wasting a valuable coupon.

"Yes," Tully said firmly.

Wayne nodded curtly. "By tomorrow morning."

"You'll contact me?"

"Yes." Wayne stood. Tully, taking the cue, also stood.

"Albert will show you out."

Tully followed the giant out the door. There was no conversation. There was no intimation of any conversation.

Had he been asked, Tully would have guessed the bodyguard's name to be Tiny. But . . . *Albert*? Not even Big Al?

The journey back to the outside world was as confusing as the trek in. However Wayne had managed it, it was a damned clever maze.

As he left the Millender, Tully glanced at the directory. Whatever business Metro Development was in, Tully knew of one product. It would be whoever the street delivered to the police tomorrow through the good offices of Metro Development.

Tully felt satisfied with his transaction. But deep down he wondered if he might have squandered a most valuable marker, as Wayne had implied.

Whatever. The die was cast. More than likely he would soon slap cuffs on the killer of Bishop Diego.

TWENTY-TWO

Tuesday was drawing to a close. A fatigued Father Koesler drove over to Ste. Anne's for the vigil service for Bishop Diego. The funeral, or Mass of Resurrection, would be held tomorrow morning. The vigil, as well as the Mass, essentially was a prayerful expression of faith in a life after death in the heaven promised by Jesus Christ.

The church was fully lighted. It had been a long time since the old structure had held so large a congregation. Special police detachments were handling crowd control. Officers were stationed throughout the church for security purposes.

Also in the church, making a nuisance of itself, was the camera crew from Los Angeles. In an unguarded moment, Father McCauley had signed a document giving permission for the filming on parish property.

Near the sanctuary, before the altar, Bishop Diego's coffin lay on a bier. The corpse was dressed in Mass vestments. The vestments were white, as was the miter on the bishop's head.

Ste. Anne's might have passed for a ski lodge housing an extremely affable group. The crowd, largely Hispanic, moved about the church in serpentine fashion, people greeting long-lost friends and friends they'd shopped with this morning. There was even a mariachi band playing in what used to be known as the organ loft.

The only activity that might be termed "orderly" was the double line that stretched from the sanctuary to the front doors. The lines were for people who wanted to "pay their respects" at the bier.

A generous supply of clergymen was in attendance. Most of them joined the viewing lines and, after a moment at the casket, gathered in the gospel side of the sanctuary. It was not a section reserved for priests;

the first two or three had probably wandered over there and the precedent was set.

Two more priests arrived at the casket. They peered in, vacuuming every detail from the supershined black shoes to the bejeweled miter.

"Looks pretty good, doesn't he?" said Father Henry Dorr.

"For a dead guy, yeah," Father Frank Dempsey replied.

"Don't be funny." Dorr bent from the waist and studied the right side of the corpse, particularly about the neck. "Look here. They said he got whacked on the back of the head. It must've been some blow to kill the guy. But I can't see anything."

Dempsey, following Dorr's observations, also bent down to see if he could find the indent. "No. I guess they must've patched it up somehow. I don't know how they do that. Like Ronald Reagan used to say, 'Progress is our most important product.'"

"That was about General Electric, not mortuary science."

"That reminds me . . ." Dempsey straightened up and leaned over the body, studying Diego's bishop's ring. ". . . did you hear about the couple who got a marriage license and went to a judge to get married?" He didn't wait for a response. "The judge looks at the license and says to the groom, 'Are you John A. Brown?' And the groom says, 'No. My name's John B. Brown.'

"The judge says, 'Take this back to the clerk and have him correct it.'

"So the couple comes back, and the judge looks at the license again, and says to the bride, 'Are you Mary B. Smith?' And she says, 'No. I'm Mary C. Smith.'

"So the judge sends them back again for a correction. Then, they appear again before the judge. The license is correct now. But, for the first time, the judge notices a small boy standing between the bride and the groom.

"'Who is this young lad?' the judge asks. The groom says, 'That's our son, judge.' And the judge says, 'I hate to tell you this, but he's a technical bastard.'

"And the groom says, 'That's a funny thing, judge. That's what the clerk just said about you.'"

"Very funny," Dorr said, "but what's the point?"

"Your remark about Reagan and the product he used to peddle. You're being a technical bastard."

"This is a church!"

"Perfectly good Anglo-Saxon word."

What with the hubbub in the church, no one else could make out what the two were saying. But, hey, they were priests. And they were paying special attention to the dead bishop's neck and to his ring. There must be something going on.

The interest was passed from person to person so that from that time on each of the faithful who reached the casket bent double to see—God knew what—at the back of Diego's head. The procedure slowed the line considerably.

Dorr and Dempsey moved on to join the other priests.

"Hi, Bob," Dorr greeted Father Koesler, who had already been through the viewing line. "Good crowd."

"Numerically, I'll give you," Dempsey said.

"What's that supposed to mean?" Dorr asked.

"Well, look at who's here." Dempsey's gesture encompassed everyone in the church. "You see any of Diego's fancy friends? Any of the money people?" The question became rhetorical. The church was filled with blue-collar Hispanics.

"So? All the better for the bishop. The common people are represented," Dorr said.

"Not all the common people," Dempsey corrected. "See any of the Hispanic leaders? These people here are the ones who didn't have a clue to what Diego was doing. These are the people who were just happy one of their own became a bishop to take special care of them. They rejoiced when he came here. They never saw him except maybe at a confirmation or a parish festival. They heard he gave money to the deserving poor. They didn't know he didn't give a damn about them."

"That's a generalization," Dorr protested.

"He's got a point, Henry," Koesler said. "Go ahead and take a careful look. None of the local leaders are here. I guess Diego didn't fool all of the people all of the time."

"And," Dempsey added, "the priests are here just to make sure he's dead."

"Speaking of priests," Koesler said, "I wonder why there aren't any Dallas priests here for the funeral? Maybe they'll get here for the Mass tomorrow."

"The Dallas contingent?" Dempsey snorted. "They're having a fiesta down there."

"Come on," Dorr protested.

"It's true," Dempsey insisted. "They knew he was a three-dollar bill before we got to know but not love him."

"Really? I thought his social climbing started when he became an auxiliary here," Koesler said.

"Down there," Dempsey explained, "he traded on his good looks. That's how he made a name for himself. He also had a talent, even down there, for raising money. His archbishop got nothing but glowing reports about him. Well, why not? He was popular. And with his movie-picture looks, there wasn't a hint of any hanky-panky. And the SOB poured money into diocesan collections. That's how come, when Boyle went looking for an Hispanic auxiliary, the Dallas power structure pointed their collective finger at Diego."

*   *   *   *

Ted Walberg and Armand Turner had worked out a deal whereby they each had been named coproducer of the made-for-TV movie, "Death Wears a Red Hat." As the filming progressed, they were beginning to work out a marginally acceptable relationship.

Just now, Turner, complete with sound and camera people, was working the church floor, while Walberg was supervising the filming from the organ loft and other precarious vantages.

"This is very good," Walberg said into the mike that connected him with Turner. "Lots and lots of action. Maybe too much. I'm not sure anybody will believe this actually could happen in real life."

"I tend to agree, Teddy," Turner said. "But we can always edit this down, or out. What'll definitely be a keeper are these lines of people waiting to view the body. They get serious when they get in these lines. No more dancing to the mariachi band."

"You're right, Mondo. But there's something going on up front in that line that doesn't play."

"What? What's that?"

"The people, just recently, seem to be bending over when they get to the casket. They seem to be looking for something. But I'll be damned if I know what."

"Okay. I'm making my way to the casket. But can you say again? What is it they're doing?"

"Bending . . . bowing . . . I'm not sure."

"A curtsy?"

"No, dummy! I know a curtsy when I see one. They're bending from the waist. But I'm damned if I can figure out what the hell they're doing."

"I'll check it out." Turner, complete with camera, sound, and lighting people, made his way through the crowd to the front of the church. He watched the odd ritual, as people continued to do precisely what Walberg had described from his perch in the organ loft.

Turner approached a woman who had just completed the bow and was moving away from the casket. "Can you speak English?" he inquired.

"Yes."

"What was it you were just doing?"

"When?"

"Just now . . . when you bent down by the casket."

"I don't know."

"You don't know? Then why did you do it?"

"Everybody else was doing it. I think maybe it's got something to do with the dead bishop. I was never at a bishop's funeral before. Maybe that's the way we pay our respects to a bishop . . . I don't know."

"Did you get that, Teddy? She doesn't know. We'll have to check with some expert . . . no, not Lieutenant Quirt—hey, wait a minute! This is good! There's a woman sobbing—real quiet like—right next to the camera. Real emotion! The real stuff! Did you get that, guys?"

"I missed it," the cameraman admitted. "I was tight in with the dame you were talking to. But she's still doing it. I'll get her now. Lenny, turn the sun-gun around."

The woman, startled by the sudden flood of light, and sensing she had become the center of attention, stopped in midsob. A tear hung halfway down her cheek. A surprised look on her face, she just stood there, bewildered.

Turner approached her and, in a reassuring tone, said, "That's all right. We wanted a shot of you crying. Could you do it again?"

"*Que?*"

"Could you cry some more? Nothing hysterical. Just the way you were doing."

"*Que?*"

"Don't you understand English?"

"*Que?*"

"Oh damn! Goddam!"

The man next in line after the now-dry madonna said, "This for TV?"

"Well, the movies, really."

"Movies! You turn camera on my wife here. I make her cry!"

*　　*　　*　　*

Father Henry Dorr motioned for both Fathers Koesler and Dempsey to lean in so they could hear him.

"Have you noticed," Dorr said, "who isn't here?"

"You mean," Koesler said, "besides the aforementioned wealthy friends of the late bishop, and the Hispanic leaders?"

"Yeah. Who else?"

"I suppose you're referring to Ernie Bell and Don Carleson," Koesler said.

"The suspects," Dempsey said with a broad grin. "They didn't return to the scene of the crime . . . eh?"

"Don't you ever get serious?" Henry Dorr chided. But then, somewhat thoughtfully, he added, "Wouldn't you expect them to be here? That is, unless they feel embarrassed to be here. Unless they feel guilty about something." His tone made their absence seem singularly significant.

"You mean," Dempsey countered, "the fact that both Bell and Carleson are absent tonight means there was a conspiracy? They both killed Diego?"

Dorr clearly had not considered that possibility. His original, not articulated, point being that at least one of the two had a guilty motive for not showing up for the wake. But now that a connection had been drawn between the two priests, Dorr liked the idea. So he adopted it. "Well, why not? Maybe the cops haven't thought of that. They both had a motive and the opportunity. Maybe one held Diego while the other hit him."

"Henry!" Koesler was horrified. "I can't imagine any priest killing a bishop . . . anybody, for that matter. And you've got two priests in a murder conspiracy? Really, Henry, that's too much!"

"Oh, all right," Dorr said. "But if that's the way this works out, remember you heard it here first."

"We'll remember, Henry," Dempsey said. "And, speaking of confusion . . ."

"Nobody said anything about confusion, Frank," Koesler said.

"I know, I know," Dempsey replied. "But I heard this joke about confusion today—"

"Frank, this is a wake!" Dorr reminded.

"It seems," Dempsey plowed on, "that this Irish maid went to confession and confessed that the butler had his way with her. So the priest asked, 'Was this against your will?' 'No,' the maid says, 'it was against the china cabinet . . . and it would've done your heart good to hear them dishes rattle.'"

Dorr affected shock. Koesler's shoulders shook with laughter.

"Well," Dempsey said, "will you look who's coming down the aisle!"

"Stan Kowalzki." Koesler identified the bishop, the center of his procession.

Garbed in a flowing white cape, holding his crosier and wearing the tall miter and preceded by some priests in cassock and surplice, the retired auxiliary bishop smiled and nodded to everyone as he passed by.

"Well," Dorr said, "that'll tell you something. They send an auxiliary bishop for the vigil service—and a retired one at that!"

"I don't think that's so odd," Koesler said. "The Cardinal will probably be here for the Mass tomorrow. He's probably busy tonight."

"This isn't a mere priest lying in state," Dorr insisted. "This is a bishop. Boyle should be here. Mark my words, there's a statement being made here."

*   *   *   *

"Mondo! What the hell is that going down the center of the church?"

"I don't know, Teddy," Turner said. "Wait! I've seen this getup before. Richard Burton in *Becket*. It's a bishop."

"Get this! Get as many closeups as you can," Walberg directed. "Great panoply! Right out of the Middle Ages. God, don't Catholics know how to throw a funeral!"

CHAPTER
TWENTY-THREE

It was now 11:00 P.M. Tuesday. The vigil service was long over. The boys had gathered in a couple of the large rooms on the first floor of Ste. Anne's rectory. Clerical collars and vestments had been put aside.

It was customary when a significant number of priests gathered that they would engage in shop talk, friendly conversation, and a bit of clerical gossip. And when the opportunity presented itself, someone was likely to break out the cards and poker chips.

And so it was tonight. The only thing different from the days of yore, some twenty-or-so years before, was that now the rooms were rarely smoke-filled and the stakes were generally not as high.

The game was going on in the large dining room. The smaller room was given over more to conversation, plus, in one corner, Bishop Kowalzki was playing chess with Father Dempsey. Standing near the chess players, only vaguely interested in the game, were Fathers Dorr and Koesler.

"Does this sort of give you the creeps?" Dorr asked.

"What?"

"Being so close to where Diego was killed."

"I hadn't thought of it . . . until now. I wish you hadn't mentioned it," Koesler added. "I guess I just got lost in having the gang around. But, okay, now that you brought it up, yeah, it *is* creepy being just a few rooms away from a murder scene. I don't think I want to think about it."

"I suppose Don Carleson is upstairs in his room." Dorr's eyes lifted in the general direction of the second-floor bedrooms.

Koesler turned a trifle edgy. "Any particular reason why you want to connect the fact that Don's room is not all that far from Diego's office?"

"No, no . . ." Dorr was patently apologetic. "I was just wondering how he can sleep."

"You mean with his conscience?"

"No, with all the noise going on down here. You're getting awfully defensive, aren't you, Bob?"

"Maybe. But I have it from your own lips that you think he did it. Maybe even in a conspiracy with Ernie Bell!" It was obvious that Koesler considered both theories preposterous.

Their attention was drawn to the chess game. Bishop Kowalzki was telling a story while continuing to move his players. And when the bishop told a story, he expected others to listen.

"I think you were there—at Jimmy Welch's retirement party. . . ." The bishop was speaking to Dempsey, his opponent in the chess game.

"That was back in September!" Dempsey wondered about the odor of a story that old.

"Yes, it was," the bishop acknowledged, "but if you haven't heard it yet, you should. You remember it was very warm that day."

"Not really."

"You didn't think it was warm?"

"No, I don't remember."

"Well, it was warm, unseasonably warm," the bishop said. "I remember because I was just in shirtsleeves, no clerical collar. When I came up to the back door of the rectory, who gets there at the same moment but Irene Casey, the editor of the *Detroit Catholic*. Well, anyway, the housekeeper is waiting at the back door to welcome the guests. For a moment no one says anything. Then I remember I'm not wearing anything that would show I'm a clergyman. But I figure the housekeeper will recognize my name. So I just say, 'Kowalzki.' And the housekeeper smiles and says, 'The party is downstairs. You can go right down, Mr. and Mrs. Kowalzki.'"

"Checkmate."

"What?"

"Checkmate." Dempsey indicated the chessboard now almost emptied of the bishop's men, with Kowalzki's king decidedly mated.

The bishop smiled and swept his king from the board. "Another game?"

"I don't think so. Thanks," Dempsey said. "It's getting kind of late.

I should be heading back soon." Dempsey stood and joined Koesler and Dorr. He yawned elaborately, striving for a convincing indication that he was indeed tired. The truth was that he didn't want to go through another game with the bishop.

The bishop, receiving no takers, left the room and prepared to depart the party.

"Nice enough guy," Dempsey said, "but he plays chess like a member of the hierarchy."

"What's that supposed to mean?" Koesler asked.

"Sort of a full-court press . . ."

"To mix metaphors."

"Yes. Well, he just comes at you with everything he's got. Tries to overwhelm you. It works only if he catches you unprepared. It's sort of strange seeing everything used like a pawn. Knights, rooks, bishops—anything but the queen—and sometimes even her. It's an interesting maneuver the first couple of times you see it. After that, it gets dull in a hurry."

"But he's a nice guy," Dorr said.

"I said that," Dempsey said.

"And he conducted a sensitive, touching vigil service, I thought," Koesler said.

"Yeah, I thought so too," Dorr agreed.

"And he had determined opposition," Dempsey said.

"Huh?"

"Those Hollywood freaks who're doing the movie. They were about as intrusive as they could get. Cameras and those bright lights right in the bishop's face. I swear, I don't know how he kept from telling them to get the hell out of there."

"For the life of me," Koesler said, "I can't figure out how they can make a movie out of this when no one knows for sure or how it's going to end."

"They'll probably film the guilty party from a great distance," Dempsey said.

They all laughed.

"Did you see how they had good news and bad news in the paper today?" Dorr asked.

"The movie company?" Koesler said. "No."

"They lost Chris Noth."

"The detective from 'Law and Order'?"

"Yeah. He was supposed to play a Detroit Homicide detective in this movie."

"I assume that was the bad news," Koesler said. "What's the good?"

"Charles Durning is supposed to play Bishop Diego," Dorr said.

"Charles Durning as a Hispanic bishop!" Koesler said.

"He can do anything," Dorr affirmed. "There goes somebody who could play himself."

"Huh?"

Dorr inclined his head toward the window. Koesler and Dempsey followed his gaze.

Clearly visible just outside the rectory was someone bundled up in a black overcoat and black hat. He was entering an automobile. There was no doubt who it was. It was Father Donald Carleson.

* * * *

The car moved slowly down St. Antoine. Not so slowly that it would attract attention, just well within the speed limit.

It was close to midnight and bitterly cold. The actual temperature was fifteen above zero. The wind coming off the river chilled the skin to ten below.

Encountering another car was an infrequent event. People out driving at this hour in this area and in this weather were going to night jobs, or coming home from a party, or were cops, or criminals pushing women or dope or stealing cars or parts of cars. And there were few of any of the above.

The car slowed as it approached Detroit's Receiving Hospital. There was no thought of parking on the street. Odds heavily favored the vehicle's disappearance before the owner's return.

Instead, the car glided down the drive to the parking garage. A parking stub jumped halfway out of the machine. The ticket was plucked; the bar lifted. At this hour there were few other cars. The driver pulled into the nearest empty space.

He got out, paused, and looked about. He could see no one.

He turned and retraced his direction. He walked toward the Emergency receiving area. He paused and looked through the glass exterior of the Emergency Department. A nurse and an intern looked up from their preparation of an empty gurney. They looked in his direction for a few seconds and waved.

He proceeded past the Emergency Department and entered the hospital proper.

The attendant at the information desk near the far wall looked up with drowsy eyes and nodded at the visitor.

He took an elevator to the third floor. He was the only occupant.

When the elevator doors opened at the third floor, he leaned out into the corridor; finding it empty, he left the elevator and walked at a normal pace down the hall.

The lighting was dim and restful. Soft sounds came from rooms as he passed. In a few, television told bedtime stories. The low hum of hospital machines and monitors was a backdrop to sounds of misery and pain, fitful moans and sporadic sharp cries.

He halted. At the end of the corridor, some fifteen or twenty yards away, was a brightly lit nursing station, the nerve center of this floor full of illness and affliction.

He stood motionless. The nurse at her station looked up. She was startled to see him. She would have been startled to see anyone at this hour. She recognized him. Reassured, her head bent again to her task.

He entered a room. It was a double room, but only one bed was occupied.

He approached the occupied bed. For several moments, he stood looking down at the patient wordlessly.

In the dim light, the patient was almost indistinguishable from the white sheets and blanket.

He felt along the patient's neck for the carotid artery. There was a pulse. A very, very weak pulse.

His hand moved across the patient's face. There was no oxygen tube in the nostrils.

He carefully removed the pillow from behind the patient's head and placed it over the patient's face.

He held the pillow tight down over the patient's face. There was no resistance. The patient's fingers moved as if reflecting distress.

There was no change in the position of either person for several minutes.

Finally he removed the pillow and felt once more for the carotid artery. This time there was no throb. He checked carefully. No pulse.

He lifted the patient's head and carefully replaced the pillow, resting the dead patient's head on it. He stood for a moment with head bowed. Then he left the room and, without looking back, went directly to the elevator.

On the main floor, he exited the elevator and walked briskly out of the foyer.

He stopped the car at the exit attendant's booth, handed him the parking ticket, paid the fee, stuck the receipt in his pocket, and drove off into the night.

As he headed away from the hospital, he shuddered. He turned the car's heater on full blast.

CHAPTER

TWENTY-FOUR

Lieutenant Alonzo Tully was the first to arrive each morning. He had added reason yesterday and today. He was walking a fine line.

Officially, as far as Homicide was concerned, the investigation into the murder of Bishop Ramon Diego was concluded. There was no dearth of other homicides waiting to be solved.

But Zoo Tully, with the rest of his squad, continued the search for Diego's killer. Much of this work had to be done on a volunteer basis on the officers' own time.

Now, Tully was playing catch up, trying to dig into cases to which he would be giving his complete attention were it not for the Diego case.

As Tully studied the folders on his desk, Sergeant Phil Mangiapane entered the squad room. They greeted each other in the morning manner of co-workers not yet fully awake. Mangiapane sat at his desk and checked his calendar for the day. Then he looked over at Tully. "Did you get your phone call yet?"

Tully, without looking up, shook his head.

The phone rang. Mangiapane looked startled, as if his question had caused the phone to ring. He looked at Tully, who sat eyeing the phone but making no move to answer it.

The sergeant picked up the phone. "Homicide, Mangiapane. Yeah, just a minute." He looked across at Tully. "It's for you, Zoo."

"Tully."

"Lieutenant, the one you're looking for is at 3330 West Lafayette. There will be several people at that address, all stoned out of their minds. You should have no trouble getting in."

Tully was sure he recognized the voice. It was Tony Wayne's man-mountain bodyguard. Tully, who still thought of him as "Tiny," was amazed that Albert, as Wayne had called him, was this articulate.

"Are you calling for Mr. Wayne?"

Albert completely ignored the question. "Your subject's name is Julio—that's spelled with a 'J'—Ramirez."

Tully whistled soundlessly. "The kid brother of Pedro Ramirez?"

There was a slight pause. Tully took the pause to mean this was an accurate identification. Tully was certain that had he been mistaken, Albert would have corrected him.

"That is all you need to know." The connection was broken.

"Let's go, Manj. We got some garbage to pick up."

*   *   *   *

Brad Kleimer had been awake for some time. He had eaten break- fast and was on his second cup of coffee. He gazed out the picture window of his downtown high-rise apartment. He was thinking of a million things. The buzz of the phone brought him back to reality.

"Kleimer."

"Brad, this is Quirt. I got something I think you oughtta know."

"Yeah?"

"That old man died last night . . . the old geezer that Carleson visited all the time."

"Who?"

"The old man. You remember. . . ." A pause. "Demers, Herbert Demers. He was in Receiving. You remember. . . ."

"Okay. Herbert Demers. So?"

"Well, they were going to release the body to the next of kin. But I put a hold on it. I figured we better not miss a single bet."

"What do you mean, George?"

"What I mean is the old man probably just croaked. But Carleson used to visit him just about every day."

"Is there any indication it wasn't natural causes?"

"Well, no. But I didn't want to take any chances. . . ."

"So what've you done?"

"I sent the body to the morgue. Asked Doc Moellmann to give it top priority." In the face of Kleimer's silence, Quirt began to have doubts. "You got a problem with any of this—what I've done?"

"No, no, George. You're absolutely right. We shouldn't overlook anything.

"By the way, while I've got you on the line, did you hear anything from Williams yet—from Maryknoll in New York?"

"No. Wasn't he supposed to report to you?"

"Yeah, that's right. But I haven't heard from him. I thought maybe you had—"

"Nope, not a word."

"Okay. Keep me posted."

Kleimer hung up.

*   *   *   *

"The big question is: Is he gonna live?" Mangiapane wanted to know.

Tully's mouth tightened. "The answer is: I don't know."

"It was the easiest bust I ever was on."

"Yeah, it's not hard to bring 'em in when they're half dead."

Tully and Mangiapane had gone to the Lafayette address, a house in the shadow of Ste. Anne's church. There were three occupants, a man and two young women. All were unconscious. The officers were able to rouse one of the women sufficiently for her to identify herself and the other two. The man was, indeed, Julio Ramirez.

Two EMS vans transported all three to Receiving Hospital. All three were placed under arrest and a police guard was assigned to them. The women, Estella and Victoria Sanchez, were sisters. The prognosis for Victoria—Vicki—was guarded. She was labeled "serious." Estella drifted in and out of consciousness. She it was who identified everyone.

Julio was critical. The ER staff feverishly bent every effort to save him.

According to Estella, Julio somehow had come into a ton of money sometime Sunday or Monday. Enough to afford more crack cocaine and heroin than the women had ever seen in one user's possession. The three of them had leisurely proceeded to get higher than she'd ever been. She could only guess that, after she had passed out, Vicki had kept at it. Julio had a long and storied history of use. To damn near kill himself, he must have set a world's record of drug consumption.

No, she claimed, she, Estella, did not know where Julio had scored. But it was a significant buy.

And that was, sum and substance, all the police had. Three crack heads; one recovering, one likely to recover, and the third—the one the cops needed and wanted—likely to die.

* * * *

Inspector Walter Koznicki had been called away from his desk. Tully and Mangiapane waited in Koznicki's office for his return.

Koznicki entered the office behind the two men, who were seated facing the desk. They felt his presence even before they saw him.

"The investigation into the murder of Bishop Diego was concluded yesterday," Koznicki said. He stepped in front of them and seated himself behind his desk.

"We haven't let our work go, Inspector," Mangiapane protested.

"He knows that," Tully said.

"I know that," Koznicki said. His statement was for the record. The inspector knew full well that Tully and his squad were working on the Diego case on their own time. But lest anyone surmise that he would relax good order, he stated his official position clearly. Having done so, Koznicki was eager to know what they'd uncovered.

Tully knew this. He began to fill Koznicki in. "First, we discovered why we were getting nowhere on the street. Our guys tapped every snitch we knew about—and then some. We couldn't get a single lead even though our best people had the gut feeling there was something vital to this case out there someplace.

"The reason we were getting nowhere was because the guy we were looking for was Julio Ramirez."

Koznicki's eyes widened. "Pedro Ramirez's brother!"

Tully nodded. "No one would cross Pedro. Not if they wanted to live long enough for another snootful of coke."

"How did you break it?"

Tully shifted in the uncomfortable straight-back chair. "Remember way back when the Kingfish wiped out almost all Mad Anthony's brain trust?"

Koznicki could not suppress a brief smile. That incident had marked the beginning of his near father-and-son relationship with Tully. "I remember it well. You were in the forefront of that investigation. You were as responsible as anyone for getting the conviction of Kingfish and his men."

Tully's hand attempted to wave away the accolade. "In any case, right after that Tony Wayne gave me one wish—sort of like a stingy genie. I didn't take him up on it then. Yesterday, I called in my marker with Mad Anthony. He gave me Julio Ramirez."

"You have him?"

"He's in Receiving."

"Receiving! What is his condition?"

"O.D. He's critical."

Koznicki shook his head slowly. "He may die. If he lives, he may be brain dead. Of what—"

"He's the one," Tully interrupted. He seldom did that to Koznicki. "It's Julio. Wayne gave him to me on a platter."

"That is all very well," Koznicki said, "but he may be dead on that platter. Do we have any witnesses? Any corroboration?"

"Not yet. We're still working on it. The important thing is we've got the perp. Everything else should fall into place. How about letting us work up this case full time?"

Before Koznicki could reply, there was a knock on the door of the glassed-in office. They could see it was Lieutenant Quirt.

"Come," Koznicki called.

Quirt had news that he knew would displease Tully. He knew Tully hadn't bought Carleson as the killer. But now there was no longer any doubt. "Walt, it's a new ballgame." He paused to let the drama he was trying to create sink in. The three looked at him expectantly.

"He did it again," Quirt announced.

Still no reaction.

"Carleson—the priest. Last night. He killed again!"

"What!" All three were as a Greek chorus.

This was the reaction Quirt wanted.

"Explain!" Koznicki demanded. Koznicki disliked such showboating. He considered it unprofessional.

Quirt, oblivious to Koznicki's reaction, forged on. "Last night, around midnight"—Quirt referred to his notes—"Carleson left Ste. Anne's rectory and drove to Receiving Hospital. There he went to the room of an elderly man, a patient that he, Carleson, visited regularly. He entered the man's room and smothered the patient, probably with a pillow."

His listeners appeared dumbfounded.

"How do you know all this? Do you have proof?" Koznicki asked.

"Okay." Quirt was on a high. "First: This elderly patient was one Herbert Demers. He was a parishioner at Ste. Anne's. There are so few people still living in that parish, we were told, that it isn't uncommon for there to be just one parishioner in the hospital at one time.

"Second: After Carleson got out on bail, we did some backgrounding on him. Part of his routine was visiting this guy almost every day. Along the way, Carleson got chummy with a lot of the hospital personnel.

"Third: This Demers was in a coma pretty much all the time. He couldn't speak for himself, and the last word of his next of kin was 'to do everything.' So they were keeping him alive—and that's about all.

"Four: One of the nurses stated that Carleson had talked to her about euthanizing the old man. She said Carleson had told her that the old guy somehow got a message to him to 'help me die.' Anyway, that's what Carleson said. She also said that just yesterday she heard Carleson shouting to the old man to let loose and die. That didn't work.

"Five: Two of the Emergency personnel testified that last night, just before midnight, they saw Carleson going into the hospital. The night nurse on duty on Demers's floor stated she saw Carleson go into the old man's room.

"This morning they found Demers dead. They were about to release the body when I recognized that the dead guy had been visited all the time by this priest who had already been indicted for one murder. Plus the priest had been a one-man cheering section to put this old guy out of his misery. So I ordered an autopsy.

"Six: I just got word from Doc Moellmann that Herbert Demers was murdered. The doc said there were pinpoint hemorrhages in the old man's eyelids and cheeks. There were bruises on the gums. The nose was almost broken. The doc said it was . . ." Quirt paused for effect. ". . . homicide."

There was dead silence in the room for several long moments. Not one of the three officers could make sense of what Quirt had just said. It was like going from A to Z without touching any of the intervening letters.

They were convinced Julio Ramirez was the killer of Bishop Diego. The only question was whether he would survive to be tried for the crime. It was as if a puzzle had been solved and all that remained was to put the pieces together. Having solved the puzzle, everyone expected that putting those pieces in their proper places would be simple.

Now, out of the blue, here was Quirt with a story that blew the pieces in every which direction.

"Has Father Carleson confessed to any of this?" Koznicki asked.

"No." Quirt seemed unconcerned by the priest's denial.

"His explanation for all this?"

"Well," Quirt began, "he was smart enough not to deny that he went out last night. See, there was a service for the bishop in Ste. Anne's church last night. Carleson didn't attend. But after the service, some of the priests got together in the rectory. Carleson had no way of knowing whether any of the priests would go to his room—see how he was, that sort of thing. Since Carleson was out murdering that patient, he couldn't claim he was in his room. Someone easily could've known that he wasn't home—"

"So," Tully broke in, "if he didn't claim to be home, where did he say he was?"

"A sick call." Quirt was near laughter. "He claims he got a call about 11:30. He and the bishop shared a private line. He claims someone called and gave him an address on McKinstry near Clark Park . . . said there was a dying woman there who asked specifically for him. Says he went immediately."

"And," Koznicki said, "at the house, is there anyone who can corroborate?"

Quirt smirked. "No such address, Carleson says. He says he drove to the spot where the house should be. The address he says he was given doesn't exist. Says he drove around for a while. He thought maybe the guy had been confused and had given him the wrong numbers. He went up and down the street looking to see if he could find any commotion. Maybe somebody on a porch looking for him. Maybe an EMS truck. After all, the guy said the woman was *dying*; maybe the guy called 911 after calling him.

"Anyway, that's what he *says*. A whole load of hospital people say something different. They put him at the scene of what Doc Moellmann says was a homicide.

"What we got here, obviously," Quirt concluded, "is a real wacko priest. You remember, Walt—you okayed the voucher—we got Williams at Maryknoll HQ in New York checking for anything fishy in Carleson's background. As time goes on, we need that less and less. Now we know we got a priest who sees a bishop making life miserable for a lot of people—hell, maybe that's what bishops do. So, what does Carleson do about it? He offs the bishop and tries to make it look like a B and E. But he doesn't realize he's got the bishop's blood splashed in his car.

"So he's indicted. But he makes bail. Now he's got a poor old duck who just won't die. So what does Father Carleson do? Even though he just got out of jail on a murder charge, he puts a pillow or something over the old geezer's face and smothers him. It's supposed to be a natural death. But Carleson forgets that a good number of hospital personnel can recognize him. And they do. On top of that, he doesn't know that the method of murder he used leaves evidence—evidence that Doc Moellmann found.

"We got a wacko priest. He goes around killing people who cause problems." Quirt's voice rose. "This guy is damn dangerous!"

Koznicki appeared—reluctantly—convinced. "What action have you taken?"

Quirt hesitated. Before reporting to Koznicki, he had called Kleimer. In retrospect, that didn't seem a smart move. He hadn't done this by the numbers. So he mentally erased a few moves and hoped he could retrace a few steps. "I think we have to contact the prosecutor."

Koznicki would have wagered his last dollar that Quirt had already briefed Kleimer.

Perhaps it was the expression on their faces or their overall reaction to his news; Quirt had the impression that Tully and Mangiapane had also been talking to Koznicki about the Diego case.

Why were they in Koznicki's office? Even more, why weren't they at all enthusiastic about the final nails in Carleson's coffin?

At length, Tully spoke. "I'm afraid we have an embarrassment of riches. We've *got* the Diego killer!"

"What!" It was Quirt's turn.

Tully explained, with some patience, how he had come upon his version of Diego's murderer. Patience was required in the fact of Quirt's frequent protestations that the case had been closed and the task force dissolved yesterday—as in, "How could you continue working the streets? The case is closed!"

Finally, Tully managed to complete his explanation.

"One thing seems clear, gentlemen," Koznicki said. "We have two disparate and distinct suspects in the murder of one man. They could not both have done it."

"Look, George," Tully said, "from the beginning of the case we've been torturing the flow of the investigation to try to come up with a priest suspect."

This statement stung Quirt—because it was true. Kleimer wanted the scenario to read, *Bishop killed by priest*. That way lay global headlines. But Quirt would refuse to admit the truth even if now he was sincerely convinced they had the right man in Carleson.

Tully continued. "If we had let the evidence lead us, we would have seen it as a street crime. Someone who knew Diego kept a significant stash on hand just got in, killed the bishop, and stole the money. It was that simple. And the guy who did it is Julio Ramirez."

"And where did that name come from?" Quirt immediately answered his own question. "From Tony Wayne—Mr. Crime of the Metropolitan area. What a fantastically reliable source! And that's it: You got no eyewitness or confession. And if this guy croaks, you don't even have a suspect.

"Where we got the killer priest. The kind of ink he's been getting up to now makes him look like a male Mother Teresa. So he helps us by offing the poor old vegetable in Receiving. If there wasn't anything else going down, Carleson certainly would be in Jacktown for the Demers killing. But now he's gonna be sent up for Demers *and* Diego. Or," he nodded at Tully, "do you have another explanation for the Demers murder?"

Tully wished to high heaven that he had some reasonable, credible explanation for the idiotic, self-destructive action taken by Father Carleson last night. But Tully could find nothing that would explain away the killing of Demers. So the lieutenant sat and steamed.

There was a short period of silence during which Quirt savored his victory.

"George, you had better inform the prosecuting attorney," Koznicki said finally. "They will want to get a judge to revoke bail. And then prepare to take Father Carleson into custody and process him all over again. Make sure that this is done by the numbers."

With a smile he couldn't contain, Quirt nodded and left the office to continue the process he had already begun. He would do this by the numbers. But the numbers would be slightly shuffled.

Largely because there was nothing left to say, there was no further conversation in Koznicki's office. In a matter of moments after Quirt had departed victorious, Tully and Mangiapane wordlessly left.

As they walked back to the squad room, Mangiapane suggested softly, "I think I smell an insanity plea coming up."

"It's about the only thing that might save him. But I don't know if even that would work."

But Tully had all but dismissed Carleson's plight. The lieutenant's thoughts were absorbed by Tony Wayne's contribution to this case: one Julio Ramirez. With this latest development, it now seemed certain that Carleson had killed both Diego and Demers. Demers, as far as Kleimer was concerned, was frosting.

Tully could grasp the connection between Demers and Diego even better than Quirt.

If Carleson had been innocent of Diego's murder, there would be no reason to act precipitately regarding Demers. But if Carleson knew himself guilty and was convinced that he would be convicted of killing Diego, the priest would know he would be imprisoned and thus unable to free Demers from pain and helpless misery.

Yeah, it all made sense. The killings went together. But what in hell was going on with Tony Wayne? Did he turn in Ramirez as a sacrificial lamb? And why?

As Tully and Mangiapane entered their squad room, which was now filling, Angie Moore called out. "Zoo, you got a call from the patrolman at Receiving who's baby-sitting Ramirez. He says there's a big guy who wants to see Ramirez—a really, really big guy. Says his name's Albert, Albert Salveigh. The patrolman says it's urgent."

Albert. Big Al. Tiny. Wants to see Julio Ramirez. Now that is interesting.

Tully wanted to see Albert Salveigh see Julio Ramirez.

TWENTY-FIVE

Tully was amused.

A young patrolman stood at parade rest in front of the door to Julio Ramirez's hospital room, blocking entrance. Directly opposite him in the corridor was the entire body of Albert Salveigh. If Salveigh had decided to march forward, the officer could have testified to how it felt to be trampled by an elephant.

Tully nodded at the patrolman, who quickly relaxed, relieved that a superior officer was here to deal with Ursus across the way.

"I've got a problem with Mr. Wayne's 'gift,'" Tully said to Salveigh. "We've rearrested Father Carleson and he's going to be charged with two murders . . . and one of them is Bishop Diego's."

The deferential look did not leave Salveigh's face. "I don't think Mr. Wayne is aware of that."

"He will be. It just went down. The media have probably already got it."

Salveigh digested this new development.

"Mr. Wayne would be the last one to claim infallibility," he said finally. "But I was part of the effort that found Julio Ramirez. And I still think we have the right person. However, I need to speak to Ramirez. He's been unconscious since before we found him. Perhaps I could communicate with him now."

"Let me check."

Tully consulted the floor nurse.

"She says he drifts in and out. We can see him for only a little while. What do you want to see him about anyway?"

Salveigh shrugged. "I just want to assure him that Mr. Wayne is responsible for his hospitalization and responsible for his arrest as well.

We want to be sure that he is convinced that he should cooperate with your investigation."

"Sounds okay. Let's go."

They entered the room. The light was soft. The single bed held an inert body.

Tully remained near the door while Salveigh went to the bed. Whatever he said to Ramirez was uttered just above a whisper. Yet Ramirez seemed to hear and understand. His head moved in what Tully took to be an affirmation. Then, after a slight nod to Tully, Salveigh left the room. He had delivered his message in less than two minutes.

Tully moved to the bed and identified himself. Ramirez's eyes were glassy. He was nowhere near recovered.

"Julio, do you know where you are? Do you know what happened?"

Ramirez nodded, almost imperceptibly. He tried to speak, but his lips were caked. Tully took a handy cloth, dipped it in water, and moistened the young man's lips.

"Am I gonna make it?"

"I don't know. You're pretty bad off. But you look like you might. Julio, I got to know: Did you kill that bishop—Diego?"

"I don' wanna think, man."

"Julio, you know who tipped us. You know who wants you to cooperate with us."

Ramirez seemed to wince, but he nodded.

"Did you kill the bishop and take his money?"

Weakly, "Yeah."

"How did it happen? You know the money was there?"

"Yeah."

"How did you kill him?"

"A gun?"

"No."

"Uh . . . a knife?"

"No."

"Uh . . . I forget."

"You killed him and you forgot how you did it?"

"My head hurts. My balls hurt. Ever'thin' hurts."

"Are you sure you killed the bishop?"

"I dunno. I musta. There was blood all over. I gotta sleep, m'n. . . ."

Ramirez's head rolled slightly toward the shuttered window. He appeared to lose consciousness.

A nurse quietly entered the room. "You'll have to leave now."

"What are his chances?"

"Improving. He took in a ton of dope. Time is the only thing that can tell now."

Tully left disheartened. If Ramirez died without a coherent confession, they had no case. Even if he lived, he could be so spaced out he'd be useless.

Then he recalled what Salveigh had said . . . something about Mr. Wayne not being infallible. Maybe this whole thing was just a dead end. Tully figured he'd better start getting used to the idea that, as ugly as that possibility was, Quirt might just be right.

By the time he'd walked back to headquarters, Tully was feeling glum. A number of phone messages were stacked on his desk. He thumbed through the pile. One of the calls was from Father Koesler. Tully decided to return that one first. Koesler had been most cooperative. He deserved consideration.

*   *   *   *

The murder of Herbert Demers had happened far too late in the night for inclusion in Detroit's morning *Free Press*. But the news was on radio. Television was trying to catch up.

Koesler watched as Father Carleson was once again taken into custody. Avery Cone, Carleson's attorney, was shielding his client from the intrusive cameras and responding over and over, "No comment!"

Koesler was sitting transfixed before the TV set when the phone rang. It was Lieutenant Tully returning his call.

Tully brought Koesler up to the moment, after explaining all the overnight developments. "The thing of it is, Demers was terminal. Hell, he could have checked out last night on his own."

"The thing is," Koesler responded, "maybe he wouldn't have died last night. From all you've said, Mr. Demers has been dying for a long time. He could have gone on a long time more. Father Carleson had no way of knowing."

Tully was surprised. "Hey, you don't think Carleson did it, do you

Somehow, I thought no matter how convincing the evidence might be, you wouldn't believe it. I mean, I thought euthanasia or assisting suicide was against your religion."

"Well . . . yes."

"You have doubts?"

"Not doubts so much as developments." Koesler realized that expounding on this topic might compromise Father Carleson, but it seemed important to be candid with Tully. After all, they had confided in each other throughout this case.

"There's been a lot of talk among theologians," Koesler said, "about what happens when one's productive life is over. When all that a person planned to do is accomplished and all he or she faces is pain and vegetation.

"See, the Church teaches that it is not necessary to prolong life if the only way to do it is by extraordinary means. This—euthanasia—is the next step. This is not pulling a plug to let nature take its course. This means actively doing something that will take a life.

"There hasn't even been much written on this. The theologians that propose these ideas are afraid of retribution. The present Pope would not tolerate such an idea. The next one might."

"Uh-huh," Tully said. "Would Father Carleson know about this kind of talk?"

Koesler hesitated. "I don't really know. We haven't discussed it specifically. But he strikes me as being well informed. I still don't believe that he was involved in a mercy killing. It's just that I can sympathize with him if he was. I've watched people die too slowly when there wasn't any purpose left to their lives. It's one of those things we might be able to do something about someday. But not yet."

"And Father Carleson is not the type to wait, is he?"

Koesler considered the question rhetorical. Though unconcerned with replying to that, another question occurred to him. "What does Father Carleson say he was doing last night?"

"I didn't tell you?"

"No."

"It slipped my mind. He claims he had a sick call. At just that time."

Koesler was relieved. He'd half feared Carleson might have claimed he hadn't left the rectory. "That must've been where he was going when we saw him."

"You saw him?"

"Yes. It was late in the evening . . . 11:30, as I recall. Father Dou and I happened to look out and saw Father Carleson getting into his car. And then he drove off."

"Did you hear the phone ring before that?"

"N . . . no. But there was a lot of conversation going on. And also, Father Carleson and Bishop Diego had their own line. So the phone would've rung upstairs in his room. With all the noise downstairs, we probably just didn't hear it.

"But that would confirm his alibi, wouldn't it? I mean, whoever called him could testify for him."

"If such a person exists."

"What?"

"He claims there was no such address. He says he drove around for a while to see if he could see any signs of anything going on in case he'd gotten the wrong address."

"Bad luck! But it's happened to me, Lieutenant. I've been called out on an emergency on a false alarm more than once. What sometimes happens is that the person who calls is so caught up in the excitement that he gets the house number wrong, or maybe the wrong street name, or both. So for the priest it's a wild goose chase.

"Then, usually the next morning, someone will call, angry because you didn't show up, or apologetic about giving the wrong address."

"Only thing is there hasn't been anything like that. Nobody's gotten in touch with anybody. We've got nothing but Carleson's story. And nothing to back it up. He says he was called out on an emergency—that no one else knows about—at just the time a bunch of hospital personnel claim he was *there*. When he gets to talk to his lawyer some more, he may want to retract that statement and claim he never left home. But now that you've said you saw him leave, he's not going to be able to back away from his first statement."

Koesler got the clear impression he hadn't done his friend any favor.

"Funny thing," Tully said, "he was sailing pretty well on that firs charge. It was all circumstantial. And I had a pretty good lead on a suspect. If only he hadn't pulled the second murder.

"But I suppose he's saying that same thing to himself right now. . . .

"Well, anyway: Does all this answer your questions?"

"I guess so, Lieutenant. I think I'll just wander over to Receiving later to set my mind at ease about a couple of things. Any objections?"

"Nope, none. And thanks for all your help, Father."

As Koesler hung up he realized that Tully's last statement seemed to indicate that his further services would not be required or requested.

Maybe this case was closed, and all the hope in Koesler's heart would not change that.

CHAPTER

TWENTY-SIX

By the time Father Koesler's last appointment left, it was almost 10:30—much later than he had planned. He was tired. A perfect time and a perfect mood to call it a day. Maybe jot a few notes about tomorrow's schedule. Maybe have a little nightcap, watch the late news on TV, and then to bed.

But he was all too conscious of what he had told Lieutenant Tully earlier in the day. In effect, he had asked Tully if visiting Receiving Hospital would interfere with the ongoing investigation.

Koesler didn't have any clear plan; he just wanted to help Father Carleson in any way possible. Not only was a fellow priest in trouble, but also Koesler felt that, in a brief period, a budding friendship had begun.

With no other strategy in mind, Koesler thought of just walking through what Carleson had done last night. Perhaps something would surface. *What?* He had no idea.

He drove to Ste. Anne's rectory. Everything was quiet. Quite a change from last night.

Diego's funeral had been held this morning. But last night had marked the clergy's celebration of what was hoped to be Diego's entry into heaven. Whether or not the bishop made it, the clergy had had their little celebration.

Last night, almost all the lights on the rectory's first floor were burning bright. There had been a good bit of noise. If any of the faithful had lingered after the vigil service, they might have been slightly scandalized. Certainly that was possible if they'd thought all the visiting clergy went home after the service. Or if the faithful assumed the clergy did not celebrate every chance they got.

Koesler glanced at his watch. It was about 10:40, almost an hour earlier than when he and Father Dorr had seen Carleson leaving last night. But Koesler figured he was in the right time frame.

He drove to Receiving Hospital and swung his car into the parking garage on St. Antoine.

At the bottom of the incline, an automatic machine spit out a parking ticket. Koesler removed it from the machine's mouth, and an automatic arm raised and beckoned him enter.

There were many open spaces. He took the first slot he came to.

He put the car in park, turned off the engine, and sat and mulled.

He hadn't given this maneuver a moment's thought or hesitation. Yet there were lots of places to park on the street. Many of the No Parking signs had an expiration time. But he had given no consideration whatever to parking anywhere but in the garage.

Why was that, he wondered. But not for long. There was a good reason why drivers chose not to park on the streets of Detroit, especially at night. It was almost an invitation to the criminal mind to take the hubcaps, the battery, the tires, the wheels, the contents, or, of course, the entire vehicle. That's why it was so common, so natural to swing into the garage. This, undoubtedly, is what Father Carleson had done last night.

Good! He was off to a good start.

He tucked the parking ticket in his wallet. Another automatic action. The ticket would be safe there. He wouldn't have to try to remember where he put it. And he'd have it handy when it came time to pay for the parking.

Koesler wanted to be consciously aware of everything he did as he attempted to retrace his friend's movements last night.

He stood on the sidewalk looking at the hospital. Yes, he thought, Don must've stood at this point. Lieutenant Tully said Father Carleson was first recognized by a couple of attendants in the Emergency Department.

Koesler was standing about fifteen yards from the Emergency entrance. As luck would have it, three attendants were standing in conversation just inside the door. Not unlike last night when, according to Tully, a couple of people were working over a gurney when they looked up and noticed Carleson standing right about where Koesler now stood. Conditions could scarcely be better to reenact what had happened last night.

So Koesler turned up the collar of his overcoat against the cold and stood there. And stood. And stood. He kept thinking that any moment now one of those people should look out to see if someone, anyone—the injured, or very ill—was approaching or trying to enter Emergency.

At length, he concluded it was a matter of chance. Eventually, someone would look up. But in the meantime he was freezing waiting for that glance. As luck would have it, last night someone had looked up and out as Carleson had reached this point. It just wasn't worth it to Koesler to become an ice sculpture while waiting outside for that eventual notice.

Tully said that Carleson, after being spotted by the Emergency people, had entered through the main entrance.

Koesler would do likewise. But first he hoped he would be able to speak with whoever had identified Carleson.

As the automatic doors slid open, Koesler had everyone's attention. He explained to the threesome what he was looking for.

"You want Lenny and Frank," a young man said. "They're the ones who spotted the priest last night. Lenny's taking sick time. But Frank's the redhead over there." He indicated a man inventorying supplies in a cabinet.

Koesler approached and identified himself. He explained that he was checking out what had happened last night.

"I told this to the cops already, you know," Frank said.

"I know. I talked with Lieutenant Tully of Homicide earlier today." The name seemed to make no impression on the young man. "He told me what happened. But I wanted to check it out for myself. If you don't mind . . . ?"

Frank shrugged. "All I can tell you is what I told the cops. Lenny and I were working out there in the corridor near the entrance. Lenny's the one who first spotted Father Carleson. When he said something, I looked out and, sure enough, there he was."

"Was he standing or walking?"

Frank looked at Koesler. "The cops didn't ask that one."

"Okay . . ." He gave the question some thought. "He was like making up his mind about whether to come in through Emergency or not

He was standing. But as soon as we saw him, he turned and went toward the main entrance. See, he usually comes through here. We all know him. He's a good guy. Knows a lot about medicine too. I guess he picked that up in the missions.

"Too bad what's happening to him. Lenny and I hated to dig a hole for him, but we had to tell the cops what we saw."

"Of course. I understand. But are you sure it was Father Carleson you saw? I mean, I just stood about where he must've been standing last night. It's not exactly close to the door. The part of the pavement that leads either into the main entrance or into Emergency is about fifteen yards from the doors. Add to that you and Lenny must've been inside the doors some way back. No?"

"Yeah . . . yeah, that's about right for him. And us? We must've been maybe forty-five or fifty feet inside. But we saw him clearly. The first thing you spot is the all-black clothes. Then that spot of white in the front of the collar—like you've got. The white hair showing at the side of his hat—your know, by his ears. Same height, same build.

"Okay, so we weren't standing right next to him, but it was him. It was Father Carleson. Yeah, it was Father Carleson. Lenny and I agreed on that. He'd tell you the same if he was here."

"Well, thanks very much."

Koesler retraced his steps to the point where the walkway forked, one path leading to the main entrance, the other to Emergency. Now he walked toward the main entrance.

Still following Tully's description of events, Koesler went immediately to the bank of elevators, making no attempt to attract the attention of the individual in the information booth.

Tully had given Koesler the floor and the room number. He took the elevator to Herbert Demers's floor. Exiting the elevator, he walked slowly and softly down the corridor, through the mesmerizing sounds of labored breathing, pain, loneliness, support machinery, and the ever-present opiate, television.

As he reached the room in which Demers had lived and died, he noted he was not far from the nursing station. He was surprised to find not one, but two nurses occupying the station.

He was not as surprised as the nurses were. One of them let out a little screech. *"Who are you?"* the screech demanded.

Smiling, Koesler approached the station. "I'm sorry. I didn't mean to startle you. My name's Koesler, Father Koesler. I'm pastor of Old St. Joe's downtown. I'm a friend of Father Carleson."

"You gave me a start," said the screecher. "For a second there, I thought you *were* Father Carleson." She spoke more calmly. "Is there something I can help you with?"

"Maybe. I'm walking through where Father Carleson was last night . . . sort of hoping to find something that might help him."

"Well, good luck. He's a nice guy. Nobody here can believe that he killed that bishop."

"The bishop, eh? What about Herbert Demers? You believe that Father Carleson killed Demers?"

"What can I say?" Sensing this conversation was going to go on a while, the screecher introduced herself. "I'm Alice Cherny and"—turning to the other nurse—"this is Ann Bradley. I'm on night shift. She's afternoon."

"And neither of you doubts that Father killed Mr. Demers?"

"The thing I'm uncomfortable with," Alice said, "is the word 'kill.' It was more like snuffing out a candle. A tomato has more life in it than Herbert had. We're all glad Father did it. If the truth be known, we all would like to have done it. We're just sorry he got caught."

"It wouldn't have happened if that detective hadn't ordered an autopsy," said Ann. "Until then we just assumed that Herbert slipped away during the night. The cops were sore that we'd sent down the linen to the laundry. They thought they might have picked up some fingerprints. But how were we to know?"

"The worst part of this," Alice said, "is that we had to answer the police officer's questions honestly."

"I had to tell them how Father and I talked about helping Herbert die," Ann added. "That's what Father said Herbert asked him to do. He said that just a couple of days ago, Herbert communicated in gestures and asked Father to help him die. Then yesterday, I heard Father fairly shouting at Herbert to let go of life and die.

"Naturally, the police thought all that was very relevant. Nobody in the hospital wanted to end Herbert's suffering more than Father Carleson. Unfortunately, that's still called murder."

"And then," Alice said, "my testimony was more damning than

anyone's. I actually saw him go into Herbert's room—just about an hour later than right now."

"You got a good look?"

"Oh, yes. Of course, it's kind of hard to see down the corridor. The lights are so bright here around the station and so dim in the hallway that it's a little hard to focus quickly. But it was Father Carleson. I haven't seen him as much as Ann, of course." She thought for a moment. "Now that I think of it, he seemed to have put on a little weight. But it was him." She looked at Koesler. "When you think about it, who else could it have been?"

"Were both of you on duty here last night when Father Carleson came?"

"No. No," Ann said. "This is report time. Actually, I'm on duty till 11:30. But Alice is my replacement, and she comes on duty at 11:00. The half-hour overlap gives me a chance to advise Alice about the state of things as she replaces me. I sort of bring her up to speed before I leave."

"So," Alice added, "last night Annie briefed me from 11:00 to 11:30, when she went home. It wasn't until near midnight that Father Carleson came in."

"One last question then: Last night—and tonight—did you talk about Herbert Demers and Father Carleson and what's happened to them?"

"Sure!" Alice said. "Why shouldn't we be talking about what everybody in the city is talking about?"

"And you didn't come up with anything that might help Father?"

"Boy, I wish we could. Like I said, he seems to be a genuinely nice guy. And what he did here—no matter what the law says—was a favor for everybody—especially Herbert Demers."

"Well, thank you both very much."

In leaving, Koesler was painstaking in continuing to follow in Carleson's footsteps, as Lieutenant Tully had described the event.

He took the elevator to the lobby and quickly walked through it, staying some distance from the information booth. Once out the door, he turned up his overcoat collar and went straight to the parking garage.

He entered his car, started the engine, and turned the heat on. He shivered. It would be a while before the engine would heat the forced air.

He found his wallet, took out the parking stub and the single dollar that was the fixed night rate.

He stopped at the attendant's booth, gave him the stub and money. Without Koesler's asking, the attendant gave him a receipt. Koesler figured so many medical and legal personnel used the garage, the receipt was automatic. He stuffed it in his pocket. The parking arm lifted; Koesler exited the garage and drove away from the hospital.

What, if anything, had he learned? He was not at all sure. He would have to think this through.

He let himself in through the kitchen of St. Joe's rectory and checked the answering machine. No calls. Good.

He could catch the final few stories on the late evening news. It was sports, weather, and a cutesy closing bit. He was sure the lead story on all television and radio stations had been the rearrest and incarceration of Father Carleson.

He made sure the lights were out and the thermostat turned down.

He had recently begun an interesting book on the Jesuits in America. He tried that for a few pages, but he was suffering from major distractions.

He turned out the light and pulled up the blankets.

He tried to find the precise key that might unlock this puzzle and cast a fresh light on static presumptions. But he was too tired.

He had to agree with Scarlett O'Hara: *I'll think about that tomorrow.*

CHAPTER

TWENTY-SEVEN

"Brad, this is Quirt, George Quirt."

Brad Kleimer propped the phone between ear and shoulder as he swiveled his chair toward the window. "George" was redundant; how many Quirts could he know? "Okay. Good morning, George. Whatcha got?"

"I just got done talking to Williams."

"Yeah? He home now?"

"No . . . and that's the problem."

"What's wrong?"

Quirt did not have happy news. But since sending Williams to Maryknoll had been Kleimer's idea, the problem was Kleimer's. "Williams hasn't been able to see the Maryknoll assignment book."

"Why's that so tough?"

"Well, he got to Ossining okay, and eventually he touched base with the local cops. He let them know what he needed, but it took a helluva long time to get their cooperation. He finally got one of the guys to go with him, and then they spent pretty much all day yesterday trying to find a judge who'd issue a warrant."

"What?" Kleimer came to his feet. "Why didn't he just go to Maryknoll and look at the record?"

"Well, he did, Brad—go to Maryknoll, that is. But they wouldn't let him see it."

"They're hiding something."

"Maybe. Probably. But the guy he talked to—a Maryknoll priest with the title of procurator—said it was the policy of the order not to disclose the record of any of their missionaries.

"I got all this from Williams . . . it probably makes more sense to a Catholic—"

241

BISHOP AS PAWN

"Get on with it."

"Yeah. Well, this procurator explained that the missionaries' activities could be compromised if this stuff got into the wrong hands."

"Williams is a cop, for Chrissake! What does he mean 'get into the wrong hands'?"

"The procurator says it's the rule—their rule. The records of the missionaries are strictly confidential and they don't share 'em with *anybody*. That's the only way they can be sure they're not gonna get into the wrong hands: They don't get into *any* hands."

"So? That's one guy."

"Williams says he went to the rector of the seminary and even to the superior general—which, I take it, is the top guy. Same song and dance . . . matter of fact, the superior general said this rule originated with him. That's when Williams went to the cops. He thought it would be a snap to at least get the cooperation of the police. But, it wasn't. Then, like I said, he finally got one guy. But they spent all the working hours yesterday trying to find a judge who'd issue a warrant."

Kleimer was irritated and growing more so. "What's the problem with the warrant?"

"The judges they saw had pretty much the same reaction: 'The Maryknoll order has every right to keep confidential the activities of its members.' And the judges weren't about to tamper with that secrecy just on the 'intuition' of some out-of-state cop. That's the word they used, Brad: 'intuition.'"

"Intuition, my ass!" Kleimer's fist hit the desk. "Williams is no dame. He's a damn good cop! We don't get jerked around by some hick cop department!"

"Yeah, Williams said the term 'hotshot Detroit Homicide dick' did get thrown around a lot.

"Look, Brad, I know you're pissed off. So am I. But the bottom line is Williams is gonna have to stay in Ossining another day. And there's no guarantee that he's gonna get a peek at that record anyhow. The department okayed just enough for an in-and-out. We're just about at the end of that chit. Me, I'd tell him to get his ass back here. But you were pretty strong on sending him there . . . if I remember right, you said something about financing this trip yourself. Well, now we gotta fish or cut bait. What'll it be?"

It didn't take Kleimer long to decide. "Hell, reel him in. Things were getting kind of thin on that first count of murder. But now that we've got Carleson for the Demers killing, we can't miss. I still think Williams was on to something, but we've got a while before we go to trial. Hell, if those people in Ossining want to play hardball, we'll just be better prepared next time we go for those records."

"Lucky we caught that Demers killing," Quirt said.

There was something about Quirt's tone. It took Kleimer a moment to realize that Quirt was fishing for a compliment. "No luck about it! That was just good police work on your part. It would've slipped right by if you hadn't been on your toes, George. Good going! That put a few more nails in Carleson's coffin."

"All in a day's work, Brad. But not bad if I do say so myself. Of course, you won't forget this when things open up here in Homicide, eh?"

"Bet your bottom dollar on it, George. I won't forget."

Quirt broke the connection. Everything was working out well. He felt very good.

*   *   *   *

"What's up?" Tully asked.

"There's no problem with Julio," Sergeant Angie Moore said. "Even if we turned him loose, he couldn't make it down the hospital corridor. We've got him under guard. Same with Vicki Sanchez. She's lots better than Julio, but still needs care. She's under guard too. Estella either has better tolerance or she didn't snort as much as the other two. We've got her in holding upstairs."

"What're we charging?"

"For now, we've got her on possession with intent to deliver. I suppose it could be true. There was such a collection of dope in that apartment they'd be dead before they could use half of it. So maybe they'd turn it up and sell it."

"Good."

Moore shook her head. "This is kind of weird, Zoo. I've never been on anything like this before."

Tully looked up, near expressionless.

"I mean . . . we've got a guy locked up for a murder while we're holding somebody for the same murder. The second guy—Julio—isn't even charged and hasn't been arrested. He's just trying to hold onto life. This is a whodunit! A real-life whodunit!"

Tully smiled. "I got my chips on Mad Anthony. I haven't seen him since the other day. But he knows we got Carleson back in jail. And he knows that Carleson's charged with two murders—and the second puts the seal on the first. But Wayne hasn't blinked. I think if he had any doubts about Julio, he'd get in touch. But: nothin'."

"Did you get anything at all from Julio?" Moore asked.

"Only that he 'did it'!"

"That sounds pretty convincing to me."

"Yeah . . . except he's not too sure whether he used a gun or a knife or a voodoo doll."

"Not exactly the kind of defendant you'd want to put on the witness chair. I can't think of too many judges who'd accept multiple-choice weapons.

"But, Zoo: What about this? What if Julio comes out of this completely and remembers everything? Suppose he says he did it and identifies the weapon—the correct weapon? Then what? What happens with the prosecutor who keeps on insisting that he's got the perp? And that he's got motive, opportunity, and means? He's got a half ton of circumstantial evidence. . . . And the priest claims he's innocent, while Julio claims *he's* guilty. What happens then?"

Tully seemed to be considering these contradictions for the first time. As he returned his attention to the file he'd been studying, he said, "Angie, we live in interesting times."

*   *   *   *

Father Koesler was getting through this day in a more or less mechanical manner.

The high point of Father Koesler's day always was his celebration of Mass. Each day he tried to prepare well for this sacred ritual—the essence of his life. But this morning Mass had been filled with distractions. As was the rest of this day.

Mary O'Connor, the parish secretary, had sorted the mail, pointing out that the separate pile needed his immediate attention.

He tried to give it undivided concentration but found himself re-reading paragraph after paragraph. Somehow he got through it all. But it took up to three times what it normally would have.

It was the same with his appointments. He conscientiously tried to focus on what his visitors said, the problems they brought to him. But if their presentation was at all on the dull side, they would lose him. He could not count the number of times he had punctuated the conversation with, "Sorry, could you repeat that?" or "I beg your pardon . . ." or "What was that you were saying?" As he saw each of these visitors to the door, he felt the need to apologize.

Mary O'Connor left for home about 4:00 P.M. She was worried about him. There had been distractions before, but not a whole day full. She had tried to make things as easy as possible for him, but nothing seemed to help. She could only hope that a good night's sleep might set things straight for him.

After Mary left, Koesler donned his sweats and went into the basement for the series of exercises that had been suggested by a physical therapist. Requiring attention was a shoulder that had lost its rotator cuff to a stray bullet, as well as a creeping arthritic condition.

Mercifully, the exercises helped clear his mind. He returned to his second-floor suite perspiring, but much more organized and put together.

It was in the shower that the puzzle began to unravel. Why, he wondered, did this sort of thing so frequently occur while he showered? Possibly because during showers he almost always was thinking of nothing. And in that vacuum that nature despised, fresh ideas were born.

He'd been trying to recall a simple statement Lieutenant Tully had made when last they'd talked. About Father Carleson's apparent involvement in the death of Herbert Demers. Tully had said something to the effect that it was too bad that he—Father Carleson—had done it.

The gist of the remark was that it was the second murder that gave crediblity to the first.

The immediate and growing reaction to Father Carleson's arrest for the murder of Bishop Diego had been disbelief. The media accurately reported what they discovered. Which was that everyone who knew Father Carleson knew him to be dedicated, generous, peaceful, kind, thoughtful, gentle—and very long-suffering—the very antithesis of a murderer.

What circumstantial evidence the prosecution was gathering had begun to pale in the face of the spotless reputation that continued to emerge.

Then came the death of Demers. Carleson's image took a sharp downturn. It wasn't so much that people and the media suddenly pictured him as a ruthless criminal and murderer. The figure that now emerged was of a priest gone mad.

Here was a priest who—with or without the best of intentions—could snuff an elderly person's life simply because nature wasn't doing its job fast enough.

If Carleson could deliberately kill a helpless old man—and he most assuredly had—then it was safe to believe he could and did kill a bothersome bishop. Demers's reality gave credibility to Diego's murder. Too bad Carleson had killed Demers. It proved he was capable of killing, and probably had killed Diego.

Not a bad argument, Koesler had to admit.

But . . .

But some of the things Koesler had experienced last night as he'd retraced Carleson's steps had planted some doubts.

To reverse the current supposition: If Carleson indeed did not kill Demers, he probably hadn't killed Diego either.

Who, then, did kill Diego? Lieutenant Tully seemed to have a likely prospect in a young man from the Ste. Anne neighborhood.

But if Carleson did not murder Demers, who did?

Somebody who looked like a priest and who resembled Carleson would have to be the murderer if Carleson were not.

What had Koesler learned last night?

The night before last, somebody—a man, presumably—was seen by a couple of attendants outside the Emergency entrance. The man was standing approximately thirty yards away from the attendants. He was standing still. Was he trying to decide whether to enter through

Emergency or the main door? Or was he waiting to be seen by somebody—anybody—in Emergency?

What did the attendants see? They saw a man—a person—dressed in black. A black hat covered the man's hair, except for the small tuft of white at his ears. They saw—or thought they saw—the narrow white tab that marked a clerical collar.

If anyone had happened to glance out the door last night, they would have seen a man standing in about the same spot where the man had been standing the night before. They would have seen Koesler all in black. Discernible at the sides of his black hat beneath the brim they would have seen gray instead of white hair.

But they would not have seen the white tab of his clerical collar because he had turned up the collar of his overcoat. It was bitter cold both nights. The most natural defense against the cold was to bundle up as much as possible.

The earlier figure was standing half facing the Emergency door making his clerical collar evident. Everybody had been talking about Father Carleson. Carleson had frequented the Emergency Room. They expected to see Father Carleson. They *did* see Father Carleson . . . or so they thought.

After visiting Emergency, Koesler had continued tracing Carleson's path of the previous night. When Koesler arrived at the late Mr. Demers's floor, the priest walked, just as he imagined Carleson had, to the room Tully said Demers had occupied. Just as he turned to enter the room, the floor nurse, Alice Cherny, looked up from her paperwork. As they talked, Alice admitted that for a moment she'd thought it was Carleson going into the room.

She admitted that it was difficult to see distinctly down the corridor due to the lighting. Then, too, she and Ann Bradley, who was going off duty, had been talking about Father Carleson.

And that's exactly what had happened the night before. The light was uneven—quite bright in the nurses' station, dim in the corridor. She and Ann had been talking earlier about Father Carleson. So he was on her mind.

Last night Alice Cherny thought she saw Father Carleson approaching Demers's room. She was mistaken; it had been Father Koesler. The night before, she thought she had seen Father Carleson enter Demers's room. Was she mistaken that night too?

All of this Father Koesler thought interesting. But that's all: just interesting. It merely suggested that it was possible—just possible—that it had not been Father Carleson who, dressed as a priest, entered Herbert Demers's room and suffocated him.

And Koesler was positive that's what the police would say if he were to present this theory to them: "Very interesting." But all it indicated was that someone else might be the killer. *And* the murderer still could be Father Carleson. And he was the one under arrest. He was the one who had been closest to Demers. Carleson was the one who claimed Demers had begged his help to die. Carleson had tried to give Demers permission to die. In all the world, neither the police nor the hospital personnel knew anyone more wishful for Demers's death, more ready to help him die, than Father Donald Carleson.

If Carleson did not murder Demers, then who?

Koesler almost felt like taking another shower.

If Carleson didn't do it, then whoever did do it, did it either out of mercy or—? A moment's thought turned Koesler's mind from a mercy killing. That would've been Carleson's motive. But no other priest—at least none that Koesler was aware of—had such a motive. And if it had been one of the hospital personnel, it wasn't likely such a person would masquerade as a priest. It would be far easier for a member of the hospital staff to walk around freely in his or her own uniform.

But suppose someone wanted to frame Carleson?

Why would anyone want to do that?

The obvious reason would be to cause precisely what had happened: a fresh start on the prosecution of the first case. The creation of a new image of the accused. Now, not a holy priest to whom any hint of violence was utterly foreign. Now, a not-quite-balanced individual who was capable of even murder in order to resolve a problem. If Herbert Demers was lingering too long—kill him. If Bishop Diego was manipulating good people—the murderer among them—and harming them—then kill him.

But who?

Gradually, an image took shape in Koesler's mind. The more he thought about it—! Still, it was no better than a wild guess. And, in any case, he didn't have a shred of evidence.

Ordinarily, Koesler would not have pressed on immediately—not in this unprepared, unorganized state. But he sensed that the longer he deferred action, the more difficult it would become to pursue this theory.

* * * *

". . . so," he concluded, "what do you think?"

Koesler had phoned Lieutenant Tully. He had explained his theory as logically and chronologically as he could. Now he waited for the lieutenant's response.

"Interesting."

Damn, Koesler thought. Just what he had anticipated. "Is there anything you—I—*we* can do about it?"

"Nothing comes to mind." Tully sounded calm, cool. Actually, Koesler's hypothesis excited him.

"Can't the police get into a suspect's place and look around?" Koesler asked.

"Not legally. Not without a warrant."

"Can't you get a warrant?" he pressed.

"Not without a specific reason. And you don't have a specific reason," Tully reminded him. "When it comes right down to it, you've got nothing more than a hunch."

"Is that what they call 'a fishing expedition'?"

"That's what they call a fishing expedition."

Koesler thought for a moment. Tully was silent.

"Wait a minute," Koesler said with some intensity. "What if *I* went in?"

"How would you get in?"

"He invited me."

"He what?"

"A few days ago. He invited me to visit him."

"The good guys just scored. But the ballgame is far from over."

"But if—Lieutenant, if I were to find something I thought was incriminating . . . if that happened . . . ?"

"Then you call me, no matter what time it is. You've got my all-purpose number?"

"Yes."

"Then give it a whirl."

"Pray for me."

"I'm tempted to."

CHAPTER
TWENTY-EIGHT

Wisely, Father Koesler did not rely on Lieutenant Tully's inclination to pray.

But Koesler prayed. He asked for God's presence with him. Of course he believed that God was present always and everywhere. But this was an intensified moment. He was convinced this would be his one and only chance to uncover the truth and, in so doing, free an innocent man from prison.

So Koesler prayed for enlightenment. He didn't know what he was supposed to be looking for. He didn't know what clue to be listening for.

What this came down to was that the police were forbidden by law to invade an individual's castle merely in hopes of coming up with incriminating evidence. They had to have a good reason to believe they would find something specific in order to be permitted entree to look for it. The police were not allowed to engage in such a "fishing expedition."

But the law did not forbid a private citizen who had been invited into the castle from keeping the fish that jumped into his boat.

The looming problem was that Koesler had no pole or line. He had no special skill in this sort of venture. He did not know what sort of fish he was looking for. He did not even know whether there even were any fish in this pond.

He needed help.

And that's why Father Koesler was praying fervently even as he lifted the knocker to rap on the door.

Why did he have this sense of déjà vu? Then he remembered: It was another time, some years back, when he had been trying to help another priest who had been accused of murder. He, Koesler, had accepted an invitation to dinner at the apartment of a man involved in the case, and, that night, had noticed something in the man's apartment that had led to the solving of the case.

Koesler fervently hoped that the same thing would happen tonight—that somehow, history would repeat itself, and that he would again come across something—anything—that would prove that Father Carleson was indeed innocent of the killings he was accused of committing.

But hope was not enough. Father Koesler went beyond hope: He continued to pray, even as the door was opened by a smiling Brad Kleimer.

"Well! Come in, come in! Good to see you. Glad you could come." As the two men shook hands, Koesler wondered at his host's effusiveness; even Koesler's own friends rarely welcomed him so heartily.

"Here, let me take your hat and coat. . . ." Koesler, feeling curiously as if he were divesting himself of armor, handed those garments to Kleimer, who stood waiting in front of the hall closet. Kleimer put the hat on a shelf, hung the coat on a hanger, closed the closet door, and turned back to Koesler with a smile.

"Kind of you to see me on such short notice," Koesler said.

"Your call *was* a bit of a surprise," Kleimer admitted, as he motioned Koesler into the living room. "But heck, I invited you to visit anytime . . . it was after I consulted with you about Carleson witnessing my wife's marriage, wasn't it?"

"Yes, that was it. I just had some spare time tonight, and took the chance. . . ."

"Fine, great! Can I get you something to drink? The bar is well-stocked." He gestured toward an army of bottles. "What'll you have?"

Koesler did not really want anything to drink. But balancing a cocktail of some kind might extend the visit. "How about a gin and tonic . . . heavy on the tonic."

"Sure thing! Uh . . . by the way, what do I call you?"

"At the risk of seeming old fashioned, I'd prefer the title."

Kleimer grinned and inclined his head. "Sure thing," he said again. "I'm Brad." He busied himself at the wet bar, his back to Koesler. "By the way, Father, I gotta remind you that I've got a date later this evening. So I gotta leave in about an hour. But now you know where I live you should come again sometime."

Great! thought Koesler, *not only do I desperately need God, He's got a time limit.*

Regardless, Koesler was using the formula he had so often recommended to others: Pray as if everything depended on God, but act as if everything depended on you. He was trying to use every precious second to look for something—he didn't know what. Whatever he was supposed to find.

Kleimer's apartment was on the fourth floor of the Riverfront high rise. From the vantage point this low in the building, the view needed a lot to be breathtaking. But the apartment was comfortably furnished . . . though there did seem to be a preponderance of end tables.

Hmmm . . . out of the ordinary for him to notice such an insignificant detail. Was that what God wanted him to investigate?

God simply had to make Himself more clear!

Koesler walked about the living room, examining each table as carefully as possible. Magazines; newspapers; folders—brought from work, presumably; some ashtrays; a few pieces of personal memorabilia.

Nothing noteworthy or signal, unless there was something incriminating in one of those folders. But for Koesler to have a go at checking those, Kleimer would have to be out of the room for an extended period. *Maybe if he took a shower . . .*

Koesler shook his head; his host looked and smelled as if he was ready for his date.

Kleimer returned with two drinks. The tall fizzing one was Koesler's. Kleimer appeared to have made himself a martini . . . either that or he had put ice and a large olive in water.

They sat on facing sofas. Koesler was within reaching distance of an end table—one that held several of the mysterious folders. He was sorely tempted.

"So, Father . . . you're pastor of St. Joe's."

"Uh-huh."

"And unofficial chaplain of the Detroit Police Department." Kleimer smiled at his blatant overstatement.

"No, I wouldn't say that. As I told you, it's only an occasional involvement."

"But I've been asking around. Your 'involvement' is always on behalf of the Homicide detectives and thus the prosecution. The operative word is *prosecution*. So I figured that somewhere down the line I might use you."

The operative word, thought Koesler, *is* use. As he had already concluded, Kleimer was a user, a manipulator.

"As a matter of fact," Kleimer said, "you've already been helpful."

"I have?"

"You witnessed Father Carleson leaving Ste. Anne's rectory about 11:30 the night he killed Demers. Now he won't be able to back out of that one."

Koesler was shocked. "But I only told Lieutenant Tully—!"

It took Kleimer a moment to comprehend Koesler's distress. "And you thought . . . Look, Father, I know Zoo Tully doesn't go along with the way this case is proceeding—he even has his own pet theory and suspect. But Tully works for the department, not for himself. He couldn't be the honest cop he is and hold back that information.

"But don't feel bad: Your information was just icing on the cake. This case was wrapped up the minute Lieutenant Quirt was diligent enough to order an autopsy for Demers. Pretty shrewd police work, I'd say."

"I guess that's so," Koesler said. "But if Lieutenant Quirt hadn't thought of it, you would have."

"What's that?" It was Kleimer's turn to be surprised.

"I mean, you're too efficient a prosecutor not to know that Father Carleson had almost adopted Mr. Demers. That Father was concerned about Demers's vegetative state . . . and that Father had even discussed euthanasia. All of that was common knowledge around the hospital. I'd be very surprised if you didn't know all about it."

Kleimer considered this a moment. "Well, yes, of course I knew it."

"So even if Lieutenant Quirt hadn't been suspicious, you surely would have."

Kleimer thought again, then chuckled. "Sure I would've. Of course I would've. But don't tell anybody; I want Quirt to feel good about this. He deserves it. It was a good catch."

"Very generous of you," Koesler observed.

"Speaking of Quirt, he tells me he's back in the movie business."

"Pardon?"

"You know, that made-for-TV production they've been working on even while the investigation was continuing. They came to me first. But I was up to my neck with the Diego murder, so I passed them on to Quirt. They got so obnoxious that even Quirt dumped them. Now that the investigation is completed, George got reinvolved. They promised him some bucks. So far, that's still just a promise."

"Now that you mention it," Koesler said, "I was reading something about that movie. Didn't they have . . . oh, what's his name? . . . Charles Durning signed? Hard to believe he's supposed to play a Hispanic bishop."

"They lost Durning. But they think they can get Donald Sutherland."

"Donald Sutherland!"

"Guess who he's supposed to play."

Koesler shook his head.

"Me!"

"You."

"Yes. Not bad, wouldn't you say, having Donald Sutherland play me?" The very thought of someone so famous portraying him seemed to intoxicate Kleimer. He launched into a narrative expounding on his hopes and plans. This case had already gained him national, even international, recognition. There would be plenty more to come as the trial took place and as, inevitably, he won a conviction.

Of course, Kleimer expected a defense of insanity, but he was quite sure he could defeat that ploy. And even if Carleson's insanity plea succeeded, the priest would be behind bars one way or the other. Kleimer couldn't wait to lock horns with Avery Cone. Nothing like going against the best; his victory would be all the greater.

One word leading to another, Kleimer used up a lot of time blowing his own horn.

Throughout, every chance he got, Koesler scanned the room. He had to return his gaze to the speaker from time to time; he didn't want to create the impression he was bored. He simply was searching for . . . what? He didn't know. He felt like an actor in a play knowing neither his lines nor even which play he was in.

At length, Kleimer checked his watch. "Say, Father"—he was still looking at his watch—"it's time I got on my horse or the lady will kill me." As he and a reluctant Koesler rose to their feet, the phone rang.

Kleimer hesitated. "I'll be just a minute," he said as he left the room.

"Just a minute," Koesler repeated in his mind. *Just a minute!* He could not chance picking up even one of these mysterious and strangely promising folders in "just a minute."

Once again he scanned the room. At least now he didn't have to worry about holding eye contact. But there was nothing he hadn't seen earlier. And nothing that seemed even remotely incriminating. Koesler's heart sank. *What a dumb idea this had been!*

Kleimer leaned back into the living room, a distressed look on his face. One of his hands covered the phone. "The lady wants to cancel tonight. I've gotta talk her out of that. Would you mind letting yourself out?" Without waiting for an answer, he said, "Thanks. We'll talk."

He disappeared again into the kitchen, whence Koesler could hear him cajoling, kidding, and pleading alternatively.

Koesler shrugged and headed for the closet to retrieve his hat and coat. Not for an instant did he blame God. It simply was not to be.

After all, he had no more than a theory, a mere hypothesis. For all he knew, his theory might be no more than a product of his wishful thinking. Perhaps he wanted so to help Don Carleson that his fancy had taken flight.

As he walked to the closet he became aware that his vision was slightly impaired by dirty glasses. He'd been in such a hurry since his shower and frustrated sleuthing that he'd paid no attention to how smudged his eyeglasses were.

Fortunately, he routinely kept a clean handkerchief in his overcoat for just such exigencies.

He opened the closet door and slid his hand inside the vest pocket of his overcoat. Strange, he didn't feel the folded cloth he expected. Rather, it felt like a slip of paper.

He had no idea what it could be. He was forever stuffing pieces of paper, cards, notes, in his pockets. He assumed almost everyone did likewise. It always proved a revelation, sometimes an amusing diversion, to pull everything out and try to place the source of each.

He pulled the slip of paper out.

He recognized it immediately. His only question was what had happened to his clean handkerchief. Then he looked more closely at the piece of paper.

No, that wasn't right. How could anyone have made such a stupid mistake?

Then, slowly, very slowly, it all began to fall into place.

Hoping against hope, he looked further into the closet. There was another black overcoat. He reached into its vest pocket and found his clean handkerchief.

Paraphrasing from *My Fair Lady*, he wanted to sing out, "I think I've got it! By George, I've got it!"

Hurriedly, he slipped into his coat and hat—making certain both were his own. Hurriedly, he returned to St. Joe's. Hurriedly, he called Lieutenant Tully. Hurriedly, Tully started the process to secure a search warrant.

TWENTY-NINE

"I think I'll take that coffee now," Lieutenant Tully said.

"Now that you mention it, I will too, if it is not too much trouble," Inspector Koznicki said.

Father Koesler was tempted to feel insulted, or at least slighted. Earlier, he had offered both officers coffee. Both had declined. Now Mary O'Connor had arrived. She offered to make coffee, and the two accepted readily enough.

From time to time, Koesler was almost convinced he was incapable of brewing coffee to anyone's taste but his own. Then something would happen to restore his confidence. Why just a few evenings ago Father Carleson had welcomed not only Koesler coffee, but warmed-over Koesler coffee.

And of course it was Father Carleson who brought them together this frigid but clear and sunny February morning.

The priest and the police officers had gathered in St. Joe's dining room to, in effect, celebrate the conclusion of the police investigation of the Diego and Demers murders. The court trials were yet to come.

"It was almost a miracle that led you to that receipt," Koznicki said.

Koesler laughed. "If you could have seen me—if you could have read my mind while I was in Brad Kleimer's apartment, you wouldn't have a single doubt that it was a miracle. But, then, as someone once said, 'More things are wrought by prayer than this world knows of.' Did you pray, Lieutenant?"

Tully wore a bemused smile. He considered the question rhetorical. He could not argue that prayer mightn't work if one believed in it; but prayer played an almost nonexistent role in his life.

"I literally didn't know what I was looking for, and I was afraid I wouldn't recognize it even if I found it. That's how bad off I was," Koesler said. He had already, at least in part, explained to Tully what had happened in Kleimer's apartment. He would go over what had transpired for the benefit of both officers. It was a ritual they had gone through in the past and would repeat now.

"Things happened in that apartment that some might ascribe to chance, but I think it was Providence," Koesler said. "Starting with Mr. Kleimer's invitation to visit him sometime. I have no idea why he did that."

"He would have found *some* use for you sometime," Koznicki suggested.

"I suppose. Anyway, I had no idea then that I would be taking him up on that offer."

"And he had no idea his invitation was going to backfire," Tully added.

"That's right," Koesler agreed. "Anyway, just as he was about to usher me out, his phone rang. If that hadn't happened, he would certainly have handed me the right black overcoat."

"And if the call had been from almost anyone but his date for that evening, he would've ended the call seconds after he got it. 'Cause his prime concern was that he was almost late for that date. It was because he was trying to talk her out of breaking the date that he asked me to show myself out.

"That gave me the time and the notion to clean my glasses before going outside. After that, it was just a matter of how we—or most of us, anyway—have a habit of stuffing things in pockets—particularly overcoat pockets.

"I remember when I went to Receiving last Wednesday night, I had to take the card out of the parking machine before I could enter the garage. Then, after I parked, I put the card in my wallet. That way, I wouldn't lose it or forget where I'd put it.

"When I drove to the exit ramp on my way out, I had already buckled the seat belt, which made it very awkward to put the parking receipt anywhere but in the vest pocket of my coat. Fortunately, Kleimer had the same experience.

"And it's so easy to go unrecognized by a parking attendant. They don't even bother looking up; all you have to do is stick your arm out the car window with the ticket and money in your hand. The attendant takes them and, in the case of Receiving, automatically gives you the receipt."

Mary O'Connor brought the coffee, fresh and steaming. She also brought some sweet rolls. She was appreciated.

"So"—Koznicki anticipated the next point—"you reached into the pocket of what you thought was *your* coat to get a handkerchief, and instead pulled out the parking receipt."

"Exactly. At first I thought it was *my* receipt. After all, it was *my* coat—or at least I thought it was. Then, as I glanced at the receipt, it was all wrong. It gave the wrong date and the wrong time. Instead of recording the entry as February 9, 10:40 P.M., and the exit as February 9, 11:30 P.M., it read, 'Entry February 8, 11:32 P.M.' and 'Exit, February 9, 12:12 A.M.'

"This clearly indicated the wearer of this coat was at Receiving Hospital when Herbert Demers was murdered. It was the first solid evidence that Brad Kleimer was the one who'd killed Mr. Demers. Until then, it was just a theory I had that Father Carleson was not the killer, and that Kleimer was.

"Brad Kleimer's plan was the soul of simplicity," Koesler continued, warming to his story. "There are lots of people wandering around almost any hospital with no permission or identification. Chief among them are people wearing hospital greens or white hospital coats or black clerical clothes. Doctors, nurses, hospital personnel, and clergy generally don't need permission—or any further identification.

"Kleimer is a bit shorter than Father Carleson. But he wears lifts. And that makes them about the same height. The two men are similarly built. Father's hair is totally white, and although Kleimer's hair is still turning, his sideburns are white. So, wearing a hat, the hair color appears the same.

"Then it occurred to me, when I visited the hospital Thursday night, that if it was Father Carleson, he'd certainly acted strangely. He stood outside in the cold with his coat collar turned down. He seemed to be making sure he would be seen and recognized as a priest. And, with everything else going on, Kleimer would be identified as Father Carleson, because that's who he resembled.

"Before going into Demers's room, he made sure the nurse got a look—just a brief glimpse—at him. He left it to her imagination to figure out who he was supposed to be. And it didn't take much imagination.

"*And,* Brad Kleimer has handled enough murder trials and been associated with enough autopsies to know that pressing down forcefully with a pillow to smother someone will leave evidence—evidence a brilliant medical examiner like Dr. Moellmann would never overlook.

"Finally, if Lieutenant Quirt were to miss the coincidence of one of Father Carleson's parishioners dying—when Father so obviously wanted him to die—Kleimer was perfectly capable of demanding an autopsy."

Koesler seemed finished with his summary.

"I wonder," Koznicki said, "if we might have a bit more coffee?"

Koesler called the request to Mary O'Connor. She entered the room with a pot that she placed on an electric warmer.

"The trouble with Kleimer," Tully said as he poured his coffee, "is that he's an arrogant bastard."

"Giving him his due," Koznicki said, "he was pressed for time. There seemed to be a ground swell in support of Father Carleson. Kleimer was beginning to doubt he could get a conviction with no more than the circumstantial evidence he had. There were unexplained doubts. And a jury cannot convict when there is a shadow of doubt."

"Williams's hunch that Maryknoll headquarters was covering up something didn't pan out," Tully said.

"Williams is a good detective," Koznicki said. "But, with one thing and another, his Maryknoll theory might very well have been proven groundless. For Kleimer, time was running out. The perfect ploy was to frame Father Carleson for a murder. No victim would be more tailor-made than Herbert Demers. Demers was dying anyway. But his lifetime was growing very short. If Kleimer had not acted when he did, there might well have been no other opportunity to implicate Father in a murder."

"I agree," Tully said. "But once we got onto his trail, it was pretty easy to tie up the loose ends. Mary, the clerk at Fuchs religious goods store, picked Kleimer out of a bunch of photos as the guy who bought a clerical shirt the day of Demers's murder.

"Then there was Michigan Bell. They found that a call had been placed from a neighborhood pay phone to Carleson's number at 11:15

on the eighth of February. Which proved that Carleson really got the call he said he did. The healthy presumption is that Kleimer made that call. He called from a nearby pay phone so he could check and make certain that Carleson took the bait. If Kleimer had called from a private phone, Ma Bell would not have had the record. Chalk up a couple for the good guys."

They chuckled.

"But Father"—Koznicki grew serious—"this all began with your suspicion that Brad Kleimer had killed Herbert Demers. I can understand why you were reluctant to believe Father Carleson was guilty of either murder. But what made you suspect Kleimer?"

Father Koesler, in turn, was serious. "I didn't, at first. Of course I couldn't bring myself to believe that Don had murdered the bishop. And nothing in the evidence that was found shook my belief. But I must admit that when Don was charged with the Demers killing I had my first serious doubts. It seemed so logical that if he had killed Demers—and that likelihood I had to admit was strong—why could he not have killed the bishop?

"Then, something that Lieutenant Tully said pricked my curiosity. You said, Lieutenant, something to the effect of, 'If only he hadn't done it.' If only he hadn't murdered Demers, there wouldn't have been such renewed belief that he had committed the prior murder.

"So the only remaining supposition had to be: What if he, indeed, hadn't? What if he hadn't killed Demers? How could someone else do it while implicating Don?

"And, who would, or could, do such a thing?"

"Well, impersonating a priest was not all that difficult. No one in the hospital got a really good look at the 'priest' who was seen—from afar—entering the hospital, and then seen almost out of the corner of her eye by the floor nurse.

"Everybody—with good reason, I'm sure—assumed it was Father Carleson.

"Who might have done it? Several people came to mind. Father Bell—to remove himself from any suspicion in the bishop's murder. He would have the added advantage of being a priest and not having to impersonate one. Honestly—and I'm a bit ashamed to admit it—he was my prime candidate.

"Then there was Michael Shell, another suspect and possible killer."

"He had an alibi," Koznicki interjected.

"See? I didn't even know that," Koesler said. "Then there was—almost for lack of any other suspects—Lieutenant Quirt. Or, perhaps, one of those crazy movie people trying to steer the story their way.

"Or, it could've been almost anybody. One of the hospital personnel intent on a mercy killing. A relative of Mr. Demers trying to hurry nature along. But none of those candidates seemed a logical choice.

"Then came Brad Kleimer. As I said a while ago, he fit the bill physically. Of course, a lot of people could qualify in that category—especially with the brief glimpse he gave the hospital personnel.

"The ultimate reason why I zeroed in on Brad Kleimer was his motive—or what I suspected his motive to be.

"You see, granting that Father Carleson did *not* do it, whoever killed Demers did it to reinforce the charge that Father Carleson killed Bishop Diego. So I thought, in this scenario, whoever killed Demers didn't really care one way or the other about Demers's death. Demers's death only served to help convict Don of the bishop's death.

"Something I heard in Ste. Anne's rectory last Wednesday evening sort of came to mind. One of the priests was complaining about an opponent's high-handed way of playing chess: He used his more precious pieces—knights, castles, and bishops—as pawns.

"That seemed to be it in a nutshell. Bishop Diego, Lord rest him, used others as pawns in a game for his own advancement. And now somebody was using the death of Bishop Diego as a pawn in a game for that somebody's advancement.

"And that someone was Brad Kleimer.

"Kleimer saw the trial over the bishop's murder as a grandstand opportunity. It was drawing national and international coverage. For the trial to work to Kleimer's benefit, the killer should be a priest and Kleimer should convict the priest.

"For the bishop to be murdered by some drugged kid would be news. But not the sensation that would come from a priest who murders his bishop with premeditation and in cold blood. If he could make this charge against Father Carleson stick, Kleimer would become a household word.

"Still and all, I didn't think that even this fantastic reward would be enough motivation to cause an otherwise sane prosecuting attorney to actually murder an old man whose life hung by a thread. I could understand how fame—celebrity stardom, if you will—could make Kleimer at least consider murder as a means to this goal. But I couldn't envision his actually doing it.

"But you see, what impressed me most about Brad Kleimer in the brief time I've known him, is the degree of vengeance he has toward his former wife.

"I wish we had the time . . . and—" Koesler chuckled. "—I wish you were interested enough for me to explain how very complex and intricate are the marriage laws of the Catholic Church. Not to mention their number.

"Before being engaged to a Catholic girl, Brad Kleimer had been vaguely aware that the Roman Catholic Church had an enormous number of laws governing entering matrimony and another pile of laws regulating getting out of a marriage once entered.

"He actually made a painstaking study of these laws. I've never before experienced a similar case. Why, there are priests who aren't as conversant with these laws as Kleimer was!

"And he did all that with one thought in mind: to hold his wife in—as far as the Church was concerned—an inescapable bond. He contrived to make sure that should their marriage fail, his wife could never get an annulment.

"I've known people, especially those in failed marriages, to be unhappy in direct proportion to their ex-partner's current happiness. But Brad Kleimer took the cake. The whole purpose of all that study and those precautions was to lock his wife in marriage in the eyes of the Catholic Church—*her* Church.

"This would be of no concern to him personally. He didn't care about Church laws as they affected him, because as far as he was concerned they *didn't* affect him.

"But they *did* affect his Catholic wife. And, sure enough, after their civil divorce, his wife discovered that as far as the Church was concerned, she would be considered married to him until one of them died.

"Now his wife did eventually marry. But she had to marry without a Catholic ceremony. And, just as Kleimer had planned, at her core she was miserable.

"Then Father Carleson came on the scene. To make a long story shorter, he passed over every single one of those many, many Church laws and witnessed the marriage vows of Kleimer's former wife and her present husband.

"Kleimer didn't discover this until after Father Carleson was indicted for murder. Kleimer was already determined to convict Father. Imagine how he felt when he learned that his former wife was happy and there wasn't much of anything he could do about it? Even if he tried to get some ecclesiastical action against Father, he'd likely not be successful in this diocese. And even if he *were* successful, it wouldn't take away his wife's bliss. She had her marriage in the Church; she had returned to her sacramental life.

"And that was it!" Koesler concluded on a triumphant note. "That's what tipped the scales in my mind toward Brad Kleimer as the murderer of Herbert Demers. It wasn't only the fame he saw slipping from his grasp; it was that Father Carleson had utterly destroyed Kleimer's carefully planned revenge against his ex-wife.

"I think it was almost a miracle that he killed Demers and not Father Carleson. But he had better plans for Father—plans that included shame, disgrace, conviction, incarceration." Koesler shook his head in sorrow. "Not, all in all, a very nice person."

Koznicki and Tully had listened with rapt attention. Each realized how truly helpful this priest had been in this case, as well as in past cases when a crime carried an essentially Catholic character.

"Now that Father Carleson is no longer behind bars and Kleimer has been charged with the murder of Herbert Demers, how goes the case against Julio Ramirez?" Koesler asked.

"Better than I had any reason to expect," Tully replied. "Ramirez and the two Sanchez girls are out of the hospital but in custody. Julio's memory is improving. And the details he can't recall, Estella Sanchez is supplying.

"According to their three individual statements, they knew—as did lots of others—about the bishop's stash. It was Julio's idea to take it. His plan was to just go right up to the rectory when they knew the bishop was in his office. They staked out the rectory Sunday afternoon. They spotted the bishop and Carleson when they got back around 5:00. They waited till the lights went on in the bishop's office. Then they just walked up to the door, rang the bell, and waited while the bishop deactivated the alarm system. He let them in. They gave him a sad song-and-dance about Julio's mother being in great need. None of them had eaten in days, so they told him.

"It hadn't occurred to Julio they'd have to kill the bishop to keep him from identifying them. Vicki Sanchez had brought along a piece of lead pipe. When the bishop was sitting in his chair, she passed the pipe to Julio and whispered what he must do.

"So he clobbered Diego in the back of the head. One blow did it. They got the money. They ditched the pipe a few blocks away. Then they bought enough crack to keep a pretty big gang senseless for a long while.

"They even brought us to the pipe. So now we have the murder weapon, complete with prints. We even got it down to this: Doc Moellmann estimated—based on the height of the bishop, the fact that he was sitting down, the angle of the blow—that the perp was about five-six or -seven. Julio is five-seven."

"One thing, Lieutenant," Koesler said, "I don't understand why the kids are being so cooperative. . . ."

Tully smiled. "Mr. Anthony Wayne. Whatever we could do to them is absolutely nothing compared with what Mr. Wayne's organization would do to them if they didn't cooperate with us and tell us the truth."

"So," Koznicki said, "it is as Lieutenant Tully thought in the beginning: robbery and murder for drugs. It happens so often. If we had not been sidetracked from the beginning with that preoccupation with Father Carleson, much of this might not have happened."

Koznicki did not mention Quirt, who was responsible, as far as the police were concerned, for the Carleson preoccupation. It was not in the inspector's nature to needlessly place blame.

"Kleimer," Koznicki continued, "might have ended up prosecuting the guilty parties. He might not even have learned what happened to his former wife and her reconciliation with the Church. He definitely would not now be accused of murder. Fate is strange.

"By the way . . ." Koznicki turned to Tully. ". . . have you heard who will be defending Kleimer?"

Tully chuckled. "Yeah. Avery Cone. He's got some free time now that he's no longer retained by the Church to work on Carleson's case."

"And Father Carleson," Koznicki asked Koesler, "what will he be doing?"

"He hasn't decided. So much publicity! But I think he's going to continue his incardination procedure with the Detroit archdiocese. He is, naturally, quite impressed with Cardinal Boyle. And I'm particularly pleased: He has become a dear friend."

Tully picked up the coffeepot from the hot plate and tipped it over his cup. Nothing emerged.

Koesler reached for the pot. "It's empty. Here, let me just go fix another pot—"

"No!" Tully responded, somewhat more forcefully than necessary. He glanced at his watch. "I've got to get back to work. But thanks anyway."

Koesler looked invitingly at Inspector Koznicki.

"No, no . . . none for me either. We must be back at headquarters. There is always so much to do."

Once again, Koesler had to wonder. Oh, well; at least his newfound friend Father Carleson liked his coffee.

The two officers were getting into their overcoats. Tully, head tilted toward Koesler, said, "By the way, I've been meaning to ask you . . ." His tone indicated a facetious question ". . . Is there any possibility that something Catholic —something spectacularly Catholic—is scheduled for next year?"

"Well," Koesler said in utter sincerity, "there has been talk of a Papal visit to Detroit—"

Koznicki's mouth dropped. "A Papal visit! Good Lord, save us!"

To which Koesler replied, "Amen."

*   *   *   *